Sexy Little Numbers
Best Women's Erotica from Black Lace
Volume 1

Look out for other Black Lace short fiction collections

Wicked Words 1–10
Quickies 1–10
Sex in the Office
Sex on Holiday
Sex and the Sports Club
Sex on the Move
Sex in Uniform
Sex in the Kitchen
Sex and Music
Sex and Shopping
Sex in Public
Sex with Strangers
Love on the Dark Side (Paranormal Erotica)
Lust at First Bite – Sexy Vampire Stories
Seduction
Liaisons
Misbehaviour

Paranormal novella collections:
Lust Bites
Possession
Magic and Desire
Enchanted

Sexy Little Numbers
Best Women's Erotica from Black Lace
Volume 1
Edited by Lindsay Gordon

This book is a work of fiction.
In real life, make sure you practise safe, sane and consensual sex.

Published by Black Lace 2009

2 4 6 8 10 9 7 5 3 1

First published in Great Britain in 2009 by
Black Lace,
Virgin Books,
Random House, 20 Vauxhall Bridge Road,
London SW1V 2SA

www.blacklace.co.uk/www.virginbooks.com/www.rbooks.co.uk

Addresses for companies within The Random House Group Limited can be found at:
www.randomhouse.co.uk/offices.htm

The Random House Group Limited Reg. No. 954009

Distributed in the USA by Macmillan, 175 Fifth Avenue, New York, NY 10010, USA

A CIP catalogue record for this book is available from the British Library

ISBN 9780352345387

The Random House Group Limited supports The Forest Stewardship Council [FSC], the leading international forest certification organisation. All our titles that are printed on Greenpeace-approved FSC-certified paper carry the FSC logo.
Our paper procurement policy can be found at www.rbooks.co.uk/environment

Typeset by Palimpsest Book Production Ltd, Grangemouth, Stirlingshire
Printed and bound in Great Britain by CPI Bookmarque, Croydon CR0 4TD

Contents

Content

Rebecca
Kristina Lloyd

Last night I dreamt he came on my face again. Men stood around me, menacing and lustful, and I was naked and scared, kneeling on the floor. Smudges of neon edged into the dusk, blooms of pink, violet and electric blue. My arms were trapped behind my back, fingers gripping my flesh. All I could see was a confusion of legs and leering faces, their eyes fixed on me while I watched the swift shuffle of his hand.

The moment was held. I waited for him, my arched back making my breasts jut and my belly curve. In the gloom, I was pale, smooth and slender but then I'm often at my best in my dreams. It looked as if I were offering myself to the men. No, it looked as if I were *being* offered with no say in the matter whatsoever. And that's how it felt. No choice, no control. Occasionally, I wriggled in protest but that appeared only to amuse and encourage them. I had a sense they were calling me names like 'slut' and 'whore' but, as is the way with dreams, the words went unheard. All that remained was a deep sense of shame and a sombre, sulky pleasure unfurling inside me. I hated it and I loved it. I wanted it and I didn't. And strange though it may seem, the urge to flee fuelled the longing to stay.

Max tapped my face, landing a couple of mild slaps on my cheek. The message was I should open my mouth. So I did. I no longer saw myself and instead I, the dreamer, slipped behind my eyes. I was surrounded by engorged cocks, white knuckles, crisp thickets of pubes and hairy thighs. Hands pumped, eyes gleamed, muscles tightened and mouths laughed. But the only thing that mattered, the only thing I truly saw was Max's cock. In the half-light, it was a ruby flare shuddering as he worked his shaft, his thumb and forefinger dancing a frenzy below his glans.

I noted his wrist, strong and thick, blurred by dark hair. Even in my dream I was aware of how his wrist's vulnerable underside, with its blue veins, pale skin and delicate tendons, contrasted so beautifully with his jerking forearm's easy masculinity. His fist speeded up, he edged closer, and then he peaked, the liquid pearl of his come shimmering in arcs and spurts before splashing onto my shame.

I woke, sticky-eyed, but it wasn't the sticky I wanted. Drowsily, I rolled over in search of him, humiliation and need muddling my brain. Next to me, the pillow was empty, just a dent where his head had been and a single dark hair, curled like a question mark. I knew at once he was with her. Oh, sure, I realise that to most people it would simply look as if he were making toast in the kitchen. But I am not most people, and nor was Rebecca.

I slipped my hands between my thighs. I was slick with moisture. Briefly, I regretted Max not being there to sort me out but then I worried I may have been talking in my sleep. He was better off downstairs with Rebecca. Once, I saw photographs of her in the room I'm not supposed to go in. Don't get me wrong. I'm not trying to make out Max has forbidden me from entering but when I first came to this house, a week before I moved in, I asked what was behind the closed door and he said, 'Rebecca's stuff.' For a long time, that was as good as a lock to me. Not any more.

Those photographs practically destroyed me. I couldn't stop looking at her. She was stunning, a tall, boyishly athletic woman with jet-black hair spiking softly in an urchin crop. She had a finely boned face, made for magazines, and lips which were intriguingly neat and narrow. There was something cruel yet beautiful about those lips and, in every picture, she exuded serenity and self-possession.

I'd always known I walked in her shadow and when I saw what I was up against, I realised I could do nothing other than fail. People look at me with barely veiled pity when they discover I'm the new girlfriend, and I can't say I blame them. I haven't a cat in hell's chance, have I? They must wonder about Max too and why he's now prepared to settle for so little. They probably think he's given up after losing Rebecca.

I can understand their concerns. After all, our relationship happened so fast. One minute we're shagging on my best friend's sofa after getting off at a speed-dating event hosted by a local night-club, Azure Blue. The next minute, I've got my own key and I'm moving in. Well, my landlady was selling my old place so I was between flats and Max offered. It's temporary while I find a new home, and it's more comfortable than Vanessa's sofa. Plus, Max and I were so horny for each other that my moving in felt quite natural.

As I lay in bed, I could hear him pottering about in the kitchen, the TV babbling away, the smell of toast and coffee drifting up the stairs. I blame what I did next on the dream. It lingered in my mind and swirled between my thighs, an awful yearning to taste more shame and to suffer. I had a sense of regret – strange to regret a dream – and yet stronger than the regret was a longing to be there still; to be trapped in that neon-lit pit, a bunch of crude, randy brutes jeering and jostling as he came on my face.

Those dark needs made me feel scorched inside, hollowed out with loneliness. I had the impulse to share my dream as lovers often do and yet I feared his response. Max didn't know I liked that sort of thing. Most of the time, I try to fool myself into thinking I don't like it either. It's so vulgar and debasing. But I've had my dreams long enough to know they're not going away. The trouble is, they're getting worse. I often wish I could shut my stuff away much as he's shut away Rebecca's stuff – her real stuff; I don't know about her dreams – but what I crave can't be boxed or caged.

I stretched, rubbing sleep from my eyes. My cunt was soft and swollen, a beat of need ticking there. I couldn't bear the thought of joining Max at the breakfast table as if this were just another day. After all, people can let their entire lives pass by doing that, can't they? So I slipped on my dressing gown then crossed the landing to shut the bathroom door, hoping to fool him into thinking I was in there. I didn't have a plan so much as a compulsion which had me tiptoeing up the steep, narrow stairs to the closed room in the attic. I imagine at various points in the house's history the attic's been used as a maid's room, a nursery and perhaps, more recently, a guest bedroom.

As soon as I walked in, I felt Rebecca all around me. Beneath the sloping, primrose-yellow walls, her clothes were racked on rails draped with ghostly white sheets. Her perfume hung in the air, an exotic heady scent mingling with the mustiness of neglect. A small sash window in a dormer recess left the room's shadows untouched by daylight. Knowing the view from there was the best in the house, I went directly to it. Spring sunshine glittered on the sea down in the bay, and the forest leading to the beach was bright with the fresh green of new growth.

Rebecca like to swim, didn't she? I could see her slicing through the water, arms flicking, elbows high as she crested the waves. Later, she would emerge onto the sand, her wet hair a glistening cap of jet. She would jog inland, muscles flexing in her perfectly toned thighs, her small breasts bobbing inside her black Speedo. Around her, drops of water would shimmer like a halo of silver sparks.

I could see how all the men would be hot for her. They'd watch from the corners of their eyes and, across the beach, cocks would be twitching and lifting inside the swim trunks of so many beautifully burnished sunbathers and surfers. They would always be hot for her, and I, dreamer at the window, would always be hot for them. All of them. One after the other. Or maybe one at either end. Two inside me, or maybe even three.

I picked at a blister of paint on the window frame, desire throbbing between my thighs. I imagined a gang of hard horny men gathered around me, water sliding along their muscled contours, caught droplets glinting in hair on shins, thighs, arms and chests. One would tenderly draw my hair back from my face, holding it in a ponytail. Then he'd pinch my jaw with his free hand, forcing my mouth open, and he'd say, 'OK, who wants to fuck her face?'

I broke off from my fantasy, suddenly aware of a presence in the attic. My heart began to race and my palms prickled with heat. I turned, convinced I was being watched. Had Max crept up the stairs? Something brushed my leg. I squealed and jumped. That fucking cat! Max has a black Siamese called Danny. It hates me, I'm sure. And yet there it was, sidling up to me and trying to slither around my ankles. I didn't trust it one iota.

I raised the window, hoping to get rid of Rebecca's scent. A warm soft breeze touched my face, and gulls wheeled in the blue sky, their cries shrill and noisy. I could picture the attic as Rebecca's dressing room where she would wander through, selecting clothes for the day. She had so many clothes: three rails plus a broad oak wardrobe I hadn't even looked in yet.

In the corner was a cream loom chair, empty save for a cushion featuring a sequinned elephant. The wicker creaked when I sat and I stayed there a short while thinking, I am Rebecca and this is my domain. Then I tried to repeat the sentence using my own name but found I couldn't do it. So profound was my inability to reclaim the space by substituting my name for hers you could be forgiven for thinking I didn't even have a name. The conclusion was obvious: Rebecca ruled this space and, though she was gone, her reign would continue for many more years, most likely for ever.

I sighed and crossed to the wardrobe. Being with Max was hopeless. He'd never be able to see me for what I was because his eyes were fogged with Rebecca. There was a tiny key in the wardrobe but the doors were unlocked. Again, it was as if Rebecca's name were enough to keep people at bay. The hinges groaned and I gazed at a shuffled rainbow of clothes. Pale rose, shrimp pink, candy, fuchsia and scarlet were interrupted by a wedge of khaki and bottle green before resuming at cherry, burgundy, magenta and purple. I fancied they'd once hung in a neat spectrum of grouped colours then someone had transferred them to this wardrobe by moving them in great armfuls, paying scant attention to the order. Max probably, emptying a bedroom wardrobe to offer space to his new lover, me. I ran my fingers along the fabrics, breathing in small pockets of fragrance released by the movement.

I wondered how it must have felt to be Rebecca, to have lived in this fabulous house in this sweet seaside town with Max's unconditional love. I tried imagining myself as her, browsing the wardrobe on an ordinary Sunday morning, mulling over the perfect outfit before choosing one to make his eyes light up. I wondered if anything would fit me. Something loose or adjustable, perhaps.

Pink tends to drain me and I find black too harsh for my

complexion but they were clearly colours Rebecca favoured. I riffled through her clothes, wincing when the coat hangers squeaked. But Max was two floors below; he would never hear. I was hoping he would take the dog out soon, as was his routine, and I was listening for the slam of the back door, eager to have the house to myself.

I selected a couple of dresses – one in a turquoise floral print, another a slinky little number in claret threaded with silver. Standing in front of a cheval mirror, positioned as if someone might still use it, I slipped off my robe and held the dresses to my body in turn. My reflection was about two stone too heavy. I tossed the dresses aside, held up a cherry-red shift dress. Same story. I continued, selecting and rejecting before finally wriggling into a tight black pencil skirt. There was some give in the fabric but even so, once I'd tugged it over my hips, I couldn't get the zip higher than a couple of inches. Ah well. I turned to check my rear in the mirror, amused to see the split of my buttocks bared by the gaping fabric, flesh spilling over the waistband, seams puckering around fat. It felt so wonderfully disrespectful.

Next, I chose a delicate, flamingo-pink chiffon blouse with daisies embroidered on the collar. My shoulders are narrow so I had no problem getting the blouse on. Fastening it, however, was a different matter. I managed to button the garment up to my breasts but when I tried the next button at cleavage height, I succeeded for only three seconds. As soon as I drew breath, the button pinged off leaving me with a neckline that was far beyond plunging and far beyond decent. The cat darted after the button while I tucked the blouse into the waist of my half-open skirt. In the glass, I grinned at the sight of the tiny buttons straining against their holes, of my bulging breasts and my nipples pressing against the sheer fabric. How lewd they looked, two big rosy blooms mocking those demure little daisies.

I thought of my fantasy guys at the beach and imagined, if I were at their feet and dressed like this, they'd know exactly how to treat me: like a dirty, greedy slut. My thoughts pulled me away from the present once again and, even as I conjured up scenarios of myself being passed around and used by a bunch of strangers, I was reminded

again that it was getting worse. Or rather *I* was getting worse. My dark thoughts were breaking out of my sleeping dreams and coming to life in my daydreams. I was making them happen. I was orchestrating events in my head. I was in control, no excuses. This wasn't my subconscious running the show when my defences were down. This was me exploring my mind, chasing wanton thoughts down the corridors of my brain and opening the doors of my psyche to find big strong men in there doing unspeakable things to me.

Standing before the mirror, scarcely even registering my reflection, I pictured a guy with his hands hooked under my arm, keeping me steady while his mate fucked me senseless. Moisture seeped between my thighs and I upped the tempo of my sexy mental narrative. Being in the attic was enormously liberating. It was a secret space under the roof, remote from real life; a room that was part of the house and yet didn't quite belong. There were no rules or routines here so I was free to let my imagination off its leash. And let it off I did by introducing a third guy into the action. He was just threatening to fuck me in the arse when that queer sense of a presence returned.

Momentarily, I wondered if it were my own guilt seeking to interrupt the blue movie of my mind. But no, the feeling was much stronger than that. I turned, ready to glare at the cat. Instead, I found myself looking directly at Max. My stomach flipped. Oh hell. Not walking the dog then. He stood in the doorway, shirtless above a pair of baggy, calf-length shorts. His ink-black hair romped in short curls around his unshaven face, anger making his dark brows hunker down over his glinting bronze eyes. He looked furious and gorgeous in equal measure.

The attic's isolation had clearly affected me because, instead of feeling embarrassed by my transgression, I was spurred on to greater boldness. I tossed back my hair.

'I'm Rebecca,' I said defiantly. 'She was a slut, wasn't she? A slut. And she got what she deserved.'

'What the fuck are you playing at?' demanded Max.

'I want to have a good time,' I replied briskly.

His eyes scanned the room. 'What? By ruining her clothes?'

'Yes,' I hissed. 'Yes. I want to ruin her clothes.' I gestured around the attic at the garments I'd flung to the ground and those on rails cloaked by dust sheets. I was about to stride over to one of the rails but, when I moved, I realised the skirt was too tight to afford me dignity. I stayed still. 'No,' I said. 'I want *you* to ruin them. Was she a slut? Tell me, Max. Was she? Is that why you never speak about her? Because she was a slut and you're ashamed?'

Max cocked his head, looking thoughtful. He narrowed his eyes at me. 'Do you want her to be a slut?'

'Yes,' I said. 'Yes. And I want you to treat me the way you treated her. Treat me like a slut!'

Max thrust his hands deep into his front pockets, leaned against the door jamb and looked me up and down. His gaze was deliberately lecherous as he trawled my too-tight get-up, lingering on my squashed, deep cleavage.

'Well, you're certainly dressed like a slut,' he said coolly.

'I'm dressed like Rebecca,' I replied. 'So treat me like her. Do to me what you did to her. Call me names and fuck me. Go on, do it! Fuck me like you would fuck Rebecca.'

The cat slunk out of the room as if offended, tail waving grandly in the air. Max swaggered towards me, his lips tilting in an arrogant grin. I wondered if I'd said the wrong thing. Had I pushed it too far? Was her perfume addling my brain?

Standing a pace or so in front of me, hands still in his pockets, Max smirked, nodding almost imperceptibly. In his eyes was a dangerous gleam full of plots, plans and perversions. I'd never seen him look at me that way before. Presumably I was seeing the Max Rebecca used to see. My jealousy quadrupled.

He made a loose fist and gently chucked me under the chin, tipping my head back a fraction. 'I've always known you wanted it like this,' he said, smiling. 'Hot little bitch.'

My groin liquefied at the sound of those words. 'Sweetpea' and 'babes' do nothing for me but 'hot little bitch' has me weak. Max dropped his hand and nudged me under each breast, lifting my flesh fractionally. Across my tits, the blouse was as tight as strapping.

'Aren't you?' said Max smoothly. 'A hot little bitch who likes it nasty. Aren't you, Rebecca? Huh?' My nipples crinkled to hard nubs and Max, as if he had all the time in the world, scuffed his thumbs over them, flicking back and forth like a metronome. 'Look at these tits,' he said. 'So obvious. I don't know why you even bother wearing clothes.'

With that, he grasped the neck of the blouse and tugged so fiercely I might have been in a bodice-ripper romance. All the buttons popped off, exposing me to the waist. Max shoved the collar past my shoulders then deftly tucked the blouse either side of my breasts. 'There,' he said. 'Let's take a look at what we've got, shall we?'

He thrust his hands into his pockets again and strode slowly away, eyeing me with the possessive glee of a man relishing his authority. I was panting a little, shocked and excited. The heat in my cheeks was strong; my head was pulsing with a rush of blood. Max began circling me at a distance, smiling enigmatically. He looked so hot, his skin creamily pale from the winter months, the dark hair of his chest thinning to a narrow line on his belly then disappearing into his low-slung shorts.

For a long time, he said nothing and with every second of silence, I felt more and more exposed. Before long, I was positively cringing to be standing alone in the middle of the room, clothes arranged to display my breasts and their taut, flushed nipples. I grew desperate for a word or touch, for anything to take the emphasis off me and reduce the intensity of Max's scrutiny. I had no idea what was running through his mind but the more he stalked and pondered, prowling in circles like a careful predator, the more convinced I became that it would be twisted and relentless. And the more convinced I became, the wetter I became.

Max moved towards me. 'Excellent tits,' he said. He bounced each one, tapping their undersides as if checking out their springiness. 'Yes, very good. Now open your mouth.'

'Max, no,' I protested. More than anything I was starting to feel silly.

'Open your mouth,' he said, his tone so light and patient it brooked no refusal.

Reluctantly, I did so. Crouching down a little, Max peered inside my mouth, tilting his head this way and that. Clearly, I was no gift horse.

'Hmm, looks fine,' he said, as if to himself. Then louder, 'Obviously, I don't want to go sticking my dick into any old hole.'

He stood straighter. I gawped at him.

'Close your mouth,' he said. 'You look foolish.'

I clamped it shut. Max smiled faintly as if pleased his new tricks were working. Standing sideways on to me, he gently rocked his pelvis forwards. His crotch nudged against my hip so I could feel the swell of him inside his shorts. He rubbed back and forth, making sure I knew he was hard. 'Gonna get that dick inside you soon,' he murmured. 'Where do you want it? Mouth, pussy or arse?'

I stayed silent. He kept on slowly rocking.

'What's up?' he said. 'Cat got your tongue?'

I continued to say nothing.

'Well,' he said. 'Let's see what your cunt says, shall we?'

He moved in front of me and began pushing the skirt up my legs but it was so damn tight it got stuck around mid thigh. Max cursed, spun me around, tugged at the skirt's back slit and ripped. I immediately felt more comfortable.

'Better access,' said Max, resuming his position by my side. He bent to caress me above one knee then slid his big broad hand to the top of my thigh. He rested it there, firmly massaging the flash. Goosebumps of anticipation prickled across my skin. I did my best to be stoic but his massage tickled wisps of my pubes and the nearness of his hand had me dizzy with need. He trailed his thumb along my folds, brushing so gently I couldn't help but whimper.

I wanted so much more and Max seemed to take great delight in denying me that. He trailed his fingers around my thighs, painting shapes on my flesh. He strummed my clit once or twice. He reached below to caress my buttocks, smiling all the while at my clear discomfort. I ached for the solid penetration he withheld and, though I tried to suppress my cries of want, several bleats and groans escaped me. I could feel Max's smile grow with every sound, his touch becoming lighter. I had not known sadism could be so tender.

When he finally pushed two fingers inside me, it was with the softly condescending words, 'There we go. Better now?'

My senses spun, heat rising to fill my head. He hooked his fingers to press against my sweet spot, and every rub against my inner wall heightened my arousal. My cunt seemed to simultaneously open around his fingers, as if I were blossoming like a flower, and yet also seemed to thicken and swell, my pulpiness clinging to those clever fingers. I tried to conceal my hunger, knowing the revelation of it would prove me a slut, but my pooling moisture and shallow breath betrayed me.

'That nice?' he asked kindly. He stood so close his words tickled my ear. I whimpered quietly in response, and then again more loudly when I felt the sure touch of his thumb on my clitoris. 'Are you going to come?' he murmured. 'Going to show me what a greedy whore you are?'

He nudged my clit, a heavy, leisurely rock that had me melting onto his fingers. I didn't think I had much choice. My orgasm rose, fluttering closer and closer while two conflicting emotions danced inside me. On the one hand, it thrilled me that Max had responded so eagerly to my sluttish desires. But I squirmed inwardly from knowing that he knew I liked this. My secret shame was no longer quite so secret.

'Come on, babes,' he murmured. 'Show me what you're made of.' He sounded so deliciously sleazy, so sure of his ability to get me off. And he had good reason to be confident because my climax was coiling tighter as his thumb worked me faster. And then I was there, right there, clenching on his fingers and crying wantonly as white-hot stars flared in my mind. Release surged up to my head and down to my toes, and I was left feeling zonked with bliss.

'There's a good girl,' he said gently, withdrawing his fingers. He was talking to me as if I were his new pet. I wouldn't have been surprised if he'd stroked my hair or made me sit up and beg for treats. His tone irked and excited me in equal measure. I wasn't sure if I wanted more or less of it. As it turned out the choice wasn't mine. In a firmer voice, he said, 'Now get on your knees then I can test your mouth.'

I was more than ready to kneel, my climax having drained all strength from me, so I fell to the ground, my ragged clothes proving no hindrance to ease of movement. My dreams, sleeping and waking, came back to me in a flood of images as I opened my mouth. Max freed himself from his zip and his cock bounced out, ruddy and stern, only inches from my lips. Without delay, he slotted himself hard and deep into my throat, his fingers tangling in my hair. I spluttered a little, desperately clasping his hips and trying to hold him steady as I drew back on his length.

'This is what you want, isn't it?' cooed Max. 'A mouthful of cock.'

He was dead right. At my own pace, I slurped back and forth, opening my throat to him as best I could and making his head butt deep. My greed urged him on and before long we'd found our rhythm. It felt as if he were being mean to me by recklessly fucking my mouth but I knew deep down he was attentive to my comfort. Nonetheless, his zest made my eyes water.

'Look at me,' he said, and I did, peering up at him through a veil of tears glittering like the sea in the bay. I blinked them away, clearing my vision. Max looked down at me, smirking cruelly as he focused on his cock pumping into my snug lips. As he thrust, I pictured a kaleidoscopic fracturing of his erection, a shifting honey-comb of flushed knobs, tucked-up balls and veined shafts, all eager to take their pleasure from my mouth.

After several minutes, Max withdrew. His breath was ragged, his eyes glinting with enthusiasm and drama. I was breathless too but Max was in no mood for resting. He leaned down to tap the side of my arse, chivvying me along. 'Come on,' he said. 'On your back, legs spread. I want to check out this other hole.'

His crudeness thrilled me though I muttered my distaste. Hitching my skirt higher, I assumed the position while Max undressed, kicking his shorts aside. The spring sunlight carried a soft silvery quality, edging into the shadows and smudging the attic with a mercury haze. Naked, Max looked superb. His skin gleamed like ivory and in sharp contrast, his body hair was scraps of rich black velvet. His cock angled obscenely from the cloud of his pubes and

I opened myself wide as he joined me on the floor. He pushed my legs back so my knees were against my breasts and I heard fabric tear. I couldn't tell if it were the skirt, the blouse or both, but who cared? The only thing that mattered was my overwhelming need to have Max's hard cock inside me.

When his stout head rubbed at the slippery crevice of my cunt, I couldn't help but wail, 'Oh, please, please.'

'Please what?' asked Max. He hovered at my entrance, nudging and teasing.

'Please, just . . .'

'Just what?' His tone was stern and impatient.

'Please fuck me,' I breathed. 'Please fuck . . .'

'Slut,' said Max, sounding rather gratified.

His cock pressed slowly forwards, prising my wet flesh apart, and then he was lodged deep inside me, his solid girth filling me so beautifully. I cried out, hooking my legs over his shoulders to secure our position. With leisurely ease, Max drew back, holding himself at his furthest reach before ramming home once again.

'Slut,' he repeated. 'Begging for my cock, begging to get fucked.'

Over and over, he plunged into me.

'Yes, yes,' I gasped, hardly knowing what I was affirming.

The shaft of his cock slid over my G-spot, and the bump of his lunges rubbed the bump of my clit. My nearness swelled, my body so sensitive to pleasure. Then I remembered I was meant to be Rebecca, that Max was treating me like a slut because I'd stepped into her shoes. Well, I thought, if that's what's required, so be it. I would gladly take her place time and again if it meant seeing action like this.

'Yes,' I said. 'I'm a slut. I'm Rebecca, I'm your greedy little –'

'No, you're not,' cut in Max. 'You're not her. You're nobody, you hear? Just some whore I picked up. I don't even know you. Don't know your name. Don't care either. You're just a fuck to me, a slut. Just a . . . a cheap, nameless slut!'

His words shivered through me. His callousness, his demolition of my identity was exquisitely freeing. We might have been strangers, wanting nothing but satisfaction from each other. It was all about sex – heartless, greedy, passionate sex. How strange and heavenly that we could unite in lust by conjuring up this distance and anonymity.

'You don't count,' he gasped. 'No name, no nothing. Just a hole.'

He made me think of those lost lonely places, outskirts of towns, warehouses by the docks, empty cottages, forgotten alleys and valentine's roses crushed underfoot. Like the attic, they didn't belong; they were places for secrets, shame and safety, places where you were answerable to no one but yourself.

'No name,' gasped Max, and he bent closer, his body grinding on my clit. My climax fluttered higher, tighter, then, with a few more thrusts, I came hard, three distinct clutches of ecstasy squeezing at my core. Max didn't even pause.

'No name,' he said again.

I heard the familiar rise in his voice, the gathering groans and urgency. I knew he was close but then, as if he'd seen my dream, he pulled out and moved hurriedly up my body. With his cock in his hand, he jerked hard and fast then he came on my face, his bursts of warmth splashing onto my cheek and spicing my lips.

Max rolled onto his back with a groan of exhaustion and I smeared his come into my mouth. He tasted sharp and briny, reminding me of the sea Rebecca once swam in.

After an uncertain silence, I asked, 'Is that what you used to do together? Was she a slut?'

Max scoffed. 'I wish.'

'Tell me,' I replied.

For a long time, he didn't answer. Then, 'Let's just say, if she'd been as interested in fucking as she was in clothes, I'd have been a very happy man.' He rubbed his hand over his face. 'Um, actually, that's not true. There'd need to be a lot of other changes as well. Starting with personality.'

Max leaned away, grabbed his shorts and fished out his cigarettes. I was confused. He'd said so little about Rebecca since we'd met and I'd assumed his silence meant he was still broken-hearted from her dumping him.

'I thought she was a goer,' I said. 'And she ran off with your best mate.'

Max laughed as he flicked open his Zippo and struck the cog. The flame shot high and bright, the gas purring faintly. He drew on his cigarette, the tip an ember-red glow.

'Nah!' he said, snapping shut his lighter. 'And I hardly knew the bloke to be honest. Just knew she fancied him cause he had an Aston Martin. Poor sod did me a favour really.' Max exhaled a stream of smoke. 'I'd wanted out for ages. Next step, she collects her stuff. I'm sick of it hanging around here. I've half a mind to torch it.' He pulled hard on his cigarette again, and I watched the column of ash gathering at the end.

'I'd rather have your stuff around,' he went on. 'Your stuff and you.' He grinned, smoke trickling from his lips. 'Especially now I know you're a dirty little slut.'

I inhaled the smell of his cigarette. Outside, a gull cried in the clear blue sky. I could feel the spectre of Rebecca leaving the room, leaving us in peace as Max's cigarette smoke strangled her perfume, the last intangible vestiges of his ex.

And I reached out to touch him, wanting to reassure myself this wasn't a dream. Then I licked my lips, tasting him there, all bitter, burnt and salty, and I knew for certain this was wonderfully real.

Kristina Lloyd is the author of the Black Lace novels _Darker Than Love_, _Asking for Trouble_ and _Split_. Her novella _The Vampire's Heart_ is published in the Black Lace collection _Lust Bites_. Her short stories appear in numerous Black Lace anthologies.

Slut

Charlotte Stein

I couldn't put a name to him at first. I'm not used to using a name like that for boys. But he is nonetheless: slut.

He isn't a slut in the same way that some guys are – players and bounders and cads. The word 'slut' doesn't quite seem to apply to them. But it applies to him, when we're in the stationery cupboard together.

We're in there, and he smiles his little sly slut's smile at me. At the time I didn't know what that smile meant, but I did soon after. I did when he turned around and bent over as though to reach for something on a low shelf, and his bum very obviously pressed into the front of my skirt.

Not even the front of my skirt. Into my groin. Definitely against my groin. He even had to kind of crouch to do it, because he's very tall. But he managed it nonetheless, and I felt those firm buttocks push into the place where my pussy is.

He did it like a woman urging her bottom back for a man's cock. He did it like an animal seeking a mounting. I had no idea how he expected me to mount him, but after the initial shock that's what I thought of anyway.

I've never wished so fiercely that I had a cock. A big fat cock that I could have plunged into his tight little arsehole – made him beg for it, made him whimper and whine and twist on me.

It occurred to me later that he was gay and some kind of fascination with me had gripped him. Perhaps he felt that I was a rather mannish woman, perfect for trying out straightness.

But that misconception didn't last long.

It stopped when I caught him looking down my top. It stopped even more when I deliberately leaned forwards and let him see further, and he couldn't even contain his little sigh of satisfaction.

He didn't even look embarrassed when I flicked my gaze to his face and finally, finally, his eyes drew up and away from my tits to meet mine. I think he tried to contain that sly slut's smile of his, but other than that he did nothing. Because sluts never do anything about getting caught, being a slut.

He became even more flagrant when I ogled him openly and lewdly. I caught him changing in his cubicle – just his shirt, nothing more – and instead of walking away and giving him his privacy, I stood there and ogled him. I did it like a challenge. I drew my gaze over his long lean torso, the slow slide down into his narrow hips, his thickly broad shoulders and his skin, oh, his lovely pale milk skin. I didn't apologise for it; I didn't let myself be nervous. I imagined what it must be like to be a man, if he were the woman. His sluttishness would make me confident, horny, unabashed. Why shouldn't I look if he delights in it?

And he did delight in it. Far from stopping, he had worked his vest oh so slowly up, up over his thick chest, fingers skimming his gorgeous skin as though wanting them to be my fingers, burning dark eyes never leaving mine.

Right at the very last moment he had bitten his lip, and dropped his gaze. I think I loved him, for that.

He does more things that I love him for. Many more things. Many more things that my pussy loves him for. He becomes a clit-tease, a filthy little temptress, pushing on my nerves and my restraint.

Surely he knows. Surely he knows that soon I won't have any.

When in a board meeting, an important meeting that he is only present at to take minutes in his silly too-big handwriting, I know that he looks. I can feel his eyes ever returning to me, waiting for me to look back. Sluts are only satisfied when you look back. He wants my attention on him, confirming his attractiveness. Making him sure that what he has worn that day pleases and excites me.

And it does. I have no idea how he knew, but I have a thing for men in V-neck jumpers. Buttoned up like a female relic from the eighteenth century, tie knotted too tight for comfort, material clinging in a way that suggests the wearer is not aware it is clinging. No one who wears V-neck jumpers could be aware that they're in something clingy.

Except for him. He obviously designed it that way: the perfect trap for my desire.

But clearly, he isn't satisfied with the effect just yet. It isn't quite enough for me to occasionally admire his shoulders, or to wonder what it would be like to hook my finger into the loop of his tie and lead him around the office like a dog. That dog who wanted me to mount it, back in the stationery cupboard.

No. He has to go one step further. He has to push it. He has to lean back in those thankfully smooth and soundless meeting room chairs, stretching his glorious body out for my delectation. He has to take his pen, and pat it lightly against his full lower lip. That lower lip I want to bite.

Even worse, he then decides to part those biteable lips, and just ever so slightly nudge the pen inside. I see his perfect white teeth bite down – not hard enough to leave any sort of mark, but not lightly either. The perfect biting strength for, say, a nipple. And then maybe his tongue could ... oh yes. Just flicker against the thing in his mouth. And maybe he could then ...

Suck.

I watch his cheeks hollow, just a little, just enough to put a person in mind of a little boy sucking on a lollipop, rather than anything lewd. But, of course, it's lewd to me. It's lewd because I know what he is and what it means, the tease.

Because that's what he's doing, really. He's teasing me with his perfectly cut features and his broad shoulders and his limpid eyes and his sucking mouth. He probably thinks I won't do a thing about any of it, because how could such a lovely creature as him be interested in me?

But he's a fool. I would say he's playing with fire, but fire has nothing on my libido.

When the meeting ends, I line my voice with calm cool iron and say to him: 'Can I see you in my office, Brad?'

Of course he has a name like Brad. Something wholesome and cute. If he were a girl, he'd be called Candy.

'Of course, Ms Layton,' he replies, and oh the devil pushes just the right hint of bemusement into his voice. Why, he has no idea what I might want with *him*. He is only a little insignificant peon. What on *earth* could he have done wrong?

I am going to show you what you have done wrong, Brad.

I hear him lolloping after me. He's very tall and near gangly, despite the bulk of his chest and shoulders. I suppose that's why I don't feel intimidated by his size, though I accept that there are other reasons.

It's hard to be intimidated by a floozy.

Even though I think he wants me to be intimidated. I think he wants me to be in awe of his sexual power, in thrall to him. I should be hypnotised and tormented by his behaviour and the way he looks. Big boss woman Ms Layton brought low? We'll see.

Once we're inside the safety of my office, I close the door behind us. I lock it. He jerks a little when I do, but it's too late for him to be surprised and innocent. Now he's going to have to pay the piper.

'Have I . . . ?' he starts to say, but I think something in my expression stops him.

'Yes. You've done something very wrong. Very wrong indeed.'

His face falls – and he does it well, too. It hardly looks put on at all.

'I'm so sorry, Ms Layton,' he says. 'How can I make it up?'

Again, it's all very convincing. He's a clever boy.

'Bend over that desk, and write on the notepad I have there exactly what you've done wrong, and how you expect to resolve the matter.'

He hesitates for the barest of moments. I see his tongue touch his upper teeth. And then he does exactly what I've asked.

He presents his rump to me perfectly, just like in the stationary cupboard, and then he takes up my best pen and starts scribbling with it. Each time he scribbles, his bottom wiggles just a little bit.

It's delightful. It's begging for my hand. I don't know why he makes that little shocked sound when I whack my palm against that begging flesh.

'Hoh!' he gasps. But he doesn't stop writing. He doesn't even turn around. It's the third slap he looks back at me on, and I see his eyes so naked and his cheeks flushed and that mouth hanging open. Shock and sex and hunger all stirred up together.

'Eyes front,' I tell him. 'While I punish you.'

'Is this how you punish all your staff?' he asks, so I reach around and unbuckle his belt. Clearly he needs something more severe, and he doesn't deny it. He doesn't even go to stop my hand or ask again if I do this with all staff, he just moans and whispers something I can't hear.

'Louder,' I say, so he shouts out with a break in the middle: 'I can't believe this is happening!'

'What did you think would happen, tease?'

'I –' he starts to say, but then I yank his Calvin Kleins down to meet the trousers that are now around his ankles, and he groans for me some more.

He has stopped writing altogether now. The pen is still clutched in his hand, however, though that doesn't last long. Once his underpants hit the floor so does the pen, and though I can't see, I know exactly what he's doing: jerking off. His thighs butt against the desk. His hips roll. I hear that slick clicking of a hand shuttling up and down a stiff cock, and he must know I can, too. But he doesn't stop. Not even when I slap his bare buttocks hard enough to leave a mark.

Instead he gasps: 'I'm going to come all over the nice neat writing I've just done for you.'

'Bad slut,' I tell him, and slap right over the handprint I've just made.

Unfortunately, this only makes him groan and fuck himself harder. I actually think he's really going to come that quickly; I can see his bum cheeks clenching and he's making far too much noise and soon he's babbling: 'God, I'm sorry, I'm sorry, I need to come so bad. God, I've been thinking about your tits all afternoon.'

I yank on his arm and get his hand away from his cock as punishment. He squirms with frustration, but doesn't try to start it up with his other hand, as though he was just waiting for me to stop him and a show of stopping him is enough.

'All afternoon?'

'Yeeessss,' he whines, and I want to turn him around so much. I want to see his gorgeous face all crumpled with impatience and lust, and then I want to watch him tug his cock until it gleams.

'Is this something you've done before?'

Oddly, I feel like a doctor. It isn't a terrible feeling by any means.

'What? Think about ... your tits ... or jerk off at work?'

That last bit comes out in a rush, and sets me glowing. Oh, to think of him doing himself in one of the stalls or in his cubicle under his desk! My clit twinges in sympathy.

'Usually I ... Usually I have to ... you know. Because I've been thinking about you.'

'What do you think about me doing?'

'I catch you. I catch you playing with yourself. Playing with your nipples, with your shirt open and your skirt up.'

Oh Jesus, that's nice. I've done it before, too, in my office. With the door locked, of course, but sometimes I'm daring enough to leave the blinds open, hoping that some beefy window cleaner will chance by and see me as lewd as can be, legs spread open, fingers strumming my clit to a great big juicy orgasm.

I need to come so bad now that I can feel my clit straining against the material of my panties, and I'm wet enough to feel it when I move. Maybe I'll make him watch while I bring myself off with that little buzzing dildo I keep in my bag. Maybe I'll make him lick my clit with his hands tied behind his back so that he can't do himself. Maybe I'll let him fuck me over the desk, great handfuls of my tits in his big hands, some window cleaner watching with his cock in his fist.

Oh, the possibilities are endless when you've got a slut on your hands.

'You like my tits and my nipples, huh?'

'Yes,' he gusts out.

I circle the desk slowly, leaving his sore arse and all that shameful need to not look him in the face behind. My legs almost buckle when I get a look at him – firm, endlessly curving prick as red and glistening as you please, shirt tails flapping, face flushed and slack. He looks like he could devour just about anyone right now. I could probably bring in Margot from accounting, and have him hump her over my couch.

'Would you like to see them now?'

'Seriously? Jesus, yes.'

I think it's the most sincere I've ever heard any man sound. I don't think he knows how to be anything but, though I suppose that's what sluts are really made of – honesty. He cannot be anything but honest about his own desires.

So I reward him by unbuttoning my shirt. He answers me by breathing hard and going for his cock again, but I tell him no. No, the price he has to pay for the sight of my breasts is keeping his hands by his sides.

It delights me that when I tell him this, he closes his eyes and clenches his teeth, but still obeys. The hands at his sides become fists – I hadn't realised how much fun sluts were to play with. Do men do this all the time? Make them beg and plead and clench their teeth? What fun.

I slide my shirt all the way off and then unfasten the front clasp of my bra. His eyes have completely forgone my face but I can't blame him. I'm too flattered to blame him – he looks like he's about to see God.

My sensitive nipples brush the lace of the cups as I peel the material away, but the soft sigh of my pleasure is freely given when he sighs too.

'Are you turned on?' he moans – I think more because my nipples are so small and tight than because I sighed. 'Does it turn you on, screwing around with me like this?'

'You know, I think it does,' I say.

His eyes shutter closed again for the briefest moment. 'Can I jerk off?'

'Not yet.'

'Please. Please. I think I'm gonna burst.'

'You'll live. Now, I want you to come here and play with my tits. Do you think you can do that?'

I don't think he can do it fast enough. He almost trips over his own trousers getting to me, and then his hands lunge at my breasts as though magnetised. I slap them. He says sorry. But even when he's saying it he can't stop ogling them. I suppose they're nice breasts – firm and full, nipples spiking upwards, skin as soft and fair as his – but even so. I just hadn't realised, in between all of his teasing and cheekiness, that he might be so horny for me.

'Lick your fingers, first,' I tell him, and he does so real quick without any kind of teasing show. But then he waits, he waits, and that's even better. 'Now gently pinch and stroke them.'

He's not a bad boy at all; I was wrong. He's very, very good. He licks and strokes and thumbs my nipples, sometimes lightly pinching, other times just circling, ever slick and smooth. The ache from those tight tips soon transfers itself to my swollen clit and my empty, creaming pussy, but I squeeze my thighs together against it.

'Suck them,' I say, and he immediately falls to it, licking and sucking and mouthing until I'm shivering with pleasure. I even let out an 'Oh yes, just like that,' and he groans into the flesh of my breast.

It makes it so that I can't wait any longer. I slip my knickers down while he's still licking and playing with my breasts, and then I pull away briefly to sit on the desk, legs spread. The cool air feels wonderful against my heated cunt, my stiff bud, but God his mouth would feel so much better.

I don't even have to order him either. He pushes up my skirt immediately, exposing my slick spread sex to his gaze.

'You've done that to me, tease,' I say, and part my sex lips with two fingers to give him a better view. My clit stands out proud and coated in my own arousal, and I can't resist stroking it, lightly. 'What are you going to do about it?'

He drops to his knees immediately. I am reminded of someone

about to die and praying to God to deliver him, and, I have to say, I don't mind that at all. He can pray all he wants at the altar of my pussy.

He hesitates before he leans forwards, but all that does is remind me how little he has hesitated so far. Not even at the lines I made him write. Not even at the spanking. But then again, you can't exactly hesitate when you've rubbed your bottom into someone's groin. It's like a game of chicken, and no one wants to be the one who puts their foot on the brake first.

I wonder where my brake would have been, if I hadn't decided to punish him. Would I have let him keep pushing me, going further and further? How far would he have gone?

Dirty pictures in my inbox, I think. Naughty emails and memos and oh, I should have let this game go on longer. I miss what I never got to see – him jerking off, just for me.

But now he's licking at me, fingering me, fucking me with his mouth and hands and I can't complain. He laves his tongue over my clit roughly at first, but soon more softly, more teasing, more exploratory.

Occasionally he replaces his flickering tongue with two fingers, scissoring around my clit and rubbing while he laps and mouths at the entrance to my pussy. The back and forth is maddening, but the caress of his tongue around every part of me sends slivers of sensation up my spine and back again. He coaxes out sensitive places I didn't know I had, ever eager.

It's the eagerness that makes him good really. But then he has to be – good I mean. He probably services women all the time.

Finally I give in and order him to bring me off, tugging him up by the thick hair at the nape of his neck so that his tongue can work my clit. Hearing my urgency, he laps quickly, pushing two thick fingers inside me and twisting them as he does.

It's too much. My body seizes and my clit swells against his tongue, fresh liquid spilling over his fingers as I orgasm with a fistful of his hair clenched in my hand and my back arching. I grunt like an animal and tell him mindlessly, 'Yes, I'm coming, I'm coming.' Mindlessly because of course he can't fail to realise what's happening.

He moans and pants against my slippery flesh, doing his best to draw every last drop of pleasure from me, before I finally push him away.

He sprawls back, cock now so stiff and angry looking that I actually feel bad for a moment. Even if he is a dirty tease, that can't be comfortable. He actually seems to have leaked pre-come all the way down his shaft, and I can see his hands clenching and unclenching at his sides.

When I stop leaning back on my hands – relishing the slow dissipation of everything he has just given me – and move towards him, his cock jerks. He jerks. There is heat high up on his perfect pale cheeks now, and soft dark tendrils of his hair cling to his temples. He looks like a livewire, juddering with too much electricity. He wants me to cut it in two, and let the snapping sizzling power out.

Which I will do.

I feel as though I'm prowling towards him. I am flushed and full up and he lies prostrate before me, back on his elbows, shoulders jutting forwards, lips parted. He tosses his head and his cute little sweeping fringe is out of his eyes. Sometimes they're puppy dog and sometimes they're sultry and right now they're burning black and deep.

'That was very good, Brad,' I say and he smiles – not quite that sly smile, but one that says he knows. He knows he's good at worshipping pussy. He even replies in a delightful sort of confirmation, plain and as sincere as he had seemed before: 'I love pussy.'

I stand astride his near-spread thighs, and look down into his upturned face.

'Tell me how you love it,' I say, and when he speaks it's in tumbling, never halting, barely sentences.

'I love licking it and tasting it and smothering my face in all that hot wetness – your clit, too, I love your clit when it jumps against my tongue and when you squirm, I love it when you squirm, Ms Layton, I love it that you're at my mercy at the same time that you're not.'

'I hear that's why girls like giving guys blow jobs, Brad,' I say, but he doesn't flinch. He doesn't look embarrassed.

'Is that why you like giving blow jobs, Ms Layton?' he asks, but I don't think he really expects an answer. I think he's amused, but his amusement doesn't anger me. It angers me even less when he tells me: 'I don't care about what I am or what you think of me. This is what I like, and I don't care if you think it's the wrong way round.'

I wonder how many people have told him before now that he's the wrong way round. I wonder if they told him so because of how terrifying he is. His power over me is terrifying. I've locked the door and spanked him and made him write lines and had him lick my pussy, and all without him telling me to – not even a little bit.

I wonder if he's made other girls do things like this, hypnotised them into dominating him with just the power of his good looks and his boyish appeal and his teasing.

I sink to my knees astride him, his bobbing cock occasionally patting between my legs when he stirs or it jerks. He lets me push his jumper up over his head, and then his shirt too, but I leave the loop of his tie around his neck.

It makes a handy leash, to wrap around my fist and use to pull his mouth up to mine.

The groan he pushes into me echoes through my body, tying me up in knots once more and making me thrust my tongue into his mouth. He responds eagerly – I'm sure eagerness is all he knows – stirring his own tongue wetly against mine, letting his mouth fall slack as I force myself over him.

He tastes like me. I've never tasted me before. Not like this anyway. I taste sweet, so sweet, as sweet as sweat on the back of the strapping young man you hired to mow the lawn.

One of his hands leaves the carpet and grasps me at the small of my back, urging me forwards, urging me harder down on him. His cock finds its way underneath my ruffled-up skirt, and the more he pulls at me the more flesh it makes contact with, until finally I feel the soft-hard slick head of it split my slit and rub up roughly against my oversensitised clit.

I don't stop it happening. Instead I reach between our bodies and press his cock right into the seam of my sex, feeling the lips there close around it almost as my wet hole would. When I lean forwards and rise up just a little, the fit is almost perfect, and I rock my clit against the sensitive underside of him.

He bucks up against me, now shamelessly moaning into my mouth. I rub him against my flesh, striking just the right amount of pressure to eventually bring myself off – not that he's going to last that long. He's trembling and, when I reach down with my free hand and cup and massage his drawn-up tight balls and the soft moist place just behind, he lunges up hard against me and draws his mouth away from mine.

'Oh God, make me come, Ms Layton,' he pants against my jaw, my cheek, everywhere leaving wet trails and hot breath. 'Ah yes, rub me there.'

I do. I have to prove, after all, that I'm as good as he is.

'Wait,' I tell him. 'Wait. I want you to come in my mouth.'

He likes that. He likes that, oh yes, he does. He lets his head fall back and the column of his throat presents itself to me, stark and strong, ready to be bitten. I had a boyfriend once who loved nothing better than to bite me, to mark me, to leave little circles all over my body. And I liked it too. I have always liked the sensation of teeth sinking in.

But this is the first time I've wanted to sink my teeth into someone else. Not just *wanted* to, but *craved* it. I want to mark all that perfect pale flesh, to scatter myself all over him in nips and bites, and see what I used to look like reflected in his midnight eyes. Shuddering, shivering, beneath another person. Pulled taut against nearly pain.

I want to teach him more about what nearly pain is. Of course I'm sure he knows already. I'm sure he knows a lot of things already, horny and gorgeous as he is. But he's also delightful enough to pretend for me, I know.

I bite him just at that place where his throat meets his shoulder. That little cup made for my teeth. And then he gasps and hisses and that meaty pressure satisfies my teeth – that lovely tensing and releasing feeling that I've only ever felt with my own hand pressed to my mouth, something buzzing between my thighs.

'Please,' he begs me, with his hand in my hair. 'Please.'

But I know he doesn't mean *please stop biting*. In fact, he presses my face harder into his throat, and sighs when I'm done leaving my little mark.

He rubs his fingers through the wetness I leave there, an expression much like wonder on his face. Wonder that's mostly a show, just for me.

But a little red pattern can't hold his attention – faux or otherwise – for long. He cocks an eyebrow at me, head still turned to one side, fingers still on the bite mark. Now, I suppose, should be the time when the tables will be turned, if he wasn't the wrong way round.

Instead he goes with: 'What do I have to do to have you?'

He really shouldn't give me such possibilities. I don't think I'm a very nice person when I get possibilities. Maybe that's why all my other boyfriends liked to tie me up. Maybe that's why I liked to be tied up.

Maybe that's why I'm suddenly not as sated as I was before. My teeth and gums hum with the memory of his flesh. My clit swells against his trying-to-rock prick.

'Tell me a story,' I say. 'Tell me the hottest story you can think of, and don't come all the way through it.'

A shadow of bashfulness falls over his face. He looks rueful, humble. I want to eat a slice of him.

'I was never a very good storyteller.'

'Try. And while you're trying, you can dress for the occasion. If, of course, I allow the occasion to come about.'

I stand, leaving his cock wet and bereft of the enclosing warmth of my pussy. He groans, but in no other way protests. He takes the condom I retrieve from my purse without a word. Sticks his tongue into the corner of his mouth as though concentrating hard – whether on rolling the latex down or inventing a story, I have no idea.

But I want to eat a slice of that, too.

'Hottest story . . .' he says, and it sounds almost as though *he's* toying with *me*. Except for the up and down quaver in his voice, of course. 'Hottest story . . .'

I retrieve my knickers from the floor.

'You know, I'm completely satisfied, Brad,' I say, even though that's now a complete lie. He looks absolutely incredible stood there, mostly naked. Tie around his neck, pants still kind of around his ankles, condom-clad cock trembling. I've never wanted anyone to fuck me more, and more than just once too.

I'm unlikely to be giving him up any time soon. I do so hope he's prepared.

'No – no, wait. No, give me a chance. I've got one.' He actually looks panicked. I don't think he's prepared at all.

'OK, OK. So there's this woman, right?'

'I see,' I sigh, and hop back up onto the desk. I cross my legs, knickers still dangling from one finger. Bored, bored, bored – only, you know, wet enough to ruin my mouse pad at the same time.

'And she's a real tease. She's the biggest horniest tease there is. And she has all these little minions at her beck and call, and they just have to watch as she stalks around in her tiny tight skirts and her blouses that show off all her cleavage.'

'Does she have nice cleavage, Brad?'

'Gorgeous cleavage. Her tits are like ... They're like ... moons.'

I'd laugh, if it were not for the enthusiasm he packs into this ... 'story'. He's practically spluttering with it. And it's obvious that he's getting off on it in some way too, because his stiff prick is now almost touching his belly.

'And there's this one guy ... this one guy she loves to torment more than the others. She loves to stand real close to him so he can smell her perfume right down to his cock. She likes to bend over him and show him everything she's got. She likes to lick her lips and get his mind stuffed full with how it'd look sucking on him. He can hardly think straight and keeps doing things wrong because everywhere she's there, begging for him to just ... fill her mouth and her pussy and her ...'

'Yes, Brad?'

'... her ass.'

There are so many things that I don't mind about Brad, this story included, but I think I like the little swallow he does after 'ass', the best.

'I bet you'd like to do one after the other, wouldn't you, Brad?'

He swallows again, harder this time. Takes a calming breath.

'If I say the wrong thing am I gonna get cut off?' he asks, so plaintively that I actually *can't* stop myself laughing, this time.

'I tell you what, Brad. Why don't you start with my mouth, and we'll see how far you get.'

'I think about right here,' he says, half-amused with himself, half-tremulous.

I laugh again, and reach for him. He does not come to me easily. Now that his finger's on the trigger and there's so much on offer, he's reluctant to start.

'You know, I can usually go forever.'

'What's different about now?' I ask, as I slither off my desk and down, down his body until I'm on my knees. He looks gargantuan from down here.

'You,' he whispers, before I run my tongue along the rubber-clad underside of his cock. It should taste bitter, I suppose, but it doesn't at all.

'Keep talking, Brad,' I say, between licks. 'What happens next?'

'Next she ... Oh! Next ... Jesus ... she ... she decides I need to be punished, for all the things I've been doing wrong ... no don't. Don't suck me. Not yet – don't!'

I squeeze the base of his shaft and cock a look up at him. 'You're doing *really* well, Brad,' I say, and he tries to fumble on with his story.

'I ... uh ... where was I?'

'You were about to get her on your desk and fuck her with your big prick.'

'I don't think I got to that part yet.'

'Yes you did, Brad,' I say, as I stand up and lead him by the cock to my waiting pussy.

I go to hop back up on my desk, but now that story time's done, he grabs me around the waist – just two big hands, practically swallowing me – and picks me up. Sets me back down and barely waits for me to steady myself or cling to him or anything. Just yanks me forwards with his hands on my ass, and shoves in.

I think I shout. It sounds very high-pitched and too loud. He apologises when my hands clamp on to his shoulders, but then just falls to rutting against me, grasping my ass cheeks and tugging hard when it's not enough for him.

He feels too fabulous, too hard against the soft sweet place inside me – I can't stop myself from rippling my pussy over his stiff flesh. He groans in protest when I do, but that just starts the cycle up all over again: he groans, I spark with pleasure, my pussy shimmies and shivers, he groans again.

Until, finally: 'I'm gonna come – damn. Damn. I wanted to fuck your ass.'

'Then do it,' I say, cool as you please while my insides boil and my pussy creams and I wonder what, exactly, the wrong way round actually is.

I didn't think it was a thick hard cock skimming and slipping through all the juice that's made its way between the cheeks of my ass. I didn't think it was him saying: 'I don't think –'

Before my clenching asshole gives way to his cock. But maybe it is, because now I'm getting fucked in the ass on my desk in the middle of a work day, and any second someone's going to knock on the door, and I'll have to answer full of cock. Stretched and fucked and the dirtiest I can be.

Though in all honesty, I think I can be dirtier. I wonder if he'd like me to fuck *his* ass.

'Jesus Christ, you're choking me,' he gasps, but he doesn't stop jerking against me and clasping my spread thighs and running all his little 'uhs' together.

'You can't come until I do, Brad,' I say, but that's too cruel even for the person I'm being now.

Even so, he obeys. He presses the heel of his palm to my straining clit and makes me come without me even knowing what does it. His trembling does it. The way he bites his lip and can't control his jerking hips. The way he moans: 'I'm gonna go, I'm gonna . . . I can't stop, oh man, oh man . . .'

It's always the sights and sounds of someone else that set me off. And I *do* set off. I shake with it. I clasp his hand to my pussy, I clasp him inside me. I moan loud enough for everyone to hear – even worse, I moan his name. He wrings it out of me, all these great surges of sensation. It's like being washed in orgasms.

And then it's all done, and he collapses over me on my desk. The desk where I once responded to an invitation from the prime minister.

'Behave yourself in future, Brad,' I tell him. 'No one likes a tease.'

I have to say, it's somewhat disconcerting to see the flash of purest confusion cross his perfect open features. He looks almost stupidly baffled, like a cartoon character of a real boy. But he pauses, and considers, and finally tries to formulate words. 'I . . .' he begins, then takes a step backwards, back towards safety. Though he doesn't look unsafe exactly. He smiles faintly, as he leaves, settling on acquiescence that seems as pleased as much as it is confused: 'All right,' he says. 'All right, Ms Layton.'

I don't know what to make of that. I don't know what he means by 'all right', and I have even less of a clue about what he was going to say after that first halting 'I'. But then I look down on the piece of paper he half-filled for his punishment, and see that he has written, over and over in his silly too-big handwriting: 'I have no idea. I have no idea. I have no idea.'

Charlotte Stein's first single author collection, *The Things That Make Me Give In*, is published by Black Lace in October 2009. Her short fiction appears in numerous Black Lace anthologies.

All in the Details

Rachel Kramer Bussel

'Tell me about it,' I whispered in George's ear. 'I want to know every detail.'

'Esther, that was such a long time ago. You don't really want to know about it. I never really talk to anyone about it.'

'Then why'd you let it slip? Why tease me like that?' Just the thought of him sucking another guy's dick had me soaking wet. We both know that I have a higher sex drive than he does, so I'm always looking for ways to add to my arousal. George doesn't mind if I watch porn or even go to sex parties, as long as I restrict myself to watching and making out. Oh, and talking dirty. He knows that there are plenty of potential lovers waiting in the wings who know about our arrangement. One way I satisfy myself is by whispering to them what I would do to them, with them, for them, if I could. What I'd want them to do to me, and to George.

We haven't ruled out the possibility of opening up our relationship sometime in the future, of letting a friend slip between our sheets, between our bodies. Until now, I had always thought of our third fantasy partner as a woman but a whole new world had just opened up to me, and my inner fag hag was all ears.

'Please, baby.' I grabbed his fingers and placed them between my legs, rubbing against the centre of my panties. 'That's how wet you're making me. I want to hear about it. Who was he? What did you do? Who started it?' I was as eager to hear the naughty details in order to get off as I was to get a little insight into who George had been before he met me. I knew the basic outline, but we'd both steered clear of any detail about our past sex lives, perhaps worried about rocking the boat or inciting jealousy where none had previously existed.

'OK, OK,' he said, turning me around so we were spooning. I let him pull my hips close, his breath hot on my neck, knowing that he needed it to be this way, without me watching him as well as listening.

'It was my college room-mate, Jason. He was a swimmer, and smelled of chlorine. He had this muscular but lean body, and he was full of energy. He was always doing jumping jacks and sit-ups while I sat in front of the computer. To me, he was just this blur of energy. I never really thought much about his dating life; he didn't seem to have one as far as I could tell.' George paused, his hand on my hip dipping beneath the edges of my panties. I pushed back against him to let him know I wanted more – of his fingers, and his story.

'He also never drank. Well, until this one night. He had lost a swim meet and came home in a really crappy mood. I was usually the one moping around, hung up on some girl or worried about a test that might jinx my scholarship. I told him I was taking him out drinking. Right away, he had an objection. "How will we get into the bar?" We were only eighteen then. I told him not to worry about it, to just put on his best outfit.

'Well, he must have been hiding some of his wardrobe, because he walked out wearing this really sexy sweater. That's the only way I can describe it; it made me want to pet him. Plus he had on this perfect pair of jeans that just made his legs look beautiful, and loafers. He looked like a model and that was the first time I thought I might be bi, or bi-curious. I wanted to kiss him, the same way I'd wanted to kiss all those girls in my classes. "Excuse me," I told him, and went into the bathroom to take care of my erection.'

I had already slipped my fingers between my legs. This was the best foreplay we'd engaged in in years. I was smitten with the idea of my very manly, hunky boyfriend jerking off in secret as he lusted after his male room-mate. It was so forbidden and naughty and hot. I've long loved looking at men kissing, whether in photos, porn or real-life opportunities, and have even initiated male-on-male action from some of my friends who've seemed interested but tentative, though those forays had never yielded more than a few moments of mutual pleasure. And while watching bonafide gay guys make out is arousing, getting two men who wouldn't otherwise be drawn to their own sex to discover the thrill of kissing another man, making another man hard, is the sexiest power trip I know. My friend Belinda taught me how to go about it, and it's been a little party trick of ours over the years, but one whose excitement was fleeting and impossible to predict; some guys can, indeed, resist a pretty girl pouting and begging him to pucker up.

So knowing that my lover, the man I'd shared a bed with for the past two years, had just such an episode in his past, was making my wetness practically spill onto my fingers.

'I was going to just try to make my cock calm down, but I wound up beating off as I thought about him down on his knees sucking me off. I had to shut my eyes and soon I was coming, biting my lip to stifle my moans. Then I quickly cleaned up and headed back out, trying to keep my dirty thoughts to myself, even though I knew there was no going back. Once I'd pictured him swallowing my seed, I knew we'd be naked together by the end of the night.' He paused to kiss the back of my neck, almost absently, like he wished it were Jason's. Then he came to life, nuzzling against me, breathing in the scent of my grapefruit shampoo, so he got to be there and here at once. We both did, and I was getting such a vivid picture in my mind, I was starting to regret that we hadn't met back then and could've devised a way for me to watch this gay seduction in action.

'I took him to a bar off campus that most students shunned because it had nothing fancy to offer. But, as you know, I have a soft spot for dive bars, and the darkness there was the perfect cover for me to both cheer Jason up and make him think our getting together was his idea. I bought us both beers, whatever was on tap, and then made him chug his. Then I got us another round and suggested we play photo hunt – you know, that game you love, with the almost-naked girls you have to match up with each other.'

I giggled, because it was true; just like his former friend, I get beyond excited when I see that a bar has those video games. They bring out my competitive spirit along with my desire to check out other women.

'I figured that if we were both safely looking at women, women in glistening bikinis, picturing what we'd do with these girls, we'd both get turned on, but the chances of any real-life women entering our realm were slim. The chances of them coming on to us were even slimmer, so the result would be that we'd head back to our room a little buzzed and a lot horny. And that's pretty much what happened.'

George's fingers found mine inside my panties as he pressed his hard-on against my backside. I was glad this wasn't just some chore he was doing as a favour, recounting the time he got it on with another guy. I'd done the same for him: told him about fiery kisses with other girls, my friend who attacked me one night and wouldn't stop until I sucked her nipples to orgasm, or my ex-girlfriend who delighted in lifting up my skirt and giving me spankings anywhere and everywhere. I loved sharing those details because I'd been with too many guys who were close-minded and felt threatened by even a hint of lesbian lust. Here I'd found a hot guy who not only wanted to hear about my dykey past, but had a little contribution of his own to our bisexual relationship.

In other words, I knew that at the end he'd fuck me senseless. 'Keep going,' I murmured, meaning both his fingers and his tale.

'So we played a few more rounds, wound up getting free vodka shots from the bartender, and capped things off with a final beer. Jason was grinning and, when I asked if he was feeling better, he looked at me like I was speaking in tongues. "What do you mean? I've never felt better," he said, with a little slur in his voice. "Let's get out of here," he said and winked.

'We walked the three blocks back to our room, and by the end he was leaning against me, and my dick was once again totally hard. When we got inside, I immediately put on the TV, needing a distraction. *Saturday Night Live* was on, and, just my luck, there was a Hanz and Franz sketch. I usually watched from my bed, and I urged Jason to get in with me. He sized me up for a minute, as if wondering if I was playing a prank, then kicked off his shoes and got in bed. "Keep me warm," he said, and I realised he'd been shivering, perhaps because of the drinking. He was pressed right up against me, and I had trouble focusing on the show. His breath was on my skin and when I turned towards him he looked me right in the eyes. We didn't talk about it, we just moved closer and soon we were kissing. Girls always talk about how kissing another girl is soft and sweet; this was kind of like that at first, but it quickly turned rough. He shoved his tongue inside my mouth and got on top of me, pinning me down. I had made the first move, but he had taken the second and run with it.'

George's breathing was getting heavier, and I couldn't resist reaching behind me to stroke his dick.

'Yeah, do that, baby. And so he was kissing me, and rubbing his cock against me through his jeans. "George, you've made me forget all about the swim meet. But there's something else you can do to really make my night." "What?" I whispered, hoping he was going to request the very thing I suddenly wanted to do more than anything else. While I'd made myself come by imagining his lips on my cock, it was my mouth I was now concerned about. I wanted to feel him inside me, to see if I could do it, to give him that pleasure. I wanted the whole experience. He made me say it. "What do you think?" I reached for his jeans and unzipped them, and his dick sprang free.'

I was rubbing his cockhead by then, feeling the round, swollen tip get nice and wet. I wanted to suck him as I heard how much he'd wanted to suck his friend, but I also wanted him inside me. I shifted so I could pull my panties all the way down and placed his cock at my hole. He took the hint and I rolled onto my stomach while George got on top of me. He's never been all that great at sustaining a steady stream of dirty talk while we're fucking, but I figured his story was almost over, and I was dying.

He entered me in one fast thrust, and started talking faster. 'Jason wouldn't let me suck him until I said exactly what I wanted, spilled my now not-so-secret lust. He was kind of like you in that regard; he liked to hear the dirty words. We'd watched porn together before, and whenever I'd suggested we mute it, he'd argued in favour of hearing every moan, every lustful bit of dialogue. So when I said, "Jason, I want to suck your cock," I worried for a minute that he might come just from that alone.

'But instead he shifted around so I was hovering over him. "Suck it, George, suck my big fat cock like you've always wanted to." I was in no position to argue that I'd only really wanted to for a little while, and I was starting to get the idea that he'd wanted this for longer than I had. But I was so turned on by what was happening that I just opened my mouth and started to lick him. I'd only been with three girls, I think, at that point, and mostly we'd been focused on fucking, so my blow job experience was limited. Certainly, I couldn't have been the best at it, but I tried. I shut my eyes and focused on the head, the way I had discovered I liked. But Jason wanted me to take the whole thing. Soon his hands were on my head. I'd always heard that was a no-no for girls, but I liked it, a little. I liked that he was telling me how to please him, rather than just making me guess.'

My boyfriend's words were coming out faster and faster as he pumped into me. Our fucking was so energetic that the bed was squeaking. I was on the verge of coming, picturing his mouth full of this guy's dick.

'He urged me to keep going, and I did, wondering exactly how big his cock was. I got to a point where it felt like there was nowhere else in my throat for him to go, but I was determined to deep-throat him; who knew how many more chances I'd have? I breathed in through my nose, opened my eyes briefly and stared at his pubic hair, then swallowed him whole. I could only do it for a second or two before I had to come up for air. Then I mostly focused on going about halfway down, then coming back up. I was so hard by then I was ready to come, and with Jason's hand on my neck guiding me, he basically fucked my mouth until he came. He let me know, right before, and I made a split-second decision to stay, to taste his come, to try to swallow it. I didn't exactly succeed, in that he spurted so much that some of it dripped down my chin, but he seemed to like that. He wiped some off my chin and fed it to me.

'And then, oh my God, I'm gonna come soon, and then ... he did it to me. He sucked my dick and I got to watch. I got to stroke his hair and watch him go down on me with more gusto than any of those girls ever had.'

George took a break and rested his head on the back of my neck as he slammed hard in and out of me, holding my hips down. We both breathed silently, each of us picturing this scene, one where a totally new (to me) side of my boyfriend was coming to light. He didn't have to tell me when he was about to come – I can usually tell – and I was rubbing my clit so hard I knew it was going to be sore later, but I didn't care. When I came, about five seconds before he did, I was glad he was on top of me to keep me in place. It was one of the most amazing orgasms of my life, one I'd need to recover from. Far from being jealous, I was delighted; we were now co-conspirators in cock-sucking, each with a wild and crazy past we could share and build on. Then it was George's turn, and he bathed my pussy with his come, just the way I like it.

'I came in his mouth pretty soon after he started. I didn't even give him a warning I was so excited. He seemed to like the surprise and managed to swallow up most of it. Then he put his head on my chest and I stroked his hair while the end of *S.N.L.* played. We fell asleep like that, but at some point in the night he went back to his bed and I turned off the TV. I couldn't sleep actually. I just watched him most of the night, wanting to curl up next to him, but he hadn't invited me. The next morning he just gave me his usual smile and showered and went to practice. We never talked about it even though I certainly thought about it and jerked off to him. But I was too scared to ever approach another guy, and wanted to try to figure out women first. You're far more mysterious. I was working on getting up the courage to finally flirt with another guy when I met you,' he said. Then he turned me over and kissed me hard on the lips. I put his head against my chest, his favoured resting place.

I stroked his hair much like I imagined he'd stroked his friend's hair. 'What if . . . we found a way for you to explore this side of you? Together, I mean. I could help. Maybe I could even watch,' I said, and felt him stiffen.

I hoped I hadn't said the wrong thing. 'You'd do that for me?' He sounded awed.

'Well . . . not entirely. I mean, yes, I would, but I'd do it for me too. If you didn't notice, hearing you tell me about sucking another guy's cock made me a little wet.' We both laughed at my understatement. 'Imagine what watching you would do to me.'

'I love you,' he said, and I said it back, glad that I had a big mouth and had used it to get him to tell me his story. We'd had a perfectly hot sex life up until then, but suddenly, I felt like I had the whole picture, or at least much more of it, and I wasn't about to put that particular gay genie back in its bottle, not when the promise of so much more awaited us.

Sexy Little Numbers sees the first publication of Rachel Kramer Bussel's short fiction in Black Lace.

The Number
Justine Elyot

'9.45 a.m. from Colliton South.' That had been the text message in its entirety.

Anyone scrolling through Charlotte's inbox would infer that this bald line of digital information had come from a timetabling service or similar; its true provenance was known only to Charlotte herself. And even she only knew that it had come from The Number. Identities of the sender or senders could not be revealed.

She screwed in her iPod headphones and looked again at the message – so perfectly straightforward and yet so unutterably cryptic. Arrowing down to The Number provoked a shiver of delicious nervousness. How many people had The Number? How many people were involved in this game? And how would it play out? She did not even know where she would be this time tomorrow.

All the same, she supposed she had better prepare to play, and she took one of her college texts, *Social Psychology of the Workplace*, from her tote bag. Within a few minutes, her absorption was such that she huffed under her breath at the click of the compartment door before she remembered what she was actually doing here and looked up.

'Mind if we join you?'

She looked swiftly away again, the paragraphs swimming under her eyes. *Them!*

The men from the station; pinstriped professionals, both in their forties, both carrying large briefcases, one bespectacled, one silvering at the temples. If this was Fantasy #3, as she presumed it was, they fitted the bill perfectly. She had spent the twenty minutes by which the train was delayed sizing them up sideways along the platform, and they certainly seemed to be doing the same, but more openly. If they were simply innocent bystanders, they were not very well-mannered ones.

The train had drawn in just as Charlotte could have sworn they were talking about what she was wearing, causing her to flush hotly and cross her arms over her chest, hiding the swell of her breasts in the light white silk blouse she wore on that May morning. Could they see the outline of her white lace bra underneath? she wondered. Was her mid-thigh plaid skirt too short? Had one of her nude hold-up stockings fallen to her knee without her knowledge? It was a relief, and yet also a disappointment, to hoist herself up in the carriage away from their predatory scrutiny.

When, after fifteen minutes, she still found herself alone in the compartment, she had assumed they were not involved; that the players would embark later on. But it seemed now that she might have been mistaken.

The taller and senior-looking of the two men stood in the doorway, one hand keeping the sliding portal from springing back, staring down his bespectacled nose at her with an expression that owed less to query than coercion.

Charlotte was a courteous, rather shy young woman; a people-pleaser by upbringing, and answering his request in the negative would have been as unthinkable to her as a plain 'fuck off'. Besides, there was something effortlessly intimidating about this man, a sense that, for all his outward civility and charm, you would not want to mess with him. Exactly what she had ordered up. Surely he must be . . .

He smiled, entered the compartment, and his companion followed. He wore a lighter suit, and seemed lighter in almost every other sense, including his manner and the piercing grey blue of his eyes. Charlotte expected them to sit at the far end of the compartment, by the door, and she was instantly disconcerted when they slid their briefcases onto the rack directly above her. The older man – whom she thought of as Alpha Male – sat down by her side, his friend opposite her, smiling ingratiatingly.

Defensively she turned her eyes down to her book and made to switch on her iPod, but before she could drown out the suddenly scary reality of her situation, the man opposite her spoke and she reluctantly halted her fingers in their mission. It would be rude, she supposed, not to engage in conversation if that was what they wanted, even if they were just simple strangers on a train.

'*Social Psychology of the Workplace* – now that sounds like a nice bit of recreational reading.'

'Oh, no, it isn't for pleasure. It's for a course I'm doing.'

'Shouldn't you have read that before setting off to college?' The other man this time, his tone mock-censuring. Or was it mock? Perhaps it was real. 'I hope you're up to date with your assignments.'

'How do you know I'm on the way there? How do you know I haven't just left college and I'm so keen I'm doing the assigned reading already?'

The men raised eyebrows at each other. 'Feisty,' noted Alpha Male.

'Isn't she?' responded his colleague.

Charlotte flicked her eyes nervously out of the window towards the sheep and trees rolling past. If it was nothing to do with the game, this was wrong somehow. This was not normal. But she had the oddest tightness at the base of her belly and her heart was racing. Were they flirting with her or ... what? Perhaps she should not go through with this. Perhaps she should leave now, but something held her back. The same thing that got her into trouble time and again. She loved a story and she always had to know the ending.

'So what do you read for pleasure?' The Alpha Male again, his voice rich and alluring with a flirtatious edge. It was a voice he used, she thought, perhaps professionally. Extremely distinctive, rather wicked, a voice that could seduce without the aid of its corporeal host.

'Oh ...' Charlotte was overcome with confusion. She had not signed up to discuss her literary tastes with these men.

'I'm guessing –' the man opposite took up the conversation; his voice higher in register, clipped and well-bred '– you seem like a classics sort of girl to me. Jane Austen? The Brontës? Perhaps a little Thomas Hardy when you're feeling melancholy?'

'Oh, I don't know,' Alpha Male interrupted before Charlotte could confirm or deny. 'I think there's a little undercurrent of darkness there. Something a little bit … wanton. Perhaps Henry Miller, or even Anaïs Nin. Hmmm?'

He was looking directly at her, one long finger against his lips. Full lips. Cruel lips. Charlotte felt a creepy-crawly ripple from the base of her spine to the nape of her neck. Was this what they called 'hackles rising'? Or was it something else? She felt caught out, as if he could read her mind. How could he have guessed that? Did she have some kind of aura marking her out as a lover of kink-lit? Perhaps she did. Still, there was only one course a nice girl could take when confronted thus. Resort to outright lying.

'No,' she stammered. 'No, just … the ones you said.' She shot a look of appeal to the man opposite, hoping he would pick up on her misgivings.

But if he did, he wasn't going to pay any attention.

'You know, I think you're right,' he said to his friend. 'Judging by the luscious blush that's spreading from her cheeks to her ears … you might just have hit on something. Are you a connoisseur of erotica, my dear?'

'You're certainly a transparently bad liar,' Alpha Male averred.

'I'm not! I don't know what all this is about!' But in that moment, Charlotte knew exactly what it was all about. These men had come from The Number. This was what she had ordered. All she had to do now was play the game.

'Oh really?' Alpha stood suddenly, extending his lean frame to its full height, a couple of inches over six foot, and retrieved his briefcase from the rack.

No! Don't go, thought Charlotte in a panic. Things are just starting to happen.

But he seated himself once more and snapped the case open, plucking from its depths ... yes ... Charlotte mock-gasped as he laid his briefcase aside and brandished in front of her nose the notebook she had been instructed to leave in the station phone box.

She made a wild swipe for it. 'What are you doing with that?' she cried, her voice cracking in alarm. 'It's mine; give it back!'

'Oh, you want it now? You need to learn to take care of your property, young lady. We found this on the station forecourt, where you dropped it.'

'Yeah, well, thanks,' said Charlotte, trying to keep the tremble out of her words. 'Thanks for bringing it to me.' She flung out her arm, but her tormentor flipped it out of her reach.

'Patience, Charlotte,' he said. He knew her name. He had opened it. He had read it. No wonder they had been watching her with such avidity on the platform. 'I just wanted to clarify a few things before I return it. This *is* your notebook, isn't it?'

Charlotte bit the inside of her cheek, considering lying just to see where that would take the action, but she knew there was no point. She nodded, caught between the twin beam of her companions' intense attention.

'You've quite a talent, Charlotte,' the man opposite paid tribute. He appeared to be the good cop of the duo.

'A talent for getting yourself into trouble. How much of what you have written about here is based on fact, I wonder?'

Charlotte knew how the script went now. 'I've ... most of it. All of it,' she mumbled.

'Really? You have picked up strangers for money in the bar of the Colliton Grand?'

'Well ... I'm a student. I have to pay my way. I was just doing favours ...'

'Interesting defence,' remarked Alpha Male to his friend. 'Extenuating circumstances; first offence. Though of course she seems to be under the impression that the law recognises gradations of sexual transaction. Of course it does not, as we know.'

'Indeed,' his friend backed him up. 'All instances of giving sexual favours for financial remuneration are illegal.'

'Punishable, according to the judge's discretion, by custodial sentence.'

'Harsh but true, Charlotte.'

'And even if you keep your pretty arse out of prison, the local press will make sure you can never show your face in town again.'

They both watched for her reaction, Alpha Male holding the book very deliberately within her reach if she wanted to snatch it away. Now was the time. Laugh it off or go with it. She could take the book and thank them for their gesture; say it had been a fun idea, but she had had second thoughts. Or ... *a chance like this might never come again*.

She swiped overdramatically for the notebook. '*Give it back!*' She hoped her manner would make her response to their unphrased question clear.

'I'm not sure I care for your tone.' Alpha Male frowned and replaced the notebook in his briefcase, snapping it shut with near-vindictive finality. Charlotte yelped and lurched forwards, almost launching herself into his lap. 'You certainly don't appear to appreciate the gravity of your situation.' He placed one finger on the bridge of his spectacles, his eyes boring into the helpless young woman before him.

'Please,' she whispered.

'Better.'

'Just be a good girl, Charlotte, and do as you're told,' the man opposite advised, his voice strangely soothing.

'Yes. Can you do that?' The older man's slender fingers reached for her chin, holding it in a firm grip while his eyes roved slowly around her face and body. 'Can you be a good girl and do as you're told?'

An incoherent 'uh' sound was Charlotte's only response. She was committed now to following the story to its end.

'We know what you like, Charlotte,' said the older man. 'We were very interested when we read your story.'

'We like what you like,' contributed his colleague. 'Isn't that a pleasant coincidence?'

'Yes,' said Charlotte dreamily, finding that the way her neighbour stroked her hand, rhythmically, gently but inescapably, was pushing the waves of anxiety far back, back behind their barrier.

'She likes this,' remarked Alpha Male. 'She's like a skittish pony; just needs a firm touch to keep her docile. Take her foot and give it a rub.'

The younger man crouched forwards and did just that, lifting one of Charlotte's legs so that her foot nestled between his thighs. He removed her sandal and began to massage the ball of her foot with both hands, moving slowly around, then dipping into her instep in a feathery-tickly way that made her shiver. Alpha had moved her hand to his lips and was kissing the knuckles, prior to taking her fingers into his mouth and sucking on them. His other hand rested on her skirted thigh, feeling hot and heavy, as if it clamped her in place.

Alpha Male removed her final finger with a popping sound and squeezed her hand tightly within his. 'Now listen carefully, Charlotte. This is what will happen now. You will refer to me as "Master" and my friend as "Sir". You belong to us until we say otherwise, and accordingly you must be obedient and respectful. We do not intend you harm and will endeavour to give you the pleasure you seek, but you must not question our orders or our motives. Is that understood?'

'But where are we going?'

'Is that understood, Charlotte?'

'Oh . . . yes.'

'Yes what?' Master hauled Charlotte to her feet by the elbow and laid two hard smacks on her bottom.

'Yes, Master.'

'I hope you're a fast learner, young lady, or you will find this afternoon both long and painful.'

'Oh, I am.'

'I'm going to advise you not to speak unless explicitly questioned, Charlotte. Do you think you can do that?'

'Yes, Master.'

Charlotte was still standing, facing away from her interlocutor and towards the man she was to refer to as 'Sir'. She felt the indignity of her position, standing up on the grimy carriage floor with only one shoe on, giving her a perilous lopsided feel.

'What a lovely figure you have, Charlotte,' said Sir. 'I'd very much like it if you could give us a little twirl. Nice and slowly. That's the ticket.'

Charlotte pivoted on her one sandalled foot, trying her best not to rush the process and incur either man's displeasure.

'She has an hourglass shape,' said Sir to Master. 'My favourite kind.'

'Yes, and the skirt is tight enough to cling nicely to her hips and backside. We can get a good idea of what might be in store for us.'

'That blouse is perfect; almost transparent. More a promise than a garment, don't you think?'

'I do. Charlotte, stand facing me and unbutton your blouse, please.'

Charlotte's impulse was to stall, to stare, to stammer, but when she caught sight of Master's gimlet eyes and straight-set mouth, she knew that she had no alternative but compliance. Her fingers flew to the little pearly buttons, slipping them carefully out of the slits, mindful that a couple were hanging by loose threads. The thought that she really ought to buy a sewing kit flashed through her head, almost occasioning a giggle in its incongruity.

The blouse hung open, exposing a column of pale skin from navel to throat, interrupted by the white lace of her bra.

'Pull it aside; show us your breasts,' instructed Master. Charlotte draped the edges of her blouse carefully at either side of her bosom so that the frothy twin cups with their spillage of flesh were plainly visible, along with the gently convex expanse of her belly.

'Good girl, turn around and show Sir.'

Sir nodded and gave her a warm smile of encouragement. He was much easier to face than Master, Charlotte thought. He seemed as if he might actually be quite nice, whereas Master was simply cold and terrifying, seductive voice notwithstanding.

'Now raise your skirt to your waist, Charlotte.'

Charlotte continued the languid movements her new owners seemed to favour, edging the rough cloth up her thigh, past the lacy elasticated top of her stockings until nude flesh felt the cool air. She had just hiked it past her white mesh knickers when a click of the door made her jump a foot in the air.

'Tickets, please.'

In a confusion, she bent forwards, desperately fumbling to adjust her clothing, but a cold and irate, 'Hold it there; don't you dare cover up!' caused her to freeze with a bunched-up handful of skirt and an arm across her chest.

From the corner of her eye she could see that the ticket collector was a skinny, acne-scarred youth fresh out of school. Far from looking shocked and appalled, a voyeuristic leer plastered his face. 'Thank you, gents,' he said thickly as Master and Sir flashed season tickets.

'Straighten up,' commanded Master. 'Skirt back up now. Give the man your ticket.'

Charlotte, feeling slightly seasick from the motion of the train and convinced she must be the hue of beetroot all over, reached into her bookbag for the ticket. She handed it to the guard without looking at him.

'Very nice, luv,' he said, clipping it and handing it back. There was a moment that seemed to last an age during which the guard just stood there, lapping her up with his eyes on stalks, holding on in the hope that he might be invited to join in the fun.

'Thank you,' said Master dismissively, and with a shrug and a slump, the ticket collector went on his way. 'As for you, miss, you had better rid yourself of any notions of false modesty. If we want you on display, we will have you on display, no matter if the massed ranks of the Scots Guards pass through this carriage. Bend over and grab your ankles now.'

Charlotte swung over as quickly as she could, hoping the speed of her response might garner her a little of Master's hard-won approval. The tight white mesh of her knickers stretched taut over her straining bum, which was directly in Master's line of sight. She gasped and almost toppled over when a volley of hard, loud smacks lit up her bottom.

'You-will-do-as-you're-told,' Master punctuated the impromptu spanking. 'Do-you-understand-yet?'

'Yes, Master.' Charlotte gulped, swallowing back dry sobs of mortification and shock.

'Good. Turn around and show Sir your bottom now. Any more of this nonsense and you'll be getting off this train and parading through the terminus naked on a leash. Would you like that?'

'Oh. No, Sir,' she said, avoiding his stare from beneath sulky lashes. 'I mean, Master!' she amended, shocked to find that Sir had clearly leaped up behind her and was adding to the spanking tariff. She had thought he was on her side!

'Hmm, I'm not convinced. I think you probably would. Anyway. Pull your knickers down to your ankles.'

Charlotte pouted, biting the inside of her lip, as she eased the thin knickers over her glowing pink bum and down past her knees where they dropped of their own accord to her ankles.

'Quite nice; do you wax, Charlotte?' asked Master conversationally.

'I do, Master.'

'I approve. Now, Charlotte, until we reach Capital City, I would like you to take a seat in that corner and sit there with your legs spread as wide as you can manage. That way, both Sir and I can get a good long look at you whenever we need a break from our work.'

Blinking at this slightly unexpected turn of events, Charlotte backed over to the corner seat indicated, next to the compartment door, diagonally opposite Master and at the far end of the banquette from Sir. She shuffled down, feeling a little sting on her backside, both from the after-effects of the men's hard hands and the stiff fuzziness of the upholstery on her bare bottom. As instructed, she parted her thighs as wide as she could muster, so that her seated lower body described a rough diamond shape, flaring out widely at the knees then tapering back to where her ankles were restricted by the knickers.

'Very nice. Now pull down the cups of your brassiere so that your nipples are visible, please. That's right. And I'd like you to hold the lips of your pussy apart so that nothing is hidden at all. That's it. We need you fully and completely exposed to our view, Charlotte. That's excellent.'

'Exquisite, dear.' Sir smiled, all friendliness and reassurance once more.

And then, as if this were any ordinary commute from a provincial town back to the capital, the two men clicked open their briefcases and took out sheafs of reading material and mobile phones, into which they intermittently barked orders and information.

Charlotte sat in this uncomfortable position for more than half an hour, screwing her face up every time shadows passed beneath the blinds. If she could make out their shapes behind the thin cloth, it stood to reason that they might be able to discern her erect nipples and the awkward sprawl of her legs and put two and two together. Master and Sir did not allow her discomfiture to influence them for one second though, occasionally looking up from their absorption in work to drink in the view or issue a curt, 'Keep those legs spread, Charlotte.'

It was a curious realisation for Charlotte that she would prefer to have her two mysterious 'owners' paying attention to her, even if that attention was humiliating, than all but ignoring her in this way. Even more curious was the way the air at the top of her thighs was cold with that particular chill that affects wet skin. If her skin was wet, did that mean she was ... turned on? She had to be honest with herself; this scenario was one that had come from her own brain on one of those nights when unfulfilled longing for sensual domination kept her awake. She blushed with recollection of the story she had penned a few days ago, in which she was taken blindfolded to a gentleman's drawing room and violated repeatedly in every orifice by a succession of anonymous men. In front of a roaring fire, of course. Master and Sir had read it, undoubtedly. It was obvious that they would draw certain conclusions from it.

But that story did not form part of Fantasy #3. Surely they

would stick to that particular narrative. Wouldn't they? She shivered, wondering if the rest of the day would really go according to her design. Would it be the only day? Master had said that she belonged to them until they released her. What if they never released her? Indeed, who were these men? An impulse of panic led her to remove her fingers from her prised-apart lower lips and shuffle to her feet, intending to retrieve her mobile phone and send a text update on her whereabouts to her flatmates. The look Master gave her on registering her unbidden movement, however, pinned her back into place, shrinking against the dusty fabric of the seat.

'I don't recall giving you permission to move,' he said icily. 'There will be a punishment for that.'

'Please, Master,' she said, trembling, 'may I send a text message ahead to my flatmates? They will expect me home by a certain time. Perhaps I could tell them . . . When *will* I be home?'

He stared at her just long enough to lead her to wonder if the blood had actually frozen in her veins, then said, 'Speaking out of turn too. Well, well, we will have some issues to address later, won't we?'

'It's not a bad thought though,' struck up Sir, and Charlotte mentally cheered him on. 'We don't want anybody making inconvenient waves if they have been expecting Charlotte back. I mean, we have plans for the rest of the day, don't we?'

Phew! Only the day, not her entire life then.

Master contemplated this, then reached into Charlotte's bookbag and retrieved her mobile. But her hopes were dashed when he flipped open the cover and began jabbing at the buttons himself.

'What's her name? Your friend?' he asked. 'Or is it a he? Do you have a client to cancel?'

'No, I don't!' retorted Charlotte, stung. 'I don't have "clients". They're just people who don't mind paying for my company when they're lonely.' *And I'm only an escort in the fantasy*, she held off from saying.

'How touching. You're quite the charitable soul, aren't you, Charlotte? I didn't catch your friend's name.'

'Lynnie,' groused Charlotte, and she watched with her lower lip stuck as far out as she could muster while Master scrolled through her contacts and began composing a message on her behalf. Charlotte was desperate to jump up and read it over his shoulder – he could be saying *anything* – but something kept her glued to the seat in her inglorious position as the buttons bleeped. She shifted uncomfortably, feeling a familiar and inconvenient urge. Would they grant permission for a toilet break? It was worth a try. But she would ask Sir, not that Master bastard. She cleared her throat timidly.

'I beg your pardon, Sir, but could I ask you something?'

He turned to her, smiling gently but reprovingly. 'You know the rule, Charlotte.'

'I'm sorry, I know, but I . . . need the loo. Really urgently.'

'I'm afraid it will have to wait. Only ten minutes to go now.'

'But I can't hold on!'

'Of course you can. Now keep those lips spread good and wide for us, my dear, or there will be serious consequences. You can do it. Good girl.'

Still smiling, he began folding his papers and replacing them in his briefcase. Charlotte noticed that the bucolic landscape outside had been exchanged for brick villas, then tower blocks. The corridor beyond began to bustle with passengers preparing to alight. Any one of them could bend down to push a case along on its casters and peer through the crack of window that was not covered by the flimsy blinds.

Master closed his case and began fiddling with his tie. Glancing over at Charlotte, he said, 'Take off your knickers and give them to me. You won't be needing them today.'

Charlotte swallowed at this blatant statement of intent. She eased the knickers off her feet and handed them meekly to Master, who put them in his breast pocket, leaving a portion visible at the top like a pornographic handkerchief.

'Thank you. Now you may lower your skirt and button up your blouse again just for as long as we are in public. But . . . no! Do not replace the cups of your bra. I want you to be conscious of your nakedness and availability beneath your clothes.'

Charlotte gasped, trying to appeal with her eyes, but it was no use. The blouse was so thin that surely everybody would be treated to the sight of the dimpled silk that outlined her nipples. Still, at least she could be assured that there would be no visible panty line under her tight skirt.

The train lurched to a halt, and Charlotte was escorted out into the corridor in single file, Master ahead and Sir to her rear. Master helped her down off the high step, but his apparently gallant gesture concealed his true intention, which was to see that he had a firm hold of her in the wide open space of the terminus, precluding any chance of escape. Sir took her other elbow and the trio paraded swiftly down the platform, Charlotte's shorter legs struggling to maintain the rapid pace of her two tall companions. To outsiders, many of whom gave the group covert glances, it must have looked exactly like what it was: two professional men with their owned girl, their possession, spiriting her away to be . . . what? Oh God. What?

Charlotte kept her eyes to the ground, beyond mortified. 'Keep up, Charlotte; no dawdling,' chided Sir, and he gave her bottom a resounding smack that rang out like a pistol shot in the echoing space. Several bystanders jumped and all eyes swivelled towards them, but thankfully they were nearly outside now, heading away from the prurient peepers and towards a row of taxis.

Something caught Master's eye though, before they could hail a cab and he doubled back, stopping abruptly before it. It was one of the silver toilet cubicles that had sprung up on the pavements of the capital recently. Charlotte breathed out, wondering if she had misjudged Master, and he possessed a hitherto unrecognised quality of thoughtfulness. She was quickly forced to reassess that idea though, when the door had slid aside and he stepped inside himself, dragging her and Sir after him.

The door shushed shut. Charlotte, squeezed into the tiny space with two men, simply gaped at them. Did they really expect her to relieve herself in their presence?

'I thought you were desperate,' said Master mockingly. 'Come on then. You can't say I'm an unreasonable man.'

'Can't you wait outside?' stammered Charlotte.

'No.'

'Relax, Charlotte,' said Sir, with a reassuring rub of her upper arm. 'It's really nothing we haven't seen before.'

'What a strange time to decide that you are coy, Charlotte,' whispered Master. '*After* you have shown us everything. It's just a bodily function.'

'Like fucking.'

'Exactly. Like fucking. You like to be watched fucking, don't you?'

Charlotte allowed them to push her down, a hand on each shoulder, until she was hovering above the cold steel of the lavatory. She squeezed her eyes shut, unclenched her bladder and let her body follow its course.

'Good. That's very good, Charlotte. You are such a quick learner.'

'A true submissive,' contributed Sir. 'I am so looking forward to our afternoon now.'

They left the cubicle, heedless of some double-takes from onlookers, and marched her along the taxi rank, past the waiting cabs to the back, where a maroon-painted vehicle waited a few spaces behind its more traditional company. They processed into the back, Master leaning forwards to speak to the driver in a low mutter, which Charlotte could not quite make out. She made to sit down, but Sir caught her shoulder and said, 'Lift your skirt first, please.'

Charlotte made a great effort to lift the skirt so that the back rose high enough but the front still covered her with some semblance of modesty. She sat carefully, drawing in a small breath at the cold smooth leather of the seat against her nude bottom.

'Your tie,' said Master blandly to Sir, and he immediately loosened it and handed it to the senior partner. 'Unbutton your blouse, Charlotte, and expose your breasts as before.'

Charlotte gave a meaningful glance towards the cabby, who was sitting at the exit of the station forecourt, indicating steadily. Surely he could see them in the rear-view mirror.

'Don't worry about that. He will have seen it all before. Do as you're told, or he'll be seeing a lot more.'

Charlotte's fingers set to work on the buttons once more, while Master wrapped the tie around her head, blindfolding her against the view of the passing urban streets.

'I feel I should be scared,' she mumbled, feeling the trousered legs of her owners nudging up either thigh above the elasticated lace of her stockings.

Two hands alighted on each expanse of bare flesh, kneading and stroking.

'There is nothing to be afraid of,' said Sir's voice on her right.

'Nothing will happen that you don't want,' confirmed Master in her other ear. 'We are taking you on a journey into your own needs and desires.'

'We are going to pleasure you.'

'And punish you.'

'Punish you with pleasure.'

'Pleasure you with punishment.'

'Because that is what you want.'

'Because that is what you need.'

The words were sufficient to quieten the nagging doubts that had prevented Charlotte's full immersion into the experience. A weight lifted; she rolled her head back on the seat and breathed a heavy sigh.

The hands were moving inexorably higher, underneath her skirt. Another hand cupped her right breast while mouths pressed against her neck on the other side. Fingers arrived at her outer lips, prising them apart then dipping into the waters with a luscious slicking sound.

'Well, well, something tells us our Charlotte is enjoying herself.' It was Sir's voice, just above her shoulder.

'Did you ever doubt it?'

Two sets of fingers delved the velvet depths of Charlotte's most intimate places, while mouths breathed warm air across her swollen nipples, then flicked the tips with their tongues.

'When we get to the hotel, Charlotte, we are going to make you come, over and over and over again,' Master informed her, half-eating her ear as he poured his voice down it.

'Until you can't walk.'

'Or talk.'

'Or think.'

'Or move.'

One finger, two fingers, three fingers, more, scissoring inside her, scattered across her clit, pushing, poking, pressing, arousing every one of her nerve endings all at once. Her thighs spread wider and wider, until they were hooked over forearms, the skirt having now ridden irrevocably around her waist, no further thought given to the cab driver. Every part of her body was under sensual attack, defences stripped down, surrender ignored by the marauding hands and mouths and tongues and teeth. Charlotte felt herself to be no more than one gigantic pulsing organism; every pore in her body shot sparks down to her clitoris, which seemed enormous now, and rapacious in its need.

Twenty fingers worked at her core while two sets of lips caressed her breasts. She was pushed back in the seat with her legs forming a wide V in the air above her; one calf held firm while the trium-phant digits invaded further and further across her borders, pillaging her most intimate parts.

When she came, writhing on fingers that thrust down and down while others circled her swollen clitoris, she kicked so hard that a shoe fell off and clattered to the floor of the cab.

One tongue then two plunged into her mouth before it had finished its broken keen of defeat. They drew back, the fingers leaving with them to remove her blindfold with a flourish, so that Charlotte lay, legs limp and loosely spread, skirt around waist, shirt wide open and bra cups down to reveal sorely reddened nipples, hair wild and eyes glazed, in a post-orgasmic slump.

'I think you needed that,' proclaimed Master. 'Don't you think she needed that?'

'She needed that,' confirmed Sir with a nod. 'Do you agree, James?'

'She got what she needed,' said the cab driver in a rough Cockney brogue.

'You did, didn't you, Charlotte? Say it.'

'I needed that,' whispered Charlotte, her tongue rolling around hugely in her parched mouth.

Sir chuckled. 'You need to smarten up your act, Charlotte. Wake up. This is simply an introduction.'

'We have many more plans for the afternoon,' agreed Master. 'We have booked the room overnight. We thought you would probably need a full night's sleep after we leave.'

Charlotte struggled to bring her shattered consciousness back into one piece. What happened in Fantasy #3? Could she even remember? It had been months since she wrote and submitted her desires to the site. Two men … silk ropes … unfeasible number of orgasms … double penetration … was that it?

'After all, this is what you asked for,' Master reminded her as the taxi stood still, indicator clicking, outside the façade of a large hotel.

'We are here to please you.' Sir smiled, fussing with her blouse until it was buttoned back up. 'And you are here to please us.'

'It's all too good to be true,' mumbled Charlotte, trying to reconfigure her body into something she recognised, allowing Master to pull her to her feet and yank her skirt back down over her soaked thighs.

'I'm not sure good is the word,' he said, and he winked. The strict taskmaster of the train journey actually winked. He was human, somewhere inside the granite.

Charlotte giggled, her heart suddenly light and optimistic. Here she was outside an exclusive hotel, with two attractive men who meant to ravish her until she could be ravished no more. This was exactly the kind of story she wanted to follow.

'Shall we?' she said, offering an elbow each to her distinguished escorts.

'We'd be delighted,' they replied in unison. The cab driver was tipped, the door opened and the three stepped out onto the bustling pavements of the capital, drawing a small wave of attention from the passers-by as they paraded along the marble concourse, past the doormen and into the Hotel Luxe Noir.

Justine Elyot's collection *On Demand* is published by Black Lace in December 2009. Her short fiction appears in the Black Lace anthologies *Liaisons* and *Misbehaviour*.

Fireworks Inside
Portia Da Costa

Fireworks! Bloody fireworks. I hate fireworks.

I throw myself into the walk-in coat cupboard and slam the door behind me. I can't take much more of this! They're supposed to be celebrating Cecilia's lavish society wedding, not blowing up a medium-sized city. What the hell are they using out there? TNT? Surface to air missiles? Semtex?

'They're too close to the house, you silly mare! They'll burn the place down, and fry all your guests, and then where will you be?'

Slithering down, I cower in the corner, in the darkness. It's as pitch black as a witch's coal scuttle in here, and there are layers of old coats hanging on pegs above me, and some rather dubious feeling carpet beneath my thighs as I tuck my legs beneath me. I can hardly breathe, but it's still better than enduring the noise outside. The dust makes me cough, and something smells distinctly mildewed with a side of mothball, but I'll take this over my pathological fear of fireworks any time. I've been petrified of the things since I was a kid, and someone set a giant firecracker off right next to me. I usually spend Guy Fawkes Night tucked up with a couple of sleeping pills, but I can't really get out of attending one of my best friends' wedding, can I?

If only the bloody things weren't quite so loud.

Bang! Boom! Boom! God, I swear they're nearer and/or even bigger now.

'Please stop. Please stop. Please stop.'

But no amount of hands over ears and cringing in a tiny bolt hole of utter blackness seems to be helping. So much for enjoying a glorious knees-up with champagne and a groaning buffet and dancing and a selection of the groom's tasty friends to cop off with. Even on a good day I couldn't pull a tasty bloke in a coat cupboard.

I'm bordering on snivelling and feeling very sorry for myself, when, during a lull in the shelling, the cupboard door flies open, and a large, generally man-sized shape hurls itself inside with me and slams the door shut again.

'Fucking, bloody fireworks,' growls a gruff voice, and suddenly there's a nice smell of spicy high-end cologne to take the edge off the aroma of fusty coats.

The new firework-phobe is right up against me, but I'm not sure he actually knows I'm in here. Should I announce myself, or keep quiet? It's only a *very* small cupboard and he's bound to knock into me any second.

'Don't you like them either?'

The man-shape leaps. 'Fucking hell! You frightened the life out of me. I didn't know there was anyone in here.'

Nice.

'I was here first.' Almost before the words are out, there's another huge detonation, and I screech in terror . . . and throw myself wildly in the general direction of Man-shape.

Luckily, he opens his arms and wraps them around me tight. I don't know whether he's comforting me, or himself, but there's a part of me that's suddenly miraculously immune to the conflagration outside. And much more interested in the idea of fireworks of another kind.

'Sorry I shouted.' It's momentarily quiet again, but I notice he doesn't let go of me. 'It's just that I *really* hate fireworks. It's embarrassing, but I had a bad experience as a kid, and they do my head in.'

'Me too. Incident with a jumbo firecracker . . . Now I can't bear the bloody things.' I sigh. 'I didn't know Cecilia was having a display.' Mm, his arms feel nice, and quite big and strong for someone who's hiding in a cupboard. 'I'd still have come to the wedding, but I might have got a good deal more booze down my neck if I'd known . . . and maybe a few tranquillisers as a chaser.'

'Ditto.'

There's another boom or two, but – and I might be imagining things – they don't seem quite as loud and threatening now. And I'm starting to feel very interested in my companion. He's smelling, and feeling, better and better to me all the time. When I hitch around a bit and manage to stretch my legs out in the darkness, he adjusts his position beside me with his arm still around my shoulder.

During the course of a bit more rearrangement, our faces accidentally brush against each other and, without stopping to think, I go for it and navigate my mouth towards his.

Another firework goes off, but this time I couldn't care less.

Man-shape's mouth is delicious. He tastes of wine and something as sweet and spicy as he smells. I think it might be wedding cake. And then I'm sure of it when he presses his tongue into my mouth.

My nipples start to tingle and, between my legs, my clitoris throbs. I don't know whether this is fight or flight instinct, or a lingering fear of being blown to bits, but suddenly I really want Man-shape. I really, really, really want to fuck.

And he wants me too, it seems. Half-dragging me against him, he acquaints me with his cock, which is as hard as steel inside the fine suiting of his trousers. As I curve my fingers around it, I wonder what he looks like. Is he one of the groomsmen? There was quite a troupe of them, and I must admit they were all pretty fanciable.

'Um, sorry about that.' As he hefts his hips to push his hard-on against my hand, he doesn't seem sorry in the slightest. 'I suppose it's my subconscious trying to take my mind off the fireworks.'

There's nothing subconscious about an erection like that, but I'm not arguing. I need something to take my mind off the fireworks too, don't I?

In an attempt to further distract himself, he starts kissing me again, really hard, but in a good way. He's got a cheeky, mobile tongue and it seems to get everywhere. Well, not everywhere, but if I play my cards right, it might get *there* too.

His hands are as naughty as his tongue and his lips and, while I'm still clinging on to his goodies, he goes after mine. I'm wearing a strapless top, and Man-shape exploits its advantages. All of a sudden, the top's around my waist, along with the saucy strapless bra that used to be beneath it.

Ooh, I'm half-naked in a cupboard with an unknown man! The darkness is like a tangible force in itself and the close air stimulates my skin. My nipples are like stones when he starts drifting his fingers across them, delicately teasing.

'You feel nice, love . . . I bet you've got absolutely gorgeous breasts. Your nipples are so hard.'

It's a bizarre sort of conversation from a complete stranger, but I like it. I'll take any compliment I can get and it's a wonderful distraction.

He cups me with one big, warm hand, rolling my nipple between his fingers and his thumb. And as he rolls, I roll too. I can't help myself. I just have to wiggle about as my pussy tingles and clenches. His cock pulses too, warm against my palm.

We've reached action stations from a standing start in the space of about a minute. I can't believe this is happening, but I'm not arguing with fate. Or a huge delicious erection like the one Man-shape has.

We kiss again, devouring each other as we touch and explore. He's quite rough with my breasts, but the more he mauls me, the more I *want* him to maul me. It's raw animal fun, with no inhibitions, no outside context.

After a few moments, he leans me back against some tumbled coats and then kisses his way down my jaw, my throat and my chest until he's mouthing where his fingers once were. His lips and his tongue are simmering hot, and I can imagine him painting the sweet cake taste over the crinkled skin of my teat. When he sucks hard, I moan out loud, grabbing at his hair. His teeth close ever so slightly, a delicate threat that makes my pussy ripple and my honey surge and flow. My posh panties are swimming and saturated.

'Mm . . .' he purrs against my breast, then sucks again, tweaking at my other teat with his warm, clever fingers.

I'm half off my head now, desire grinding low in my belly. My hips surge, blindly trying to get my crotch in his general direction so I can push it against him and get some sort of ease. He helps by surging back at me, and even though we're an ungainly heap of limbs and torsos, I manage to rock myself against some part of him, rubbing my aching pussy against a bit of his suited body.

After an indeterminate period of this tussling about, he lifts his head. I can't see his face in the blackness, but I know he's smiling. And I know that if I could see his eyes, they'd be as black as our little sanctuary, black with lust. His hand goes up my long skirt, and starts hiking it towards my waist, where the bundle of my top and bra sits. Pretty soon, everything's in a bunch around my midsection, and he's fingering my panties.

First he strokes me through the drenched silk of my gusset. He probes and presses and works at the cloth and my pubic hair until there's just the one thin delicate layer between his big square fingertip and my swollen trembling clit. I grab wildly at him as he starts to masturbate me through it.

'Oh God, oh God,' I chant as sensations gather. My pelvis is lifting, wafting about, but that doesn't put him off. He still manages to keep contact with my clit through the silk. He even gets creative. I could swear he's trying to bring me off in a figure-of-eight pattern.

I grab at him, clutching his shoulder and his hand between my legs. I don't have to direct him, because he's doing fabulously on his own, but I can't seem to control the actions of my own hands.

Of course, it doesn't take long and, before I really know it, I'm coming like a train.

My pussy clenches and lurches and boiling waves of pleasure crest in my belly. If I had a functioning brain cell, I'd take note that this is probably the best orgasm I've ever had, but as I've temporarily lost my mind, I just come and come and come.

And I've still got my pants on.

A few moments later, he says, 'All right, love?'

Sex still glowing and fluttering, I gasp, 'Hell, yes!' And with the words still barely out of my mouth, he starts kissing me again, tantalising my tongue with muscular swirls and stabs and lunges.

What a man, eh? He makes me come, takes nothing for himself yet, and still he's happy to serve up more kisses.

Eventually though, he does start to get a bit proactive. He takes my hand and draws it back to his bulging groin. Which is bulging more than ever now. In fact it feels like he's got an anaconda in there!

Time to have a proper feel, even if I can't actually see the goods. He seems to think that's a good idea and helps.

Between us we unfasten his leather belt and his trousers, and then push them and his boxer briefs down his thighs. His monster of a cock bounds when it's released, and I gasp, 'Crikey!' when I take it in my hand.

He's big and hot and hard and just how I like them. If I wasn't so desperate to get him inside me, I swear I'd get turned on by just the prospect of licking and sucking him.

Before I can stop to think, I offer, 'Would you like a blow job? After all, you brought me off without getting anything yourself.'

'What an incredibly sweet offer,' he says, a laugh in his voice. 'And I can't say I'm not tempted.' His gorgeous organ pulses in my fingers as he speaks. 'But I'd really, really like to fuck you, if that's all right?'

'Are you sure? I really don't mind.'

'Oh, all right then, I can't resist . . . Just give me a bit of a once-over with your lips and tongue first, and then we'll shag. How does that sound?'

'Like a plan.'

Surprisingly, I have no trouble orientating myself towards his penis in the darkness. I swear I could find it via heat-seeking alone. He's so hot, and so delicious, and fine and salty and a little bit sweaty and foxy too in a very good way. I flick him with my tongue and lick around beneath his glans, and then suck his knob into my mouth. He makes very raunchy, animal-like sounds in his throat as I work on him. Delightfully uninhibited, he doesn't hold back, and he growls out some purple profanities of appreciation.

After a while though, he says, 'Time out, babe! I need to fuck you now, or I'll unload into your mouth.'

It sounds incredibly crude, but somehow, in a strange way, almost poetic.

We start to wriggle around again, and in the darkness I feel him fishing in his pocket. Ever the opportunist, eh, Man-shape? Condom to hand? But then again, *I've* got some in my handbag. It is a wedding after all, and a traditional occasion to get lucky.

He rips off the foil then, taking hold of my hands in his, puts the rubber between my fingers and guides me to him. Working as a team, we roll and roll the latex down his length.

'Ready?' he murmurs when he's covered.

'Absolutely. But how are we doing to manage this?'

'Don't worry, you feel like a very flexible girl to me.' He laughs wickedly and starts to manhandle me – in the nicest possible way – into position.

We bump and grapple and tumble and wiggle, but eventually I'm on my back, knickers off, with my knees in the air, and he's between my thighs. His yummy rubber-clad cock butts at my entrance, and he reaches down and precision locates the target area. Then he pushes in, with a lurch of his hips, deep and home.

Oh great God Almighty, he feels amazing. I've never been so stretched, so filled. And the awkwardness of our position and the tension in our limbs only make the way he thrusts feel more dynamic and sweet than ever.

He pushes. He shoves. I push and shove right back at him, every action and reaction tugging and battering at my clit. My legs flail about as much as they can in the confined space and coats collapse onto us, wrapping us in a blanket of heat that only makes things feel even more crazy-sexy and frantically hot.

A tumble as mad and wild as this can't hope to last long, but who cares? Within a few moments, I'm coming again, and moaning and groaning. I sense he would have liked to have lasted longer, but he just laughs and curses madly as he comes too. His powerful hips pound me like a pneumatic drill, and as he shoots his semen inside me, he grabs my bottom and holds me nice and firmly in place.

Afterwards, we lie panting like a pair of beached hippopotami in a mangrove swamp. We're a messy tangle of bunched clothes, sticky, sweaty limbs and coats, lots of coats. I'm almost suffocating, but gently and considerately, he digs me out of the hot stuffy bundle.

It's several minutes before we come back to earth and realise that outside the fireworks have stopped and all is quiet. I've no idea *when* they stopped, but they could probably have dropped a cruise missile on me in the last ten minutes and I wouldn't have noticed.

Suddenly, I start to feel awkward. Should I introduce myself or what? I do think I want to get out of here, because for the first time since I entered this closet, I feel claustrophobic. I start to wiggle my way back into my clothes, hauling up my bra and top, and then setting my skirt to rights. It's tricky, but by silent agreement, Man-shape helps me. The only thing neither of us can find though is my knickers.

'Look, I don't think it's a good idea for both of us to emerge together, do you? It'll look ... um ... suspicious.'

I sense him frowning. Have I offended him? Oh, I hope not.

'Good idea. Shall I leave first? Then rap on the door for you if the coast's clear?'

'OK ...'

When the door opens, the light from the corridor dazzles me and I clap my hands over my eyes. But when I peek out from between my fingers again, blackness has descended once more.

For a minute, there's silence, and then comes a solid rap on the door.

I start to open it, then snatch it shut again, hearing laughing female voices approaching. I wait and wait in the darkness, until I can't wait any more, but then when I inch the door open a crack and peer out the corridor is empty.

No Man-shape. I think I want to cry.

Throughout the disco afterwards, I don't see any of the groomsmen. Too busy adorning the going-away car, I suppose. Blowing up the obligatory inflatable sheep and getting busy with the shaving foam. If Man-shape *is* one of them, he might be staying out of the way on purpose, not wanting an embarrassing confrontation with his hasty cupboard shag. I thought he was nicer than that, but maybe he isn't.

When the evening winds to a close, fleets of taxis have been hired to take everybody home that's going home and, feeling deflated, I line up with friends from work, and members of the families of the bride and the groom. I know I shouldn't feel like this. It was just a bit of wedding fun, a tradition as much as the white veil and the confetti.

But just as it's my turn for a taxi and I'm about to step forwards, a hand on my arm stops me in my tracks.

'Can I give you a lift?' says a wickedly familiar voice, and I turn and there's a tall and exceptionally male figure beside me.

Oh goody, it's *the* most handsome of all the groomsmen, the one I really, really hoped it would be. But still I hesitate.

'Don't worry. I had two glasses of champagne earlier, but that's the lot. I'm safe to ride with.' But the way his eyes twinkle suggests a different kind of danger.

'Ooh, yes, in that case, I'd love one. That'd be great.'

Is it him? His voice sounds the same, but then the acoustics in the cupboard were very different.

I follow Mr Tall, Dark, Handsome and Safe to a parking area around the corner, still not sure whether he's my sex-friend from the cupboard. Even if he isn't, I'm not going to argue. He's really mighty fine.

But then, just as he opens the door of a large, dark and rather swish-looking car, I catch a glimpse of something in his top pocket, tucked in there like a handkerchief . . . and it reminds me keenly of the draught that's teasing my pussy.

He notices me noticing my knickers in his pocket and grins. He's got a rather hawkish face, but it's also dreamy in a kind of secret agent way. I really cannot believe my luck tonight.

'My name's Drew, by the way. Drew Richardson. Pleased to meet you.' As he settles into the seat beside me, he offers his hand and I have to laugh out loud.

'Pleased to meet you too. My name's Susan –'

'Susan Grey, yes, I know . . . I asked.'

His fingers are warm and, at their touch, my clit actually tingles, remembering them.

'So, Susan Grey,' he says, looking at my mouth. I can't help but lick my lips. 'Did you enjoy the fireworks?'

I'm puzzled for a moment, then I laugh again. He's a devil.

'Absolutely, Drew Richardson, absolutely. They were awesome.'

Drew Richardson gives me a wink, then releases my hand and starts the engine.

I wink back at him ... and plan the next display.

Portia Da Costa is the author of the Black Lace novels *Continuum*, *Entertaining Mr Stone*, *Gemini Heat*, *Gothic Heat*, *Gothic Blue*, *Hotbed*, *Shadowplay*, *Suite Seventeen*, *The Devil Inside*, *The Stranger*, *The Tutor*, *In Too Deep* and *Kiss It Better*. Her paranormal novellas are included in the Black Lace collections *Lust Bites* and *Magic and Desire*. Her short stories appear in numerous Black Lace anthologies.

The Colonoscoper and the Snake Charmeuse

EllaRegina

V's cock, like his reputation, precedes him, reaching almost to his knees in its semi-erect state, wagging from left to right, clearing the way to the sofa like a blind man's cane. His excitement is apparent; a clear filament – similar to the dewy radius of a spider's web – extends from his prick's winking eye, a laser beam descending towards the ground.

Our clothes and footwear came off immediately once beyond V's apartment door and now lie in a cashmere, wool and leather pyre on the floor beside it. He wants me to put on the wide belt I was wearing so I pick it from the jumble and fasten it tightly around my slender naked waist. We have kissed, inhaling the other's breath nearly to the point of fainting. We have touched almost every square inch of each other's warm damp skin.

The sofa is curved – resembling a banquette in an art deco restaurant – the remaining half from a pair that together made a circle; one crescent mirroring the other. It is upholstered in shiny patinated leather the colour of burgundy. V lifts me up – he is a big strong man, his body in supreme condition from biking, swimming and weight-lifting; I am a 98-pound ex-baton twirler – and plants me atop the piece of furniture in a sitting position facing away from him; my feet resting on the seat cushions below, my rear end a ripe peach hanging invitingly over the tall sofa back.

I spent all day preparing myself. A morning enduring high colonic irrigations in an aromatherapised room complete with fake waterfall, Yanni and Enya – thankfully played at barely audible levels – followed by an afternoon home-administered reload of sorts, using an enema bag filled with lubricant. I wanted nothing to impede this man's path.

V gently bends me forwards so that my head rests on my knees. He inserts a finger into my pussy, exploring its eager status, teasing me with a second finger, and, for an instant, a third, moving the troika as a unit leisurely in and out. He brings his hand to his face, favourably evaluating my private scent and flavour, then reaches towards me, offering his fingers which I smell and taste with glee, adding the moisture from my mouth as I suck and lick them clean. He comes before me momentarily and we kiss again, my personal sap now in the tongue mixing.

V returns to his post behind the sofa and begins his Long March. Using his saliva for assistance he insinuates his thinnest finger into my rear and is surprised to discover that the wheels, so to speak, have already been more than adequately greased. There is a pump bottle of lubricant nearby on a low black slate table but I do not think we will be in need of it; the tunnel is properly primed and all set for his invasion. He penetrates me again with a larger finger, then the largest, and finally with two digits together until he pronounces me ready to admit him – all of him, or at least as much as I can handle.

But first he must enter my pussy – just long enough to incite me – and in doing so thoroughly varnishing his prick with my plentiful yield. He moves to my anus and commences: tentatively pressing his swollen glans against the yawning opening as he tests my receptivity, then sinking himself inside me by millimetric increments, with each anal advance asking if I am in any kind of pain. Amazingly, I am as relaxed as I've ever been, remarkable considering the magnitude of the impalement equipment at hand. I breathe profoundly and slowly, as pregnant women are instructed to during in extremis labour.

V is gradually filling me up, moving steadily forwards – the bulbous *Soul Train* cartoon locomotive logo lurching rhythmically onwards – until I feel that he has somehow managed to reach a virgin spot, a tight, hot, slippery, hospitable place where no man has gone before him. He is the Sir Edmund Hillary of my rectum. I wonder what kind of flag he will plant at the end. Or is there a terminus? The horizon appears infinite.

He proceeds further, pressing ahead and withdrawing – now in true ass-fucking mode – going yet deeper with each investigative propulsion. I grip him firmly as he moves through my tube, holding his probe like the woven bamboo cylinder of a Chinese finger trap. Otherwise I am as limp as an abandoned marionette. V raises my upper body to match the angle of his trajectile. He clutches my belt – horse-rein style – so that at any particularly vigorous juncture I am not catapulted off the sofa onto the wall as if I were a rock in a slingshot.

It is the ultimate pole dance, with V providing the endless upright. I wiggle my ass a bit as he progresses, his pipe plunging into me – a butter churner's dasher stick – edging along my spine. I am on the ride of my life. His prick swells inside my intestines, bringing to mind those flat travel sponges that assume their regular size after being dropped into water – he is lengthening and expanding with each surge. I finger my flooded pussy.

After some time there is a new sensation, unlike anything I've ever felt – unfamiliar yet not unpleasant. I realise what it is. Something is poking against my throat. It is V's prick, which has succeeded in reaching my mouth from behind, and in the process miraculously bypassing my gag reflex. He continues his back and forth movement. Not only is my hungry derrière getting royally plugged but I am performing a reverse act of fellatio, breathing only through my nose by now, draining the sweet preliminary liquid emanating from his long staff, my salivary glands on overdrive, at once sucking and swallowing – not an easy task with a heating riser in my oesophagus. I no longer have the capacity for speech but am able to exude a long guttural glottal hum of encouragement.

The tip of my tongue darts in a playful spiral around the head of V's instrument, sharply scoring its centre underside in a single continuous lick as it passes by, until, with one final thrust, the prick definitively emerges from my mouth, well beyond my clamping lips – a baby entering the world – pointing upwards at the ceiling like the thick bell of a tenor saxophone. I am completely pierced; an animal on a spit.

I play his didgeridoo with my marionette fingers, giving long milking strokes, slowly reaching one hand after the other as if I were climbing Tarzan's vine, all the while continuing the workings of my mouth and tongue. I collect some pussy discharge to aid my manual labour.

I want it all – I want V to come in my mouth, on my face, in my hands, out my nipples, in my ass – at the same time. He begins to convulse in a shudder that runs, literally, through my core, vibrating my entire body. His prick shakes within me – a rattlesnake, a spirit possessed – its heated fluid starting to emit with more force; but he controls it by some means and starts to recede in stages, leaving my hands feverish and wet (I smear their coatings on my face) depositing a serving in my mouth to savour. He continues his rearwards slither and, as he goes, releases a stream of molten lava inside me like a line on a map, finally halting in my ass – about eight inches from its portal – where he finishes his output, serendipitously triggering my uterus and rectum to contract simultaneously. V pulls out of me and spills his last hot drops on the ballerina curve of my quaking rump. I am both very full yet acutely empty without his imposing interior presence.

I slide down from my roost, my ass landing on the sofa seat in a comic book *splat*! V retrieves an indigo-blue towel from the bathroom, places it underneath my seeping cavities and moves in next to me. We kiss once more, his creative juice now present in the melange, and thirstily drink from each other's mouths, fiercely competing for the sexy blend. We sit shoulder to shoulder as if in a car, and I cannot help but caress his shaft in awe as it resumes its 'normal' size. We fall asleep, our heads together – Siamese twins joined at the skull – my hair lightly draping his face, my hands a warm tea cosy securely wrapped around his still turgid prick. That entire night I dream of sliding down the brass pole at Hook &

Ladder Company #20 on Lafayette Street, over and over and over and over again.

Sexy Little Numbers features the first appearance of EllaRegina's short fiction in Black Lace.

Michelangelo's Men
Janine Ashbless

Bourbon is the colour of autumn; I always start to drink it again as the nights close in. Bourbon ushers in gas-fire evenings and too much TV, it snuggles up under the duvet with us while we're waiting for the heating to come on and murmurs oak-matured confidences. When Trent, stretching one bare foot along the sofa and poking me in the bum cheek with his toe, asks, 'What do you want for your birthday, then?' I've drunk enough to answer unguardedly.

'I'd like to see you fuck Mike.'

Trent pulls a face over his glass; an aghast grin. 'Danielle!'

'What?' Then I press my knuckles to my lips, catching a giggle. 'Don't you fancy him?'

'That's not the point, is it?'

'No? What is the point?'

Trent's eyebrows – he has these great dramatic eyebrows – peak quizzically. 'Well, (a) he's straight.'

'What's the difference between a straight guy and a bisexual one?' I say, quoting a very old joke and not waiting for him to answer. 'About four pints of beer – boom-boom!'

'And (b) he's your boyfriend.'

'Yeah.' I smile dreamily. 'I'd like to watch you fuck my big straight boyfriend.'

I've always liked men. That makes me straight, I'd say, not kinky. I like the way men are; their bulk and their hairiness and the way they don't look like me. I like them muscular and unselfconscious and a bit careless, and I don't mind it rough sometimes. I like a man with a powerful sexual appetite and the confidence to pursue it.

Good-looking, but masculine not pretty – the willowy youth thing doesn't do it for me. No twinks, no skinny-boy models, no gawky students. Plain old-fashioned masculinity.

Isn't that ordinary? A bit dull even?

I always fuck with the light on. I like to see a man at work, whether looming over me or bowed between my splayed thighs or beneath me as I straddle his face or his cock. If he's fucking me from behind I like to face a mirror and watch. Yeah – I love that best of all. He's not thinking about me then but just concentrating on the job, his forearms taut, his shaft thrusting away, his fingers digging into my flesh. Enjoying himself with my ass. I'm sort of a voyeur then, as well as a participant. Some ex-boyfriends have taken that for vanity, but I'm really not bothered about seeing myself. It's all about him.

I guess you could say I'm visually oriented. Seeing is a turn-on. Hey, it comes with the arty thing: I make jewellery in my spare time to sell online, and if I could make enough money at that I'd do it for a living. On the other hand if I hadn't been temping I wouldn't have met Mike, so work's not all bad even though I have to take most of my earrings out and dress my hair and make-up down so much that hardly any of my friends would recognise me. I can pretty much pass for normal so long as I keep my clothes on. Mike on the other hand really *is* normal: he's something with the word 'manager' in it in the IT department and he wears a shirt and tie and he goes home once a month to see his mum and he drinks lager and buys a lads' magazine with reality TV stars showing their tits. He actually looked shocked the first time he got my clothes off and saw the rings through my nipples and my tattoos – a Celtic knotwork circle around my navel, an ivy garland right the way round my hips and a tribal pendant on my breastbone – though he did his best to hide it. I did think for a moment he might bolt, but he got stuck in. Like a man.

I like it when he surprises me like that.

People wonder what Mike and I have in common. Sometimes I do too, and he's certainly nothing like my previous boyfriends. He loves his family, I never see mine. He went to business college,

I went to art school. He likes to stay in and play on his PS3, I like clubs and festivals. And yet ... he's grown on me. Two things help. The first is that he really *really* likes to fuck. It wasn't just a start-of-a-relationship buzz that wore off after a few weeks; he wants it every day, at the most inappropriate moments like when I'm getting ready to go out or talking on the phone or cooking. He squeezes into the shower with me or – Jeez, this one surprised even me – sticks his cock in my mouth while I'm sitting on the loo having a pee. He'll wake me in the middle of the night with a stiffy nudging my bum. And when he is too tired to get it up he loves to eat my pussy. Now that's a precious thing in a man. Don't ever undervalue it.

The second thing in his favour is that he plays rugby – union, not league – and he's built like a brick shithouse. It's all natural muscle too; he doesn't go to a gym to tone anything or worry about his weight, which shows a bit around the jawline and I find quite endearing because I've met far too many narcissistic men. I started to go watch Mike play sport at weekends, and believe me it's little short of full-on porn watching thirty men charging about colliding into each other, filthy with sweat and mud and sometimes blood, smashing each other to the ground and swearing and grinding down together into a scrum, every muscle straining.

You see, I always knew I liked watching men. I didn't know I liked watching them together until a few years back when I went to a friend's wedding. It took place in a northern castle, which sounds flash and bits of it are, but it's been converted into a university college so actually there are a lot of pokey little corridors and student rooms hiding away behind the banqueting hall and the medieval galleries. I ended up late at night climbing a turret staircase and switching on lights as I went, like someone in a fairy story exploring the forbidden wing of their palace. What I found up the tower wasn't a wicked fairy with a spinning wheel but a unisex toilet, which suited me fine. I was in a state that night, having just quarrelled with my boyfriend of the time – I can't even remember what had set it off now, just that he'd said something and then I said something and then he said something else and I'd walked off in tears. So I was pleased to have a room miles from the party, all to myself. The room was L-shaped with five cubicles and I sat down behind the row of sinks, next to the hot water pipes, and had a good weep and felt self-righteously tragic like you do when you're young. After a while the room light, which was on a timer, went off and I sat in the dark and sniffled.

Then I heard feet coming up the stairs. I thought it might be someone looking for me so I just scrunched down into my space and said nothing when the door opened. It was two men; I saw that as the fluorescent tube flickered on. They weren't looking for me or anyone else; they had eyes only for each other. One of them I sort of recognised – he was the groom's uncle, I think: middle-aged and blond going silvery at the temples, but fit looking, in a raw-boned Scandinavian sort of way. He was wearing a tux, I remember, and a blue cummerbund. I recalled even at the time that he'd sat at the high table with his wife. He set his back to the door as it closed and pulled the other bloke to him, firmly. That guy was younger and darker and it was obvious he wasn't quite keen on kissing, but that's what the older man did; gripped the back of his head and pulled his mouth to his own.

Two guys kissing. I froze, hoping I was invisible behind the sinks, hoping that the blood that'd rushed to my face wasn't lighting me up like a neon beacon. Then, as the tongue-wrestling went on, I gradually let myself focus on the action. Those men kissed like they were starving to death and fighting over the last scrap of food. Stubble scraped stubble. Teeth flashed. Little gasps broke free of their lips. And their hands – they were all over each other, pulling at shirts and grabbing for crotches. Flies were yanked down releasing twin erections that butted up together aggressively, hot sticky lengths rubbing one on the other. The younger guy groaned and babbled a string of swear words. The older one caught him by the short hair at the back of his scalp and pushed him to his knees, while his other hand mastered his own erection. It was a big, gnarly, tough-looking cock, I thought. The guy on his knees stared at it with an expression of awe and stretched to lick it. No way was that allowed; fingers tightened on his scalp and his head was jerked back.

'Ask nicely, bonny boy.' The heavy cockhead bobbed.

'Please!' His eyes were bright with need. His lower lip trembled.

The standing man grinned. 'OK then.'

That's when I saw for the first time one man take another's cock in his mouth. It changed me for ever. I watched a cute, dishevelled-looking guy who I wouldn't have minded chatting up myself eagerly swallow the rigid length of a man twice his age, and I heard them both make noises of gratitude in their throats, the giver with a whimper, the receiver with a huffed 'Um.' I saw blue cheeks stretch to take the girth and then skin shining with spittle withdrawing momentarily, only to plunge in again. And I thought I was going to dissolve into a puddle of my own juices, so wet and hot and weak was I, my whole body pulsing to the beat in my sex. All my old self-pity was blown away, like I'd been struck by lightning.

You've got to realise this was in the years B.H.B: Before Home Broadband. I'd not really seen that many erect cocks either in the flesh or in photographs, never mind two blokes at it together.

The blow job was quick and efficient. The groom's uncle lurched and grabbed the other guy's head in both hands and pumped into his mouth and ejaculated down his throat. For a moment they separated and the guy on the floor knelt back, breathing hard and licking his lips, his own hard-on standing ruddy and stiff despite comparative neglect. He took it in his sweaty hand and began to jack it.

'Hey.' With a monosyllable the older man brought a stop to the masturbation. Kneeling himself, he faced his fellator and took his frustration in hand and the younger man leaned back, visibly surrendering control. Up and down slid that big, masterful hand on that stiff cock. Firm and then fast – faster than I'd ever managed giving a handjob – until strands of pale spunk were squirting between his fingers. He captured most of the sticky mess in his hand, anointing the guy's purplish cock with his own ooze. The younger man gasped and gasped and shut his eyes, seeming to sink into a trance.

Then the groom's uncle stood, quite matter-of-factly, to tuck his own cock away. It was when he turned towards the sinks to wash his hands that he saw me. He stopped.

'Oh shit,' said the younger guy, his eyes open now, fixed in my direction.

'Why . . . I don't think there's anything to worry about.' The older man had a much better view of my flushed face, and could read my expression rather more clearly. He stepped towards me and I just stared. I couldn't even blink. 'You're not going to tell anyone, are you, hinny?'

He held his hand out. His sticky fingers. He touched my parted lips and I opened them and let him slip his spunky fingers into my mouth. Believe me, my whole body was so fucking wet and yielding then that if he'd put a loaded gun to my mouth I would have wrapped my lips around it and sucked.

'Canny lass,' he said. He left me with the grassy, salty taste of his lover on my tongue.

That was it: my first time seeing two blokes together. I knew right then that this was it: this was my Thing, capital T. And finding the internet was like coming home.

Even if I hadn't been into man-on-man I would've ended up surfing the gay sites anyway. If you want pictures of men, that's the place to find them. Sports stars in their underwear, brooding models, just nice-looking guys in the buff – you've got to go gay even if you're a straight female, even if you're not looking for hardcore. Which I was. Heterosexual porn is made for men, that's the trouble: it's wall-to-wall snatch and boobs and lipsticked mouths. Men often don't feature at all, and if they do they're often ugly bastards because the focus isn't on them. If you want men as objects of desire you've got to hang out with the boys.

Men turn me on. The thick bulge of a bicep, the dusting of hair down a flat stomach, the jut of a hard arse. Thigh muscles hewn in improbably sharp angles, like they're sculpted from wood not flesh.

The sleek chamois of a soft cock and the almost rubbery ridges of a hard one. The asymmetry of a hanging ball sac, and the gathered wrinkles on the pouch. I want to look. I want to touch. I want to lick. Guy on guy sends me into meltdown. It's hotness squared, it's pure lust: desire untainted by distraction. I'm not going 'I don't like her make-up,' or 'She's too fat' (or worse: 'She's skinnier than me!'). I'm not trying to imagine myself in the scene, in fact I'm not thinking about myself at all. I'm just consuming, my eyes eating them all up: magnificently burly bears and sleek otters, heroes and warriors. Don't ever listen to anyone telling you that men are not beautiful. It's a lie, a nasty modern lie, that says male bodies are faintly ridiculous. If art history taught me anything it was that through the centuries it was men who epitomised the aesthetic ideal.

Michelangelo could show you all about that. His saints and patri- archs are massive, granite-hewn figures, gods in human form. Look at the Sistine Chapel: it's a bathhouse eulogy to the male body, a sanctified Pride march. Even his female nudes are just men with implausible breasts stuck on to broad masculine torsos.

Mike doesn't know any of this stuff. He doesn't guess what sites I surf when I'm on my own in my room. He knows I get turned on watching him play rugby and that I don't always let him shower afterwards but drive him quickly home instead so that we can fuck while he still smells of sweat and crushed grass and battle. What he doesn't realise is that when he does clean up with the other guys I'm fantasising about him naked in the team showers with all those heavyset hairy men.

Trent on the other hand knows exactly how I feel. We've never talked about it, but we share an understanding. We've been friends for that many years that we have very few secrets. In fact, I can tell whether he's serious about a guy as soon as he brings him home. If he thinks it might be serious, or hopes it is, Trent shuts his bedroom door. If it's just a one-night stand then he leaves it ajar with the bedroom light on, so that if I'm very quiet I can sneak up in the darkened hall and watch them fucking.

It's a good job that one's a secret, because Mike doesn't really like me sharing a flat with Trent as it is. It's not that he dislikes the guy

– they get on fine if a bit awkwardly, though I'm pretty sure Trent sees him as a joke – but the arrangement makes him anxious. 'He's gay,' I explained on our first date.

'But you're not,' he answered grumpily.

Mike's basic problem is that he's unimaginative. He can't work out how I can live with a good-looking bloke and not be tempted to fuck him. And certainly Trent is hot enough, but I don't want to jump his bones: I just want to watch him buggering other men. I want to stand on the landing in the early hours and watch two tight sweaty bodies ferociously entwined and hear the deep throaty grunts of both men as they power their way to orgasm, and feel the sex juices melting down the insides of my thighs.

But yeah, I can understand Mike feeling a bit insecure around Trent. My boyfriend might have the advantage in mass but Trent is smart – caustic too, on occasion – and talented and really obviously more my type. I remember the look on Mike's face the first time he came round to our flat and saw Trent's canvases: huge intricate monochrome hatchwork that redefines the urban landscape in terms of Piranesi's *Prisons*.

'Is he famous?' Mike asked in a small voice.

'He ought to be. He's a freelance graphic artist at the moment. Does illustrations for leaflets and advertising brochures.'

Then he met Trent in the flesh – barefoot and shaven-headed, rings through his eyebrows, a bolt through his lower lip, a barbell through his tongue. And those deep-set, mocking eyes. And the talk about deconstructionism and post-modernist irony which, I've got to say, Trent laid on with a trowel in order to sound him out.

No wonder poor Mike feels like a himbo.

But he puts up with my choices. He might look like an alpha but he's out of his home territory when he's with me. I think I'm his door to a weird new world he's only heard of, and he's curious enough to hang on in there in the hope of further glimpses.

It's a dangerous combination that: insecurity and curiosity. It can lure you into doing things you shouldn't.

* * *

And in the end, it doesn't need beer goggles to lead Mike to places he's never been before. Though certainly there's alcohol consumed on my birthday, I think we've danced most of it off by the time we return to the flat. We've clubbed till we dropped, with most of my friends turning out to join me during the night, but now it's just the three of us in the back of the black cab and I'm practically in Mike's lap, snuggled up against him, my boobs popping out of their little cross-laced leather top, my stockinged thigh over his, my hand in his crotch, my face nuzzling his cheek. Trent takes no notice; he's just staring out of the window, anxious for a cigarette. Mike's flushed and cheery and he's got a semi-hard-on which I'm doing my best to encourage.

'Did you have a fun evening?' I ask, licking the salt from his neck with the tip of my tongue. I'd deliberately picked a club that was just out of Mike's comfort zone, with enough punters in fetish clothing to make him self-conscious: bright slick PVC and bondage cuffs and supple skintight rubber. Even one pair in insectile latex masks, leashed to their leather-clad mistress.

'It was fun.' He's playing with the bulge of my breasts as they threaten to spill from my bodice, jiggling a naughty finger in the gape of my cleavage.

'What did you think of Leanne?' I giggle, squirming. Leanne had done her bit to advertise my work by hitting the dance floor topless except for a fine chainmail pectoral that attached to a silver necklace and matching nipple jewellery. It's one of the best pieces I've made. She'd certainly pulled enough attention, shimmying with arms raised and the mesh dancing over her perky little breasts. I was touched by her loyalty.

'Very cute.' His smile is slightly shamefaced; he's wondering if I'm trying to entrap him. Which I am I suppose, just not in the way he thinks. I run my thumb along the bulge that's sandwiched between his thigh and his trouser fabric and I feel it thicken and solidify under my caress.

'Want me to do something about this when we get home?'

'Uh-huh.' He shifts his hips, trying to make room in his pants for his swelling erection.

'Want me to lick it?' My breath is moist in his ear. 'I'm in the mood for sucking something big and hard.'

He covers my hand with his as if that will disguise what I'm doing from Trent. His own breath is coming quicker now. 'Whatever you want, love,' he says. 'It's your birthday.'

He can't see my grin. If he could maybe he'd worry.

But when we pile out of the taxi and into the flat I don't hurry Mike to the bedroom the way he wants. Instead Trent and I neck some water and look for glasses and bottles in the kitchen while Mike first of all hovers and then sits uneasily on the edge of the sofa, watching us at the other end of the open-plan room as we chat and chuckle. 'You want to take these into the bedroom?' he asks when I come through to his side at last, glasses in hand.

'No,' I answer cheerily. 'I'd like to sit here a while.'

Mike tries to disguise the disappointed downturn of his mouth and sits back on the sofa while I pour bourbon into three glasses. Trent parks himself in the armchair facing us and sets his tin of rolling tobacco out on the low table, his attention focused on skinning up the first of a series of stingily thin cigarettes. I pass a full glass in his direction and he nods.

But I don't hand Mike his. Instead, taking one in hand, I climb onto the sofa and sit astride his thighs, looking down on him with a smoky smile while Mike's eyes widen questioningly. Taking a sip of the whiskey I stoop to kiss his lips and the dark liquid passes from my mouth to his. Our tongues lap cautiously, then deeper. There's no hurry, no urgency, just a savouring of the layered tastes of the bourbon and each other. I slip my hand into Mike's lap and find that it's still there, his semi, still restless and eager for my touch. We laugh together, silent and private. Mike slides his hands up my legs, unable to resist my spread thighs, and I'm not surprised – I'm wearing this ridiculously provocative outfit: black fishnet stockings and a blue faux-snakeskin miniskirt. His thumbs find the gap of silky flesh between stockings and knickers and caress my innermost thighs, easing up towards my gauze-clad pussy. I squirm against him and moan in my throat, nipping at his lips. I feel his cock surge, protesting at the confines of his trousers. Soon I'm absolutely sure it's a full-on erection, and his hands are, under the very inadequate cover of my skirt, making incursions under the edges of my panties in a manner that makes me gasp. And every time I gasp, he twitches with arousal.

'Come on, love,' he says under his breath. 'Let's go.'

I slide sideways off his lap onto the cushion, one fishnet thigh still draped over him, and look over my shoulder at Trent, who is drawing with satisfaction the first lungfuls of tobacco. 'Mike's after a blow job.'

'On your birthday?' His brow puckers. 'Shouldn't it be your turn?'

Mike seems dazed by the unexpected interruption to events, but he's adaptable. He swallows hard.

'Oh, I like sucking him off. He's got a lovely cock.' I squeeze the member in question, finding it rock solid still. 'I could suck it all night.'

'Or at least until you get bored.' The quirk of Trent's lips is patronising.

'Hey, you: I'm really good at it!'

'Yeah, right.' His tone is unmistakably derisive.

'She could wake the dead,' says Mike in a hoarse voice, and I feel my heart warm: he's coming to my defence. But this time Trent actually snorts.

'What?' demands Mike.

'Women don't give proper head. They don't know what they're doing with a dick: it stands to reason. You want a really great blow job, you need a man.'

'Like you know what women can do, mate?'

'I've given it a couple of tries, a few years back.'

'But not with Dani.' Mike is pugnacious.

'No.'

'Then you don't know what you're talking about.'

Trent exhales a long cloud of smoke, his eyes narrowing wickedly. 'Show me then.'

'Huh?'

His eyes flick to me, glinting. 'Show me. Reckon you can eat his meat good enough to make me eat my words?'

I straighten my back, thrusting my tits and my lower lip out. 'Hell yeah.'

Mike grins, not quite certain where all this came from but appreciating the novelty. He's sort of aware that this is crossing a boundary he's never previously approached, but he's a bit punch-drunk from the sensory overload at the club and he's stand-up horny from my teasing, and the caresses I'm still lavishing on his shaft are stopping him thinking clearly. He even helps by uncinching his belt as I set my glass aside. 'She's going to make your eyes water, mate,' he promises. He's being possessive; he thinks it's us as a couple against the gay bloke.

Poor unimaginative Mike.

His cock is straining the seams of his fly as I get started and the teeth part with a staccato purr. Out pops Mike's cock, hot and eager and flushed dark, his foreskin already being shouldered aside by his swelling glans. God, I love the way cocks stand up like that, so uncompromising and unambiguous. There's nothing half-hearted about an erection. Nothing that says, 'Well, I'm not really bothered but ...' It's a demand made physically incarnate.

Trent brings his drink and his smoke and comes to sit on the near edge of the coffee table so that he can get a good view. I flash him a conspiratorial look before I crouch down on the sofa and take that great big meaty length in my mouth, sliding it all the way to the back of my throat and bathing it in the taste of sour-mash spirit. Mike lets out a little grunt and shifts his position, getting a good angle as he lays his hand on the back of my head. I'm aware at the very periphery of my vision of Trent taking a drag on his cigarette and rubbing his knuckle over an itch in his nose, coolly appraising of my performance. So I give him one, though it's all supposed to be for Mike's benefit. I make sure there's plenty of visible tongue and lots of movement, my head bobbing up and down as I suck that cock as far down my throat as it'll go. I make sure there's audible sucking and little grunts of erotic shock as it pushes to its limit in my throat's sheath. I can't really take him all the way, he's too long for that, but I can have a good go. Mike's certainly moved by my efforts: after a few minutes he pushes his jeans down from his hips to expose himself further, releasing his scrotum into view. A big, furry ball sac matches his big exuberant cock. I take it in my hand, playing with his nuts through the tightening skin.

I know Mike. I know all his little tells – the catch in his breath, the sudden surge of sweat to the skin of his crotch, the ooze of clear lube from the slit of his cock – well enough to be sure that he's reached the Zone, that he's no longer conscious of anything but the need to orgasm. That's when I stop, lifting my open lips from his cock, washing its crown only in my hot wet breath. It twitches with frustration.

'Not bad,' says Trent softly. 'Want something to compare it to?'

Mike swears, helplessly. Then as I stick out my tongue and explore the slit of his glans very delicately he lets his head fall back against the back of the sofa and shuts his eyes. It's hard to tell whether he's refusing to respond to the offer or incapable of doing so; either way, Trent takes it for assent. Stubbing out his cigarette he slides off the coffee table and kneels before Mike. I forestall any negative reaction by swirling my tongue around the cockhead like it was an ice cream, and as I caress that solid column of flesh Trent joins me there, his mouth fastening to the shaft, his breath mingling with mine, his tongue lapping and inter-twining with mine. I taste the cigarette he's just smoked and the absinthe he downed earlier in the evening, a minty undertone to the smoke. For a few moments we're sucking Mike's cock together, then I withdraw and sit back slowly. I want to watch. I want to watch as my best friend blows my boyfriend, one beau-tiful man moving on another. Trent, I note with envy, can take it all the way: every thick inch. Mike groans and groans, linking his hands behind his head as if he's scared what he might do with them if they are loose, and his hips first recoil and then buck.

He's going to come in Trent's mouth, I'm sure of it. It's so fucking beautiful and so fucking hot and so fucking dirty what

I've done; I'm the Wicked Witch of the West and I'm melting right here on the sofa, turning into a molten puddle. My pussy's swollen and running wet, but I don't stick my fingers down there. I don't want anything to distract me from this vision. He's going to come.

Then Trent frustrates us both. He quietly lets go and sits back on the table. Mike is left with a glazed cock and an even more glazed look in his eye as he lifts his head and the two men stare at each other.

'So how was that? Want me to finish you off?' Trent's voice is low, but there's a challenge in it. Tricking Mike, I realise, is not enough for him. Mike swallows, his Adam's apple punching the air. There are bright red patches burning on his cheeks.

'Not bad.' He echoes Trent's own words to me earlier, just as sarcastic, and I'm truly impressed by his efforts to master himself. He lowers his hands carefully to his sides; a couple of strokes and he'd be able to bring himself off I'm sure, but he doesn't touch anything. This is about some bizarre measure of masculine cool. 'It's the tongue piercing, I suppose,' he adds, clearing his throat. 'That definitely makes a difference.'

'I've got others. Want to see?'

Mike doesn't nod, but makes a twitch suggesting casual consent. Trent stands, pulls his T-shirt off with one smooth motion and opens his trousers. There's no stripper-style lingering tease here, just a straightforward, almost aggressive unbuckle and drop.

'You look after yourself,' Mike allows.

Oh Trent. His body is a work of art. Not a big bloke, not like Mike; tight and wiry instead, and there's no body hair allowed to soften the lines. He doesn't wear as much metal as you might expect from seeing his face but a whole lot of ink instead; his torso and arms are tattooed with tribal thorns so sharp you'd worry you'd draw blood if you licked him. Under his skin his muscles stand proud in layered groups as defined as one of Vesalius' anatomical illustrations. His pubes are shaved to a stubble, and his foreskin is cut so that even when he's only half-hard like now, dangling in a long curve, he looks eager. The shaving and his pale skin make his blue veins almost as prominent as the tattoos. He's got an ampallang barbell through his shaft just behind the head, ending in steel balls, and a captive bead ring through the opening of his urethra. It makes his cock look like a weapon. His scrotum in contrast to Mike's is hairless and satin-skinned, hardly wrinkled, and hangs low and heavy. Little gold rings pierce folds of skin either side of his cock.

'They make a difference too, do they?' Mike says with a nod of the chin to the piercings, still determined to sound bluff and easy even with a full-on boner and his pants around his thighs. I put my hand over my mouth to stifle a giggle.

'Yeah.'

'To you or the . . . the guy you're fucking?'

'Both.' Trent's eyes are bourbon dark. 'You can touch me if you want, Mike.'

'That's all right.'

They're ignoring me. I am forgotten. A witness only.

'What do you think will happen, Mike?' Trent is amused. 'You scared I'm going to turn you?'

Mike laughs too, uncomfortably. 'I'm just not . . .'

'You not curious then? D'you not want to know, just once, what it feels like to have a man's cock in your mouth?'

'Ah . . .'

'This is your chance, Mike. Suck my cock.'

'It's not my thing, mate.'

'Suck it.'

Maybe he's just mesmerised by Trent. Maybe he's so self-conscious that he'd rather suck a prick than look like one. Maybe he's just out-of-his-mind horny right now. Or maybe he really does want to try it out – but whatever the reason, Mike takes a deep breath, sits up to the edge of the seat and leans forwards to take that heavy strop of meat between his lips.

'That's it,' says Trent.

I don't believe it. I don't believe it! This is incredible. I could punch the sky and run round the room whooping, but I sit close and tight and don't dare to move a muscle, terrified of drawing attention to myself, terrified of breaking this spell. Mike's wearing a slight frown of concentration as his tongue fumbles with the unfamiliar shapes and tastes. Then I see the surge and swell as Trent's cock thickens and I can't stop a sigh escaping my lips any more than I can stop the wet that's flooding my knicker gusset.

So. Fucking. Hot.

It's a minute of pure heaven. It's a picture that burns itself into my brain: my boyfriend blowing my best friend. His big masculine face wrapped around that stiff dick. The bob of his larynx as he sucks and swallows.

But when Trent starts to move his hips and push to the back of his throat, Mike pulls away. He drops his eyes. 'Like I said, mate,' he mumbles, 'it's just not my thing.'

Liar, liar, Mike, though it's my pants on fire. If you're not interested then why's your big dumb cock still standing between your thighs so stiffly that there's pre-come weeping from the glans? Why does it twitch as you brush it with your fingertips? You're just scared because this is going too far and too fast for the ordinary bloke you think you are. I bite my lip in frustration.

Trent though takes a different tack. 'You prefer pussy?' he says with a ghostly smile.

''Fraid so.'

'Give him pussy then, Dani.' His eyes flash me a command. 'Sit over his face.'

So as Mike leans back once more against the cushions, I stand. He rests his head on the sofa back and I turn and present him my bum in its little skirt, the transparent gauze straining over my labia, and the wild perfume of my sex. I settle, wriggling, over his face and he pulls my gusset aside and sinks into my swollen juicy pussy grate-fully, lapping at me. I let him pretend this spree is entirely heterosexual as he gobbles my clit and Trent kneels before him to go down again on his cock. Mike groans once. I make a higher keening moan, but it's not the press of his face and tongue and teeth that does it for me, delicious though they are, but the sight of Trent's tattooed back bent between my boyfriend's thighs, the sight of his head – glossed with perspiration – rising and sinking over his cock.

This time there aren't any interruptions. This time Mike's whole body goes as hard as a board, quivering with tension. This time all the heat that's been building and building inside me incandesces at once and I mash myself down on his face not caring if he can breathe or not, and as Mike heaves and bucks beneath us both, spurting his jizz into Trent's eager mouth, I come too, harder and longer than ever before. I nearly drown the poor bastard, I reckon.

Trent lifts his head and runs his tongue around his lips.

My trembling legs give way and I tumble onto the cushions. A good job too, because Trent hasn't finished. He stands, climbs up on the sofa to get one knee astride Mike's shoulders, and before the other man has time to get his breath back or react in any way slaps his scrotum to Mike's mouth. 'Lick my bollocks,' he rasps, taking his erect cock in his hand and glaring down at the face between his legs. 'Go on: fucking lick them.'

And Mike does. As Trent jerks off, Mike licks and sucks his balls and even laps at the underside of his cock so that Trent shoots his load with a gasp; splash after splash onto the living room wall.

In the right clothes I can pass for a nice ordinary girl, but I'm not: nice girls don't do that to their boyfriends. They don't lure people over the rainbow and then leave them to find their own way home. If getting home is what they want, after all.

I don't know what Mike's reaction is going to be. He got up this morning and made me a cup of tea and went into the bathroom. He's been there a while. I imagine he's looking into the mirror and trying to work out what he can see. He didn't say anything much to me in that brief space before disappearing. I mean, he didn't act weird or anything, he didn't give the impression of being pissed off; he simply didn't mention it. It's just not the sort of thing he talks about.

He's a man, after all.

Janine Ashbless is the author of the Black Lace novels *Divine Torment*, *Burning Bright* and *Wildwood*. She has two single author collections

of erotica, *Cruel Enchantment* and *Dark Enchantment*, also published by Black Lace. Her paranormal erotic novellas are included in the Black Lace collections *Magic and Desire* and *Enchanted*. Her short stories are published in numerous Black Lace anthologies.

The Test
Dianne Dawson

'Amanda Trewen.' Randall spoke grandly, enunciating every syllable of the name as though he were making love to it. 'That's the contract that's up for grabs. She wants to completely revamp her Jackson Street estate, and we're in the running: against those whores from Pacifica Design.'

A murmur of hushed exclamations filled the room. Amanda Trewen, only one of the most noted socialites in the city. Her family owned a substantial portion of San Francisco, not to mention the state of California. Their achievements, both commercial and political, extended back to the colonial era. By New World standards, she was practically royalty.

'So who gets to go?' Melanie demanded. Her massive head of varicoloured ringlets seemed even more frenzied than usual as she leaned forwards anxiously. She clearly wanted to be selected, but so did everyone else in the room. I prayed silently and crossed my fingers under the table. Randall seemed to be very pleased with my performance lately, so maybe I had a chance.

Surveying the faces around the table, Randall dragged the moment out as long as he could. Flaming queen that he was, he couldn't resist an opportunity for the dramatic. 'It was a hard choice on this one, you've all been absolutely brilliant over the last few jobs. When it came down to it, though, the choice was obvious. Jenna, you'll be representing the firm on the Trewen account.'

I exhaled a breath I hadn't realised I'd been holding, and the room erupted in congratulations, both sincere and false. As the clamour died down, Randall returned to the business of existing projects and updates. I couldn't really focus on all of it, and from the smirks that

Randall kept tossing my way, he understood my state of mind. Any designer would have their head in the clouds after receiving this kind of news, but as the meeting progressed, the enormity of the responsibility dawned on me. This kind of contract would bring more money into the firm than ten average jobs, not to mention the prestige, photo shoots and publicity that could ensue. Nothing of this scope had ever been in my hands before, and that realisation gave me pause. I stared into the table's polished black surface, mesmerised by these thoughts until the grating of chairs against the floor pulled my thoughts back to the present. Everyone filed out of the room, chatting amiably, but Randall hung back, casting me a compassionate smile.

'You'll do fine,' he assured me, leaning against the table. 'I wouldn't have chosen you if I didn't think you were the best person for the job. I know you probably want to get down to it, but take the night off. Go out: celebrate! You deserve it.'

After patting me on the shoulder he, too, left, and I was alone with my thoughts. Surely, Randall was right. I was the best person for the job and, for now, it was time to party.

I frowned at my reflection as I prepared myself that evening. I dabbed foundation on my trouble spots, then ended up coating my whole face with it. I'd never been fond of the redness of my complexion and, though the coral pink of my new halter dress complemented my dark-blue eyes and blonde hair nicely, it did bring out the ruddiness of my skin. As I popped a pair of dangly earrings into place, impatient knocks sounded from my door and I rushed across the living room to open it.

'Hey, sweetie!' Trish gushed, filling my small apartment with her exuberant presence. 'Congratulations!' She grabbed me around the middle and delivered an enthusiastic hug before making way for the couple behind her. Trish was always a diva and tonight was no exception: designer skinny jeans hugged her enviably round bum and highlighted her small waist, which was left exposed below a black satin cropped blouse with billowy sleeves. Her mass of shiny black braids ended below her blouse, and bounced against the naked small of her back as she walked. Only in my dreams was I that sexy, and the fact that she was gay frustrated men on a daily basis.

'My feelings exactly,' Anne's voice rang out as she and Ian entered the room, hand in hand. I hugged them both and exchanged smiles of sympathy with Anne. We both lamented our inability to equal Trish's looks, though Anne's sentiments were always a confusing mix of envy and lust.

'So where are we off to tonight, kids?' Ian asked, burying his hands in his pockets. Between his good looks and his sensible attire, he looked like a model out of a Sears catalogue. Anne never seemed to object to his lack of fashion savvy, and frankly, neither did I.

I'd selected the restaurant already, a chic new Asian fusion bar that promised both a sexy atmosphere and good food. The restaurant was just as posh and popular as I'd heard: only by virtue of it being a Tuesday night did we manage to get in.

Delicious food and several bottles of champagne were delivered to our table, inspired by my good fortune and an unusual feeling of wealth among us. We raised our glasses in my honour repeatedly, and wound up as inebriated as we could get while maintaining any dignity. The venue was as much of a nightclub as a restaurant, and we all made our way to the dance floor, some more willingly than others. By the end of the night, the combination of alcohol and dancing had inspired multiple make-out sessions between Trish and Anne and, when the night came to a close, they left together, bound for Trish's trendy Chinatown apartment.

The soul of chivalry, Ian escorted me back home, and I invited him in for one last glass of wine. As he lounged on my couch, I poured us each a glass of Shiraz, and he smiled in thanks as I handed one over.

'So it's another lonely night for both of us,' I said as I settled myself on the couch next to him. He nodded and I took the opportunity to broach a topic I'd avoided for some time. 'Are you really OK with Anne seeing people outside your relationship?'

He laughed a little, though it sounded forced. 'Only women,' he answered defensively.

'I know it's only women. Still, she's been spending a lot of time with Trish, and you're left alone so often. You really don't mind?'

Sighing, he looked me straight in the eyes. 'OK, it's starting to get on my nerves. We used to have the most amazing sex after a night out, but ever since I gave her these freedoms, I lose her on nights like this. I'm horny as hell and she's gone. It's not right.'

For a few awkward moments, we sat in silence.

'I guess it's good that we have each other!' I commented playfully, placing my legs in his lap. It was meant as a harmless gesture, but he smiled thoughtfully and began to trace patterns on my bare skin, sending shivers up my spine.

'I guess it is,' he answered, his fingers travelling further and further up my thighs until they were outlining the edges of my lacy new thong. I gasped and he leaned forwards, muffling my surprise with a deep kiss. I ran my fingers through his strawberry-blond hair as he settled himself atop me, manoeuvring his hips between my legs. In one smooth motion, he swept my dress past my head and onto the floor, leaving me in the sweet little pink lace lingerie set I'd purchased after work. Pulling my breasts out, he wrapped his lips around each nipple in turn and a mixture of pleasure and guilt rippled through my body. His lips landed in hot kisses along my torso and I pulled down my panties eagerly as he progressed between my thighs. The feeling of his tongue on my clit sent me reeling and I bucked against his face in excitement. It had been so long since I'd been with anyone.

It didn't take long for him to drive me over the edge, and my body was still rocking with orgasm when he entered me, not even bothering to undress. His stiff cock filled me and pounded away my many nights of solitude as we cursed and moaned. My finger on my clit brought me to another hard climax before I felt him spill himself inside me with a desperate cry that sounded as though he hadn't come in months.

We were both shaking when he pulled away to fix his pants, and I grabbed my dress to cover myself in a sudden fit of modesty.

He didn't look back at me as he gathered his things and left the apartment, and I shared his shame. From across the room, my golden retriever, Dobby, regarded me with a reproachful expression.

'Oh, shut up,' I said, throwing my dress in his direction. 'You have five girlfriends.'

The next day, I managed to rouse myself early enough to walk Dobby and prepare for my first meeting with Amanda, despite a righteous headache and plummeting self-respect. I chose a pair of designer faded jeans and a burgundy velvet jacket to convey both casual coolness and a sense of occasion and pulled back my shoulder-length blonde hair, leaving a few tendrils to frame my face. Satisfied with the effect, I gathered my samples and portfolio, and made my way to the Victorian mansion on Jackson Street.

The door to the imposing home was answered by Ella, a neatly dressed, gorgeous Latina with skin the colour of cappuccino. She spoke with an air of authority and announced herself to be Amanda's personal assistant. I spent the day in her presence, along with a twin pair of China dolls from Pacifica Design. True to form, their every idea hinged on transforming the authentically Victorian home into a trashy homage to contemporary design. How long did they believe Lucite chairs would stay in style? Apparently, for ever.

They hovered nearby and snorted unprofessionally as I made my suggestions. Instead of ignoring the home's existing charms, I offered to complement them by updating the colour schemes and replacing most of the furniture with current incarnations of classic forms. A few period pieces could remain, and would stand out in their modern surroundings. Ella's mouth approached a smile as I spoke, though I never received so much as an unambiguous sign of approval. As we passed through the salon, I was struck by the sight of an ugly, rough-hewn wooden chair that was already bizarre in its refined surroundings. I pointed out that I would be sure to remove it during renovations, and Ella's look of displeasure made me wonder if I'd lost the account in one fell swoop.

It was mid-afternoon before we were finished, and Ella ushered us to the front door with disconcerting speed. She assured us that our firms would be contacted shortly with Amanda's decision. The door closed abruptly, and I paused on the porch feeling utterly deflated by Ella's attitude, and by not having met Amanda herself. The pair from Pacifica Design was clearly disappointed as well, but after throwing me a look of disdain, they hurried away, teetering dangerously on hot pink platform heels.

I followed at a leisurely pace, contemplating the estate and, as I did, a black limo pulled up to the kerb. Shock and delight riveted me to the spot as I realised the person exiting the limo was Amanda, clad in a stunning body-hugging red dress, which made her look like sex incarnate. Glossy deep-brown hair rippled down her back, and her skin was a flawless bronze tan. Her eyes were masked by oversized black sunglasses, and she wore red ballroom gloves, which very few women could have pulled off. The chauffeur draped a black trench coat over her shoulders and she proceeded through the gate. I thought she would ignore me completely, but as she approached, she slowed to a stop and removed her sunglasses. Even narrowed against the bright sunlight, her hazel eyes shone like polished gold.

'Hi,' I said dumbly, breathing in her exotic perfume and struggling to come up with something – anything – to say that might inspire her to invite me back inside. Her presence was overwhelming and intoxicating.

'Hello,' she answered, her full lips curving into an amused smile. Without another word, she continued up to the house, and I remained where I was, feeling like an idiot.

I stood there only long enough to watch her pass through the front door, then departed, walking quickly to my car as though I could outrun my embarrassment. Vaguely, I registered a voice calling my name, and I turned round to see Ella following me, hurried and breathless.

Catching her breath, she shot me a dagger-sharp glare and smoothed her skirt primly. 'Amanda would like to see you again tomorrow,' she announced darkly. 'Be here at 7 p.m. sharp. You've got the job.'

* * *

Randall was thrilled and I threw myself headlong into preparations. I stayed at the office late, assembling fabric swatches and paint chips into design schemes, and visualising the house interior in different shades and designs. I grabbed our very best manufacturer catalogues and sample books, wanting more desperately than anything for Amanda to be glad she chose me. In my mind I replayed our meeting over and over again, analysing each minute detail of her expression and body language to glean some knowledge of who she really was. Her beauty was undeniable, but it was her presence that had surprised me. Her every move seemed purposeful and perfect and, when I was with her, my mind seemed to melt away into oblivion. For one exquisite moment, I'd forgotten about my indiscretion with Ian, and my anxiety over winning the contract. No person had ever filled my mind so completely, and I longed to feel that again.

I returned the next day exhausted from a night of fantasy and obsessive planning, but the very thought of being in Amanda's presence again had my adrenaline pumping so hard that I was completely alert. Ella answered the door dressed in a creamy white pantsuit, and led me through the corridors to the rear dining room.

Amanda was waiting, and when she turned and laid her eyes on me, my breath caught in my throat. Again, she was stunning: a strapless gown of black embroidered silk encased her lithe, bronzed body as though it had been sewn on. Boning neatly corseted her tiny waist and, though the dress was as short as decency would allow in the front, a train fishtailed from its corseted middle to sweep grandly to the floor.

'Thank you for coming, Jenna,' she said in her rich, melodious voice, and the fact that she knew my name filled me with embarrassing joy.

'Thank you for having me,' I answered, surprised I was still in possession of my faculties. I entered the dining room with my books and spread them out on the table, keenly aware of her proximity. The exotic smell of her perfume surrounded me once more, but this time I was close enough that it mixed with the faint smell of shampoo from her wavy chestnut locks. It was all I could do to resist the compulsion to bury my face in their glossy depths as we discussed my ideas.

It didn't take long for me to lose track of why I was there. Colour schemes and textiles lost their importance: instead my eyes swept the curves of her shapely body. I knew I wasn't getting away with anything. Her presence was all-encompassing, as though even as she considered the swatches and palettes, she was aware of all things around her, and controlled them in equal measure. Perhaps she even controlled me.

'I like the red suede and cool neutrals in this palette,' she said, straightening her back and watching me with golden eyes that seemed to know exactly what I'd been thinking.

I cleared my throat nervously. 'I'm so glad,' I answered, grabbing a sample book and clutching it in front of me like a shield. Under her stare I was torn between the impulse to run and to bow at her feet.

'Are you quite all right, Jenna?' she asked, and again I thrilled at the intimacy of her address.

'I'm just fine,' I lied, nonchalantly setting the book back on the dining table. I had barely a moment to feign composure before it crashed noisily to the floor. Cursing, I bent to pick it up, placing myself level with the soft black miniskirt that covered only a few inches of her shapely thighs. From my new vantage point, I could see the hint of bare skin exposed by the tops of her sheer black stay-up stockings. Is she wearing anything underneath? I wondered.

'Are you certain you're all right, child?' she asked, placing a gentle palm on my head as she spoke. Child, I thought. She could barely be a handful of years older than me. Clutching the book again, I dared to meet her gaze. Staring into pools of liquid gold, I wished so powerfully for her lips to meet mine that the desire left me breathless. Succumbing to lust, I tossed my book aside and buried my face in her thighs, clutching them to me as though they were my salvation. I was shocked to feel tears rolling down my cheeks as I kissed her thighs over and over, inching upward until

I was pushing black silk aside to reveal her beautiful naked cunt.

Gasping in anticipation, she braced herself on the table and parted her legs, revealing the slippery, pink flesh that I longed for. I continued delivering my kisses to the bare skin of her thighs, and didn't hesitate a moment before pressing my face between her legs, landing my tongue in her sweet wetness. I swirled my tongue across her tiny, pearl-like clitoris and she moaned, clutching my head close. I could feel the moisture building between my own legs, and I longed to touch myself, but my focus on Amanda was so complete that I couldn't possibly bring myself off. Instead, her moans of pleasure seemed like fingers, nudging my clit repeatedly. When she finally came, drenching so much wetness on my face that I feared I would drown, I almost felt as though I'd reached orgasm as well. As she regained composure, she looked down at me with such love that I radiated with pride.

'What do you want from me, child?' she asked, continuing to address me as though we were separated by decades rather than years.

'Everything,' I whimpered, her juices still covering my face. I inhaled to elaborate, to tell her how perfect and beautiful she was, but my words were cut off by a voice from the kitchen.

'Mistress?' the voice said, and I turned my head to see a nearly nude man emerging from the darkness, his defined, muscular body covered only by a small black loincloth. A leather collar encircled his neck, and the silver ring at its front sparkled in the firelight. Shock registered on his face as he realised what he was seeing.

'Derek, what are you doing here?' Amanda demanded, and his face fell, lips quivering slightly as he realised the gravity of his error. 'You know you're forbidden to address me in this manner when we have company.' Amanda's low voice took on an aggressive edge that made even me feel penitent. As she continued to scold him, the fog of desire lifted from my mind and I began to process the situation. *Mistress ... Mistress!* It explained so much: Amanda's dramatic wardrobe, her overwhelming presence, her unquestionably dominant personality. Was she little more than a sadistic prostitute, financing her lavish lifestyle with money from people who would give anything to be denigrated and used? The idea was so vulgar it made me feel ill. Forcing emotional distance from the deep connection I thought I'd just felt, I returned to my feet and weighed my options. Amanda was busy with this man: it might be my only chance to escape unnoticed.

Slowly, I edged my way towards the kitchen, but they both turned to me and, panic-stricken, I fled. My heels clicked a rapid staccato against the tiled floor as I ran and slammed the door behind me. Voices distantly called my name as I circled the yard and exited through the front gate. I could still taste Amanda on my lips, but as I ran to my car, I swore I would never return to that place. Not ever.

For a few days, I managed to stay away, but instead, Amanda visited my dreams. Every night it was the same: I prostrated myself before her, landing worshipful kisses on her feet before gazing up at her face, impossibly high above me. My naked skin tingled as it grazed the silky flesh of her legs. I pressed my face into her hot, moist depths, behaving like a woman possessed. I lapped up her wetness eagerly, filled with desperate longing for a word of praise, or to feel her fingers run through my hair appreciatively. I was hers – body, mind and soul – and her approval made me feel loved in a way that was more primal than anything I'd ever experienced. I awoke each night in a sweat, my body screaming with lust, but no matter how many times I pleasured myself, I was left wanting. Some part of me needed Amanda, and I hated her for it.

When I walked Dobby, we would inevitably end up passing Amanda's house. Occasionally the front door would open and I'd dash behind a bush, my presence made obvious by the red leash and golden retriever who stubbornly refused to hide beside me. If it was anyone else, I would continue on my walk, but if it was Amanda, I would wait and watch, taking in the sight of her as shamelessly as a stalker. After she departed I would berate myself for exalting in her presence. Yet no matter how much I reprimanded myself, my feelings remained.

After a week of sleepless nights and unfulfilled desire, I could take no more. Losing Amanda's account had infuriated Randall, and I became increasingly useless in my contributions to other projects. None of my friends were speaking to me, not even Trish, and I didn't have the energy or presence of mind to figure out how to repair my the situation. I was an emotional wreck, and at serious risk of being fired.

Leaving work on Monday, I ended up wandering the streets rather than heading home. My world was falling apart piece by piece, and at the epicentre of my suffering was a woman whom I couldn't seem to escape. It was no surprise when I ended up in front of her house again.

A misty rain had drenched the city all day, and by the time I reached the front gate, my clothes were soaked and clammy, and my hair was plastered to my face. Without concern for my appearance, I pressed on, and stood shivering on the front porch, waiting for a response to my earnest knocks. They'd been so quiet, I wondered if anyone had heard me.

A whisper of footsteps and a rustle of curtains at the window preceded the door's opening. As usual, it was Ella, dressed impeccably in a black pinstriped dress suit. Her expression was mixed as she looked me up and down, a combination of distaste and self-satisfaction, as though she'd known I would return.

'Wait here,' she said curtly, allowing me into the foyer, but no further. I stood shivering by the door as she ascended the curved staircase, glancing back to make sure I obeyed. From the foyer, their discussion was unintelligible, but I could hear Ella's anger juxtaposed with the eternal calm of Amanda's rich, melodious voice. Just hearing her speak made my heart beat faster, and I dropped my face into my hands. How could I be so pathetic?

'Do you regret your choice to return?' her voice asked, shockingly close.

I looked up and there she was. Her attire wasn't nearly as grand as the last time we'd met: instead she wore well-tailored black trousers, elegant crocodile leather pumps, and a soft white cashmere sweater that wrapped neatly around her tiny waist. Even in this more casual dress she was spectacular. I'd seen her look mysterious in black, and glamorous in red, but in white, she was radiant. I wanted to reach out to her as she approached, but I stood still, shivering again, this time not just from the cold. Ella returned, standing behind Amanda with two folded fluffy towels.

'Thank you, Ella,' Amanda said, taking up a towel and wrapping it around me lovingly.

Bereft of speech I stared into her eyes as she rubbed my arms briskly, and I held the towel around me as she reached for the other, and draped it over my head. She dried my hair gently and rubbed the thick squishy towel against my cheeks as she finished. I breathed in the smell of her perfume and almost melted on the spot.

'You still haven't answered my question, child,' she said, and it took me a moment to remember what she'd asked.

'No, I don't regret it,' I said, drawing the words out of the last coherent fragment of my mind.

'I'm very glad.' Amanda smiled, and I mirrored her, suddenly feeling warm despite my clammy clothes. She walked away and I followed her quietly into the salon, where a fire burned brightly. She pulled up the strange chair that I so hated and motioned for me to sit. I lifted myself into the unusually high seat and she smiled at me again and I beamed up at her. 'Let me get you some hot cocoa,' she said, and disappeared from the room.

Ella sat to the side, watching me as I dried my legs with the fluffy towels and settled myself into the chair as best as I could. The awful thing was as uncomfortable as it was ugly. Unlike before, her expression was unreadable, but I doubted her attitude had changed. Amanda returned to the room briefly to hand me a large steaming cup. I took it and sipped gingerly before discovering the sweet chocolate was exactly drinking temperature. Of course it's perfect, I thought as I began to drink greedily, she's perfect.

I finished off the cup and Ella collected it wordlessly. Turning away, I looked towards the couch and was startled to see a man sitting there, watching me.

'How long have you been there?' I asked angrily.

'Only a moment,' he answered placidly, lifting himself from the couch with athletic grace. 'I'm Derek. I'm very pleased to properly make your acquaintance, Jenna.'

I shook his hand and watched him as he returned to the couch. His curly black hair and forest-green eyes seemed familiar, and I soon realised that he was the naked man whose appearance had shocked me into fleeing. In his navy-blue Dockers and pencil-striped shirt, he looked like he'd just arrived from work.

Movement in my periphery caught my attention and I turned to see another man enter the room, this one tall, black and broad-shouldered. He wore expensive trousers and a crisp white shirt, as though he'd just walked in from a board meeting. Nodding curtly, he perched himself on the arm of the couch, waiting patiently, and not entirely acknowledging my presence.

Ella re-entered the room and took her seat, watching the doorway expectantly. It wasn't hard to guess what they were waiting for, and I couldn't help but get caught up in their anticipation.

I gasped a little as Amanda entered, and the others gulped audibly. Her nearly nude body was wrapped in a gorgeous black and white French teddy with intricate lace work that criss-crossed her trim torso and ended in an impossibly small thong. Delicate black stilettos accentuated her shapely legs, and a black silk robe hung from her shoulders. Every exposed inch of her satiny bronze skin stood out in contrast to the black silk behind it, and we all longed to touch it. She was a queen, our queen, and we watched her with reverence as she crossed the room to sit in an oversized chair that suddenly seemed more like a throne. I turned my own ugly chair to face her, and the man who had ignored me settled himself at her feet with a barely audible sigh of pleasure. He placed his head in her lap and she stroked the back of his head and addressed him as her 'dear William'. I couldn't help but envy his position.

'Do they pay to be here?' I asked, my concerns bubbling to the surface. Three faces turned to me in anger, but Amanda remained unfazed.

'I understand why you would think that, Jenna,' she said,

nodding slightly. 'There are places in the world where that happens. This is not one of them. I have more than enough money of my own. Everyone here is a kindred spirit, and I invite them to join me because they have a need I fulfil. It's a need that's been in the background of your whole life, Jenna, I can tell. A need to give in to someone who will love you unconditionally, and will watch over you, taking away all need for you to think, or worry about the problems in your life. I can be that person for you, if you wish.

'Is that what you'd like?' she asked, and I had to hold myself back from pathetically whining, 'Please, yes.'

'Yes, I'd like that,' I answered, as soon as I could reply with some modicum of dignity.

Amanda smiled and rose. 'Very good,' she said, and nodded to the group before leaving the room. Ella exited the room behind her, and the men began to strip, folding their clothes as they went and placing them in neat piles in the corner of the room. They were both muscularly built, though Derek was more lithe, and William more bulky and several inches taller. Both were also well endowed, and a warm blush rose to my cheeks as I watched.

Ella reappeared in a tiny black thong and, in her hands, she carried two familiar black loincloths. My pulse raced with trepidation as they all turned to me, and Ella motioned for me to rise. Taking orders from Ella left a bad taste in my mouth, but I obeyed. William took my towels and folded them neatly as Ella and Derek proceeded to remove my dry, wrinkled clothes. The fleeting touches of their fingers on my skin sent ticklish little shivers of pleasure through my body. Against my will, my nipples stood erect and excited and, as Ella removed my bra, Derek fondled them gently. When they finished, they set my clothes aside with the others and sat on their knees, facing Amanda's chair. I promptly followed suit.

Amanda returned soon, carrying an elaborately carved, red-lacquered box. She set it on the table next to her chair and pulled out several collars, then fastened one around each of our necks in turn, followed by a long, deep kiss. Both the men developed impressive hard-ons, which could not be hidden by their loincloths, as she progressed through the ceremony. Finally, it was my turn, and after she fastened the leather around my neck, she lifted my chin to press her soft warm lips to mine. They were pillowy and sweet, and I held on to that kiss like a dying woman gasping for air. Every inch of my body longed for her touch, but she kept her distance, and returned to her seat too soon.

'Welcome, my darlings,' she intoned, sending frissons of excitement through the group.

'Good evening, Mistress,' they replied in unison, and I felt stupid for not knowing instinctively what to say.

'My dear Jenna,' she said, and I was overjoyed to have her attention focused on me alone. 'You are new to the fold and ripe with promise, but are you really ready?'

'Yes, Mistress,' I answered immediately.

'Well, you believe you are, anyway.' She laughed dangerously, gazing thoughtfully at the ugly chair behind me. 'You ran from me once, and that betrays a wilfulness that I will not abide. Have a seat, my pet, and we'll see how ready you are.'

Empty-headed and eager to prove my subservience, I returned to the chair, its rough surface especially unpleasant against my naked skin. Mistress whispered in each of the men's ears and they searched the box, retrieving something I couldn't keep track of as she walked towards me, filling my world with the sights and scents of her body. She held my wrists to the arms of the chair as she leaned forwards, then rained kisses on my grateful lips. Suddenly, her palms were joined by the cold, firm sensation of tightening leather, and I became aware that my wrists were being bound to the chair. A note of concern rang in my head, but I stifled it, focusing instead on the lace-clad goddess who pushed herself between my legs, and began to fondle my breasts.

The sensation of tightening leather gripped my ankles as well, and I realised I was being firmly restrained to the chair. Seeking reassurance, I gazed up into Mistress's golden eyes, but she stepped away, holding my thighs wide as Ella grabbed a notch that I hadn't noticed before, and pulled the seat out from under me. I sank into the empty space it left, before righting myself awkwardly, pulling up with my legs and resting the weight of my body on my thighs and forearms.

'What is this?' I exclaimed, my face contorted in confusion. 'Mistress, what are you doing to me?'

'Anything I wish, my darling Jenna,' she answered mysteriously.

William appeared with a large flowered bowl, which he placed under the chair ominously. I stared down at the white porcelain, and looked to Mistress again. A host of possibilities, from the strange to the horrific ran through my mind. Mistress approached me once more, but I took no comfort in her kisses.

'How quickly you distrust, my sweet Jenna. Remember, I opened myself up to you, and you threw that gift in my face. Now I need to know how much control you're willing to lose; how completely you'll give yourself to me.'

She leaned in to whisper in my ear, and her smell was still intoxicating. 'It's just a little release, my darling: a harmless bit of little more than water. But how early we are taught to hide it, to control it tightly. The conditioning runs so deep that we never give it a second thought. Tonight, my sweet, you will give that power to me. You will relinquish that control when I tell you, the moment I tell you, or you will leave, and will never again have the chance to earn a place in my heart.' The finality in her voice filled me with despair.

I barely held back the tears as they watched me, waiting silently. I knew I had a choice: I could tell her 'no' right now and be set free, but never again would I have the chance to call Amanda my mistress. Having experienced the bliss of her love, the pain of that fate was unbearable. *Yes, Mistress*, I conceded, *whatever you want, I'll give*.

'Begin, my pet,' she ordered, as though she could hear my silent surrender.

Tensing my body and fighting against powerful unconscious barriers, I forced myself to release, and a tiny trickle dropped into the bowl beneath me. Mistress laughed quietly and congratulated me, and a hot flush of embarrassment rose to my cheeks. My mind was filled with a riot of discordant emotions, from happiness to shame and self-loathing.

'Again,' she ordered, and it flowed more easily this time. Mistress smiled and instructed Derek to reward me. He stepped forwards, rested a hand between my parted legs and pressed gently on my clit, sending incomprehensibly powerful shocks of pleasure through my body. As his fingers slipped across my pussy, I realised it wasn't just my release that had made me wet. I was dripping with desire, and acknowledging my excitement sent waves of shame rippling across my skin, magnifying my pleasure tenfold

'Again,' Amanda ordered, even as Derek was touching me and I obeyed, the paired sensations making me feel dirty and turned on at the same time. I watched Mistress as William took his place at her feet. She opened her legs and he pushed the bottom of her teddy aside, slipping his tongue along the sweet wet flesh that I knew lay there. Her exquisite body twitched with pleasure as he licked, but her eyes never left me, and, as always, her attention filled me with joy.

Ella pulled out one of the chair's spindles and Derek made his way beneath me. I struggled in one final effort for decency to pull my hips out of reach, but I was firmly restrained, and despite my best efforts he began to lick and suck me. The wrongness of it so dizzied my brain with frustration and ecstasy that when she ordered, 'Again,' once more all I could do was whimper in protest.

I kept my eyes on Mistress, praying that she acknowledged the depth of my submission. Derek's tongue didn't leave me as I released, and I couldn't help but imagine my fluid streaming down his body to the floor. Yet his eagerness never seemed to wane, and when I finished and finally deigned to look down I saw his hard cock pointing up at me, his hand working it furiously. Pre-come dripped out of him and, despite myself, his excitement fired my own. His tongue rubbed rhythmically across my clit, and I pressed my hips into his face as he licked, turning my eyes up to watch my mistress again. William sat in the chair and she faced me as she bounced on his thick dark shaft, pausing occasionally to allow Ella to eagerly lick her. The firelight danced on her bronze skin and she ran her fingers through Ella's hair as she gave in to a massive orgasm that shook every muscle of her body.

I continued to press against Derek's face, and soon he was moaning beneath me. I looked down to see rivulets of come pouring from his rigid cock, and in that moment I came too, wishing my hands and legs weren't bound so I could pull him close and come hard on his face. When the tension of climax subsided, I was utterly spent, and I sagged into the gaping chair barely capable of maintaining consciousness. Ella and William held me up as Mistress unfastened my restraints, a towel was wrapped around me once again and then William lifted me easily into his arms and carried me upstairs.

I passed out somewhere along the way, and when I awoke bright sunlight was streaming through the lacy curtains of a cosy guest bedroom I remembered seeing on my first walk through the house. I felt clean and warm and comfortable, and when I cast my gaze across the room I saw Amanda in a soft flannel robe, reading a book in the corner.

'Good afternoon,' she said, closing her book. I sighed as she walked over to the bed and sat down beside me.

'Hello, Mistress.' I beamed, nuzzling into her thigh. I could not remember having felt so rested and content in years, and yet something bothered me, a nagging memory that grasped at my consciousness. Ian, Anne, Trish – they all still hated me, and my head was still on the chopping block at work, though those facts seemed to carry little weight inside these walls.

'What's wrong, my sweet?' she asked, and I poured my heart out to her, wishing she could fix it all with the sweep of one graceful hand. When I was finished, she bent over and kissed my forehead, then my lips, and stared into my eyes. 'All will be well, my darling. Your friends will forgive you: they're each as responsible as you for what happened. Your job is safe, Ella saw to that this morning. You should have no more worries in life than the silly beast sleeping in the corner,' she said, and for the first time I noticed Dobby on his back nearby, paws twitching in canine reverie. Surprised, but realising that nothing about my mistress should ever surprise me again,

I settled back in bed and smiled. Everything was perfect, and it always would be, so long as I served my mistress: and I never planned to stop.

Sexy Little Numbers features the first appearance of Dianne Dawson's short fiction in Black Lace.

Daisy's Diary
Sadie Wolf

1 January
New Year's Day

I intend to spend this year having as much sex as possible. From this day forth I am to make myself available to all. An unusual New Year's resolution, I admit. It's also a simple idea that requires a high level of commitment on my part. I must, for example:

* Shave my legs every day
* Always wear matching underwear
* Always wear a smile
* And always be available for sex

26 January
New Moon

I've always had a thing about construction workers. I like the dirt, the hard work, the blatant disregard for health and safety and above all the sheer unadulterated manliness of it all. I only have to see those yellow reflective jackets in the distance and my heart skips a beat. Between my house and work a new roundabout is being built, causing twenty-six weeks of delays; twenty-six weeks of sitting in grindingly slow-moving traffic and watching the men at my leisure.

My favourite man is usually working on the left-hand side as I go into work, so I get a really good look at him. We've even made eye contact once or twice, which I know is blatantly slapperlike of me.

All this started before New Year but even after I made my resolution, I couldn't imagine how anything could happen with him. And then this morning, I met him in Sainsbury's.

He and another guy were obviously on the lunch run, armed with tabloid papers and sandwiches. He recognised me instantly and his face broke into a smile. He looked right at me with steely blue eyes and I felt myself blushing. His friend said something under his breath, took the sandwiches and the newspapers and disappeared. I couldn't move, my knees were trembling too much.

Up so close I could see every grain of dust on his hands, every smear of mud on his jacket, the stubble on his face and every strand of his dark scruffy hair.

'On your coffee break?' His voice was deep and calm, with the faintest edge of a local accent. 'When do you have to be back?'

'I've got a day off.'

'Do you want to go for a drive?' he asked.

I looked at him, felt the strength of him, the confidence rolling off him. 'OK,' I squeaked.

Meekly, I followed him to the van. I've always liked travelling in works vans. I like the smell, the equipment, the roughness of it.

'You look very pretty today.' He glanced across at me. 'It's good to be able to see you properly. You've got a fantastic pair of legs. So . . . I know a place we can park up . . . If that's OK with you?'

'Yes, that's fine,' I said lightly, as if I were agreeing to a cup of coffee.

The back of the van was a mess and he cleared a space and laid his yellow jacket down on the floor for me to lie on. I was wearing a clingy grey woollen jumper dress, boots and sheer tights, not the easiest things to take off, so I helped him out by unzipping my boots, rolling my sheer tights down and pulling my dress off before lying on his jacket. I had kept to my rule about underwear and had on a pretty pink lacy bra with matching pink knickers.

Kissing him was such a joy after fantasising about it for so long. It was wonderful to actually be almost naked in his arms, feeling the roughness of his shirt and jeans against my bare skin. I was overwhelmed by the feel of him, the smell of him, and the longing that only got worse and worse the more he kissed me.

He pinched my nipples and stroked between my legs while I buried my head in his chest and tried to stay quiet. Then his fingers pushed inside me and I felt how wet I was. He drew his fingers in and out of me gently, caressing me with wetness.

I felt him taking me towards orgasm and I wanted him inside me. I felt down and rubbed his erection through his jeans. He sat up and rolled me over onto my front and I heard him getting undressed.

He pulled my knickers down and drew me back onto all fours. I could feel his cock against my thighs. First, he pushed his fingers inside me as if to broaden me for his cock, which followed and was pressed deep.

My eyes fixed on a toolbox on the shelf above me as he pumped deeper and deeper inside me with every thrust. He pushed me down onto my front so that my belly lay against the cool of his jacket and my thighs against the rough carpet of the floor.

One of his hands leaned on my shoulder, the other on my hip. I could feel the heat and sweat of him against my back. My breasts were pressed hard against my forearms, my face a few centimetres from the dusty carpet of the van.

He entered me at an angle, pushing inside me so that wave after wave of pleasure rolled across the inside surfaces of my body. I followed the path of pleasure in my mind, riding it. At last I closed my eyes and concentrated on the heat that was building inside me until finally I let myself fall, resting my face on the dirty floor.

7 February
Full Moon

On Saturday morning I was lying in bed reading a novel, wearing a new beautiful white silk negligee and matching wrap: attire that made me feel glamorous and sexy in keeping with my New Year's resolution. The novel I was reading was erotic and as a result my nipples had become hard. I was just about to indulge in a spell of self-love when the doorbell rang. It was my neighbour, looking rather flustered, cold and damp in an orange anorak.

'I'm really sorry, I've done a stupid thing –'

'Come in, have you locked yourself out?'

'I can't believe it, Jane's going to kill me. I just popped to the post office to collect a parcel and I left my keys on the side –'

'Don't worry, come in and get warm.'

He stepped inside, almost tripping over some shoes in the porch and filling the doorway into the sitting room, an awkward, bumbling figure.

'It's the second time I've done this, she's going to have to come all the way back from the city, she's gone shopping with her friend ... I'm going to be in the doghouse.'

'Don't worry. Listen, why don't you let me make you a coffee and you can wait here until she comes back? I don't mind a bit. I mean, I wasn't doing anything ...'

'But I'll be in your way. And I got you out of bed. I'm so sorry, what a nuisance I am.'

'Now stop it, you aren't a nuisance at all. And if Jane's busy shopping, let's not disturb her.'

He hovered awkwardly in front of the sofa, as if unsure whether or not to sit down.

'Let me take your coat, it's soaked through. I'll hang it up in front of the radiator.'

'Are you sure you don't mind?'

'Positive. Now not another word. You're to make yourself at home, do you hear me?'

He sat down meekly, as if all the fight had gone out of him.

I was quite shocked by how terrified he seemed of his wife: the poor man was practically quaking in his boots. Seeing him like that brought out my maternal instincts. It also made me think that if his wife didn't appreciate what a nice husband she had, then maybe she didn't deserve to keep him all to herself.

I made coffee, with a large slug of brandy in it. Then I sat down next to him on the sofa, letting my robe fall open enough to reveal the lacy bodice of my negligee. His eyes clocked it, only for a split second, but he definitely looked.

He kept looking nervously at his watch and out of the window, seeming for all the world like a man on the run.

But after the second coffee-with-lots-of-brandy he began to relax.

'So, is your wife a bit strict with you then?' I said lightly.

'Well, I try to avoid crossing her, that's for sure. The last time I had to spend the week in the spare room.' He smiled ruefully, but his shoulders were straighter and his face had lost its look of abject terror.

'No!' I was appalled.

'Well, about four days. She's got a bit of a temper on her.' He smiled at me, appreciating the sympathy.

'I'm afraid I'm rather old-fashioned. I believe the man should be the boss,' I said innocently.

He laughed. 'Well, I don't suppose there's many women like you left any more.'

'Perhaps there's more than you think. For me personally, I just find it so *relaxing* to let the man take charge. It makes me feel so much more *feminine*. Does that sound silly?'

'No, no, not at all. I've often thought that maybe the old ways are the best. Less cause for arguments perhaps?'

'To love, honour and obey,' I said, taking hold of his left hand and looking at his wedding ring.

'If only,' he said, and laughed, but he let his hand remain in mine.

I picked up his hand and put it on my breast. He pulled it away as if he had been burned. I pushed the wrap off my shoulders and slipped the straps of my negligee down to my waist. I picked up his hand again and put it on my bare breast. My nipple hardened against his hand.

I looked up at him and saw the struggle in his eyes. It didn't last long. Most men, when offered sex on a plate, will find it impossible to resist, and my neighbour was no different.

He jumped on me clumsily, inexpertly, as if he couldn't wait to get me undressed and have a look at me. He pulled the wrap and the negligee off so that I was completely naked. He buried his face in my breasts, pressing against them, sucking, nibbling and chewing on my nipples. His hands grabbed hold of my bum, stroking and squeezing and digging his fingers into my thighs.

He shoved his hand eagerly between my legs. He grunted, breathing hard as he found my pussy. In spite of, or perhaps because of, the rough inexpertness of his attentions, I had become very wet. He seemed overcome and pushed my legs wide apart with both hands so that the inner muscles of my thighs stretched painfully. He buried his face between my legs with an enthusiasm I have rarely encountered: licking, kissing and sucking until I was almost at the point of coming. Then he jumped up, tore off his clothes like a kid and got on top of me.

He pushed his cock into me, pressing against all the right places more by luck than judgement. I thought about the parcel he had gone to pick up, the doorbell ringing, his fear of his wife. I felt like a slut then, because a woman who fucks her married neighbour with no encouragement is surely a slut, and I embraced this feeling, this thought, and it made me come.

27 March
British Summer Time Begins

It was five-thirty on Friday night and I had that euphoric feeling that comes with the end of the working week. I walked home along the new riverside. The lights of the bars and restaurants twinkled invitingly. Small groups of smokers stood outside. I caught the eye of a good-looking dark-haired man in a suit.

'Hey, sexy, come and have a drink with us!' he called out.

I froze for a moment, doing battle with my old self – who would have ignored him and walked off huffily – and the post-new year Daisy. The new Daisy won and I smiled and walked over to him. He put out his hand.

'I'm Carl, and this is my mate Gaz.' He was wearing a nice suit and a tie, and he smelled of aftershave. He was maybe thirty years old, with sexy brown eyes and nice white teeth.

'I'm Daisy.'

'Nice name. What would you like to drink?'

We went inside and I was left with Gaz, who looked friendly enough but seemed very shy. Unfortunately for him he looked rather like Shrek, not in the least attractive.

I excused myself and went to the Ladies'. I put some lipstick on and brushed my hair. I had on a black pencil skirt, a cream camisole top, a cream fitted cashmere cardigan, sheer black stockings and kitten heels. My outfit emphasised my boobs and bum and the shapely curve of my hips and I felt pretty confident that I looked good.

'Here's to the weekend!' The three of us clinked glasses and I felt Carl's eyes resting on my face.

The bar was full of people like us: nine-to-fivers celebrating the end of the working week by getting tipsy.

'Do you smoke?' Carl asked.

'Sometimes . . .' I hadn't got any but I wanted one.

'Come on then.'

We went outside and Carl gave me a cigarette and lit it for me.

'So what do you two do?' I asked.

'Sales. Pays well when you're a charmer like me. Gaz here does the technical stuff, he's an IT geek. What about you?'

'I'm a trainee solicitor.'

'So, brainy as well as beautiful.'

I blushed and he noticed, which only made me blush all the more. I laughed. 'Is that a sales technique?'

'No, I'm strictly off duty. All compliments after five o'clock are genuinely heartfelt. Same again?' He looked at my empty wine glass.

'Oh, let me –'

'No, I won't hear of it. I asked you, remember.'

By the time we left the bar I was properly drunk. I found myself walking arm in arm with Carl, with poor Shrek following behind. Carl's flat was a typical bachelor pad, with a massive TV, storage towers of CDs and DVDs and a big glass coffee table with piles of magazines on it. Gaz and I sat down on an enormous brown leather sofa and Carl opened a bottle of wine, poured it into three big glasses and sat down next to me.

Carl put his arm around me. The room spun slightly. He stroked my leg. He took the wine glass from my hand and set it down on the glass table, then leaned in and kissed me. His mouth tasted of white wine. His hands found the buttons of my cardigan and took it off. He ran his hands over my camisole top, feeling my breasts through the thin fabric. I was dimly aware of the fact that Gaz was sitting on the sofa behind Carl but I just thought, It's Carl's flat, he can go if he wants to. And Carl's hands playing with my tits and Carl's tongue in my mouth made me feel hot, made my nipples tense and my knickers damp and I was way beyond stopping him.

Carl took my hand and put it on his cock, and I played with him through his trousers, until he stopped me, undid his trousers and sat back comfortably.

'Suck my cock, Daisy, why don't you?'

I got off the sofa and knelt down on the floor.

'Take your top off.'

I did as I was told. I was wearing a brand-new white lace push-up bra. Carl wolf-whistled softly. Poor Gaz was sitting up the other end of the sofa with a dim, faraway expression on his face. I felt sorry for him then, but not sorry enough to stop. I took Carl's cock in my mouth and sucked him and doing this made me hotter and wetter than ever.

'Daisy, come up here a minute.' He tugged at my bra strap to get my attention.

I stopped and looked up. Gaz had changed position on the sofa and was now looking straight at me with an unashamed leer.

'Daisy, we're all friends here, aren't we?' Carl seemed quite relaxed about sitting there with his cock sticking out of his trousers. 'Poor Gaz, I think he's feeling a bit left out. You don't mind if we let him join in the fun do you?'

'Do you mean you want me to –'

'No, babe, not that. I want to be the one who comes in your mouth. I want you to take off your skirt and panties and let Gaz take you from behind while you get back to sucking my cock.'

I stood up and undressed, as if in a dream. I felt faint with a mixture of desire and horror. When I was down to my white suspender belt and black stockings and heels, again Carl let out an appreciative whistle. I knelt back down on the floor.

'Good girl.'

I took Carl's cock in my mouth once more.

I was aware of movement to the side and behind me and I felt Gaz's thick hands around my hips. I then felt his fingers fumbling around my sex before they pushed inside me with some force, which wasn't unpleasant. This was followed by his cock jabbing insistently against my pussy before it pushed inside, entering me fully in one deep thrust. I felt Carl stroking my hair, reassuring me.

'You're a very sexy girl, Daisy. You make a very pretty picture.'

I let his cock slide all the way into my mouth as my throat relaxed and he moaned softly. Behind me, Gaz pushed in and out of me like a machine, hard and steady, almost hurting me at the top of his entry, and I felt my body responding to him, felt the slickness between my legs as he pulled out with each stroke.

'She's a good girl, isn't she, Gaz?'

I heard Gaz grunt in response. Carl held on tight to my hair and pushed hard into my mouth.

I tasted come on the end of his cock and knew it wouldn't be long before he climaxed. Knowing this made me try harder and I ran my tongue around the edge of his cock as he slid deeply in and out of my mouth. Carl groaned and pulled my hair hard, sending spasms of pleasure through my stomach and down to my clit. Gaz's cock inside me felt good, really good, and I focused on this feeling and stopped worrying.

Gaz's hand left my hip and slid down slowly and tentatively until it was between my legs. I held my breath and prayed. At last his fingers were on my clit, pressing, exploring, feeling and I gasped and whispered under my breath, begging him not to stop. I was terrified they would both come before I did. I needn't have worried,

I was so wet and so turned on already and Gaz's fingers were now so surprisingly gentle and nice that within seconds I felt myself starting to come.

I shook all over when I came. I thought I was going to put Gaz off and I lost my rhythm with sucking Carl. It didn't matter: my coming seemed to excite them both and they came too. I swallowed Carl's come at the same time as the last waves of my orgasm went through me.

I lay on the sofa with Carl while Gaz got his coat and said goodbye, looking sheepishly pleased with himself as he shuffled out of the door. Carl raised himself up on one elbow and lit us both a cigarette. 'You are one amazingly sexy woman, do you know that?' He looked me straight in the eye and we both started laughing.

I had forgotten how good it felt to walk home in last night's dress and make-up, as if I had a big sign above my head that all the shoppers could see saying I HAD AMAZINGLY PERVERTED AND FANTASTIC SEX LAST NIGHT. WHAT DID YOU DO?

The sun was shining and my body felt loose-limbed and free. Carl's number was in my phone; he had made me promise to call him but I didn't know if I would. It seemed a shame to risk spoiling something so perfect and, besides, there were going to be plenty of other nights, with plenty of other men.

Sexy Little Numbers features the first appearance of Sadie Wolf's short fiction in Black Lace.

Maiden Voyage

EllaRegina

I have wrangled one of just a hundred coveted seats on the inaugural transatlantic commercial flight of MaidenAir® – the first carrier devoted exclusively to female passengers. Their slogan is long on pun and short on grammar: *MaidenAir, th'AIR for Her . . .*™, as if copywritten by Lady Chatterley's lover had he been a Madison Avenue ad man; but I am enchanted by their Pepto-Bismol-pink aircraft and cartoon logo: a bulbous blushing aeroplane nose penetrating the void of a soft billowy doughnut-shaped cloud – an almost perfect smoke ring – white cotton candy against a cross-hatched pale-blue sky.

Online booking lists options, questions, an enigmatic travel wardrobe caveat – 'two-piece outfit only: top and bottom; no dresses, jumpsuits, et cetera, allowed' – and one strict directive: 'No carry-ons permitted: your every on-board need will be taken care of,' a promise at once frightening and reassuring. I choose window seat 34A, my brassiere size – a superstitious air-travel ritual – and indicate meal preference: Asian VegetAIRian. For 'sexual orientation' I scroll until the appropriate selection appears on the horizon amidst a multitude of possibilities and put my cursor arrow within the square outline next to 'Heterosexual, mostly', clicking a check mark into the empty space. Form completed, I am eticketed for MaidenAir® Flight No. 001 (MA-001), departing New York City (JFK) 2 May at 19.30; arriving seven hours and ten minutes later on 3 May in London (Heathrow) at 07.40.

Crossing the Boeing 747–400's threshold is like swimming through a gynaecological speculum into an endless tunnel of pink; I'm inside a 416-seat vagina. The colour scheme dominates the cabin interior

– carpet, upholstery, walls, storage bins, barrelled ceiling – as well as the flight attendants' uniforms: bubblegum pink on the women; a boisterous peacock hot pink for the men, down to the shoes. A fleet of attendants stand guard winging the entrance, welcoming us aboard one by one. Pre-take-off classical music pipes in at an ethereal sound level: Beethoven, 'Für Elise' – feminine, calming. Royal Class™ is enthroned behind a pink velvet curtain; Coachman Class™ is where I belong. Another phalanx of flight attendants – male and female – stands at the aeroplane's rear, hovering like a rain cloud, as we find seat assignments matching the information on our pink tickets.

For this maiden voyage only one quarter of passenger seating capacity is utilised: every ticket holder is surrounded by empty spots; alternate rows are occupied – a sparsely arranged chequer-board. I stow my jacket in the overhead bin and claim 34A, a pink burrito wrapped in absorbent towelling, window shade open – a startled eyelid – black tarmac below and beyond. On the aisle seat to my right are three neatly folded pink blankets – I can almost see static sparks radiating from the synthetic fabric – four head-sized pillows cased in same, and a pink vinyl rhomboid zippered tote with bracelet-loop handle, MaidenAir®'s logo on its front; underneath, in block capitals: SKY-BAG™. I unzip to inspect the contents:

One pink toothbrush, *MaidenAir, th'AIR for Her ...*™ along its top; *UK* on the bottom in raised letters.
A finger-length pink tube of presumably pink toothpaste.
Pink dental floss threaded on a dollhouse-appropriate spool.
A pink satin eyeshade with pink elastic band.
One pink headset.
Two pink foam earplugs.
A pen, memo pad, diminutive body lotion vial, lipstick and sealed moist towelette, all boasting the MaidenAir® logo, each item pink.
A mini-dispenser of hot pink Tic Tacs.
A pink plastic comb, embossed with the now-familiar *MaidenAir, th'AIR for Her ...*™

One pair magenta anklet socks, of a singular design: plastic Louis XIV heels, pink, adhere to the anatomically correct area, creating a hybrid sock-shoe with non-slip zig-zag-runnered traction soles.

Spiralled transparently wrapped pink condoms in five different measurements, London landmarks on the shiny packaging, keyed to symbolically denote the enclosed products' dimensions. In ascending size order: Cleopatra's Needle obelisk; Tower of London; Nelson's Column; the Monument to the Great Fire of London; Big Ben.

A pink-topped clear cylinder, the magnitude of a small cucumber, containing a gelatinous substance; printed longitudinally with the London Underground symbol and TubeLube™ in a Gill Sans font.

A thumb-shaped pink plastic bottle of the official MaidenAir® fragrance; it smells like semen mixed with pineapple and cumin but is not unappealing.

In the seatback pocket facing me, next to a pink vomit bag and *MaidenAirWaves*, the in-flight magazine, a rigid laminated folded menu board presents wordless diagrams picturing faceless human-oids performing assorted activities. On one side, the usual safety instructions; on the reverse, other visualisations – tableaux simply rendered, yet clearly conveyed via nimble economy of line: women in aeroplane seats, nude from the waist down, no features except for red 'O' mouths, no pubic hair, pink seat belts fastened, legs sloped over forward seats, also strapped down with pink cinctures – held yoga poses – limbs open and waiting like unemployed nutcrackers, the odd heeled anklet sock-shoes on all feet. Next to the battened-down women, pink flight attendants, male and female, engage the seated passengers in a variety show of sexual acts – the kinds feasible on board a 747-400 with a cruising speed of 565 miles per hour travelling at 35,000 feet. My forward seat ahead does, in fact, sport ankle-cuff-length pink belting on either side, mirroring the board diagrams.

I gaze out at the high-gloss pink wing – the aircraft body seems to have been painted with nail polish – a red light blinking at its end. I vibrate between my legs, synced to the pulsing signal. Yes, this will be an interesting seven hours and ten minutes. I have not flown in too long a time, in every sense of the word, and MA-001 could be just the ticket; I am more than ready to be launched.

Good evening, ladies and ladies! Welcome aboard MaidenAir®'s inaugural voyage, Flight No. 001 bound for London Heathrow. We are there for you! Each passenger has been assigned a personal Coachman or Coachwoman based on the collected booking form data. He or she will do whatever possible to make your MaidenAir® experience a most enjoyable one. We wish you a pleasant flight. Thank you.

My Coachman is Jamie G, according to his nametag. Salt and peppery, handsome, Beatle-inflected English, an older man: my type, on the nose. I swoon, feeling an immediate intoxicating chemistry. One hand wears a pink latex glove. Jamie G politely asks me to remove all clothing from the waist down. I hand him black garments, black underthings and black boots; he puts them in an overhead bin. My Coachman shows me how the funny sock-shoes are worn. He lays my calves over the forward seat, pink belting fixing me in place – I would open my legs for him anywhere. He modifies the seat angle so I am at an alpine pitch, genitals aligned with the forward seat top. Once limb configuration satisfaction is achieved, Jamie G's latexed hand gives my pussy a warm fondle. He sucks pink thumb and forefinger, extending the remaining three to me. I eagerly oblige. His head brushes my goosebumped thighs; burrowed in further investigation, skywriting an indecipherable message on my clitoris. Were I not moored I would be levitating. 'You're ready for take-off, Miss 34A,' he determines, restoring the seat to its default state. He unfolds a pink blanket and covers my nakedness. He knows how to find me later. I'm not going anywhere; he's got me in a holding pattern.

The aeroplane roars, taxiing down the runway with increasing velocity, and soon I perceive loss of ground contact and hear the wheel mechanism retracting. We are quickly whisked aloft as if by a gigantic pink patent-leather glove; the borough of Queens falls away outside my portal, a toy village panorama.

There is the usual wordless safety demonstration run-through but I never pay attention; I do, however, take notice of the ensuing pantomime: a menu board sexual position sampler; performed in the nearest aisle by a Coachman–Coachwoman duo and across the cabin by two Coachwomen – one tantalising preview, albeit a dressed rehearsal.

Something drops from above. It is pink, plastic, shaped like a penis and filling up with air.

Ladies and ladies! The CloudPleasers™ have descended! Place this interactive self-inflating device firmly in your vagina, secure the Velcro strap behind your waist and breathe normally. The CloudPleaser™ will expand, conforming to your interior dimensions; its sensors consistently monitoring your body temperature, vaginal wall pressure, blood flow, lubrication, pulse and contractions throughout the flight. Please observe the nearest seatback video screen. Our patented chartHERflight™ system records and constantly updates your readings in real time as well as documents the aircraft's location, ground speed, altitude and distance travelled at any given moment. You can track your comings and your goings: the pulsating pink CloudBursts™ represent your arousal; their size correlates to your excitement level; static pink circles indicate orgasms reached. Upon deplaning your complete flight registry will be automatically sent to the email address you provided when booking. Keep your CloudPleaser™ inserted during the flight at all times or until a uniformed Coachman advises you to remove it; kindly refrain from touching the device as it is set on automatic pilot. Finally, with your health and safety foremost in mind, MaidenAir® always uses fresh CloudPleasers™: 'One woman, one flight, one CloudPleaser™,' manufactured from our proprietary hypoallergenic material, MaidenTex™.

We offer every amenity to help make this a thrilling journey. Our in-flight entertainment service takes off with your SKY-BAG™ headset. Plugged into the armrest receptacle, it connects you to an array of stimulating cinematic material and audio selections designed to enhance amorous urges. We have placed a complimentary copy of our titillating in-flight magazine, MaidenAirWaves, *inside the nearest accessible seat pocket; feel free to take this with you when we reach our destination. Your overhead PheromonAir™ nozzle, releasing a customised formula expressly blended for each passenger, is sure to inspire the optimum in-seat head trip. Blast off, with pleasure!*

I lodge the ballooning gadget as instructed and twist my air nozzle open full throttle – palpably more desirous when the current is aimed at my nostrils. I rig the headset, activate the video programme and tap 'entertainment preference keywords' onto the finger-sensitive LCD panel: 'Straight'; 'Extreme'; 'Oral'; 'Anal'; 'Babymaker'. A grid of windows, each bearing a frozen image, floods the screen. I play them simultaneously, a 10.6-inch diagonal orgy: enormous engorged cocks, many hairless holes, white semen abounding in dolphin fountain spouts. Were these not obviously pornographic they would be great advertisements for Elmer's Glue. There are several audio channels: musical choices, orgasm sound effects and an adjustable click track thumping a single beat; I find the collective video Babel's accompaniment. My CloudPleaser™ steadily, actively fucks me, its rhythm ever-changing, based on what I watch, what I hear, what I inhale and my physical reactions to their commingling.

I look at the chartHERflight™ monitor. A lower-case t-silhouette representing the aircraft is situated on the map near Nova Scotia, a line from the 't' leading backwards to JFK and forwards over the Atlantic, towards the British Isles. A cluster of glowing pink round CloudBursts™ is already registered, like beads on a wire; I'm an in-progress pearl necklace being strung, jetting across the ocean.

Beverage service commences. Jamie G brings my pink-lemonade vodka cocktail, a Misty London™, no rocks, exactly as per the booking form request.

I peruse *MaidenAirWaves*: video synopses are skipped – I hate plot spoilers; enticing photographs beckon – vintage as well as contemporary – grouped by category, subject, sexual predilection; erotic writings, from Catullus to Sappho and beyond, are alphabetised by author, including my favourite, Anonymous. The magazine's pages also function as a catalogue, detailing products for sale in MaidenAir®'s bulging Cloud9Shop™: an arsenal of vibrators, dildos (one- and two-seaters, with or without harnesses); plugs; beads; gags; whips; spanking regalia; bondage toys; sex games; condoms and lubricants; DVDs of all in-flight videos – everything duty free. I worry that the potential oestrus generated by this entertainment multitasking – reading, gazing at photographs and item specifications, watching videos and listening to audio tracks concurrently – will burden chartHERflight™'s circuits, but they appear to handle, as I do, the abundance of stimuli.

Jamie G arrives with my meal, lowering the nearby tray table. I unpeel the foggy steaming cling-film topper, its exterior scribbled in pink marking pen: *34A* amid a cartoon cloud outline. Dinner is excellent: spicy chickpea and vegetable curry, cold Indian beer. There is salad but I'm full; the untouched Italian extra virgin olive oil package enters my shirt pocket – I can't let such a delicacy be discarded.

Jamie G returns and gives me a quizzical look while collecting my pink tray. I resume in-flight entertaining – multiple CloudBurst™-inducing passages scribed by my preferred author. I glance at the seatback screen whenever I detect that familiar twitter, seemingly occurring more frequently and intensely if Jamie G is within sniffing distance. My necklace is assembling quite nicely. I may have the chartHERflight™ log printout framed.

Beverages accumulating, the loo calls. I ring for my Coachman, pressing the armrest's C BUTTON until a pink light winks overhead. Jamie G resurfaces, undrapes me, disconnects the CloudPleaser™, unbuckles my legs and acts as escort to the WCs – I toddle awkwardly on sock-shoes – dutifully waiting beside me in a long queue of semi-clad women and their respective Coachmen and Coachwomen. Red OCCUPIED lights are illuminated; contented high-pitched vowels emerge from within random compartments, floating like rows of excited comic-book letters. Jamie G explains that the WCs double as menu board diagram practice rooms and fitting booths for Cloud9Shop™ merchandise; there is even a dedicated MileHighDungeon™. Flashing green VACANT, one door opens; a Coachwoman steps out, gripping two leather paddles, followed by a dazed twinkling tittering passenger wearing the same outfit – waist to toes – as mine, except for lavender-pink heels and matching stripes dividing anklet backs like seams in silk stockings. Her dimpled buttocks are pinker than anything on board.

I relieve myself and Jamie G reseats me in 34A, CloudPleaser™ reinstalled. Shades have been drawn, lights dimmed; perhaps a nap can be managed.

I leave the pink world for several hours, dreaming of cocks – flying cocks dripping with white glue, winged cocks in all variations, a rare-bird aviary comprising different flesh tones, feather curves, free-falling freewheeling flying styles – some riding the wind, others against it – making their loop-de-loop rounds in the skies. A wayward cock loses its path and flies into my mouth, a lost bird. I clamp it between lips, engulfing warmth and heartbeat. I taste its semen, which recalls pineapple and cumin. The bird is moving. I undo my eyeshade.

This is no dream. Jamie G straddles me, his Boeing 797 filling my mouth, discharging, air-dropping its cargo. I swallow avidly; I had room for that salad after all. A handful of new CloudBursts™ glimmers on the screen. And I'm not the only one: my lavender-pink-heeled aisle mate is being very well attended to by her Coachwoman, poised betwixt strapped legs, a mammoth condom-covered pink rubber phallus mounted on a thigh harness – my neighbour's mouth and pussy alternating as its target. Her unplugged CloudPleaser™ hangs in mid-air, flying solo, abandoned: a wet pacifier, temporarily out of service. The woman six rows away is a twisted pretzel, ankles flanking her head, seat tilted so far back she's practically upside down. I see glittery navel adornment and shaved landing strip. A Coachman is ploughing her rear with his oily pink cock: Cleopatra's Needle, Nelson's Column at most, but doing its job well. They caw like seagulls. All around me I hear mating calls of wild birds and can distinguish moving figures in the cabin's semi-darkness, lit only by pink safety lights tracing the aisles.

Jamie G notes my wandering magpie eyes. 'Give me your SKY-BAG™!' I hand it over, hypnotised. He rips off a condom – the Monument to the Great Fire of London – removes my blanket and flips back my seat. Cock airworthy and skywards, he applies TubeLube™ to His Royal Hugeness and the condom's pink exterior once it's rolled on. 'I'm heading towards Pudding Lane!' he declares, referencing the Great Fire's source as he skydives into my pussy. His lips find an ear. 'Actually, Miss 34A,' he whispers, rotating his monument like a propeller, stirring me up, 'this batch is improperly marked; it's really Big Ben.'

'I thought so, Jamie G!' In no way is he a mere column.

The condoms also have sensors; my chartHERflight™ chronicle is virtually uninterrupted. Mine is a Coachman *par excellence*. He contributes a strand of static and palpitating CloudBursts™ to my transatlantic pearl necklace. The towel under me efficiently absorbs all copious effluvia, my private bouquet permanently impregnated in its fibres. Truly, the whole aircraft exudes Eau de Vagina by this point, what with a hundred of them being happily serviced, one way or another.

Jamie G stores his personal gear and unbuckles me. 'Come,' he says, uncorking my CloudPleaser™, grabbing the pillow stack and a few condoms. 'We need more room for the in-flight entertainment I think you'll enjoy best of all.' He leads me to a bulkhead where a gauzy pink curtain on a ceiling track cordons off several square metres. The space is intended for wheelchair-bound passengers but there are none booked. Jamie G organises me on elbows and knees, slipping a pillow beneath each joint. He encircles my waist with a pink belt attached to the pink carpet – otherwise used for securing rolling paraphernalia. 'Safety first!' he says. After cuffing other floor belts around ankles, mine and his, he palms my small breasts, causing the extra virgin olive oil packet to cascade down.

'Aha!' he exclaims. 'Just what I was looking for! Miss 34A is a *very* naughty girl. Not only hasn't she finished her supper but she's absconded with the fixings!'

'How did you know?'

'It's my job,' says Jamie G, 'plus our sensors take inventory.'

'I'm sorry. I don't like seeing food go to waste.'

'Oh, that won't happen. Have no fear!' He rips open the plastic – I envision rich golden-green oil welling at the brim. I turn, watching him spill precious liquid into his hands, rubbing them together.

'That's pretty fancy skin cream, Jamie G.'

'Not its ultimate use, Miss 34A.'

I feel Jamie G, all hot and hot pinked against my bare thighs. One olive-oil-dressed finger makes a maiden voyage, probing an untreaded passage.

'I've never done *this!*' I say, surprised.

'I read your booking form,' replies Jamie G, 'and am familiar with the Miss 34A history. You're curious. Or . . . ?'

'Yes. I'm an intrepid traveller who believes in exploring untrampled spots off the beaten path.'

Jamie G concentrates on his spelunking, adding oil and more fingers to my chunnel.

'It's chiming time for Big Ben,' he announces, momentarily departing from my posterior. He fits a new condom on his timepiece, tossing it abundantly with salad dressing. He imitates the clock tower, gently gliding his wide-bodied fuselage inside my evacuation door.

'Dong. Dong. Dong. Dong,' he sings. 'Dong. Dong. Dong.'

He is completely within me by the fourth 'dong'.

It must be 07.00 in London. I am being driven by a piping baguette and speculate whether our destination is not Paris instead.

Jamie G's body covers my back – on top like a tandem parachutist – and begins to buck, pressing, deeper yet, transcending what I thought was the frontier; my head mashes the cushioned pink wall as if it were a pillow. His heat, his weight, his touch, his voice, his breath, his cock, his smell. He sends me into a raptus: besotted, mesmerised – I would do anything for him.

'Wait until you see the CloudBursts™ I'm going to drop,' he whoops. 'You won't believe your eyes!'

'Hold on!!' commands Jamie G between primordial squawks. Turbulence never comes at a convenient time and this occasion is no different; we are also descending. My rear is airborne but his architectural anatomy tethers me, as do strips of belting. The aeroplane rattles and shifts altitude at a jerky pace. One hundred women are screaming, whether from sheer ecstasy or fright I have no idea. Through the thin curtain I sense vague luminous rectangles: one hundred video screens flicker like winning slot machines in Las Vegas, one hundred chartHERflight™ paths beaming enough necklace bling to stock Tiffany's.

Jamie G pulls a telescopic disc, at my mouth's level, from the wall. Out pops a pink rubber cock, like a magic trick snake. 'This will stabilise you,' he says. My lips surround the pink horizontal. Indeed, with this orthodontic-retainer, his salad-dresser holding up the rear, belts cinching my waist and our ankles, the 747-400 could flip over, twirling three times like a test pilot action, and we'd still be right where we are.

I am flying. *We* are flying, high, very high, in the sky; soaring – the aeroplane's nose pointed down, Jamie G's cock ascending. A smouldering liquid oozes from the skyhook tickling my uvula. It tastes like semen, pineapple, cumin and is rather appealing. I produce appreciative noises while drinking; I am tanked.

'That's our MaidenBlaster™ fuel,' says Jamie G, hands grasping my midsection. 'All Coachmen donated. It's running this bird, too, oil prices being what they are – circulated throughout the cabin as well. But it's only to be shared with extraordinary passengers – like *you*, Miss 34A.' When he utters my name fiery oil loads his condom – I wiggle my ass in response, captivated by every word – and, at that precise moment, wheels kiss tarmac in a smooth touchdown. There is applause, maybe for the landing, or our floor show, its shadow play likely visible from behind the scrim. My rectum contracts, thirstily guzzling what remains of the olive oil, my throat behaving similarly with the MaidenBlaster™ fuel. Jamie G keeps Big Ben ticking as I shudder.

Ladies and ladies! Welcome to London Heathrow Airport. Local time is 07.40. For your safety and comfort we ask that you wait until we have come to a complete stop at the gate before summoning your Coachman to properly assist you with deplaning. On behalf of MaidenAir® and the entire crew, I'd like to thank you again for joining us on this very special voyage. We hope you've enjoyed the flight and look forward to seeing you on board again in the near future. Have a nice day and thank you for coming and going with MaidenAir®!

Once the aeroplane is halted Jamie G detangles us, tucks himself in and helps me up. I can barely stand or walk. He provides careful guidance back to 34A, unlatches the overhead bin and reunites me with my New York City mourning costume. The chartHERflight™ screen is overflowing. Static pink circles throng the original line; offshoots have blossomed, forming a flow chart – not much can be seen of water and continents. Jamie G takes a hot pink 1-inch-diameter badge from his trousers. Two yawning black 'm' squiggles, resembling tiered birds spread in flight, span edge to edge. He pins the ornament to my jacket. 'Miss 34A, you've earned your wings.'

I cannot deplane without assistance. Jamie G knows that; it's his job. He supports me as we wait to disembark. I dangle my SKY-BAG™ – it's all I can lift. We begin moving, slowly, behind other passengers – many of whom are also having trouble in the basic ambulation department – and their attendant Coachmen and Coachwomen. While vacating I glimpse the cockpit yearningly; pilot and co-pilot, sitting: grinning, sunburned, pink. Next time I'll ask if I can visit.

* * *

One hundred pink wheelchairs fringe the ramp outside the aeroplane exit door. Jamie G settles me in one and we're off. We pass the boarding gate where a batch of giggling women – gazing at us in wonderment like hungry puppies – awaits this particular aircraft, departing for JFK in a few hours, after it's been cleaned, refurnished and refuelled: one thousand MaidenAir® Coachmen are probably within a designated hangar, taking *that* matter in hand at this very instant. I am wheeled to the luggage carousel where our bags, home-delivered courtesy of the airline two weeks pre-boarding, are swiftly retrieved: one hundred identical pink rolling duffles, front and back touting MaidenAir®'s logo, with the phrase 'I'm coming and going!' – figure-eight orbits of white calligraphy – repeated in an overall pattern.

Jamie G hitches my bag to the wheelchair, rolling us towards Customs and further, through a series of automatic pink plastic-padded sliding doors – gaping swollen labia as they open – until we greet crisp English air. A hundred black London cabs are queued; one is hailed. With pink duffle deposited in the boot, Jamie G transfers my still-trembling frame onto the back seat, and bids me adieu.

'Goodbye, Miss 34A,' he says, leaning against the slightly lowered window. 'It has been my pleasure taking care of you.' Jamie G's odour perforates the confined space, entrancing me, and I realise: those were *his* pheromones emanating from the nozzle like a genie from a bottle. I was sprayed with Jamie G; held under his knee-weakening spell the entire voyage – during my occupancy of 34A, and directly from the source when unseated in his vicinity. I am too spent to do anything but smile.

I watch Jamie G's figure become a pink matchstick, then vanish beyond the plump-lipped aperture of the pink MaidenAir® terminal. I roll up the glass to contain and enjoy him for as long as I can.

I begin to doze and am roused by my burly, behatted Cockney-accented cabbie: "'Ello, lovey. Are we coming or going?"

'Both.'

He starts his engine and we launch into the thick of London, webbed in early morning haze, on the wrong street side. I hope two weeks here fly by as I'm already thinking about my return trip.

Sexy Little Numbers features the first appearance of EllaRegina's short fiction in Black Lace.

In Heat
Shayla Kersten

Miriam Lahti's day had started out fucked up and hadn't got any better. The day had begun fighting with her oh-so-hot neighbour and only emphasised her need to get laid. George Branford's precious car was like catnip to her cat. Almost daily arguments about paw prints and hairballs just added to her rising heat every time he was around.

Then work sucked. Miriam's boss had a major meltdown first thing over an irate client. Needing someone to take his frustration out on, he picked her. The rest of the day continued downhill from there.

Toss in the unusually hot summer and Miriam was ready for comfortable clothes and a gin and tonic. Climbing out of her car, she sighed with relief at being home. Her feet seemed to melt into the concrete with each step in the sweltering heat. Humid air kinked her hair into curls.

As she opened the front door, a ball of grey fur zipped past her legs. 'Fuck!' Chasing after the cat wasn't on the list of her favourite Friday night activities. Not that she had anything better planned.

Setting her purse on the table in the foyer, she called out the door. 'Max. Here kitty, kitty.' Typical cat – he ignored her.

Thick black clouds rolled on the horizon. The sunny promise of the morning had deteriorated all day as a front moved in. The heavens were ready to burst. Max hated getting wet more than he loved his freedom. He'd be home soon.

Kicking her heels off, she walked across the living room then up the stairs, unbuttoning her skirt as she moved. The clouds hadn't diminished the unusual August heat. The air in her apartment was damp and stale, even worse on the second floor. Fans didn't provide much relief. Her thin silk blouse stuck to her skin with a fine sheen of sweat.

Sliding the balcony door open, she prayed for a cooler breeze. The slight flash of lightning brightened the clouds. Thunder rumbled in the distance. The sun had dipped below the storm leaving the sky dark and foreboding.

Without turning on the lights, Miriam let her skirt drop to the floor. Her thigh-high nylons, tacky with a thin sheen of sweat, clung to her legs like a second skin. A hint of a breeze teased through the open door.

'Oh, yeah . . .' Miriam stepped into the doorway. A quick glance around revealed no one in nearby gardens. With the weather brewing bad, the private park behind the apartments should be deserted. Darkness descended like a curtain. A mist of rain blew through the door and glazed her skin. The exhibitionist hiding in her psyche escaped long enough to urge her out onto the balcony dressed only in her blouse and underwear.

The slight sprinkle of rain kissed her face with cooling relief. The damp blouse grew wetter, rainwater seeping into the thin lace of her bra. Her nipples tightened with a combination of a slight chill and the idea of someone seeing her on the balcony half-dressed.

Lifting her head, she let the light rain cover her face. The breeze cooled her moist skin. Raising her arms, she welcomed the change in temperature. With a long sigh, she released the aggravation of the day into the falling night. If only she could lose her sexual frustration as easily.

Recurring fantasies of her neighbour – dark wavy hair flopped over his frowning brow. Deep blue eyes, chiselled features. The brooding good looks were only the top of the list. A body to die for hid under the perfectly tailored suit. Well tanned, hard muscled . . . Could she help it if the view from her bedroom window looked over his small backyard?

And every time she saw him, her body heated and cream pooled between her thighs. Her imagination had her pushed over the hood of his precious car, her skirt rucked up and her underwear torn away. Hard, rough sex ... pounding into her pussy with long strokes of his thick cock ...

She lowered one arm. Her hand slid down her dripping blouse to the small triangle of cloth covering her mons. Running a finger along the seam of her labia, she bit her lip against a moan.

A loud meow interrupted her all too brief fantasy. 'Max?'

His raucous muttering seemed almost level with her but how ... The rain began in earnest and Max's cries increased in intensity.

'Max. Where are you?' Miriam leaned towards the railing. Her heart jumped as she peered over the edge in search of her cat. She didn't do heights well. She never moved more than a foot or two onto the balcony. And never to the edge. But Max ...

'Kitty, kitty ...' Another plaintive meow answered her call. This time Miriam's gaze followed the sound up the tree near George's balcony. 'Max?'

A street light on the other side of the tree revealed the silhouette of her wayward feline. Another meowed squeal confirmed her fears.

'Bloody hell.'

A low rumble of thunder sent Max into a flurry of pitiful meows.

'OK ... OK.' Miriam took a deep breath.

Max's perch on the tree branch appeared to be about a foot from George's balcony. Even if the man were home, he'd never help her rescue Max. The balconies were about a metre apart, maybe a little less. The drop between them wasn't life threatening – probably wouldn't break anything if she fell. The idea of falling, slipping between the gap and flying through the air robbed her of her breath.

'Oh, God.' She couldn't believe she was contemplating climbing onto George's side. Lightning crackled in the distance then thunder followed within a few seconds. She needed to get to Max before the full fury of the storm hit.

Max screamed his displeasure once again, prompting Miriam to action.

With a deep breath, she moved to the edge. If she didn't look down... The shadows hid the height from her view. A gutter ran along the roof of the connected houses. If she used it to keep her balance... 'Don't look down. Don't look down,' she mumbled as she climbed onto a chair next to the railing. Gasping deep ragged breaths, she grabbed the edge of the gutter. After a good tug to test the sturdiness, she stepped onto the strong metal railing.

Her nylon-covered foot didn't slip but she should have removed them first. Too late now. If she stopped, she'd never muster the nerve to climb up again. Her gaze focused on George's railing. With a quick step and a short jump, she landed on his balcony.

The shakes took over and she sank to the wet tiles. Max's meow subdued her anxiety attack a little. Focusing on her stranded cat kept her from sitting paralysed on the floor. Miriam stood on trembling legs then crossed the small space to the tree. As she reached the railing, Max leaped from his perch onto the balcony. Before Miriam could touch him, the soaked cat took three jumps to the opposite side of the balcony, up on the railing then sailed onto Miriam's side. With a flick of his tail, Max disappeared into her apartment.

'Son of a bitch.' Miriam slid back to the floor as the rain intensified, pounding hard drops against her skin, finishing the soaking of her clothes. She needed to get back to her side. But first she had to catch her breath.

A light flipped on inside George's house, shining through the glass doors. Miriam shrank into a darkened corner, pulling her knees to her chest. 'Damn!' Now what?

Fear of discovery washed away her issue with heights. She'd gladly jump the distance between their balconies if she could get across the now lit open space. George would probably call the police. She couldn't imagine trying to explain her presence or her state of dress.

Rain ran in rivulets down her face. A shadow crossed in front of the glass door as she wiped water from her eyes. The tall lean figure of her cranky but gorgeous neighbour stopped in front of the door casting a long shadow in the falling rain.

'Go away, go away, go away,' Miriam whispered. She drew back against the balcony railing as the door slid open.

Dressed in a pair of tight-fitting boxers, George stood staring out into the night. His gaze stayed up, away from Miriam hidden almost at his feet.

Eye level with his crotch, Miriam's gaze fixed on the bulge in his underwear. Even flaccid, he was enticing. In spite of the cool rain and chilling breeze, heat warmed her face. A rush of desire curled through her body. An ache settled in her pussy as her body tensed with need. Her nipples, already peaked from cold, ached to be touched.

Her gaze strayed to George's hands. Strong broad hands with long thick fingers ... Her breast would fit in his palm with room to spare. Hot calloused hands ... touching her as she ran her fingers down his sculpted abs ... down further ...

As if he could hear her thoughts, George's hand rubbed across his stomach, fingers teasing the edge of his waistband. His cloth-covered cock twitched and thickened as his hand dipped below the dark material. His fingers, outlined inside the tight material, closed around his flesh. Short fondling strokes thickened his shaft. The tip of his cock peeked over the top of his waistband as his strokes lengthened.

A soft moan almost escaped. Too long since Miriam had been this close to an almost naked man. An image of her crawling across the wet concrete on her hands and knees flashed into her head. Heat swirled through her pussy. Warm wetness seeped through the tiny scrap of silk covering her shaved mons.

Miriam's hand slipped up to her breast, cupping the cold flesh through the soaked silk of her shirt. Tweaking the hard nipple, she let a small moan escape. Her heart almost stopped until she realised a rumble of thunder covered the sound.

George's strokes grew longer and a little faster. His chest rose and fell in sharp panted breaths.

Miriam could almost hear the air rushing in and out of his lungs. Leaning into the hard wall, she ran her other hand down her stomach. Desire seared through her body, infusing her with recklessness. Slipping her fingers under the tiny line of elastic on her thong, Miriam pushed towards the pulsing heat of her core.

'What the hell?'

She froze at George's exclamation. Her heart raced but the need burning through her core didn't dampen.

The tall lean body appeared beside her on the balcony. Her gaze travelled from muscled thighs, reluctantly past the thick cock, tracing up the six-pack of abs, over the finely furred chest until she reached the angry frowning face.

George's strong hand wrapped around her upper arm. A sharp yank pulled her to her feet.

'What the hell are you doing?' Grabbing her other arm, George held her in a vice-tight grip.

'Max . . .' she stuttered through chattering teeth. Cold, fear, desire all had a hand in destroying her ability to speak. 'Tree . . .'

George glanced over his shoulder towards the tree then let his gaze travel around to her balcony with its open door. 'Is he still there?'

Shaking her head, Miriam opened her mouth to speak but words failed to come out.

A half sneer, half grin curled George's lips. 'He made it home and left you hanging in the wind.' His grip eased as he chuckled. 'Typical cat.'

Miriam nodded. Her mind wasn't on her pain-in-the-ass cat. Her skin warmed under George's hands. Desire shook through the chilly breeze and drenching rain. 'You're getting wet,' she whispered. She followed the rain dripping down his chest. Wanting to drink the water from his skin, she licked her lips.

A sharp exhalation from George pulled her gaze back to his face. His nostrils flared with short breaths. 'You're already wet.' His hands squeezed her upper arms, pressing them closer to her breasts.

Miriam didn't need to follow his roaming gaze to know what he saw. Her nipples were rock hard, poking through the soaked sheer silk of her blouse. The wet white material wouldn't hide much. The tiny scrap of silk from her thong wouldn't either.

Miriam swallowed hard and bit her lower lip before she admitted, 'In more ways than one.'

'You've been almost as naughty as your cat.' Without releasing his hold on her arms, George's thumbs ran up and down her skin. 'I might have to punish you.'

Her mind raced at the possibilities. A hard spanking followed by a rough fuck . . . Miriam gasped as a shudder ran from the top of her spine to her ass and culminated in warm heat in her pussy.

A wide grin split his lips. 'Seems like you want to be punished.'

Shortness of breath captured any words she might have said. A slight nod was all she could manage.

'Tell me yes.'

Her chest heaved with gasping breaths. 'Yes.' Her secret stash of novels included erotic bondage, submission and a few other kinks, but she'd never had the nerve to act on her fantasies. The idea of George taking her . . . 'Yes.' She raised her gaze to meet his.

With a short nod, he whispered, 'Good.' Leaning forwards, George brushed his lips across Miriam's.

Before she could react, he'd pulled away. She craned her neck to follow but he pushed her away.

'Kissing is for good behaviour.' His grip kept her at arm's length. 'You have to earn the privilege.' Thunder accompanied his frown. 'And because of your cat, you have a lot to make up for.' With a little push, he released her.

Shivering against the rising tide of desire mixed with a smidge of fear, Miriam crossed her arms over her chest.

'Drop your arms. I want to see what I have to work with.'

Miriam hesitated. Her rain-soaked clothes hid nothing from his gaze, even in the limited light from his bedroom. His penetrating gaze made her self-conscious. And the threat of violence, no matter how sexual or how much she wanted it, forced her guard up.

'I could just call the police. Trespassing, lewd behaviour, naked in public . . .' George leaned close then growled in her ear, 'And I'm sure the officers would love to see you in that outfit.'

Even though his words sent erotic heat through her body, Miriam wasn't ready to be a public spectacle. Her arms slid to her sides.

As if oblivious to the now pouring rain, George paced around her. His fingers traced a line from the back of her neck down her spine. Miriam's gasp for air ended in a small cry as George's hand swatted her bare ass cheek.

'Like that, do you?' George repeated his action on her other cheek.

Miriam's pussy clenched with each blow. Cream warmed her nether lips and her ass tingled with the heat of his blows.

George's fingers tangled in her shoulder-length hair. With his body so close she could feel his heat as he yanked her head back. 'I don't ask questions to hear myself speak,' he growled. 'Answer me.'

'Yes.'

'Yes what?'

Miriam's neck ached from the pressure of his hold. 'Yes, I liked it.' The grip tightened, pulling her hair a little harder then the pressure released and a strange sense of pleasure – relief from pain – washed over her.

'Good girl. For that, you get rewarded.' His mouth nibbled along the side of her neck. Soft kisses with the scrap of day-old beard. His hand still controlling her head, tugged until her lips met his.

This time a hint of tongue warmed her lips. Opening for more, she was disappointed as he pulled away. However, his body moved closer. His hand slid down her back and gripped her hip. The other hand slipped between their bodies, fumbling with something.

Miriam gasped as his thick hot cock slid between her cold cheeks. His chest pressed tight against her back. Water slicked his skin but didn't cool the contact.

His hands slid forwards from her hips to the hem of her blouse. 'Unbutton or I'll rip it off.'

Her hands moved at the implied command in his tone. The silk blouse was one of her best but being soaked with rain had probably already ruined it. With a shiver of desire, Miriam dropped her hands to her side.

A soft chuckle breathed against her neck. 'I like that idea better.' His hands grasped the delicate material and, with a sharp jerk, he ripped the buttons from the blouse. 'I have an interesting use for this.' Pulling away, he yanked the garment down her arms. Nimble fingers unhooked her bra next, ridding her of it as well.

Miriam instinctively covered her bare breasts with her hands.

'Modesty? A little late for that, isn't it?' George pushed her towards the small table on his balcony. 'Lie on your stomach.'

In a fog of desire mixed with fear, Miriam didn't think she understood. Lie on what? She turned around to face him.

He shook his head slightly. 'Lie across the table on your stomach.'

'In the rain?'

'Yes.' His eyebrow arched.

'But the storm.'

His frown eased. 'The lightning is far away. You can tell by the sound of the thunder. I wouldn't put you in danger.'

Miriam shuddered as his fingers caressed the side of her face.

'If you want to stop, tell me.' George leaned in and his soft lips brushed Miriam's. 'But something tells me you want this.'

Wanted, needed, couldn't stop now if the sun rose and a hundred people stood in the park watching . . . Miriam's body shivered on the edge of an orgasm and George had barely touched her. The idea of him using her on his balcony . . . She'd dreamed of George, in bed – even tied to his bed – his hard body pressed against hers, his cock buried in her snatch. But never had she imagined fucking him on his balcony in a rainstorm.

Turning around, she bent over the tiny table, pressing her aching breasts into the cold wet metal. Her hips and groin were off one edge and her head off the other. Only her torso rested on the table. George stood in front of her, his boxer-covered cock, rigid with arousal, at eye level.

His hands held her blouse and bra. With a grin, he ripped the blouse down the middle of the back. Grabbing one of her arms, he wrapped half the remains of her shirt around her wrist then around the table leg. With deft hands, he proceeded to bind her other arm as well.

Her breath caught in her throat. Excitement raced through her body. Unable to keep still, she wiggled against the table, massaging her breasts into the hard metal. Heat flushed her loins. Her pussy spasmed with need, clenching around her emptiness. She gagged against a rising scream of frustration. If George didn't fuck her soon, she'd deteriorate into a raving loon, shouting her need to the world.

'Not too tight?'

'No.' Her gaze fixed on his dick. The limited light of the doorway didn't keep her from seeing the thick crown peeking over the top of his waistband.

George stood legs wide and hands on his hips watching her. 'Very good. You look good bound.' One hand slid forwards to his waistband. He tugged the wet material down and his rigid flesh sprang free.

Miriam's throat ached with the need to taste him. Flicking her tongue across her lips, she glanced up at him, ready to beg.

'I wonder what you'd look like gagged.' His fingers wrapped around his dick in a light grip. He stroked from the base to the tip. Gripping just below the crown with his thumb and forefinger, he tweaked his swollen flesh.

The rain had slowed to a drizzle. Wetness coated her skin, teasing trails down her sides, through the crack of her ass, over her shoulders. A cool breeze sent goosebumps across her skin. The night seemed to darken even more as her gaze tunnel-visioned on the hard body and stiff cock in front of her.

Miriam nodded, licking her lips again. 'Let me taste you,' she whispered.

Shuffling closer to the table, George brushed his dick against her lips.

Not quite close enough, she strained her neck forwards in an effort to wrap her lips around him. Miriam tugged at her make-shift bonds in frustration. Want pooled into warm cream between her thighs. Her thighs clenched together over her swollen clit. 'Damn it.'

'Impatient, aren't you?' George took a half-step closer then pressed his flesh against her lips.

Miriam flicked her tongue against the slit in the crown then circled the thick flesh. As she sucked the tip, a moan of encouragement drifted from above her head. Even bound, she wasn't helpless – she had the power to drive him mad or please him.

His hands twined through her dripping wet hair, squeezing streams of water down her neck. Since she couldn't move more than an inch or two, she had to accept his slow pace as he fed her his length.

Her tongue twisted around his flesh, teasing the thick crown. Her muffled moans vibrated through her lips. The taste of rain combined with the salty musk of his skin.

Miriam's skin prickled with the sweet combination of fear and thrill. The light from George's bedroom would silhouette the action for anyone walking in the darkened park. The weather would discourage casual strollers but the possibility alone fuelled Miriam's arousal to epic temperatures.

The idea of George's flesh spearing her over-heated pussy while someone watched . . . Miriam clenched her thighs, pressing her mons against the edge of the table. She needed relief. The steady thrum of her heart pounded in her ears. The pulse point in her neck throbbed with excitement. The ache of need had already robbed her of her sense, most of her breath and, if she didn't get relief soon, she'd lose what little remained of her sanity.

'Feels good. Your mouth is so fucking hot.' George's hips pulsed in a steady rhythm, stroking her mouth with half his length. 'The first time I saw you I thought those beautiful lips would look great wrapped around my cock.'

Warm cream drizzled down Miriam's thigh mixing with the rain. Her hips pushed into the hard edge of the table, seeking exquisite pressure, fabulous release. His words added to her urgency but his slow motions frustrated her. Tugging at the remnants of her shirt did no good. She was bound tight and at his mercy.

'Too bad I'm expecting company.' George leaned forwards then reached over her back. A hard slap on her ass startled her. 'I could keep you here all night. Fuck you in so many ways.' Another swat warmed her backside. 'Of course, I could just invite my friend to join us.'

Miriam gasped around his cock. She wanted to pull away and yell, 'Yes,' but his grip kept her mouth impaled on his dick. The top of her swollen clit made contact with the table. Blessed hard contact. Her orgasm started with a long hard shudder that wormed its way deep into her womb. Muscles clenched as the spiralling sensation worked its way out from her groin to her limbs. Languorous lethargy swept through her as heat radiated through her rain-soaked body. She expected steam to rise from her skin.

'Damn. Sounds like you'd like that.'

Miriam moaned around the thick flesh filling her mouth with relief. At least he kept her from screaming, 'Bring it on.' The idea of another man joining the already erotic fantasy pushed her right over the edge again. Ecstasy stole her breath. Her heart raced at a giddy pace, leaving her body weak but still willing.

George's strong hands tightened in her hair. 'Definitely sounds like you'd like being tag-teamed. One at both ends maybe.'

His cock pressed deeper into her mouth, pushing against the back of her throat. Gagging for air, she was helpless to answer yes or no. With his fingers laced through her hair, controlling her head, she couldn't even shake her head. Or nod.

Nod yes. Beg for more. Slut out completely by letting two men, one a stranger and one who might as well be, bang her at the same time.

Her wrists pulled against her silk bindings. Her hips ground against the table's cold wet metal. George's shaft stroked her mouth with increasing speed. Short, fast motions ... tiny hints of bitter seed burst on her tongue with each pass.

'Damn,' George growled as he pulled his cock free of her mouth. 'Almost lost it.' Releasing his grip on her, he wrapped his fingers around the base of his length. 'Not ready to finish with you yet.'

Miriam gasped for air. She missed his heat, his taste already. Her neck strained towards the ruddy thick flesh. A low chuckle diverted her gaze to his face.

A crooked grin canted his lips. 'You realise that if my friend shows up, I'm going to let him fuck you.'

Biting into her swollen lip, Miriam stopped her enthusiastic approval from blurting out.

'Yeah.' George nodded as one eyebrow arched. 'Be right back.' And he disappeared from her view.

Her mind raced in a dozen different directions. She had to live next door to George. What would he think if she let his friend fuck her? She dropped her head down over the edge of the table. What a stupid thought. What did he think of her already?

Would he expect sexual favours from her in the future? Instead of the idea irritating her, it added to the swarm of arousal threatening to burn through her pussy.

It's not like she had other options. No regular lover. No lover at all in the last year. Seemed half her pay went on batteries for the vibrator.

Then again, what was his friend like? A loser? A dog? Grotesque? And how could she trust either one of them? She barely knew George.

Fingers teased the crack of her ass. 'Last chance. Andy will be here any minute. I left a note on the door to come upstairs. Said I had a surprise.'

Once again, Miriam bit back a response. Hopefully, he'd recognise her silence as implied consent. She couldn't say yes. And she bloody well wasn't saying no at this point.

'Sweet.' George's finger delved deeper until it brushed her anus. 'Maybe I'll fuck your ass while Andy takes your pussy.'

'Yes.' Miriam couldn't stop her voice this time.

Without warning, George's finger slid down her swollen clit. 'Not yet. But very soon.' His soft chuckle bordered on evil.

'Yo, George.' A new voice rang through the door of George's apartment. 'Where you at?'

'Out here, Andy.'

Miriam craned her neck around trying to see the newcomer. Her skin flushed in spite of the cooling temperatures and the misting rain.

'What are you doing out in the rain?' Andy's voice grew closer. 'Fuck!'

George laughed as his fingers pushed into her wanting depths. 'Meet my neighbour, Miriam.'

'The hot one with the cat?' Andy's amusement bled through his voice.

'That's the one.'

'Exceptionally nice to meet you, Miriam. Any rules?'

A hand slid up her spine to the back of her neck, sluicing water from her skin. Andy didn't seem too surprised to find his friend with a naked woman on his balcony. *Rules?* The question seemed familiar, as if he'd asked the same thing before.

'I don't know. Miriam seems to have lost her voice.' George's fingers found a steady rhythm, stroking her pulsing cunt, pushing her closer to the edge again. 'She seemed quite excited at the idea of being taken from both ends at the same time.'

'Sounds good to me.' Andy's hand slipped under her dripping hair and squeezed the back of her neck. 'Coin toss?'

'What?' Miriam blurted out with surprise.

'Unless you have a preference, love.' Andy's hot breath whispered in her ear.

Miriam turned her head towards his voice. Backlit by the light from the bedroom, a shock of blond hair haloed a shadow-hidden face.

'Otherwise, we can toss a coin.'

Before she could think of a coherent answer, Andy covered her mouth with warm lips. His tongue slipped past her parted lips and traced the edge of her teeth. His fingers dug into her hair, pulling several strands tight against her scalp.

Shivers of desire raced through her. Her skin prickled with cold and need. Falling into the searching kiss, she sighed.

'No need to toss,' George interrupted. 'I've wanted to fuck her since the day I moved in. You take her mouth this time.'

This time. Miriam pushed against George's intruding hand. Her toes caught the floor of the balcony and aided her efforts. The table rocked with her motions. Her moan vibrated around Andy's tongue.

Andy pulled away from her mouth. 'And she seems a little anxious.' His tall lean figure moved around the table. Standing in front of her, he reached for the fly of his slacks. 'Shouldn't keep a lady waiting.'

Miriam's gaze locked on the bulge in Andy's slacks. Her hips kept a steady rhythm against George's hand as she ran her tongue across her lips.

Andy made a show of opening his slacks. Fingers ran down the length of his zipper then back up again. The top button slipped the buttonhole. His hand paused to cup the still growing bulge.

After a hard swallow, Miriam released a breath she hadn't realised she was holding. Fascinated by the slow show in front of her, she rocked against George's hand instinctively. Then the pressure was gone. Turning her head, she spotted her sexy neighbour from the corner of her eye.

His cock glistened in the light from his room. His hands fumbled with a shiny foil package. Condom . . .

Damn. She'd been so far gone into her fantasy she almost forgot reality. Thank God, George hadn't.

With a sigh of relief, she turned back towards Andy.

The fly of his slacks hung open. His briefs were tugged down to reveal a long thick cock, maybe longer than George's. Definitely thicker. She almost opened her mouth to ask the two men to change places. The idea of Andy's monster plunging her depths . . . but maybe there'd be a next time.

Rough hands gripped her hips, tugging her backwards. Her arms wrenched a little as George's manhandling put pressure on her bonds. Then the tip of his cock nudged her swollen folds. The silken head slid down her slit, brushing her sensitive clit. Back up again, the thick flesh teased her opening.

She wiggled her hips in a futile attempt to capture his cock, pull him into her slick depths, but he escaped. Slippery with her juices, his dick rubbed against her anus. 'No,' she moaned.

'No.' His cock slid up between her cheeks as his whisper washed over her. 'Not yet.'

Andy stepped forwards. His cock brushed against her lips, leaving a trail of pre-come mixed with rain on her mouth.

With greedy abandon, she wrapped her lips around the head. Her hips pushed against George's hot flesh. She needed more.

George swatted her ass hard. The stinging flesh warmed in spite of the cool breeze and cooler rain. Another swat. Then a third. Each a little harder than the last. Each moving to untouched skin.

Moaning around Andy's cock, she wiggled her hips, not sure if she was trying to avoid the blows or encourage them.

Andy pressed forwards until her concentration needed to focus on not choking. She flicked her tongue along the hard ridge of his cock and suckled the hot flesh.

Her attention centred on Andy, she gasped when George's dick found its target. Hard silken flesh pressed into her channel. With a mouth full of cock, she could only moan her impatience.

Deeper George's length pressed until he filled her depths. His pelvis bumped her ass, pushing her clit into the hard wooden table.

Her body shuddered with racking spasms. Her pussy clenched around the hard flesh, urging him deeper as George pulled away. Another long stroke pierced her flesh. Andy's cock swept into her mouth a slight beat off from George.

First George, then Andy. Plunging from both ends. Her skin warming, sweat mixing with rain, with come. The slight irritation of inconsistency eased as the two men synchronised their movements. Each filling her with an increasing pace, almost choreographed, planned . . .

Miriam floated into pure ecstasy. Her body used by two men . . . reality surpassed fantasy.

Then the matched pace faltered. George broke stride, his hips jerking against her ass. His fingers gripped her hips with painful intensity. His loud moan echoed across the balcony and into the trees.

Another orgasm slammed through Miriam's body as Andy's hands pulled through her wet hair. With her head held immobile, his cock pressed deep but she didn't care. She rode the heights on George's cock while gulping Andy's hot gushing come.

'Damn, woman.' George's body covered her back. Warm skin, cool water and muscles ...

Andy pulled his spent flesh free. The bitter taste of come dragged across her tongue, her lips.

'You're one lucky bastard, George.' Andy's hands combed through her hair. 'With her next door, I'd never leave home.'

'I might not.' George's breath warmed her neck. 'What do you say, Miriam? Would you do this again? Or maybe even more?'

'More?' Her mind couldn't focus on his words.

'I might want to invite a couple of other friends over. You'd make a fantastic party favour – splayed, bound, ready to be fucked in every hole.'

Andy's fingers ran across her lips. 'She'd be the perfect plaything. And very convenient having her next door.'

Miriam's cunt clenched around George's softening flesh. The idea of being a toy for George and his friends sent a shock of heat through her core.

'Definitely,' George murmured against her wet hair. 'Would you like that?'

'Yes.' Anything he wanted – with one condition. 'But you have to leave Max alone.'

'Max?' Andy asked.

'The cat.' George laughed. 'Since it is Max's fault I found you on my balcony tonight, he can do anything he wants.'

Miriam sighed as she tugged at her restraints. If she could get dry and warm, she'd be as content as her spoiled cat. She might even purr.

'Let's get dry and move this into the bedroom.' George must have read her mind. He rolled off her. He knelt near her head and reached for the remains of her tattered blouse. 'And then we'll start again. It's going to be a long night.'

Miriam's body tensed with a renewed surge of energy. Max was definitely getting special treats after this.

Shayla Kersten's short fiction is also featured in the Black Lace anthology *Seduction*.

Hard at Work
Madelynne Ellis

I'm here again, staring through the sheet glass walls of the office into her den, wondering how to make my size thirteen feet move across the threshold. Isn't it enough that I've had to pass her once this morning already? I've already forced myself to make the obligatory morning greetings.

For the second or third time, I consider returning to my desk and phoning through the request. Except, even the sound of her voice makes me tremble. It's the sound of thimble winter. It makes my pulse race and my testicles freeze. She scares me. I'll admit it. Mercifully, she's not the boss. I am, as my desk tab and stationery headers proudly proclaim. I wonder if I should remind her of that? Miss Stevens ... Miss Ursula Stevens ... the She Bear.

God help me as I take the plunge. I'm about to be chewed up and spat out.

The agony doesn't end once I've crossed the threshold. I hover by her desk like some bumbling office junior while she sorts the morning post. At twenty past ten, she'll bring it to me with a cup of wickedly stewed tea and a stale custard cream. Ursula is always punctual.

She looks so ordinary as she works. Busy and neat, like a thousand other ordinary secretaries nestled between their photos of white fluffy pets and sadly undernourished spider plants, but then she looks up. Ursula has the sternest, most knowing eyes; forget-me-not blue with corollas like smoky haze. They're eyes that I could fall into and get lost for ever.

There's a moment of utter stillness as I gaze into her eyes. The sort of moment you only get in vintage Hollywood movies before the final kiss and the credits roll. Ursula is so still she could be marble. Only the deep magenta of her lips signifies any warmth.

I step back from her afraid. 'Could you come into my office,' I blurt. There, I've done it. I turn quickly away. The next move is hers. I hold my breath, because I know that something is about to change. I feel it coming in the silence of my wetted breath. I feel it in my guts as I stumble back into my office.

My mouth is all tongue. Suddenly, the collar of my shirt is too tight. I wish I'd slipped the top button open beneath my tie before I started all this, but now it's too late, because Ursula is behind me.

She closes the door with a significant snicket.

'Mr Johns,' she says.

I turn.

She's just a tiny dot of a girl, bespectacled, with a choppy bob cut, all angles really. Still, there's something immoveable about her, an impression of flexibility and strength, like a Russian gymnast. 'Yes?' She raises one eyebrow over the top of her spectacles.

I can't speak.

A devious smile briefly tugs at her lips. 'Ah. Have you been naughty, Mr Johns?' she says. The words roll off her tongue as if it's the simplest of questions, as though she's asking, 'Would you like a cup of tea, now?' or 'Shall I put through this conference call?' But the answer isn't simple at all.

'Tell me.' She paces around me, and rests her pert little bottom carefully against the edge of my glass-topped desk. 'Were you touching yourself earlier, while you were looking at me?'

Dumbly, I find myself nodding. In that moment, I know that she knows the entire sorry truth. She knows that my frantic one-handed typing – I never could touch-type – is a ruse to disguise the rude satisfaction I'm taking as my hand works my cock inside my fly, while my eyes feast on the view of her in close-up, fed straight from the security feed to my computer screen.

'That's a bad thing to do, Barry.'

She's never used my first name before. I'm always Mr Johns, but the balance of power is slipping, shifting. I see it spiralling away from me, and all I can do is gape.

'I think I'd better see if this specimen is worthy of such lavish attention so early in the working day,' she says, in a stern no-nonsense sort of voice. 'The company doesn't pay us to take pleasure, Barry.'

There it is, the repetition of my name. Now, she's taunting me.

'You do realise that there are still three sales to be settled this morning and five staff reviews scheduled for after lunch.'

One of which is hers. The thought doesn't give me any strength. Instead, I stare straight ahead through the glass walls of my office into hers, thanking God for the small mercy of venetian blinds across her door. What's happening now is not something I want the entire work floor to see.

When she reaches inside my pants and scoops him out, he stands up and peeps at her, anything but shy. From the moment I stepped back into this room with her following, I've been boiling. The freedom and her gentle inspection are exquisite. I want more, but, perversely, I don't want to just thrust inside her body and come. What I'm feeling is more complicated than that, and less crude.

She strokes a bead of pre-come from the tip, and wipes it over my lips so that I can taste the desire I've already wept. I groan, and the noise seems to come from the pit of my stomach.

'I don't think you'll be able to concentrate like this, do you, Barry?'

'No.' I bite my lip, both fearful and full of hope.

'No, Miss Stevens,' she corrects. 'I think we'd better restrain him until the work's done. Keep him out of trouble so to speak.' She pats him as if she is affably jogging my shoulder after spouting some witticism.

Ursula's punchline is still to come.

I've paid it no accord until now, but the presence of a paper bag in her hands suddenly makes me tense. It's silly really. This sort of bag is ubiquitous in our department, where they are as likely to contain doughnuts as documentation.

'Close your eyes,' she demands.

I hear the soft crinkle of paper, the pop of bubble wrap. Her arms encircle my waist. Something cold encases my cock, drawing a whimper. It squeezes, in contrast to her touch, which is whisper light.

She tucks me neatly back inside my pants and zips me up.

'Open.'

I stare straight down at my smooth trouser front. All seems normal, but I can feel whatever it is tugging at my cock.

'That should be better.' She smiles, and there's a hint of danger in her hazy blue eyes. 'Anything else and you can buzz.'

For two full minutes after she returns to her office I do nothing but stare blankly at the door between us. I wonder if I've walked into someone else's daydream. Whether what just happened occurred entirely in my head, but when I move I can feel its presence, rings of cold steel and a casing of supple leather.

I sit at my desk and pull up figures onto the computer screen, but everything is a pixelated blur. I curse. This is not how office romances are supposed to work. We're supposed to get frisky on the desk or find a store cupboard in which to consolidate our passion. I'm supposed to throw her across my knee and spank her until her cheeks are cherry red.

She can't leave me to sweat like this.

It's no good, I have to see.

I run into the executive bathroom and lock myself in the single cubicle, where I peel down my trousers and underwear.

My grin stretches from ear to ear. As suspected, I'm locked down tight, the shaft encased in violet leather and bound by four steel hoops. A tiny padlock dangles from the fastening. It's the sort of lock I could pick with a paper clip in about two seconds, but that's the point. It's my escape route. If I'm not game, I just take it off and we never speak of this again. If I'm hers, I stay locked up and wait patiently for my reward at the end of the day.

The thought of that moment makes my cock swell. The leather grips me tight. I mustn't concentrate on her, or think of running my fingers through her hair, or of touching her throat, or her delicate bust. I must keep my thoughts neutral – pure.

I return to my desk, having dashed my face with water, and concentrate. It's a hard-won battle.

The hours until lunch drag on inexorably slow. Ursula feasts on feta cheese and olives on thick slices of tiger bread. My appetite is gone. I pick at a Mexican salad followed by a chocolate eclair.

During the afternoon interviews, I tick boxes, I smile as my stomach grumbles and I give out a sunshine warning or two.

Ursula's review comes at the end of the day. The rest of the staff are pulling on coats as she strides into my domain. Her records are arranged neatly between us. They say she likes yoga and Vietnamese stick fighting. She's worked here seven years having come straight from college with impressive grades. She's still young, too, this woman who has tied me into this hideous device of pain and torture.

'Is there a problem with my performance?' she asks, deliberately charming, and flashing a hint of her lovely smile.

I shake my head, but I can't meet her gaze.

'Barry.'

That jerks my head upright. 'Yes, Miss Stevens.'

She captures me with her wicked gaze. 'Is there a problem?'

Problem. Yes there's a problem, I want to rage. I'm the boss and you're undermining my authority. You're humiliating me.

Ursula drags her plain shirt up ever so slightly as she shifts position.

'I . . .' The words just won't come and, if they did, I know it would signify the end.

The end of what though – a relationship that's barely begun?

'Yes.' She looks straight at me, holding me in that wicked gaze. She's smiling again now. This is all an elaborate tease, and, boy, is she enjoying it. What employee wouldn't?

'Perhaps you'd like me to demonstrate some of my skills,' she says.

I know for a fact we're not talking about her typing speed.

'Yes,' I gulp. 'That would seem to be appropriate.' Although, it's not something I've demanded of any of the others. But Ursula is different. Ursula is definitely a special case.

She walks around the desk, perfectly calm, as if everything is entirely normal. I squeak when she kneels and turns my swivel chair so that her chin is level with my knees. If I, or anyone else, were to adopt this pose, it would be a pose of submission, but for Ursula it's a position of command. She draws one fingernail slowly up the inner seam of my trousers.

'I think you'd better take them off,' she says. 'We wouldn't want them getting crumpled or stained.'

He smells primarily of coffee and aftershave, although a hint of dry-cleaning fluid still clings to his trousers, which I insist he folds and lays crease free on top of his desk. I'm pleased to see he kicks off his socks and shoes along with his slacks, aesthetics are important and I like seeing men's feet. They're such fragile things compared to the rest of them. Even when they're whopping great size thirteens, like Barry's.

He settles again in the leather chair, his toned thighs wide spread either side of me. When I rest my hands lightly upon his knees, and both his thighs and his cock twitch in greeting, my heart does a little somersault too, though I hope I keep it hidden. For months, I've disguised how intensely I feel about this man, concealing my high colour beneath layers of carefully applied foundation and blush. I hardly dare meet his eyes now, for fear that he'll see just how big a fraud I am. All this no-nonsense secretary lark is an act born of desperation. The first day we spent together, I was so over-awed, I turned into a stilted, super-efficient zombie, but it got me through and kept me in a role that had previously seen a very high turnover of staff despite the swish private office and a nice compen-sation package. The whole office spoke of Mr Johns as some sort of demented demon, likely to kick you into the street for picking your nose on work time. I realised pretty quickly that it's just an act for him too. A way of playing with the big boys and getting some respect when he's almost half their age.

That doesn't change the fact that I'm out of my depth here. I'm not a dominatrix, just an ordinary secretary, and my knowledge and experience of these sorts of devices are virtually non-existent. I bought it online, thinking it pretty, never expecting to find a man to encase within its steel and leather grip. I never for a moment thought I'd be fastening it around my boss, though he looks beautiful, clasped within the rings. The sight of the tiny lock dangling from the fastenings fills my stomach with butterflies.

Mine, all mine.

I dangle the key from my fingertip. The knowledge that I can ask whatever I want of him makes me curiously light-headed, but, strangely, I can't think of a single demand. Actually, that's not entirely true, it's just that all my senses are attuned to him, and quite unconcerned by material gains. I long to see him naked. Will the rest of his body live up to the promise of his hard cock and solid thighs? They in themselves are an unanticipated surprise.

Barry tugs uneasily at his collar, clearly seeking to ease his sense of confinement as I look upon him, but I don't allow his discomfort to hurry me. I take my time, admiring the shape of his cock, the slight curve in the shaft and the deep magenta of the flared head. I've not seen that many. But Barry's is nice. As I lean closer and touch the springy tuft of dark curls at its base I catch the scent of him, a perfume not too dissimilar to that of my own: rich and gamey.

'Say "please",' I insist, and he groans. My tongue flicks out over my bottom lip, and I shuffle myself nearer to the tip of his cock. He's been so obedient. He really does deserve a treat.

'Please, Miss Stevens.' He begs so beautifully, eyes downcast, just peeping up at me occasionally to gauge my responses. 'Please take it off.' There's a hint of a growl alongside his plea that makes me want to laugh. It's the same grumble of disapproval he uses as a fearsome motivational tool amongst the workforce. He's so used to being in charge, to snapping orders and having people jump.

I don't jump. We're playing by my rules today, not his. Tantalisingly, I trace a finger along his cock from the base to the tip, subconsciously counting the five steel rings. It gives me time to master my own eagerness. 'I'm not sure that's such a good idea, Barry.' I hold the tiny padlock between my finger and thumb. 'You're very excited, and I don't want you losing control of yourself.' Really, I'm just too aware of how delicate the balance of power between us is. Without the restraints, our game is merely an ordinary torrid office affair, the sort that involves fucking upright, balanced against the photocopier, or sneakingly groping one another within the claustrophobic confines of the stationery cupboard. This is too good for that, and we both know it.

Barry's pulse shows in his temple as he sucks in a heavy breath. He lifts his hips slightly – wanting, straining.

'Well, if you're sure you've been good.'

'Yes,' he hisses.

I seek deceit in his eyes, but there is none. My mouth forms a wide O as I lean forwards, hands splayed across the tops of his broad thighs supporting my descent.

'Wait! Perhaps we should take a look at what you've been working on first.' I rise up a little and tap a few keys on his computer. The fuzzy black and white security feed bleeds onto the screen, showing a camera pointed at my empty desk.

'That's hardly being good, now is it?'

'I had you minimised,' he says with a wry shrug, which startles a peal of laughter from me.

Fingers concealing my mouth, I ask: 'Do you honestly think admitting to that is going to appease me?'

He sags a little at the shoulders in response. 'I'll take whatever punishment you think fit.'

'Oh, will you?' Much to his bewilderment, I unfasten the tiny padlock and remove the leather and steel restraint.

'You're not going?' he whispers, a trace of dejection woven around the words.

'Going? I'm going to suck you, Barry. But I expect you to show some self-control. I don't like guys coming in my mouth. If you manage to keep yourself in check, then I'll give you a reward. If not, our little game is over.' One tiny glimpse at the row of buttons on my starched white shirt is enough for him to start nodding. His sign of agreement fades, and his hands tighten on the arms of the chair as I once again tilt forwards as if to taste him.

'Take off your shirt and tie.'

At the last moment, I swerve away, provoking a groan of complaint. Still, Barry does as instructed with ego-stroking quickness. Unlike his trousers, his shirt is flung upon the floor. I tut at his sloppiness, but really I disregard the rumpled shirt, my interest already focused on his body. My jaw falls slack, shocked by how pleasing his physique turns out to be. Not even his glorious thighs prepared me for what I'm now staring at. Awed, I pass a hand across his naked chest. 'You've been hiding this well.'

Barry inclines his head. 'No one's ever asked to see it.'

Dear God, we're all fools in this office. I've lusted over this man for months and I never suspected he looked like this beneath his work-soiled shirt and dodgy end-of-line suit. I make him turn before me, so that I can see every beautiful line of his body. He has the sort of abs make-up artists paint onto models before a photo shoot, and the arse of a tennis supremo. His nipples are two pale pinpoints, only a tiny shade darker than the surrounding skin, while between them a light smattering of hair covers his chest. Below his navel the hairs thicken and mingle with the wiry curls that hug his groin. As I turn him before me, he seems so vulnerable despite his obvious masculine strength that I almost forget my role as stern mistress and crush him to my breast eager to offer comfort.

Luckily, Barry is not so lost in the moment. His full sensual lips part a fraction, and his breaths burst over me in slow faltering gasps. I touch him gently, tracing two fingers over the ridge of his hip, before finally touching his cock with just the tip of my tongue. His fists clench upon the chair arms as my fingers dance over the ridges of his shaft. The knuckles whiten when that delicate exploration reaches the fuzzy weight of his balls. With whiskey-coloured eyes he wordlessly begs, wanting and arching up off the chair to plead for more. In desperation, he bites his lip, and that's when I take him deep in my mouth.

Still, even as I suck him, I demand as much in return as I give. I dig my fingernails into the hard globes of his rear and enjoy the supple spring of flesh beneath my fingertips. Tomorrow, I don't doubt he'll have bruises.

Barry's fists continually clasp and unclasp, seeking purchase and support. Eventually, his hands settle upon my head, the fingers weaving a path through my hair while little mewling sobs break from his throat. The taste of him grows increasingly thick upon my tongue. With only a fraction more effort, I know I can make him come. That glimpse of power leaves me giddy. I've told him not to give in. This game of ours is not about quick satisfaction, leastways not his alone. Once I might have been satisfied to take a lesser role, but not now I've seen what's truly on offer. Now, I want every goddamn inch of him. I'm so turned on by the whole idea; I can smell myself as I rise. Slick and eager, I roll my hips so the lips of my pussy rub together bringing a welcome jolt of pleasure. I want to be with him, to meld our bodies into one. It seems a little vanilla, but hell, the idea of a frantic union dominates my thoughts and kicks my already steaming libido into overdrive. Sex, sex, sex, echoes like a mantra inside my head. I don't want to lead him around the office naked on a length of chain or whack his arse with a table-tennis bat. I want to take this wild stallion for a steamy gallop.

'Fuck me,' I mumble into his groin, knowing that as he plunges into me, this great dividing barrier between us will smash.

Sex is such a great leveller. It exposes us for what we are – animals. It's not so easy to hide behind a façade in the midst of passion, when every inch of your skin is on show. At the moment of orgasm, we howl and shout, and strain and cry, and for just a few seconds we let our bodies rule us, and all our barriers crumble. That's what I want from this man that I admire and whom I work with, this man that I love to tease and want to be truly permitted to love.

I release him from my mouth and his low groan is plaintive enough that I feel it as a dull ache in my bones.

One hand flat against his stomach, I push him deep into his ridiculously swish leather chair. It swivels slightly as he sags into his black embrace. His eyes shine with anticipation, their golden-whiskey hue growing increasingly bright as I rise from my knees. 'Fuck me,' I whisper again.

Inch by inch I raise my straight skirt, until the tops of my stockings show and then the black and red slash of my panties. They are so wet with my arousal a pattern has formed upon the scrap of silk.

As gracefully as I can, I step out of them.

Barry looks. He can't help himself. He stares at my neatly trimmed thatch and the glistening ruby lips of my pussy, and his already rapid breath catches in his throat. 'Oh God, please,' he whispers.

'There's no need to call upon the Almighty. A simple "Please, Miss Stevens" would do.'

'Please, Miss Stevens,' he parrots and the look in his eyes is pure hunger now. The CEO could walk in at this moment and I don't think Barry would blink. His gaze would stay fastened upon my cunt and we'd fuck regardless of the crowd.

I feel giddy and high as Ursula sits astride my lap. The perfume of her body floods the space between us, and I drink it down until I'm completely drunk. She holds my cock in her delicate grasp as she sinks down on me, until I'm right inside her, and it's all we can do not to just cling to each other and shake. But this slow killing softness doesn't suit the rage burning within either of us. I grab the desk and thrust against it, to send us spinning, the chair squeaking in protest. We rise and fall. I dizzily thrust until my vision is blurred and the lines separating us blend together. Stars crash through the heavens. Falling snow clouds the view of the city outside. I forget the rules and boundaries and suck greedily on Ursula's breasts, leaving transparent wet patches on her shirt, until I have the wits to hike it up and release her from the captivity of her bra's tight grip.

Her skin is smooth and soft. The faint trace of baby powder lingers on it. I thrust and buck and watch her climb, her mouth fallen open, eyes closed, head tilted back. And I want nothing more than to last until she's reached an orgasm, and to be inside her as she quivers and jerks and every last vestige of her normal icy calm demeanour falls away. I try to think of work, of shares and profit margins and consolidating stock, but nothing distracts me from Ursula's beauty. In the end, I leave everything up to fate and explore her body with lips and fingers, encouraging her pursuit of bliss.

'More,' she gasps as I delicately pat her clit. 'Don't stop.'

I don't stop. I rub her eager bud more quickly, slicking it with the salve of our arousal. She grips my shoulders hard, rides my fingers as well as my cock.

'Oh!' Her face crumples then relaxes as she exhales and I feel the pulse of her orgasm grip me. It tugs at my cock, and I lift my hips trying to buck into her but the position is too restricting. While she's still gazing at me in a bewildered post-orgasmic haze, I ease her off my lap. Upright, behind her, I bend her over the warmed leather of the chair and push into her from behind.

She looks so goddamned elegant.

I grip her hips tightly and fuck dementedly, so that my body won't let me slow, even when my orgasm rushes up way too fast. The sensation twists and writhes inside my body. It pricks at my skin and becomes concentrated in a streaming blaze of heat through my cock.

Release . . .

The office lights hum. The snow outside continues to dapple the window ledge.

Ursula coughs then breaks into a smile. 'Do I pass?' she asks, looking back at me over her shoulder. Her gaze flicks briefly to where her review lies forgotten on the desk. There was never any question of that, and I refuse to be drawn back to concepts of work and status. I hold her tight instead, and circle the skin at the base of her spine.

'Will you come to dinner with me?'

Something unexpected sparks with the depths of her eyes – surprise? Pleasure? I'm not really sure which. 'I'd love to,' she says, 'but I fear everywhere will turn us away dressed like this.' I'm butt naked, and her clothing is damp and creased. Not to mention that we both reek of sex, a scent nothing but a shower or a nice long soak will shift.

'I don't want a torrid affair,' I say.

'Of course,' she replies with an obedient little nod. She turns and perches in my big leather chair a moment, before fishing around under the desk for her panties. She doesn't believe me, or is now expecting a brush-off.

'I'm serious. I don't see why it should be a secret. I'm not interested in providing fodder for the gossips. We're adults after all.'

'Of course we are.' Her expression tells me she's decided I've had my fun and that it's business as usual again.

'Ursula, are you actually listening?'

She stares at me. 'Yes, Barry. You want us to be ... You want us to be an item?' Finally the penny drops.

'Yes.' And a serious item at that, not just some tedious fling. How could I want anything less from her?

'Well, it's rather sudden,' she says. 'Did we just skip a few steps?'

I laugh as I shake the creases from my shirt. 'Put your knickers on and I'll see if I can fill in a few of the gaps.'

I text the florist as we venture downstairs in the lift, and order a bouquet for tomorrow morning. Then I take her home, cook her dinner, and let her tie me up and lick dessert from me.

Madelynne Ellis is the author of the Black Lace novels *A Gentleman's Wager, Phantasmagoria, Dark Designs* and *Passion of Isis*. Her paranormal novella *Broken Angel* appears in the Black Lace collection *Possession*. Her short fiction has appeared in numerous Black Lace anthologies.

Gifted
Carrie Williams

My wedding – it seems so long ago now, a lifetime and more. An unforgettable day and night, a glittering, fairy-tale affair – a remote Scottish castle, an indigo dress in silk taffeta, a manly poet of a husband gazing at me raptly as he made his vows to please me, over and over, until the end of my days.

So now, little more than a year later, what was this terrible itch in me? What was it that had me wanting to run into the street, one hand at my pale throat, and scream at the top of my lungs? What was this sense of the walls closing in on me, until the room itself was crushing me, squeezing all the air from my body, leaving me a lifeless doll on the bed?

My husband, as a bard, a sensitive man, tried hard to understand, and to help me. We travelled, near and far, in an attempt to scratch that itch. In Morocco, in the Dades Valley, we took a *grand taxi* to the Rose Festival, where he anointed me, head to toe and every part in-between, with sumptuous, sweet-scented oils crushed from the pink petals of local blooms. In Venice, we came together as if strangers at a candlelit ball, camouflaged by our ornate headdresses. And when we'd danced each other into a frenzy, rubbing our bodies together, he chased me through the labyrinthine streets and fucked me, hard, still anonymous behind the ghostly porcelain white of his mask, on a deserted bridge beneath the light of the moon, the canal rippling beneath us like a silver ribbon in the breeze, the mist shrouding us from the eyes of passers-by. Back at our hotel, in the light of dawn, I watched as the glitter that had swirled my cheeks and the geisha-gold powder on my lips rubbed onto the sheer white linen of the pillow as he drove himself inside me, insatiable, never getting his fill of me.

But it was never enough, not for me. Wherever we went, we were still us, him and me, face to face, engaged in the daily round. It was claustrophobic. I wanted, needed, more. And my poet of a husband with his big soul understood that, and he didn't leave me but said he would lead me into places new and undreamed of.

And so we find ourselves in Vienna, in a velvet-curtained box, having dined on oysters, sweetbreads and other costly things. Around us rise tier upon tier of gilded opera boxes, below us stretches the gleaming wood of the dance floor, polished to perfection. Lights and chandeliers twinkle, flowers overflow their opulent vases, sending out intoxicating aromas, and glasses tinkle as toasts are raised and champagne is poured into countless throats. It's like being inside a giant chocolate box, with the same sense of a slightly cloying sweetness. I feel drunk, though I've only had one glassful. I want to stay sober. I know this will be an unforgettable night.

Greer is holding my hand and, as the Austrian national anthem strikes up, his grip on me tightens. I still don't know exactly why we are here, at the city's famous Opera Ball, but I know what is at stake for my husband. By loosening the leash of our marriage, by acceding to my appetites, he hopes to save us. But there's the danger that I could slip the lead entirely, like a dog making free from a too-indulgent master.

I lean forwards as, beneath our balcony, a shimmering string of girls, dressed all in white like ice queens, unfurls into the ballroom to the strains – so I read in the programme – of Karl Ziehrer's 'Fächer-Polonaise'. Accompanying them, contrasting with them in their immaculate black suits, are the boys. But it's the girls who capture my attention: like the winter streets outside the Staatsoper, they glitter so very brightly, sequins glinting like the pure snowflakes through which we strolled here from our hotel. My throat becomes dry; I allow myself another sip of champagne. Be careful, I say to myself. Be very careful.

I look at my husband and, although I know he knows that my

eyes are on him, he keeps his own directed at the goings-on down on the ballroom floor. He knows how to wait, my husband. He knows how to be patient. He's brought me here, but he won't lead me, knows that there's no taming a free spirit like me. He can steer me, but ultimately I'm beyond his control.

The debutantes peel off to the sides of the room, making space for ballerinas from the State Opera Ballet, who begin to pirouette for all they're worth, stretching their pliant young bodies, making dazzling and audacious flights across the room. But they can't hold my attention: leaning forwards, my opera glasses to my eyes, I'm watching, very intently, one of the debs. I'm not sure, yet, why this one has snagged my attention, what memories or fantasies she may stir in me, but I'm determined to find out.

The girl in question has let go of her partner's hand, has brought her hand to one hip. With the fingers of her other she is fiddling with her silver necklace. Her hips, which are quite full, jut out to one side, giving her a slight slump. My eyes rise to her face, and I see that while many of the other debs have a kind of perfect, classical beauty – all rosebud lips and pink cheeks, all manes of pale-blonde hair flowing over ivory shoulders – hers is more edgy, more interesting. There's an exotic, perhaps Asian, allure to her.

With her insouciant posture and her slightly bored, maybe even rebellious, expression, she looks like she'd rather be outside having a cigarette, flirting with the waiters. Or up here, in a box, playing footsie with a gorgeous Scottish poet as she downs a glass of champagne, and then another.

Glancing back to reach for my own glass, suddenly thirsting for just a few moments' reprieve from sobriety, I catch my husband's eye. He's looking at me, and suddenly I know that he's been watching me as I've been watching the deb, studying me. He knows, almost before I know it before myself, what is going on in my head.

Greer and I have never had any secrets from each other: that was part of the 'deal'. I say deal because, from the very outset, Greer was clear that he was taking me on not only as a lover and a wife, but as his muse. He knew about my life, my adventures, and far from being jealous of my past he was aroused by it. But his interest was far from prurient. He didn't even want to hear about it: for him, my past, my pleasures, were inscribed in my flesh and in the ways I loved him. I was a living poem to him, and a constant source of inspiration. For that gift he was prepared, I now understood, to give me my freedom. More than that – to facilitate it.

Crystal clear, sharp and pure as stalactites, the notes of an aria ring out, startling me out of my contemplation. Tearing my eyes away from Greer's probing gaze, I look down. The ballerinas are exiting in a blur of rustling tutus, and the debs are taking over the dance floor again, together with their partners. The cold notes of the aria give way to the rich warm tones of violins and brass playing Strauss' 'The Blue Danube', and the couples begin to waltz. They do so faultlessly, with great assurance, and I remember the concierge at our hotel explaining how candidates had been selected by a committee and had to pass an audition before being granted a place. Many came from the upper echelons of Viennese society; a handful were from farther afield.

I seek out the girl who caught my eye. With her ebony hair, her dusky skin, her eyes the colour and shape of almonds, she stands out. She might even, I think, scrutinising her with my opera glasses, be part Indian.

I train my glasses on her partner. He's the antithesis of her: with russet-tinged blond hair, fair skin and pale-blue eyes, there's something almost Aryan to him. He oozes the money, prestige and confidence of the Viennese aristocracy, and I find him utterly unsexy. I try to imagine him fucking the girl and I can't. I know that that might be plain jealousy, this refusal to countenance the idea of her in his arms, in his bed. But to me they don't seem a natural couple. Perhaps, as a foreigner, she had to be matched up with a dance partner?

The couples swirl on, dizzying me. I can't take my eyes off the girl, even as I know that my husband's eyes are fixed on me, expectant. He's waiting for me to make a move, but I don't know what is expected of me, what is even possible. I feel out of my depth. My freedom is suddenly a burden. The girl sweeps by, again and again, her flesh glowing and lambent above the low, scooped back of her ballgown, where her hair is pulled up into a loose chignon that seems to bespeak that casual disregard for convention I thought I glimpsed earlier in her stance.

I stand up.

'Are you OK?' says Greer, frowning, reaching for my hand, a steadying presence amidst all the whirling, the lights, the overpowering scent of the lilies that were placed in our box.

'I'm fine. I just . . . I'm just going to the toilet,' I manage, then I turn abruptly, open the door and lurch along the corridor, stopping every so often to stabilise myself against a wall. The corridors are deserted – weirdly, eerily so after the bustling crowds who were surging through them when Greer and I arrived earlier this evening. Yet strangely, here alone, I feel more hemmed in and on the verge of panic than I had then. As Greer has often pointed out, my self-diagnosed claustrophobia seems to be more about me, about me being thrown in on myself, than about being in a confined space. On the contrary, I seem to thrive when there are other people around.

For a while I think I'm going to be sick, that I'm not going to make it to the bathroom and that I'm going to disgrace myself all over the plush carpets of the Staatsoper. But when I do get there, panting, sweat prickling my skin beneath the sheath of my long gown, I recover myself. For a few moments I just stand gazing at my reflection in the mirror, and it's almost as if I'm seeing myself for the first time. My deep-auburn hair, my green eyes, my freckled shoulders, bared. I'm a beautiful woman – how else did I snare one of the world's most desirable and talented literary figures? Then why isn't that enough?

Turning my back to the mirror, leaning back against the cold heavy marble of the washbasins, I hitch up my dress and, after slipping the tip of one finger into my mouth, bring my hand between my legs, slide it beneath the flimsy fabric of my knickers and touch myself. My lips are wet, sticky with my juices, my clit hard and questing. I let out a moan, my eyes flickering towards the door. It seems so unlikely that I will be disturbed, when everyone's attention is directed at the grand opening ceremony, yet I'm not sure I can risk it. The humiliation at being caught pleasuring myself by one of these well-to-do, smug, bourgeois ladies would be immense.

But even as I think this, I can't help myself. I part my legs further, using one hand to gain purchase on the smooth marble as I lean back against it, and rub furiously at my clit, annoyed at myself now. Finding it hard to get the momentum I need to scratch this inconvenient itch, I take my hand away for a moment, to use both hands to inch me up to a sitting position on the basin edge. Then I tend to myself again, this time using the fingers of one hand on my clit and inserting two, three fingers of the other into my sodden core. Head thrown back, I climax almost immediately, unable to stifle my cries.

When I come out, Greer is standing in the corridor, leaning in a rather louche way against the wall, hands in his pockets, a cigarette wedged in one corner of his mouth. He's given up, and anyway smoking inside the opera house is certainly *verboten*. But he likes the pose of it. It suits his Byronic looks, his poetic swagger.

I sidle up to him and he smiles. Even before I bring my fingers to his nostrils he knows what I've been doing in there. He inhales deeply, closing his eyes as my honey-scented juices surround him with their aroma. Then he opens them and, removing his cigarette, takes my fingers in his mouth and suckles at them, as avid as a newborn babe for its mother's milk. For a moment we just stand there, and time seems to stand still. Then the doors to tens of opera boxes the entire length of the corridor begin to open, spilling their occupants out, and we understand that it's time to descend and join the dancers on the floor. A cry of 'Alles Walzer!' confirms this.

Down the grand staircase we go and, as we emerge onto the dance floor, Greer's hand in the small of my back, reassuring me, I think of how our bodies know each other so well by now. Night after night of discoveries, in a journey that seems, in many ways, as if it must be never-ending. There is such a deep eroticism to this that I can't imagine ever being through with Greer, as I have been with so many people in the past. Lust was always a fire in me, but a violent fire that built up quickly and burned hard before dying right down, as all fires must. Is it possible that Greer has found the secret, a way of fanning the flames in perpetuity?

He holds me to him, hand still on my lower back, and for a brief interlude our torsos are crushed up against each other. My nipples are erect at his chest, and in turn I feel the pulse of his dick as it hardens against me. But the Viennese waltz is faster than I remembered, and before long our bodies are moving more freely as we become reacquainted with the figures we both learned in the past – the change steps, the hesitations and hovers, the *fleckerls* with contra checks. Constantly circling, I begin to feel dizzy again quite quickly and am glad I've gone easy on the champagne.

As we turn, the faces of the people watching flash by me. At first they're mere blurs, but as I begin to slow us down, they come into better focus, and I see how they're lightly filmed with sweat, nakedly lustful, as they in turn regard the dancers. The debs are clearly still the main focus of interest, flitting gorgeously around the floor like feathery plume moths, their white dresses as well as their dancing prowess making them stand out from the crowds.

Increasingly giddy, I begin to try to steer Greer away from the centre of the dance floor, through the 'fast lane' of dancers moving rapidly and smoothly counter-clockwise around the outside edges and corners of the room. And that's when I see her, or rather her back – that patch of flawless naked skin, burnished-looking beneath the warm lighting and in contrast with the creamy flesh of most of the other dancers. She's within arm's reach, it seems – her back is almost touching Greer's back – and it's all I can do to stop myself reaching out to touch one peachy, downy shoulder, as if I'm being lured by a particularly ripe and succulent fruit.

Greer must see it in my face, in the way my eyes brighten and my pupils dilate, in the way my lips part slightly as my breath grows more laboured and excitement quickens my pulse. Confirming what he already knows, he glances over his shoulder, then he looks back at my face, and his smile is the tender smile of a father acceding to the wishes of a demanding but much-loved daughter. He can see, I think, into my very soul.

'Let's get a drink,' he says, and although I feel a pang at being led away from the girl now I've come so close to her, I know that Greer, as ever, is thinking of me, has my best interests at heart. And so I nod and let him lead me to the *Seitenbühne*, the 'side stages', where, amidst a theatrical decor of wall frescos, heavy velvet curtains and intimate lighting, people are gathered in conspiratorial little groups, laughing and drinking and biting daintily into little canapés with the ultra-white teeth of the ultra rich.

For a moment, as we wait for a drink, I feel lost. This is not our town, we don't know anybody here: what are we doing so far from home? What is this quest we're on, and where will it take us? And then, as Greer passes me a glass and I bring it to my lips, a smile flashes in his eyes and I know before I've even seen her that the girl is standing by my side.

I turn my head to her, wondering how Greer conveyed to her the invitation to join us. Did he somehow find the occasion to speak to her or pass her a note, without my seeing, or did she merely read it in his eyes, in some gesture that he made on the dance floor, unseen, or undeciphered, by anyone else? Or did she come unbidden, having felt my gaze on her skin, scalding her with its intensity.

It matters little: she's here now and, as I pass her my champagne and she takes a hefty swig, our eyes lock and my heart flutters wildly like a bird forced into a cage.

She doesn't tell us where her partner is now, but it becomes clear that they didn't come together. She has flown from Bombay especially for the event, she tells us in honeyed tones that match the burnt-sugar colour of her skin. Her mother was a Bollywood actress, her father an Austrian count, and she spent her early teens at a boarding school near Salzburg, where she dreamed of one day being a debutante at the Opera Ball. She doesn't tell us her age, but I know that the dancers have to be between seventeen and twenty-four, and guess her to be about twenty-one. A good decade younger than my husband and me.

Greer says nothing as she speaks, and for a moment it's as if he isn't there at all, as if there is just Farah – as she introduces herself – and me in the room, away from the chattering masses. Time seems to have frozen around us, and for a while we are the only people who exist, suspended in the shiny bubble of our mutual admiration.

'I noticed you,' says Farah and, as our bodies edge closer, Greer absents himself, gesturing towards the bar.

'Yes, on the dance floor,' I reply, drinking her in with my eyes.

'In your box,' she says, mischief flitting around her awesome features. 'You were watching me.'

As she speaks she reaches out, and her slim fingers encircle my wrist, the most welcome of shackles, light but firm, as if brooking no resistance. There's no resistance on my part anyway: I am more than happy to let her lead me away through an arched doorway into another, smaller room with an equally ornate decor. Here, among lush palm trees and carved stone pillars, we lose ourselves, finding sanctuary in the swags of a curtain that tumbles from ceiling to floor. Pulling it back, Farah invites me inside and then lets it fall back over us, creating a little world of our own.

The dense velvet masks any sounds from outside, and for a moment, as we hesitate, suddenly shy, the sounds of our breathing come harsh and fast. Then, taking the initiative, Farah places a hand on one of my bare shoulders and brings her mouth to the other. I swoon back. My shoulders are my true erogenous zone, and the feel of her lips on me makes me wonder if I might faint. I close my eyes, surrender to her. With her silken palm still clad in its elbow-length glove, she massages my shoulder, gradually bringing her hand around the back of my neck, until I understand that she is pulling me into her. I shift my head around and take her ear lobe, a small fleshy titbit, in my mouth, and suck at it before nipping it gently. She pulls me still closer in response, and I feel the crush of her breasts on mine. My cunt burns for her.

She knows that, and she reaches down, gathering the hem of my evening gown and pulling and then folding it up to my waist. Sinking to her knees, she tugs at the lace of my knickers, bringing the front of them down until she has revealed the hard pink bead of my clitoris as it protrudes from the slender wisp of my Brazilian. I arch back in sweet torture as she takes my clit between her lips and then her teeth, repeating the playful nips that I gave her ear lobe. With one hand I clutch at the curtain, fearing that I will go out of my mind.

She continues working at me with her mouth, sucking and nibbling at my clit, then threading her nimble tongue through my lips, teasing at my hole before retreating and starting all over again. I thrust my pussy to her mouth, wanting more, ever more, desperate to have her inside me. She takes her mouth away, looks up at me, and in the scant light behind the curtain I see that her mouth and jaw are slick with my liqueur.

She starts pulling me down, until we are both on the floor, and suddenly she has slipped off one glove and balled up her hand and is fisting me, her face in mine, and tears are coursing down my cheeks as I feel myself losing it. For a moment I think of Greer and a stab of guilt goes through me. But then I reassure myself: he's nearby, I know it – perhaps just the other side of the curtain. Greer wanted this for me as much as I wanted it for myself. There is nothing to feel bad about. My pleasure is Greer's pleasure.

Farah extracts her hand, but it is only to bring her mouth to me now. Crouching over me, eyes gleaming darkly, she slips her tongue inside and with her fingers begins to massage the hot swollen bulb of my clit. Within my pussy it feels as if I am blooming, opening up like a flower, and I lay my head back against the stone floor, oblivious to its roughness as I writhe beneath Farah. Heedless of the scores of people who lie behind the curtain, I surrender myself to a crashing wave of an orgasm, which has me biting the back of my hand.

Once we've straightened our gowns and steadied our breathing, we step out, one by one, from the curtain. Greer is standing nearby, leaning against the wall, one ankle crossed over the other – he's lost the cigarette, but there's that loucheness to him that I love. Though his long wavy locks are caught back in a tidy ponytail, there's still a wildness to him, something of the moors from which he hails and where he feels most at home; where many of his poems come to him – the ones that are about nature and not about me. I'm more used to seeing him in a chunky Aran sweater, jeans and wellington boots than in tails. In both, though, he is a splendid creature – honed and handsome, elemental, sex on a stick.

He watches us emerge, a wry smile flitting about his lips – he is envious, I know. Perhaps no real gift comes about without a little self-sacrifice. I step towards him and he hands me a glass of champagne, then raises his own in a toast. I turn my head. Farah is walking away. I wonder if her partner is looking for her, if he fancies his chances. *Don't go*, I want to shout, but the words get stuck in my throat. It has been beautiful, but perhaps it's over already. She has played her role and now it's just Greer and me, back in our own private universe. He has granted me my taste of forbidden fruit and now real life is to resume.

'Shall we have one last dance?' he says, as if sensing my mood slump, like the champagne growing flat in the glasses in our hands.

I shake my head. 'Let's go,' I say, struggling to keep my dejection from my voice.

We leave the Opera House and walk back through the cobbled streets of Spittelberg, frosted with snow like icing sugar. We stop for a glass of hot spiced wine, talk of this and that but not of Farah. There is nothing, it seems, to say about her. Nothing to say but thanks, and I'm not sure that I need to articulate that. Greer knows how grateful I am.

It's the small hours when we get back to the Hotel Sacher, where our beautiful suite is strewn with the evidence of our other life, our real life – discarded clothes on the floor, where we made hasty love before getting dressed up to go to the ball, magazines left opened where I was flicking through them, make-up and toiletries scattered around.

'I'll run you a bath,' says Greer, and I listen as he strides across the bathroom and opens the taps. He's good to me, I tell myself. So why this constant yearning in me for more, like a flower constantly turning to face the light, never able to rest? I had a wild youth, for sure, but I've hardly settled for Greer – he is more than I could ever have dreamed of. When we got together, I scarcely dared hope it would last. When he asked me to marry him and be his lifelong muse, I wept with joy and with fear too, wondering if I was worthy, afraid that he would find me out.

I undress, slithering out of my scarlet robe, and it's as if I'm stepping out of a dream. I walk towards the bathroom and into a cloud of billowing steam scented with costly oils – ylang-ylang, sandalwood and rose absolute.

Greer appears in the doorway, places one hand on my hip and leans in to kiss me on the neck. 'A drink?' he says.

'A hot chocolate would be good,' I say. The hotel is famous for its chocolate, or its chocolate tart at least. I'm worried that I may not sleep if I don't wind down. Worried that thoughts of Farah might keep me tossing and turning until dawn.

I soak for an hour, reliving the ball in my mind. We have come so far, spent so much money: was it worth it? Am I destined to live the life of a tourist, to forever wander the globe in search of experiences that will take me away from what I fear the most – the everyday and its banality? Have I not learned by now, I think as I sip the hot chocolate that Greer brings in to me and places on the rim of the tub, that you can never escape the everyday and the banal, that it is waiting for you behind every exotic experience? Why can I not reconcile myself to living in the ordinary world?

Swaddled in my bathrobe, I lie down on the bed. Greer, also changed into his robe, is at the wooden bureau, pencil in hand, brow furrowed in concentration. A poem has come to him, or the beginnings of a poem. He, too, risks not sleeping tonight. And then we have to check out by noon and get to the airport. We'll arrive home exhausted, demoralised. This trip has brought us nothing, nothing beyond a few moments of pleasure for me, and perhaps a vicarious thrill for him.

I close my eyes, see Farah's lovely face again, and then I begin to doze off in the low lamplight, comforted by Greer's companionship, the way he wants nothing of me, beyond my presence in his life. Opening my eyes from time to time, I feel reassured by the solidity of his presence. He's my safety net, I think. Only that makes him sound boring, when he's not. Greer is far from boring. But knowing that he won't leave me makes me brave, gives me the permission to be myself. How many people can say that of their marriage?

When I wake, dawn light is seeping into the room. Greer is no longer at his desk, nor is he in bed beside me, and the bathroom light is off. I sit up, panic-stricken. Did I take him for granted after all? I find myself wondering for the first time. Has he suddenly realised what it means to be with a woman who can never be satisfied? Has he decided to seek out somebody who will devote herself to him entirely? Perhaps I have failed as a muse, now he has seen me in my true colours, now he has seen the things of which I am capable, the baseness of my appetites.

I swing my legs over the side of the bed, and rise. And now I notice a faint light emanating from the sitting room of our suite, the room we haven't even used, since our bedroom is so vast. I cross the bedroom and stand in the doorway, my bathrobe swinging loose, hair tumbling about my shoulders. There's a double chaise-longue in here, almost queen-bed size, in gold damask with claw legs. On it I see Greer, his own hair free now, rippling like dark water over this shoulders. His hands are on the arm of the chaise, and his body is moving backwards and forwards, in a slow jacking movement. I bring my hand to my pussy, instinctively, aroused without really understanding why.

I move closer, feeling as if I'm in some kind of trance. Beside the chaise I see a fake fur, cast off, like some animal huddled up ready for hibernation. Beside it is a pair of pearly elbow-length gloves, tossed haphazardly to the ground. I look at the bodies on the chaise and a physical shock runs through me when realise that there's a tangle of them: not two, but three. Limbs protrude in every direction, so that it's difficult to tell who's who, where one begins and another one ends. It takes me a few minutes to work out the configuration.

Greer, as I knew it, is on top. He's thrusting his dick into the mouth of another man, whose face I dimly recognise. It's someone, I realise, from the ball – not Farah's partner, but one of the men who stood watching as we danced, face lit up, aglow with lustful thoughts. Farah must have picked him up afterwards, after we'd gone. I'd mentioned our hotel to her, so she must have brought him here with her, as frustrated as I was by the brevity of our encounter.

Farah herself is kneeling at the end of the chaise-longue, her hair drizzling over her fine-boned face where her chignon has come down. Her mouth is wrapped around the other man's dick even as he has a faceful of Greer's, but when I look down she swivels her eyes up to me and there's a smile in them, an invitation. I step behind her, slide to my knees and push up her white dress, now stained and rumpled at the hem. Her buttocks are full and pulpy, cinnamon brown. I take a handful of each and ease them apart, then with my fingers slide the thong of her knickers from her crack to reveal her taut sphincter and the glistening slit of her pussy. Admiring it for a moment, I bring my face to her and, inhaling her musky scent, plunge my tongue inside her wet slot, repaying the compliment that she paid me earlier. Immediately she begins writhing and moaning through her mouthful of cock, and I grip her buttocks tighter as I feel myself start to lose it.

After a minute the men stop moving, with Greer on top turning to find out what we are doing. When he sees my face, my mouth on Farah's pussy, my tongue flickering inside her like a flame, he smiles, winks at me. I wink back at him, wondering if he is as surprised by this turn of events as I am, or whether he in fact engineered it. Did he, by some means, invite her and her friend to join us?

He stands up, comes round the back of me where I'm kneeling at the end of the chaise-longue and, his prick all nice and lubed by the other man's saliva, goes down on his knees between my legs in turn, pushes my lower back forwards with an authoritative palm and plunges himself into me without foreplay. The brutality of it sends me wild. Then I feel his arm wrap itself round my waist, and with one hand he starts strumming at my clit. I let myself be carried away by the discordant sensations – the violence of the thrusting versus the delicate butterfly strokes at my clit.

Extricating herself slowly from me, Farah crawls forwards, and I look up in time to see her straddle the man, who is still prone on the chaise-longue. From where I'm situated I can see her juicy cunt as it slides up and down the thick hard pole of him. It gets me so hot and horny I can't stop myself, and I fling back my head and let out a wail as my clit catches fire and my inner walls start contracting and relaxing around Greer's beautiful cock, over and over, so strongly it could almost be pain. As if he wants to take me to my absolute limits, Greer slides two fingers into my sphincter, and my climax has a terrible ferocity, my hands still gripping Farah's ankles, eyes trained on her own gorgeous cunt as it coats the man's proud cock.

Orgasms being contagious, Farah and Greer start coming too, their cries ringing out as my climax finally dies away, leaving me panting and in disarray. Their rapture, in turn, brings the other man to his threshold, and after a moment of palpable resistance he steps over it and I watch his fingers dig into the luscious brown flesh of Farah's upper back, that patch of her that first caught my eye back in the Opera House – a time that is so recent but already seems like a dream, fleeting, otherworldly, ungraspable.

Though afterwards, when we have recovered ourselves, Greer invites them to stay for a glass of champagne, Farah and the man are keen to get going, back to their own real lives, whatever they may be. Standing at the door in my bathrobe, watching them head for the lift and then disappear, I wonder, briefly, what the future holds for them. Then I turn back into the room and at look my poet of a husband, and I wonder what the future holds for us.

Stretched out on the chaise-longue, Greer is naked and as magnificent as a lion basking in the sun. It strikes me that, after all that he's given me, he remains the greatest gift of all. I walk towards him, the numbness leaving my post-orgasmic pussy, excitement fizzing through me like bubbles in champagne, happy that we're alone together again.

Carrie Williams is the author of the Black Lace novels *The Blue Guide*, *Chilli Heat* and *The Apprentice*. She has also contributed to numerous Black Lace short story collections writing as Candy Wong and Carrie Williams.

The Fantasy

Jamaica Layne

There is an object to my affection.

I sit in the front row of his lecture hall, making a point to stretch my legs out in front of me so the tips of my toes come within mere inches of his. I stare at him, transfixed, my eyes melting deep into his dark-blue pools, my ears trained upon the sound of his voice as he lectures on and on. Not on the actual content of his lectures, mind you – I've never taken a single note, and I'm sure I'm destined to fail his course as a result – but on the timbre and vibration of his voice itself, the sheer musical quality to it. If his voice were an instrument, it would be an oboe.

I desire him as I have desired no other. But alas, he is never to be mine. He is my professor, I am his student. He is married, and not to me. He is twenty years my senior. He is the eldest son of an old landed family from Cornwall, and an Oxford graduate. I am the only daughter of an electrician from a housing estate in East London, and a student here at the third-rate university where he teaches part-time out of pity for the lower classes. Our destinies are never to be intertwined, at least not in this life.

But I have other lives. Lives which I create for myself. And in those lives, he is mine, all mine, always.

There is an object to my affection. And he lives here, with me, in my own secret world.

In my real life, I don't know Professor Coventry's first name. But in my own private world, his name is Joseph. It is a simple name, yet a powerful one, ancient and biblical. It is my chosen name for my secret fantasy lover, the lover that I explicitly and exquisitely control. He is mine, and none other.

I have many fantasies in which Joseph Coventry is the star. If I were a Hollywood screenwriter creating a sex series for HBO, I would have a lucrative contract.

But my favourite fantasy is also the simplest, the most elegant.

He arrives at my dorm room late at night, wearing a cutaway and tails and a white satin cravat, carrying a bouquet of long-stemmed red roses. He's taken one of the roses and trimmed it short, then plucked it into his buttonhole as a boutonnière. His formal tuxedo shoes are polished to an otherworldly shine, and his body smells of starch and fresh powder.

He arrives at my pockmarked dorm-room door unannounced. He explains to my bewildered face that he was on his way to a formal dinner party at his family's estate, but decided at the last minute he'd much rather spend the evening here, with me, in my dorm room.

Ludicrous, of course. But it's the preposterous nature of my secret world that makes it so exciting, so tantalising, so real.

He comes into my room, shuts the battered Formica door behind him. The cheap lock clicks into its slot. He hands me the roses. I smell them – they are delicious – and find an empty plastic cup to put them in, the kind university students get for free at parties, the kind with a beer company logo screenprinted on its side. The juxta-position of his glamour and elegance with my cheapness and commonness is an aphrodisiac – for both of us. We are both step-ping into forbidden worlds together. He is slumming with the salt of the earth, and I am cavorting with the nobility. The high-born teacher will soon fuck the low-born student, and we care nothing for the consequences. We are both turned on by touching the very flesh that the world has forbidden us.

And so we touch. Timidly at first, but soon we grow bolder. We start by joining fingertip to fingertip, then sliding whole fingers into each other, building a web of hands. We stay locked that way – simply – for a moment, then open the lock in pursuit of higher planes. He takes each of my wrists into his hands, caresses the back of each of them with the tip of his index finger. He traces the lacy pattern of the blue veins just underneath the skin, gently presses on the dark-grey scar I got when a piece of pencil lead got stuck under my skin when I was but a wee girl in kindergarten. He keeps his fingertip pressing there for a moment, touching my past, bringing the child that I once was into the present.

He squeezes first one forearm into his fist, then the other, then he passes his fists up and down the narrow poles that are my arms, pushing up the sleeves of my sweatshirt. He runs feathery touches up and down the translucent pale skin on the insides of my elbows, sending shivers up and down my spine, which land between my legs. I am shaking now, trembling in the presence of a higher being than myself. Joseph is not only taller, and older, and from a higher social order than I am, he also has an wiser, more sensual soul. He knows how to touch my body in ways that are otherworldly, ways that remind me that I am but a mere mortal, while he has lived longer than for ever.

'Joseph,' I moan as he touches me, speaking aloud the name I have given him for the first time. My cries and sounds press him further, lead him to tug the tattered sweatshirt I've had for years over my head. I am braless underneath, and my breasts hang loose, frothy and pale, seeking his touch.

There is an object to my affection. And now, he is here with me, beside me, against me – and soon to be inside me.

I stand before him, my chest heaving, my bare breasts glorious. Of my own accord I step out of the ratty tracksuit bottoms I wear around the dorm room, revealing the light cotton knickers I'm wearing. The knickers are decorated with paw prints and a portrait of the Garfield cartoon character cat rests on top of my furred mons. They're my favourite and most comfortable set of knickers – I got them as a Christmas present when I was sixteen, which makes them almost five years old and very well worn. Joseph doesn't seem to mind this one bit. If anything, my trashy teenager's knickers, scented as they are with five years' worth of my pussy juice that's become embedded into the microscopic bits of cotton fibre, turn him on like nothing else could.

Joseph practically drools at the sight of my knickers. He falls to his knees, buries his face in my cotton-covered mons, inhaling my scent as if I am a bed of exotic orchids in an aristocrat's hothouse. I smell myself in the recycled air – it is an earthy scent of sweat, baby powder, washed cotton, salt, and pussy.

Joseph slides two fingers underneath the elastic cuffs of my knickers, one on each side. Slowly he pulls them down, making the gesture into a slow, steady waltz. The elastic catches on the razor stubble of my unshaved legs. Joseph keeps pulling, pulling, pulling, until the knickers pool at my ankles. I make two tiny steps, like a ballerina, and at last my body is totally free, naked as the day I was born.

Joseph, however, remains fully clothed in his cutaway and tails. This excites and thrills me, the knowledge that every pore of my skin is uncovered and open to the air, to the feel of his breath, his touch, while his remains encased in expensive, well-tailored silk and gabardine. He doesn't touch me yet though. Instead he picks up the wilted knickers that lie at my feet, and brings the gusset up to his mouth. He slides his tongue up and down the damp, wash-worn fabric, savouring my salty, musky taste like the rarest of exotic truffles. He inhales my scent deeply, even chews on a bit of the frayed elastic. Then in a move that shocks me, he unbuttons the fly of his tuxedo trousers, pulls out his erect cock, and begins to mastur-bate with my knickers. I watch, transfixed, in complete awe of his transformation from upper-crust impeccability to primal animal nature.

An English nobleman university professor is jerking off with my undies. It's the most erotic thing I've ever seen – in real life or in my mind's eye. And in doing so, Joseph takes possession of me first by proxy. He is fucking me already, even without laying a hand upon my naked body.

Joseph stops manhandling my knickers just shy of a tuxedoed orgasm, casts my now damper-than-damp undies into a heap on the floor. He reaches out to me, each hand gripping a milky white globe and squeezing. He presses into the deep tissue of each breast, then passes a thumb back and forth across each areola. My nipples stand at attention, the pale skin around them already taking on the trademark sex flush. I become hot to the touch underneath his fingers, my breasts twin hot plates, his hands two matching kettles, both about to boil.

He presses me down to the floor. My hips arch up when they contact the cold linoleum; he takes it as his cue to spread me wide. He plunges into my depths, still fully clothed except for his erect, aristocratic member. We fuck that way – me naked and he dressed to meet the Queen – for what seems like hours. Joseph's cock is big, thick – an earthy, low-class contrast to all the starch and pomp and gabardine that usually surrounds him. Sex, after all, is the great equaliser. Whether you're born in the East End or Chelsea, your shagging machinery is the same.

He thrusts into me hard, pressing into my womb with each heave. My belly quivers from within, slowly at first, then rapidly. Joseph just pounds and pounds at me, his body straining as he reaches for his climax, which for some reason just won't come. I decide that I must help him.

I tighten up my sheath so hard my body threatens to expel him completely. With each thrust he makes, I tighten and release, tighten and release, until I hear him groan and grunt and moan in time with my ministrations. Still his climax remains out of reach. I open my eyes, look at the pained expression on his patrician face, the misery he feels as his body tastes pleasure, but cannot find solace.

I must take matters into my own hands. Or rather, my own mouth.

Slowly, gently, I press my palms into Joseph's chest, pushing him away until our bodies separate. He gives a little moan of disappointment, but he will not be disappointed for long. For I am about to give him the blow job of the century, East London-style.

I lean forwards, gaze upon his thick cock, slick and shiny with my pussy juice. I take the whole thing into my mouth at once, relishing the gag reflex that bubbles up when his tip tickles the back of my throat. If he were any other man that sensation would make me nauseous, but, for him, it only turns me on all the more. He is my noble superior, I am his low-class slave, here to suck him off royally.

It is a torrid fantasy, to be sure, but it is one that gets me off every single time.

I taste the many flavours of his cock – the dusky, salty taste of my pussy, the muskiness of his unwashed foreskin, the flat, dull taste of dry skin – all of them making up the earthy palate of desire. I begin to move my whole head back and forth in long, swift strokes, deep-throating him, sucking and licking and blowing the whole time. I move faster and faster, my tongue probing at his foreskin, my lips pulled back tightly over my teeth, sneaking little bites at the base and tip, until finally Joseph comes hard, spilling his salty patrician seed into the back of my throat until I swallow, making him a part of me for ever.

Many noble – peasant fantasies would simply end here, but mine does not. For now that I have given my fantasy lover the royal tongue treatment, he does not just zip up after receiving his slumming fuck and blow job and go on his merry way (as I'm sure he would in real life). No, in my fantasy world, he stays, and returns the favour.

He parks himself between my legs, surveying the landscape – bumpy, pink and glistening. My cream is spread across my petals, making them appear as if they are melting. His mouth finally finds my clit, and settles there. He makes the tip of his tongue into a miniature whirlpool which swirls about my most sensitive spot. My orgasm approaches and, as my noble professor eats me raw, I become a live wire, electrified. The pulses begin in my clit, then reverberate upwards and outwards until my whole body is engulfed and shakes.

This is appropriate, for Coventry is a professor of astrophysics. I may understand little to nothing of his lectures, but that does not matter. For here in my fantasy, Professor Coventry – my Joseph – teaches everything I shall ever know or comprehend about the nature of the cosmos. The whole universe exists in the space between my clit and his cock.

There is an object to my affection. And that affection is boundless. Powerful enough, indeed, to create a whole separate world.

* * *

I am back in Professor Coventry's lecture hall. He has ceased to be Joseph – now he is back to being the haughty, married, no-name professor over whom I have no claim. I have heard nothing of today's lecture, for I have been far, far away in another place and time. I have had three orgasms just sitting here in my hard wooden chair, as I imagine myself naked with the rakishly handsome man who stands mere inches away from the ends of my toes. I glance down at the blank page in my notebook, which was to contain notes from today's lecture on the nature of black holes. Even after Professor Coventry's two-hour discourse on the subject, I know nothing of black holes, other than the fact that the space between my legs has just become one.

The pull of my crotch is so strong, in fact, I have my very own gravitational field.

Coventry has come to the end of his lecture ten minutes early. He seems distracted somehow, as if something is nagging at him. Or perhaps tugging.

He adjourns the lecture, writes the assignment on the board in block letters large enough to be seen anywhere in the vast hall. 'Until next week then, class,' he says, snapping his notebook shut. 'Cheers.'

He takes a small step towards me, then another. Have I caught him in my tractor beam? Could my fantasies really come true? Or is he just going to give me a tongue-lashing for daydreaming through his lectures?

'Miss Standish,' he says in his crisp upper-class accent, 'I would like to see you in my office.'

I ask no questions. I make no protests. I simply stand up and follow him down the hall, matching his long strides as best I can in my tall stiletto boots.

Coventry unlocks his office door and steps inside. I follow him, head and crotch buzzing. His office is neat and posh-looking, just as he is. An original oil painting of water lilies hangs on one wall, lodged in a heavy gilt frame. There is a marble bust of Isaac Newton on his desk, and the walls are lined with heavily laden bookshelves. There is the faintest scent of pipe tobacco, mixing with the old

Victorian building's trademark must and old polished wood. I admire the academic surroundings, meet his stern, blue-eyed gaze. I say nothing. Like a demure girl of nine, I wait to be spoken to.

'Miss Standish, I am very concerned about your progress in my course,' he says. 'First of all, when I didn't recognise you from any of the other courses I've taught, I looked you up in the university database. I found that you have a Communications concentration. Is that correct?'

I nod.

'I further discovered that you have not taken even one of the prerequisite courses for Astrophysics 203. You are aware there are multiple prerequisites for this course, are you not?'

I give a non-committal shrug.

Professor Coventry blinks twice, nonplussed. 'Ahem. Miss Standish, the minimum prerequisite for enrolling in Astrophysics 203 are two full years of university-level physics, plus one semester of introductory astrophysics, and at least one semester of advanced calculus, including differential equations. As I've said before, your concentration is in Communications and, according to the records I requested from the registrar, you have taken absolutely no university-level science courses prior to now, and your only mathematics studies here are one semester of Topics in Mathematics, which is the lowest-level course taught on campus, reserved for humanities concentrators such as yourself. I have no reason to believe that the information I received from the registrar is incorrect, but I always believe in giving students the benefit of the doubt. Is there any chance whatsoever that the registrar is incorrect?'

I give another non-committal shrug.

This just exasperates him even further. 'Miss Standish, let me be perfectly clear. You are not qualified to be taking my class. Indeed, the registrar should have prevented you from enrolling in my class altogether, but that's another matter entirely. I must advise you, Miss Standish, that I expect you to drop my class from your semester registration immediately. You do not belong here. There is absolutely no way you can possibly understand coursework at this level, given your background. Do you understand that?'

Yet another non-committal shrug. This time, I add a coy little smile, which seems to throw him off the slightest bit.

He rolls his eyes and sighs. 'You really are a difficult one to figure, Miss Standish. If you don't mind my asking, why would someone like you take an interest in an advanced astrophysics course in the first place?'

'Oh, I guess I just thought it might be interesting, is all,' I say, accenting it with yet another non-committal shrug.

'Interesting, eh? Do you have any idea how complex and difficult an advanced course such as this is to understand? Why, the calculations required to pass the first exam alone are enough to drive half the Physics concentrators out of the course within the first two weeks! There's absolutely no way you could pass tomorrow's exam if even many Physics concentrators can't!'

Exam? That takes me off-guard a bit. 'There's an exam?'

He gives me a wide-eyed stare. 'Of course there are exams, Miss Standish. Or is that a completely foreign concept to someone from the humanities quad? Who knows, perhaps it is. For all I know, all you humanities chaps do is just sit round reading books and sipping coffee all day long.'

'We, um, we have exams. Just not usually in the first two weeks of class.'

He looks down his nose at me, feigning snobbery. But I can tell from the growing glint in his eyes that he's starting to like me a little bit. 'Well, you humanities types are generally a soft lot,' he says.

'We study just as hard as anybody else does,' I retort. 'We just don't do a lot of maths, is all. But that doesn't mean we aren't important. Shakespeare was a humanities type, you know. So was Keats. And William Blake wrote about the cosmos quite a lot. I honestly thought that by studying astrophysics, it might help make me into an important writer someday. Writers are supposed to know quite a lot about how the universe works, and –'

He raises his hand to stop me. 'Look, Miss Standish. I don't know why you're in my class, and I also know for certain that you don't belong in it. But I'll tell you what. As long as you agree to drop the class from your registration, I'll allow you to continue to sit in on lectures as an auditor. I wager you won't understand ninety-nine per cent of what I discuss in class, but if it inspires you to write some Booker Prize-winning space novel someday, then I suppose we'll call things even. Sound fine?'

I nod, and can't help but feel my face nearly split open from the grin that spreads across my cheeks.

Now I know for sure that Professor Coventry has noticed me. Hell, he might even like me a little bit. Now all I need to do is try to find a way for my fantasies about him to come true.

A tall order, to be sure. But it's one I'm prepared to fill.

And I suppose if I fail, there will still be an unlimited supply of fantasies starring my very own version of Professor Coventry.

Joseph.

There is an object to my affection. And now he is one step closer to being real.

I am back in Professor Coventry's class. I dropped his course from my register as he instructed; the astrophysics department approved his suggestion I audit the course as a non-grade-earning student on the condition that I write a term paper describing what I got out of auditing the class at the end of the semester. I wonder just how honest I should be when I write that paper. Because I have learned very little about actual advanced astrophysics in this class.

I have learned a lot about how to make myself come in public without even touching myself, however.

Maybe I should write a paper about having self-induced orgasms in Astrophysics 203 and turn it in to my human sexuality professor next semester.

I am sitting in the front row of Professor Coventry's massive lecture hall, as usual. I stretch my feet out in front of me as far as they will comfortably go, sink lower into my seat so my legs will stretch out a little further. The tips of my ballet flats are just a few inches from the lectern behind which the object of my affection stands primly, pointing out the finer details of the importance of subatomic particles in the formation of pre-galactic nebulae.

The words falling out of Coventry's mouth might as well be in ancient Aramaic; I have no understanding of electrons or quarks or anything else remotely subatomic. In fact, at the moment I am so aroused by the sound of Professor Coventry's intelligent, scientific, upper-class voice that the only thing I even remotely understand is the fact that my crotch is on fire.

I slowly close my eyes, listen to the erotic buzz grow in my brain as the sound of Professor Coventry's lecture slowly dissolves, his voice swirling and melting into a wordless, primitive animal version of itself in my mind's ear. He has ceased to be Professor Coventry, and is now Joseph Coventry, my very own personal love slave.

This fantasy is much hotter, much edgier and dangerous. No more clandestine dorm-room liaisons for us, oh no. From this point forwards, in my fantasy universe Joseph and I will meet and fuck only out in the open, in public view, where anyone and everyone can see and hear and taste our illicit trysts. And I will be the dominator, while Joseph is the meek submissive. Like any addict, I need increasingly high doses of my chosen drug in order to get my fix. While a single, innocent hit might have sustained me before, I now require heavier, riskier doses.

The scene dissolves into a different version of itself, with a sensual musical background and chiaroscuro lighting. I'm still sitting in the lecture hall, and Professor Coventry – Joseph, now – is still standing behind his lectern. The lecture hall is still full of students, and Joseph still drones on about electrons, protons and quarks.

The only major difference is, we're both naked. And instead of taking notes on nebulae and particle physics, Professor Coventry's students are taking notes on how to fuck properly.

Astrophysics 203, meet Proper Fucking 101.

Joseph pauses his long diatribe on the universal nature of quarks and beams at me. 'Miss Standish, I do believe you have some special expertise to share with the class on the nature of particle physics. Isn't that so?'

I stand up, letting all hundred-odd of my fellow students take in my pale naked glory.

'Why yes, Joseph, it is,' I say. 'I do believe you have failed to describe the powerful forces that make subatomic particles stick together. And I do believe I have some special knowledge on that very subject that I can share with my classmates in a very special way.'

'Ah, good, then you should demonstrate, Miss Standish – or shall I call you Penelope from now on?'

'Yes, Joseph, please do. One of the most important components of particle-joining force is that the particles in question must call one another by their Christian names at all times.'

Joseph's eyebrows rise. 'Why, I never knew that, Penelope. Truly, the depth and breadth of your astrophysical knowledge is astonishing.'

'There's a lot of other things about me that are astonishing, too,' I say, and strut up to the lectern. I'm stark naked except for a pair of patent-leather platform stilettos, a little fashion accent I picked up in an S&M shop down a dark alley off the Holloway Road last autumn. In my hand I'm carrying a matching leather whip with a barbed tip – a little accessory I purchased on the same shopping trip. I never thought I'd have occasion to use them – let alone in public – until now.

Joseph watches my every move, his eyes widening, his mouth evolving into a naughty leer that positively drools as I inch closer and closer to him. The sound of my stilettos clicking against the pockmarked wood floor echoes throughout the lecture hall. The collective breath of the gathered students quickens; you can almost taste their voyeuristic arousal on the recycled classroom air. Joseph's cock is already fully erect and dripping with pre-come. But my focus isn't on his cock just yet. I am seeing him fully naked for the first time, and the view from here is gorgeous. His cock is old news that I've read before, but his long, hard, chiselled body is a new landscape that I must fully explore before revisiting the familiar territory between his two fine legs.

The fantasy body I have created for Joseph is a true work of art. Even though he dresses in stuffy tweeds and wools on campus, those dull patrician vestments do nothing to hide the virility of the athletic, masculine body underneath. He is fit and trim, his biceps are thick and hard from working out in the campus gym, his angular cheekbones belie the sharp corners of the pubic bone that juts out from his narrow, six-packed waist. The outline of a perfect male specimen is right there in the open for anyone who chooses to look; here now in my fantasy world, all I've done is connect the dots. And the results are truly a wonder to behold.

His six-foot-plus frame is long, lean, reminiscent of a Hellenic warrior. His chest is firm, thick, angular and perfectly hairless, as smooth and luminescent as alabaster. His torso is an upside-down triangle, with strong, broad shoulders and a firm, narrow waist which points downwards to his cock, which is itself capped by a mound of downy, sandy-blond fur. There is so much here that is so beautiful to see, it makes me wonder why he felt the need to wear that damned tuxedo during our last tryst.

Then I remember – it was *me* who made him wear that damned tuxedo. Joseph dwells only in *my* world, he does only what *I* dictate. In today's fantasy, I have more than made up for that damned tuxedo. Joseph's birthday suit is far better than anything a Savile Row tailor can muster.

Joseph comes out from behind the lectern, so everyone in the hall can see him. We each take steps closer to one another, until the tip of his dripping cock taps my abdomen. A collective gasp rises from the collected students; only now do they seem to realise what they are about to witness.

Joseph makes a move to thrust his cock between my legs, but I stop him with a gentle tap of my whip. He instantly gets the message. 'What is your wish, Penelope? I am at your command.'

'Turn around,' I say, my suddenly deep voice booming throughout the hall. 'And bend over.'

He obeys. I honour his obedience with three sharp *thwacks* of my whip across his backside. Joseph shudders with pleasure. 'More, please, Penelope. More!'

I oblige him with several more swats, until his buttocks are rosy red and stinging. He shudders with more pleasure, and his balls pull themselves up tight against his groin. With just a few smart flicks of my whip, I have nearly brought my beloved professor to orgasm.

Cosmic forces, indeed.

I forcibly turn his body to face mine. I turn to the lectern, speak into its tinny microphone. 'And now, class, you will witness just what happens when two electrically charged particles collide.'

I raise my left leg and wrap it around Joseph's waist. His cock slides into my sheath of its own accord, and he begins to thrust. I come almost immediately, my clit melting even without any external stimulation. The knowledge that I am engaging in nature's most primal, filthy act in a stuffy Victorian lecture hall in full view of nearly a hundred of my student peers is more than enough to get me hot, hot, hot. He thrusts deep and hard, the tip of his cock hitting my womb with every stroke, sending rollicking vibrations up and down my entire body. We fuck for what seems like hours, until my cunt is rubbed raw and Joseph is crying and moaning in desperate need of release – yet his orgasm is nowhere in sight. But I know my fantasy lover's body so well that I immediately comprehend why he cannot come. His body needs something that even my juicy, creamy sheath cannot provide.

Without ever breaking the connection between us, I manoeuvre my hands – one carrying my whip – around Joseph's body until they are gripping his backside. The fingers of my right hand slip between his buttocks, searching and probing until I find his back passage. I gently press into the tiny ridged rosette, lubing it with Joseph's own sweat and the pussy juice that coats his crotch from our marathon fucking session. With gentle probing and plenty of our shared natural juices, Joseph's back passage slowly begins to open like a blossoming lily. I fit in one finger, then two, then four. Then, in a gymnastic feat worthy of any Olympic gold medallist, I thrust my cunt hard against his cock, giving him the deepest penetration yet, as I simultaneously shove the braided leather handle of my whip into his asshole.

'Uhhhhnnnnuuuhhh,' Joseph groans, all traces of his upper-class origins gone. 'Yesssss.'

A little creative ass-fucking was just what the doctor ordered, because Joseph explodes into me, his seed spraying so deep and hard into my body that I can practically taste it. His come mixes with my flowing juices and runs down my leg, pooling into a small puddle on the floor.

Joseph collapses onto my shoulder, scarcely able to get his breath. I turn my head to face the astonished class. 'And that, students, is what happens when two charged particles collide in space,' I say. 'They explode upon impact. There will be a test on Friday, students, so be sure to study up.'

The movie screen of my fantasy world fades to black, and the credits begin to roll. 'The Last Of The Red-Hot Nobleman Astrophysicists,' the title card reads. 'Starring Penelope Standish and Joseph Coventry. Written and Directed by Penelope Standish. Executive Producer: Penelope Standish . . .'

A sharp tap on my shoulder yanks me back down to earth. 'Ahem. Miss Standish?'

I slowly open my eyes, and see a set of tweed-trousered legs. I slowly gaze up and see that those tweedy legs belong to Professor Coventry. The real Professor Coventry, and not the one I just fucked in my imagination. 'Y-Yes?'

'Miss Standish, were you asleep during my lecture?'

I feel my face go red. 'No, sir. I was, ahhhm, just thinking.'

He raises an eyebrow. 'Is that so? Then perhaps you'd like to share with the rest of the class just what you were thinking about with your eyes closed and your mouth hanging open.'

'I was, ahhhm, just imagining what happens when two electrically charged particles collide in space,' I say. 'Based on the information you presented in your lecture, I imagined that the collision produces an explosion, sort of a miniature black hole that results in the creation of new atomic matter.' Which is true, actually. I was thinking about exactly that. If not quite exactly in those terms, of course.

A slow smile spreads across Professor Coventry's face. 'Well, Miss Standish, it seems I underestimated you. Even with your poor science background, it does indeed seem you have what it takes to comprehend higher astrophysics. I must confess I was about to ban you from my classroom altogether, but it seems it is you who has turned the tables on me. I daresay I've just learned quite a lesson against making swift judgements.'

'Well, Professor, I am glad to have been of service,' I say, giving him a sly smile. 'I do indeed find your lectures most … stimulating.'

'I'm delighted to hear it, Miss Standish. And I would like to learn more about how a literary humanist such as yourself grasps higher astrophysics. There's always something to gain from non-traditional perspectives.' He returns my smile and, if I'm not mistaken, his blue eyes sparkle. 'Perhaps you and I can discuss this further after class? At the coffee shop downstairs? I fancy a cup of cappuccino, I hope you'll take one with me. My treat.' He extends his hand, I take it. What results isn't quite a handshake – it might even be the beginning of a caress.

I smile and nod, feeling my whole body grow warm once again as I follow my beloved professor down the wood-panelled halls to the student café. It's only a meeting between a noble professor and his adoring low-born student, but it just might be the beginning of a wild fantasy come true.

There is an object to my affection. And now, I just might have some real affection in return.

Jamaica Layne is the author of the Cheek novel *Market for Love*. *Sexy Little Numbers* features her first appearance of short fiction in Black Lace.

Set Up
Kay Jaybee

I still can't quite believe we are together. Just one glance at Jade's vastly over-dyed yellow hair, spiked up in an incongruous mass, would have been enough to make me cross the street only a few months ago, but there's something about her, something dangerous, but strangely compelling. It's as if I have to stay, just to see what outrageous things she'll do next.

I watched Jade light the row of candles that provided the only source of light in the otherwise dark room she'd hired. The glow of the flames was enough to see that the room, although basic, held everything that was required for what Jade calls the club's 'quick bonk' trade. As I stood next to her, sort of in a trance, I watched Jade's petite frame perched on the edge of the single bed, testing its bounce.

The small ring that pierces Jade's top lip reflected in the flickering beams of heat, and my eyes were drawn to it. I hate it. I've always hated it, and yet, somehow, I'm fascinated by it. Just like her tattoos. She has two, one on each bicep, a Celtic cross on the left, and a ring of thorns on the right. I hate them too. I despise how they have marked such perfect flesh, and how they'll never ever leave her, but, like the lip ring, I'm drawn to them, like scars that just beg to be scratched. Whenever we have sex I physically need to touch them, pull at them, claw at them.

Jade leaped off the bed and stood in front of me and, although I'd been semi-aroused ever since she told me what she'd planned for the coming hour, the sight of her approach caused my palms to prickle with apprehension and my dick to harden against the denim of my black jeans. I couldn't believe she'd talked me into agreeing to take part in this, but then, as I've said, I find nearly everything connected with Jade unbelievable.

Apart from the bed, the windowless room contained a single wooden chair and the table that held the candles, under which was a chest of drawers. Jade opened the top drawer as I stood mesmerised, watching her pick up a candle so she could highlight the contents. My throat, already dry, suddenly felt like sandpaper, and I licked my lips in an attempt to stop them sticking together. I shouldn't have been surprised when I saw all the paraphernalia of bondage neatly hidden away. After all, Jade likes to be in charge, and despite my more traditional practices before I met her, I like to let her, but in this case I was more nervous than usual.

She came forwards then and, leaving the drawer open, put the candle down and placed a firm hand over my encased cock. Telling me to relax (something that was totally impossible), Jade rubbed hard against me, swelling my size so that its confinement physically hurt. I took a calming breath and nodded at her. She'd already asked me not to speak. I'm not sure I could have anyway.

Her violently coloured fingernails began to undo my white shirt buttons. She always seemed amused by my clothes, as if their ordinariness was as confusing to her as her outlandishness was to me. My chest, which still bore evidence of her teeth marks from the night before, felt chilled in the cool room, but I quickly dismissed any feeling of cold when she turned her attention to undoing my jeans.

Slowly, oh so damn slowly, Jade undid my flies and tugged down my trousers, showing just how full my pants were of hard cock. I don't think I've ever met anyone who could get me so rigid with just a touch.

So, there I was, naked in a small candlelit room, standing before a strange creature wearing an off-white frilly blouse, hanging over an ultra-short miniskirt, black hold-ups (whose lace tops were no secret to anyone) and a pair of black boots. Slutty, deliciously slutty. How I longed for her to hold me, to pop my dick in her bright-red lipsticked mouth and play me around with her tongue, but tonight it was not her who would be doing the touching.

When Jade first told me she'd hired someone from the back pages of a magazine to come and, as she put it, 'fuck me senseless', I was horrified, alarmed, and so turned on that she laughed at me. It was a challenge then, once she'd laughed at me, and I had no choice.

I waited there, uncertain, my pulse banging through my veins and my heart beating in my ears. For a fraction of a second Jade watched me, assessing me, as if she was wondering if this time perhaps she'd gone too far, but then she came to herself and, after a quick rummage in the open drawer, produced a metal gag. I winced at the sight of it, but was somehow powerless to stop her. Jade's adept fingers clicked it into place, forcing my mouth to remain wide open, and my tongue to be trapped beneath a small leather depressor.

I made a pathetic whimpering noise as Jade came and licked my helpless face, muttering how much she wished she was the one who was going to fuck me. I longed to tell her she would definitely be seen to later on, but I couldn't, and simply stood, frustratingly dumb as the metal pinched at my lips.

Then came the handcuffs. Jade said nothing, but showed them to me in detail. The black wrist guards were placed further apart than usual, joined with a retractable chain, in the middle of which was a two-inch long, half-inch thick butt plug. I tried to protest, but it was pointless, it would also have been contradictory, for the second I saw the plug, my dick quivered and I'd given myself away. Jade smiled briefly. She knew I'd never even considered anything anal before I'd met her, and now I love it, although I'd never have admitted it to her, or even myself – until now. She seemed to know though.

The first wrist guard was snapped in place, as was the second, but the plug was left hanging. I could feel it dangling, teasing my butt.

Finally, she produced a blindfold, soft and black. She whispered, 'Goodbye,' to my eyes, as she pulled it across my face, effectively plunging me into an erotic darkness which left me at the mercy of my increasingly lurid imagination, and the whim of Jade's prostitute.

Jade had told me the 'hired help' would enter the room as soon as I was blindfolded and, even before I'd become accustomed to the dark, I heard the door open and felt a draught of air seep briefly across my exposed flesh. I imagined a blonde with surgically enhanced tits, long limbs and a dominant stance. When the first contact came I was convinced I was right. Unbelievably soft skin touched mine, causing little electric shocks to pulse against me as anonymous fingertips stroked my chest. I could hear Jade murmur encouragingly, and could tell by the husky tone of her voice how turned on she was.

With three people in the room there wasn't much space to manoeuvre, so I wasn't surprised when I was sat down on the edge of the bed. The foreign hands had a firmness about them, which spoke of no-nonsense experience, as my legs were widened and my balls were engulfed in a smooth palm.

A guttural noise of longing escaped from my open throat as my scrotum was massaged. I pictured the hands working against me having scarlet nail polish painted at their tips but, from the feel of her hands, I knew the nails were not as long as the claws Jade favoured.

I closed my eyes beneath the blackness of my mask as a blissfully cold moist mouth fastened itself around my shaft. This pro was an expert; the differing tensions of her mouth, tongue and throat sent sensations shooting up my dick and into my stomach like I've never known. As the mouth pumped away, deliberately grazing my delicate skin with her teeth, I felt my control slipping away. Any second now I'd spunk – but her mouth withdrew at the crucial moment.

I could have cried, screamed, except of course, I couldn't. The best blow job I'd ever received (sorry Jade), and it was gone. Taken away at the vital moment.

The unknown hands returned to me, but this time they held me around the waist, steering me so that I was lying face down on the bed with my knees crouched up under my stomach. I knew, as I felt the unused plug hanging down between my legs, what was going to happen next. I tried to take some deep breaths to relax, but it was almost impossible, with the gag so tightly in place, to do anything other than take shallow snorts through my nose.

My attempts to calm myself were sharply interrupted by an insistent tongue darting at my anus. Again and again the warm muscle poked at me, circling the velvety rim of my backside before pointing itself at the hole itself. I clutched the sides of the bed, willing her to continue, as two hands joined the tongue, kneading and fingering my raised butt, making its little mouth pucker greedily. I pictured Jade watching, and I wondered if she longed to join in.

At last, after an agony of delicious preparation, the butt plug was pushed between my yielding buttocks. I whimpered as the associated stomach cramps came and went with the intrusion of the foreign object, and whined still further when the chain that attached the plug to my handcuffs was retracted sharply, and my hands were snapped up to my backside, so that I was effectively keeping the plug in place with my own wrists.

Although my legs were still free, without my sight and with my arms captive, my movements were clumsy, and I found it difficult to comply when Jade ordered me to stand up. In the end, impatient hands grabbed at me until I stood upright and uncertain, the strain in my dick accentuated by the presence of the dildo in my rear.

The room was suddenly so silent; it was as if we were holding our collective breaths. I ached to feel this new woman's breasts against me and, as if by magic, nipples began to drag across my back. Hard tight tips that trailed softly. Then came the sound of a condom packet being ripped open. I tensed slightly, hoping I wouldn't come at just the touch of it being rolled on, but nothing happened. Perhaps it hadn't been a condom packet, perhaps I had been mistaken. I didn't really care; I was so close to the edge now, I was as desperate as I'd ever been to feel this woman around me.

Jade suddenly whispered in my ear, 'Would you like to be able to see your present?'

I nodded vigorously at the sound of her gravelly voice.

'You must promise to be a good boy though, or I'll get them to leave.'

I nodded again, wishing she'd just get on with it.

'If you make a scene I will leave as well, and that will be it for us. The end.'

I began to panic slightly. What was she talking about? I nodded anyway, my dick very much in charge of my brain, as the butt plug suddenly revealed itself to have a vibrate function, shooting quivers of hot shakes up my spine.

'OK then,' Jade murmured as she pulled the satin mask away.

It took a moment for my eyes to adjust to the dimly lit room, and I didn't understand the evidence of my own eyes for at least two seconds.

There was a man standing beside a bare-chested Jade. His dick was as hard as mine and his piercing blue eyes, surrounded by shoulder-length brown hair, stared straight into mine with undisguised, unashamed desire.

If I'd been able to speak I would have probably yelled at them, but I couldn't, I couldn't do anything. I looked at the man's firm lips and knew that they had been around my cock; that his tongue and fingers were responsible for getting the now throbbing plug in position. My stomach turned over again and my heart bashed against my chest so hard I thought I might either explode or collapse. I felt vaguely sick and, as I looked at Jade's naked breasts, more vulnerable than ever before.

Jade came forwards and stroked my short blond hair. 'You're a very good boy.' Her hands calmed my pulse rate slightly. 'I think you deserve a reward, don't you?'

I couldn't respond of course, and I'm not sure what I'd have said anyway, as Jade signalled to the man to come closer. I stood still as he began to kiss my neck, my torso and my arms, his right hand grasping my dick and firmly stroking it from top to bottom, causing a confused mixture of desire and revulsion to surge through me as my lover looked on. I kept my gaze on her as our guest put his mouth back around my shaft. I shuddered for a split second, and almost moved away, but I didn't. He was just too damn good, too many sparks were shooting through me as the butt plug quietly thumped inside my arse, and his rhythmic tongue lapped at my front. I focused my watering eyes on Jade, whose own hands began to play with her pert nipples. This was obviously doing almost as much for her as it was for me.

As he pulled away I gurgled an involuntary groan, which made Jade giggle. My brain seemed to have shut down, and I was in total denial that the source of this incredible pleasure was a man. Yet this denial couldn't be sustained as Jade turned me around and, loosening the chains a little, released the buzzing black plug. I felt so empty I could have cried, I wanted the space to be refilled, and I would have taken anything as I was pushed to my knees and leaned over the edge of the bed. The fact a man was already positioning himself up against my arse cheeks was irrelevant, and I screwed my eyes tightly in readiness for what was to come. As male fingers stretched my cheeks wider, I pictured Jade in a strap-on; I concentrated on her luscious tits as a hard dick thrust into my quivering backside.

Jade knelt in front of me and forced my eyes open. She dripped her words into my ear, 'There is a man fucking your arse, babe.' Her gruff smoker's tone continued, 'It's turning me on like you wouldn't believe.' I watched her watching me as the hired help slapped his balls against my buttocks, his expert hand snaking around to hold my swaying penis. Caressing me as he fucked progressively harder, burning my knees on the poorly carpeted floor.

I might have screamed, but I only dribbled helplessly into the face of my girl, who, in a typically sluttish move, flicked her skirt up and slid her knickers down to show me how glisteningly wet she was.

My body tightened and, as I looked at Jade's face, I understood and accepted everything. Her living out of a secret fantasy, her dishevelled clothes, her obvious desperation to be shagged and, most important of all, the fulfilment of my own most basic desire. I gave a throaty moan as creamy spunk shot from my dick towards Jade, splashing her tits as I sunk under the weight of our guest.

Without being given the chance to recover from my new mind-blowing, experience, I was hauled to my knees. I swayed unsteadily as Jade roughly grasped a handful of my hair to keep my head still, whilst the stranger's penis disappeared into my pre-opened mouth.

I almost choked as he pushed between my Sahara-dry lips. Finally though, I managed to force myself to relax enough to accept his insistent pumping, and felt the alien trickle of semen glide down my throat and spill down my chin.

The hired help nodded at me, gathered his clothes, and was gone. No words, nothing.

Standing, shaking, shock engulfed me. I'd had gay sex. I'd enjoyed gay sex, and I'd had it in front of my girlfriend.

Jade was looking at me as if deciding whether or not to take the gag and cuffs off. Perhaps she was worried I'd attack her with rage or something, but she must have been reassured by my obvious enjoyment of the situation, and released me.

I winced as she took the metal clamp away, my jaw cracking back into position, as I ran saliva around my mouth and lips. I stared at her; I had no idea what to say. She undid the cuffs, and I rubbed at my wrists and swung my arms, trying to loosen the knitted muscles of my shoulders. Still no one spoke.

I stared at her. Then, suddenly, disbelief at my situation hit me. With an aggression I'd never felt before, I lifted her across my lap, grabbed a cane from the still open drawer, and whipped her backside, until she begged me to stop, and my dick was as hard as before. I turned her over and fucked her, like I've never fucked anyone before. That was when she told me she loved me.

Jade doesn't know yet, but I've arranged a rematch. I've rented out the little room again, and another 'hired help', a woman this time – just for her. I can hardly wait . . .

Kay Jaybee's short fiction appears in the Black Lace collection *Sex and Music*.

Glove Love
Kristina Wright

'Oh, don't be a big baby. Do you have any idea what women go through – what *I* go through?' I waved my toothbrush in the air. 'It's ridiculous, the indignities women are forced to endure while you men whine.'

The topic was prostate exams; the big baby was my boyfriend Oliver. He had just celebrated his thirtieth birthday and his doctor had recommended a complete physical – complete, as in top to bottom. Problem was, Oliver wasn't too fond of anyone being anywhere near his bottom.

'I can't believe you've never had one,' I said, sizing him up from the bathroom door while he got dressed for work. 'It's not a big deal.'

He frowned at me, still boyish with his too-long blond hair falling over his forehead in soft waves. 'It's a big deal to me. Why would I have one? I'm young and healthy. I run five miles a day and I have abs of steel.'

He was right on all counts. Oliver's body was certainly a work of art – one I admired eagerly every chance I got, even after being together for four years.

'You have a family history. It's silly to be squeamish about something that could save your life.'

'Can we not talk about this, please?' He put on his trousers, pushing each leg through forcefully to emphasise his distaste for the taboo subject. 'I really don't think it's necessary for some ... some *dude* to stick his finger up my rear and fondle my balls.'

'Isn't there a female doctor at the practice? You could request she do your exam.'

That gave Oliver pause. 'How would having a female doctor feel me up be any better?'

I laughed. 'You might enjoy it. Some men do, you know.'

'Not *this* man.' He glared at me as if I were suggesting he do something perverted while wearing my underwear.

'I'll help you prepare for it,' I said.

His frown only deepened as he flung a grey tie around the collar of his black shirt. 'How are you going to do that? Hypnotise me?'

I headed into the bathroom and fumbled around in the bathroom cabinet, retrieving several purple nitrile gloves. I stood in the bathroom doorway and gave him my best come-hither look as I waved the gloves like a handful of deflated balloons. 'Bend over, big boy.'

Oliver stared at the pile of purple in my hand as if I held a very large and poisonous snake. 'First of all, why do you have medical gloves? Second of all, are you out of your mind?'

I laughed. 'I stole them from the doctor's office during my last visit. Kind of kinky, don't you think? Now I have a real reason to use them.'

'You are seriously twisted.' Oliver was still shaking his head and frowning as I joined him in the bedroom. 'No way.'

'All you need is some lube and it won't hurt at all.' I got the bottle out of my bedside table and showed it to him, trying to look like innocence incarnate. Sexy fuckable innocence who wouldn't injure his delicate butt. It wasn't easy. 'You can trust me.'

'Hell, no.'

I could practically feel him clenching his butt cheeks from across the bedroom.

'C'mon,' I cajoled. 'You play with my butt all the time.'

'You like it.'

I smirked. 'You will too.'

He got his tie knotted properly on the third attempt. I had really rattled him. 'Sorry, doctor, I have to go to work.'

I snagged his sleeve as he headed for the bedroom door. 'Not so fast,' I said, hooking a bare leg around his hip. I was still in my pyjamas, which consisted of just a T-shirt and thong. 'You're far too agitated to go to work. You need to calm down. Doctor's orders.'

'What do you have in mind?' He eyed me suspiciously, but I could feel his resolve softening even while other areas of him hardened.

I put my goodies on the dresser and reached for his belt. 'A massage with a happy ending?'

'Going to have to skip the massage,' he said, glancing at his watch. 'I have a meeting at ten.'

I reached for the purple gloves as I knelt in front of him. He took two steps back as I pulled them on and grabbed the lube. I grinned at his stricken expression.

'Calm down, Mr Nervous.' I pulled him forwards by his belt loops. 'The gloves are good for other fun things too.'

'I know that determined look in your eyes,' he said, though he didn't complain when I palmed the impressive lump in his pants. 'You are not to be trusted.'

I didn't give him too long to think about it. I unfastened his trousers and tugged the zipper down over his bulge. I slipped his pants and underwear down around his ankles and brushed one purple-sheathed finger down the length of his cock. It twitched against my touch.

'That feels weird,' he said.

I applied a generous dollop of lubricant to the palm of one glove and stroked it up the length of his cock. 'How does that feel?'

'Still weird, but a kind of kinky, horny weird.'

I took his cock in my gloved hand and stroked him, the lube making the nitrile glove slide easily along his erection. I enjoyed the visual contrast of the purple glove against his lube-slick flesh. It *was* kinky. I smiled at the slightly surprised noise he made when I cupped his balls with my other hand, then I fondled the sac until it was as slippery as his cock.

Oliver leaned over me, bracing his hands on the dresser at my back. 'Wow. I like those gloves.'

'I knew you would,' I said.

I laced my fingers together over the head of his cock and twisted them as I ran them up the length of his shaft and back down again. Over and over, I fisted his erection between my lubed, gloved hands until he was thrusting against me and breathing hard. It was supposed to be a treat for Oliver, but I felt myself getting wet as I jerked him off with the purple gloves.

As I slid my hands up his cock once more, I took the head in my mouth. He nearly knocked me out as he jerked against me. I banged the back of my head against the dresser and pressed my teeth into the taut skin of his dick as a warning to be more careful.

'Sorry, sorry,' he gasped. 'That just feels so damned good.'

I grumbled around him in my mouth, but I didn't stop. I loved having him this aroused. I knew when he was like this I could do anything – *anything* – and he wouldn't care. As he curved over me, his stomach muscles rippling as he braced against the dresser, I took him deeper into my mouth and stroked his quivering thighs. Slowly, I slipped one hand down to his balls, cupping and kneading them gently. His cock twitched in my mouth, so hard and velvety, the slightly sweet taste of the lube mingling with his musky flavour. What had started out as a tease was turning into a major turn-on . . . for *me*.

As I massaged his heavy balls, I stretched my middle finger out and reached back to rub his perineum. It was the barest of touches, but Oliver went instantly still. I kept sucking and stroking, my finger gliding over that part of him that was in such close proximity to his butt hole. The subject of ass play had never really come up before because it wasn't something I was particularly interested in. At least, not interested in *giving*. Now, having been told in no uncertain terms to stay away, I was suddenly very eager to explore the forbidden zone.

'Careful,' he said, his voice husky with lust. 'I know what you're up to, girlie.'

I dragged my teeth down the length of his cock and he groaned. I grinned as he popped out of my mouth. 'I promise I won't do anything you don't want me to do.'

'Good.'

'But I hear the orgasm is wicked intense. The best of your life.'

He stroked my hair, clearly anxious to get back to business. 'I'm sure it'll be intense enough.'

I laughed, then swirled my tongue over the head of his cock. 'Whatever you want, baby.'

'I want your mouth,' he said roughly, fingers tangling in my hair. 'I love your sexy mouth.'

I gave him what he asked for, sucking him until he made shallow thrusts against me. I was stroking his perineum again, my finger so close to his back passage I could feel the ridge. I wanted to slip inside him so badly I ached. I pressed my thighs together in the same rhythm I sucked him. I had a sudden epiphany that this must be what he felt right before he pushed his cock into my pussy. The hum of anticipation and barely contained desire – who knew that something meant to pleasure him would have me out of my mind with wanting to do it? But I wouldn't want him to force something on me I didn't want to do and, no matter how much I ached for that intimacy, I wouldn't go against his wishes.

He was fucking my mouth harder now, but I didn't complain. I wanted it. It turned me on to make him wild and out of control, so I sucked him until saliva dripped down my neck and splattered my breasts. If I'd had a third hand, it would have been between my own legs, strumming my clit to an explosive orgasm. As it was, I could only think about getting him off so he could return the favour.

Oliver went still again, though I hadn't done anything to make him feel threatened. My finger was still massaging his perineum in gentle circles, barely bumping the ridge of his tight hole, the entire area slick with lube and spit. I quickly pulled back and looked up into his eyes.

'I didn't – I won't,' I tried to say, though my aching jaw was having problems working properly. 'I'm being good!'

He swallowed hard. 'Do it,' he whispered, so softly I was sure I'd heard him wrong over the blood rushing in my ears.

'What?'

'Do it,' he repeated. 'Just be careful.'

'Are you sure?'

He sighed, his cock glistening wetly in front of me, his entire body quivering with barely suppressed need. 'Do it. I want you to. Please.'

I didn't ask again. My heart thumped as if I were a virgin about to be deflowered, but I couldn't let him know how nervous I was.

I took his cock back in my mouth. It had lost some of its rigidity during our brief exchange, but all it took was a few gentle sucks before he was back to full mast. I knew he was dreading what was to come, even if he had asked for it, so I had no intentions of dragging out his fearful anticipation. Giving his cock my full attention with my mouth and one hand, I slid my other hand over his balls and reached back towards his ass.

He jerked against me, but didn't tell me to stop. Two fingers rested over his asshole and I left them there as I took him as deep in my mouth as I could. He groaned as my throat rippled around him and I slid back off him.

'Baby,' he gasped. 'Oh God!'

I did it again, coming as close to deep-throating him as I ever could. This time, when I was so far down on his cock my nose bumped his groin, I very gently pushed the tip of my slick, gloved index finger into his butt. It was the barest of penetration, but he clenched down. Not to be deterred, I slid back up the length of his cock and sucked the head, swirling my tongue around the tip to catch his arousal. I ran my upper lip over the ridge again and again, knowing exactly what reaction I would get. When he jumped, I slipped my finger deeper into his ass.

'Oh God,' he groaned, but it wasn't a sound of pain.

I had my finger in Oliver's ass up to the first knuckle. My pussy was creaming so hard I was sure there must be a puddle on the floor beneath me. I slowly pulled my finger out to the tip as I went back down on his cock, then pushed it in again as I let his cock slide out to the head. Back and forth I went, sucking his cock and gently fingering his ass, as he pushed forwards towards my mouth. Then, somewhere in the rhythm, he switched it up and started pushing back towards the finger in his ass. That's when I knew he was mine.

With just the tip of his cock cradled on my tongue, I slowly massaged his prostate. He gasped, pushed forwards as if trying to get away from my probing, and then pushed back towards my finger. His ass clenched tight around my finger, but this time it wasn't about forcing me out – it was about his approaching orgasm.

His cock twitched in my mouth as I took him to the back of my throat once more and sank my finger in his ass at the same time. Suddenly, he was coming and groaning like an animal, making guttural noises I had never heard him make before. His entire body quaked and the dresser banged against the wall as he rocked between my mouth and my finger.

He seemed to come for ever and it was all I could do to breathe through my nose and swallow everything he gave me. My finger was buried in his ass, his body clenched so tightly I couldn't do anything except make little circles inside him. That seemed to be enough. He was completely lost in his orgasm – the orgasm I had given him. I had never been more aroused in my life.

Slowly, the tension left Oliver's body, his breath coming in pants as he braced himself against the dresser. I very gently pulled my finger away as I released his softening cock from my mouth. He was still breathing hard as he flopped back on the bed, his entire body glistening with sweat.

'Damn,' he said between breaths. 'Holy hell. Fuck.'

I giggled as I took the gloves off inside out and threw them on the dresser. I stood up, stripped off my soaked panties and flung myself across him. 'You seem to be having problems talking,' I said.

'I think that's because you just sucked my brain out through my dick.'

Grinding my pussy on his now flaccid cock, I stared down at him. 'If I didn't know better, I might think you enjoyed that.'

'You'd be right. That was fucking intense.' He wrapped his arms around me and flipped me over on the bed. His fingers found my aching clit and began stroking it roughly. 'You were right. Best damned orgasm of my life.'

'You're going to be late for work,' I managed to say.

'Work be damned.'

I moaned, already halfway to my own orgasm, but then he abandoned me on the bed. 'Come back here!'

It was his turn to laugh as he pulled on a purple glove. 'Hmm. These things are meant for smaller hands,' he said, but that didn't deter him from his efforts.

'They come in different sizes. I stole a few of the small.'

Gloved and with a dollop of lube squirted into the palm of his hand, he came at me looking like a maniacal sex fiend. A sexy-as-hell, just-got-his-ass-fucked-and-now-wanted-revenge, sex fiend. 'The doctor will see you now.'

I laughed. 'You don't need lube. I'm drenched.'

He knelt between my thighs and spread my pussy open with two fingers of his left hand, as he made teasing circles with the tip of his right index finger. 'Hmm. Yes, you are. But the lube isn't for this hole.'

I gasped as he slid a finger inside my pussy, aching for more. He pushed another finger into me, then a third. I was so wet his gloved fingers glided inside me easily. I pushed my hips up towards him, silently urging him on as I clutched at the bedlinen.

'You want more?'

'Oh yeah,' I gasped. 'A lot more.'

He chuckled. 'Yes, ma'am.'

He used four fingers to stretch my pussy, then twisted them inside me to stroke my G-spot and fill me up. I thrust against his hand and he pressed his thumb to my engorged clit. I thrashed about like a fish out of water, rocking against his magical, purple-gloved hand as he fucked me senseless. I rode the sharp edge of desire, so deliciously close to orgasm that my pussy rippled around his fingers as I concentrated on my singular goal of coming. But Oliver completely derailed my plans when he moved his left hand down between my cheeks and slipped a lubed finger into my ass.

My breath caught in my throat then whooshed from my body in a scream. With my pussy filled with his fingers, my bottom could barely accept that single digit even with lubricant to ease the way. As he slowly pushed the finger in deeper, I whimpered, caught between discomfort and mindless pleasure.

'Good?'

I nodded, eyes on those purple gloves between my thighs. 'Oh yes,' I gasped. 'I feel so full.'

'Mmm. Nice and tight too.'

I nodded, unable to speak as he began alternating between

fucking my pussy and fucking my ass with his fingers. With all my flailing about, he could do little more than rub his thumb over my clit every few strokes, but I hardly felt neglected. My need to come, having subsided for a moment when he pushed his finger in my bottom, returned full force. I arched off the bed, pushing my crotch at him like a wanton creature.

I stared at his hands, sheathed in purple and sliding in and out of my body. He glanced up from his task, his eyes meeting mine as my pussy and ass gripped his fingers.

'I think you're going to need to steal an entire box of these gloves, baby,' he whispered.

'In my size, or yours?'

He didn't hesitate. 'Both.'

I came then. Hard.

Kristina Wright's short fiction is featured in the Black Lace collections *Liaisons* and *Seduction*.

On Keeping Pets

K D Grace

'This is Tino.' Stella placed a hand under the man's chin and lifted his head so Anne could see his lovely stubbled face, blushing as though she had just caught him masturbating behind the sofa.

He nodded, then quickly lowered his head again, dark eyes disappearing behind a fringe of auburn curls.

'Tino's uncomfortable with new people,' Stella said as the two followed Anne into the lounge. 'Don't worry. He'll get used to you.'

Another one of Stella's nutters, Anne thought. Though this one was at least tall and good-looking.

In the lounge, Stella made herself comfy in the leather recliner, then turned her attention to Tino. 'Sit,' she commanded.

The man dropped onto the floor next to her, and she ran her hand absently over his unruly dark hair, then caressed the back of his neck.

Still wondering what was going on, Anne sat down across from the two. She couldn't help noticing, as Tino shifted to rest his head on Stella's knee, that he was sporting a good-sized erection beneath thin summer trousers.

She quickly averted her eyes, but not before her pussy got the message and warmed to the thought. These days Anne didn't see too many hard cocks.

Stella chuckled softly and rearranged herself in the chair so Tino could nestle against her leg. 'He's always got a hard-on, and he loves to show it off.' Then she added nonchalantly, 'How about a g and t? I'm gasping.'

Anne clambered to her feet, trying to keep her eyes on Tino's face. 'And what about you? What would you like?'

The man only buried his head against Stella's leg like a shy child.

'Tino doesn't drink, and he's already been fed.'

'Already been fed?'

Stella disengaged Tino's arms from around her leg and stood. 'Stay here, Tino, mistresses need to talk.'

'Mistresses? What the fuck's going on?'

'Shshsh!' Stella grabbed Anne's arm and hustled her off into the kitchen. 'He's very sensitive to other people's emotions. He's nervous enough just being in a strange place.' She helped herself to a glass and found the gin. 'Remember when my therapist said that with my relationship issues, before I got involved with a man, I should start with a plant?'

Anne nodded. 'And if you didn't kill the plant, work your way up to a goldfish, than maybe a cat or dog. Yeah, I remember. So?'

Stella plopped an ice cube in her glass. 'I did OK with a goldfish. But I'm allergic to cats and I'm afraid of dogs, then I found Tino.'

'What? Is the RSPCA adopting out men these days?'

'There's a site called the Kennel Club. They set people up with pets, and we're not talking cats and dogs here, Annie. It's temporary, only for a night, a weekend at the most.'

'You're kidding, right?'

'Hon, I wouldn't joke about something as yummy as Tino.' She offered a wicked giggle. 'Anyway, I find having a pet occasionally suits me better than having a relationship. And I couldn't help thinking, after our conversation the other day, that you might enjoy a pet too. You certainly seem to be responding well to Tino.' She gave Anne's tits a passing stroke with her free hand. 'Look at those nips.'

Anne slapped her away. She had lamented to Stella that, with the demands of her job, she had no time for a relationship, but someone working as hard as she did surely deserved a good shag once in a while. At the time Stella had been practically fellating a mango ice lolly in Kensington Gardens. 'I may have just the solution to your problem,' she said. And now here she was with Tino, the pet.

Anne grabbed the gin bottle and poured herself a double.

'Tino's very low maintenance, well behaved, clean.'

'Jesus, Stel, this is a bloke you're talking about, not a moggy.'

'Come on.' She grabbed Anne's hand and led her back towards the lounge. 'If he's left alone too long, he gets bored and sometimes gets in trouble.'

'What the hell's he going to do, piss on the carpet?'

'Don't be daft. He's house broken, but, unlike most blokes, he always remembers to put the seat down.'

'I don't believe we're having this conversation. How did –' Anne stopped in her tracks sending a cascade of gin over the rim of her glass onto the carpet.

There on the floor, exactly where they left him, was Tino, head thrown back, eyes closed, enthusiastically thrusting the thick cock he'd extricated from his trousers in and out of his fisted hand.

'Tino! Bad boy! You know better than to play with your thing unless you're asked.' Stella shoved passed Anne and slapped his hands away from his penis.

Anne watched in fascination as the pouting pet pushed his trousers and underpants down far enough to bare his exquisite bum. Then, on hands and knees, he presented it to Stella, who gave him a resounding thwack on each arse cheek. Anne's pussy practically gushed as Stella spanked him again, and his muscular buttocks clenched and relaxed, beautifully displaying the dark pucker of his anus. How the hell had Stella kept something like Tino and the Kennel Club a secret from her?

'I hate to punish you, darling, but you must behave. Let's get you out of those clothes. You don't mind, do you, Annie? Pets only wear clothes in public.'

Tino sat back on the floor and lifted his arse while Stella stripped him. The spanking had done nothing to lessen his huge erection. His heavy balls bounced against his thighs with Stella's efforts.

'Does he have a collar or something?'

'Could have if you wanted him to, but the Kennel Club pets are all very well trained.' Once Stella had him completely naked, she turned her attention to Anne. 'Sit there on the chair. Let him get used to you.'

Anne couldn't believe she was participating in this circus but, with her heart pounding in her chest and her pussy twitching in rhythm, she did as she was told. She was painfully aware of the weighty fullness of her breasts, feeling as if they were mostly nipple and areola at the moment. She felt as naked as Tino, who watched her with wide-eyed curiosity.

Stella was saying something about the twat in IT, who didn't know his arse from his iPod, but Anne wasn't listening. How could she when Tino had crawled across the floor, erection at full attention, and now sat only inches from her, looking up at her with those deep dark eyes.

Stella smiled her approval. 'You can touch him. He won't bite, not unless you ask him to.'

Anne reached out her hand, and he slid closer until her fingers rested in his hair just above his left ear. At her touch, his erection surged, and he moved forwards to lower his head onto her thigh.

'You see, he likes you.' Stella knocked back her drink and tinkled the ice around the glass. 'I need another one of these.' She padded off to the kitchen, leaving Anne alone with her pet.

As she stroked his hair and the nape of his neck, Tino rubbed his face against her thigh in much the same way her sister's cat did when she visited. Marking territory, her sister had told her. Was this man marking her as his territory?

He scooted still closer, making a sound at the back of his throat that wasn't completely unlike a cat's purr. He continued to nuzzle and rub his face and nose against her thigh, moving in serpentine stretches, insinuating his way into the space on the floor between her legs. Once there, he rose on his haunches and nestled and stroked until his face rested on her upper thigh. Then with another throaty moan, he nuzzled in, nose first, against her crotch.

She gave a little yelp and grabbed the arms of the chair, a move that he took for an invitation, snuggling in until she could feel his hot breath through her trousers. 'Oh God! Tino, I ... Ah!' She bit off the words in a gasp, as Tino began to lick her crotch with long wet strokes of his tongue. His warm saliva made the fabric cling to the contours of her vulva, now moist inside and out. Curling her fingers in his hair, she opened her legs, and shifted her hips. He pulled her closer to his face, sniffing, inhaling, sampling her scent. She thrust her pussy against his nose with a rush of pleasure.

By that delicious smell of cunt, mammals recognise when females are ready to be mounted, and males do whatever it takes to stimulate them to readiness. Humans were no different. She knew her own smell, when her vulva was slick with her juices and aching to be fucked. And Tino was sniffing her, testing her, familiarising himself with that intimate scent. Male dogs in the wild were always horny. They lived to copulate, and here was Tino with a hard-on almost from the moment he met her. He really was like an animal!

'Tino! Bad boy! Get back.' Stella stormed into the room and grabbed the man by the hair, pulling him away from Anne's cunt.

'What the fuck are you doing?' Anne gasped, using every ounce of her control to keep from dragging him back to her.

Tino wrapped both arms around Stella's leg until his full cock rubbed against her calf, then he began to hump.

'Bad boy!' She shoved him off. 'You know you don't lick someone's pussy unless they ask you, and you don't hump my leg.'

She turned her attention to Anne who was still struggling to catch her breath. 'I'm sorry. He's usually better behaved, but he's uncomfortable. Look how full his balls are. The Kennel Club keeps their pets horny to heighten the pleasure for their mistresses, but that's no excuse for his bad behaviour. He can't go bashing around like a randy baboon.

'Bend over, Tino, take your spanking.'

To Anne's surprise, Tino turned his lovely buttocks to her. Bracing with his arms against the coffee table, his arse was practically in her face, his little back hole clenching nervously. Both intrigued and aroused, she brought her hand down with a stinging smack against his pale bottom. His cock twitched; her wet pussy got wetter. As she spanked him again, he grunted and humped air.

Stella chuckled. 'Poor thing. He's so horny. He's not used to waiting this long before he comes, and it's pretty clear he's got your scent.' She nodded to the wet spot between Anne's legs.

Before Anne could respond, Stella took Tino's face in her hands and kissed him. The pet responded enthusiastically, and the delicious tongue that had lathed Anne's cunt only minutes before now ate Stella's mouth as though she were the flavour of the month. She reached down and cupped his balls, kneading them until he whimpered. Then she turned to Anne. 'Whatever you want him to do, just ask.' She looked down at her watch and heaved a sigh. 'I'd love to stay for the fun, but I'm off to Bath for the weekend. I've left the Kennel Club instructions in the kitchen. If you have any questions just text.'

'What?' Anne catapulted from her chair and grabbed her friend as she headed for the door. 'You can't leave me. I don't know what to do.'

'Oh come on, Annie, it hasn't been that long. He's yours until Sunday evening. My treat, so enjoy.' Then she was gone.

Sure enough, on the kitchen table was a list of instructions from the Kennel Club entitled 'On Keeping Pets'.

1. *Get to know your pet. Your experience will be more enjoyable if you are comfortable with each other.*

Anne felt something warm and wet against her hand and looked down to see Tino kneeling next to her, his tongue flicking over her fingertips, his eyes locked on her.

'I'm sorry, Tino. It's just I've never had a pet before.' She reached out and stroked his head.

Still holding her gaze, he stood and led her back to the lounge. When she sat, he sat on the floor in front of her, watching her expectantly, shifting uncomfortably around the weight of his distended penis, clenching his buttocks and rocking his hips. She couldn't take her eyes off such blatant, insinuating arousal, and found her own hips rocking, rubbing her swollen cunt against the chair.

'According to the Kennel Club rules, if I tell you what to do, you obey because you want to please me. Help me get undressed, then.' She tried to sound commanding. 'Hurry up. I need to come.'

Once again he knelt between her legs, fumbling enthusiastically at her blouse until she was out of it, then he practically ripped her bra off. His erection rubbed against her calf, then her thigh until he was almost thrusting. He nuzzled her zipper open, and she could feel his hot breath on her pubis. With a groan, she lifted her hips, and he freed her of the last of her clothing, burying his face in her pussy, licking and suckling, making her buck against his mouth.

'No!' In a frenzy of sensation, she clawed her way out of the chair onto the carpet with Tino nipping and tonguing her the whole way. 'I didn't tell you to lick my pussy.'

She half expected him to break into a lupine howl of frustration. On hands and knees, she caught her breath, then she wiggled her arse at him and spread her legs to show off her heavy pout. 'Fuck me,' she growled. 'You've smelled me, tasted me. You know I'm ripe for you. Fuck me, and make me come.'

Tino obediently positioned himself behind her, spreading her labia with wet fingers. She reached between her legs and guided his jutting cock into her dilated pussy then thrust back onto him hard, crying out with the first stretching impact. He grabbed her hips and humped, grunting and groaning, his hands moving first to cup her bouncing tits and thumb her nipples, then to knead her buttocks in sinuous bruising grasps.

As he found his rhythm, he slid a hand down over her pubis and rubbed the hard node of her clit to delicious raw fire until she could stand it no longer, and she came. The clenching of her pussy sent him over the edge, and he emptied his balls into her with great gasping moans. Then together they crawled in front of the fireplace and he wrapped himself around her for a little rest before round two. She drifted off to sleep with his fingers curled in a gentle caress against her cunt.

'He fucked me like an animal, Stel! I couldn't get enough. Even thinking about what he did to me makes me wet.'

Stella shushed her when the people at the next table gave an irritated glance in their direction.

Anne leaned closer and spoke in a more subdued tone. 'Whatever I wanted, he did. He always touched me just the right way, almost like he read my mind.'

'Pets can be very intuitive.'

'God, I never dreamed sex could be so good. Do you know who he is in real life? I'm dying to find out.'

'No idea.' Stella ran her spoon around the rim of her cappuccino, then licked the foam. 'Pet identities are strictly confidential. Besides, don't you think knowing names would ruin it?'

'I thought it would drive me crazy, all that silence for a whole weekend, but it was so freeing, no pressure to make witty conversation, no dressing to seduce, no trying to impress, and he adored me anyway! He does speak, doesn't he?'

'Pets aren't allowed to speak, or they wouldn't be pets, would they? The Kennel Club does the talking.'

'I figured as much. I want him again, but I can't access the Kennel Club website.'

'It's by invitation only, but once you've had a pet, your password is your pet's name. If you change pets, your password changes too. I have to warn you though, Tino's not easy to get.'

Stella was right. Once Anne had accessed the Kennel Club website, Tino only had one opening for the next three months, and that was because of a cancellation in three weeks. In spite of the high fees the Kennel Club charged, Anne took the opening and scheduled him for the whole weekend.

For the first few days after her encounter with Tino, Anne was content to let him simply be the pet from the Kennel Club, but as the euphoria of the weekend wore off and the real world returned, she found herself wondering who Tino really was.

His Kennel Club bio said only that his full name was Valentino, height 6'1", weight 190 pounds, hair auburn, eyes brown. The bio was followed by a long list of testimonials from Tino's previous weekend mistresses. They were all rave reviews. Suddenly Anne didn't feel so special any more.

Still, she couldn't stop thinking about him. Tino invaded her dreams, nibbling smoked salmon from her hand, curling up on the floor by the bed, waiting patiently until she invited him to join her, until she told him how she wanted him to touch her, to taste her, what she wanted him to do with his cock. He was so obedient in such delicious ways. No matter how ridiculous it was, she missed him. She missed the way he listened, the way he looked at her with those adoring eyes, the way he stretched and moaned when she caressed his perpetually heavy penis.

He had only been with her for a weekend, she reminded herself angrily. And what was he, anyway, but a glorified prostitute? Yet how could she endure being without him for two and a half long weeks? One night she even fantasised that she asked him to move in with her, and he accepted.

A week later, her work took her to the States, to Portland, Oregon. It was a whirlwind trip, a day of meetings, a night at the airport Sheraton, then back to London. At least that had been the plan.

When room service arrived the morning she was to fly out, with her mushroom omelette and a copy of the *Oregonian*, her plans changed.

On page four of the newspaper, she was greeted by a smiling photo of Tino! She plopped her teacup down on the tray, slopping Earl Grey over the crisp white napkin, and read the caption as the scent of bergamot filled the air.

'Vincent Evanston, reclusive philanthropist, to dedicate new wild-life preserve near Lincoln City.'

The ceremony was this afternoon. Forgetting all about her omelette, she held the paper up to the lamp and squinted hard at the photo. The hair was styled differently. The face was shaved clean, and the man in the photo wore an immaculate suit, which made him look older. What would Tino be doing in America? Perhaps it was just someone who looked like him. And yet she had to know.

An hour later, she was in a hired car, road atlas open on the passenger seat, heading for the Oregon Coast and Lincoln City. If she hurried, she could just make it.

* * *

It was not without considerable effort that she finally found the Fireweed Nature Reserve at the end of a not-so-well-maintained gravel road. When she arrived, even the journalists were dressed like adverts for an outdoor magazine. She wasn't likely to blend in with her clingy summer dress, as her kitten heels slid treacherously between the cracks in the boardwalk over the marsh which led to the viewing platform where the dedication was to take place. Tino wouldn't have cared what she wore, she reminded herself angrily.

She stumbled up the boardwalk just as the introduction finished, nearly falling against a man draped in half-a-dozen cameras.

And suddenly there was Tino, looking rugged and considerably less vulnerable in his khaki trousers and cotton shirt. He waited politely for the applause to die down, then he spoke. 'As most of you know, I grew up not far from here.' The resonant voice and the American accent sounded strange coming from her pet. 'My best memories are of a pair of barn owls who took up residence on our farm the year I turned twelve. All that summer, my brother and I watched those owls, even rigged up a camera and got some pretty decent photos. In fact, we were so obsessed with those birds that we started a secret club in their honour. We called ourselves the Night Owls. Those owls successfully raised five chicks that year, and I fell in love.

'Places like this are important, not just because of the sanctuary they give wildlife, but because they offer all of us an opportunity to fall in love with nature.' His gaze moved over the crowd, came to rest on her, then moved on. She felt as though she had been slapped, and yet how could she be stupid enough to expect he would recognise her? Surely this man couldn't be her Tino.

He continued. 'I have a reputation for being a recluse, but I'm not really.' He offered a mischievous chuckle. 'I just prefer the company of the residents of a place like this over you lot.'

To the sound of laughter and applause, he cut the red ribbon stretched across the viewing platform and stood smiling, shaking hands while cameras snapped and reporters asked questions. People adorned in binoculars and bird scopes now lined the rail of the viewing platform. The chill in the air as the sun fell below the wooded hills of the coastal range made Anne's nipples ache through the ridiculously thin dress.

She was halfway back to her car, feeling stupid and self-conscious, when a strong arm slipped around her waist, and a familiar scent filled her nostrils. She looked up into Tino's dark eyes.

'What are you doing here?' It was still a shock to hear her Tino speaking.

'I came on business. I saw your picture in the *Oregonian*. You are Tino, aren't you?'

'Tino's not here.' With his arm around her waist, he guided her away from her car to a waiting limo. Once they were inside, he knocked on the privacy window and the driver took off.

'But you have to be Tino, or you wouldn't have recognised –'

He covered her mouth in an insistent kiss, teasing her lips apart, sparring with her tongue, making her insides feel like warm toffee. 'Tino's not here,' he whispered against her lips, then flicked them with his tongue. 'There's just Vincent.'

'What are you, schizo then?' She let out a little gasp as he nibbled her ear lobe and kissed the hollow of her throat.

'We all have more than one person living inside us, Anne, and you came here today because you wanted to know who else lives in here with Tino, didn't you?'

'Where are we going?' she asked, feeling suddenly frightened as the driver turned on to the main road and picked up speed.

'Portland.'

'But my car. It's a hire, and my bags.'

He kissed her again, and his hand moved up the inside of her thigh. 'Don't worry. My people will take care of everything.'

'But I thought –' With a sharp little gasp, she suddenly forgot how to speak, as his fingers slipped inside her knickers.

'We have until we get to Portland, Anne. You can waste time trying to find out about Tino or –' he slid his middle finger into her moist pout '– you can spend that time with Vincent.' His thumb pressed tight little circles around her clit. 'It can be such a pleasant drive to Portland.'

'I don't even know Vincent,' she gasped.

'You will by the time we get to Portland.' He burrowed, face first, into her well-displayed cleavage, wasted on the herons and otters at the nature reserve. He shoved aside the plunge neckline and push-up bra, until her breasts tumbled over like ripe fruit ready for his tasting.

The seat in the limo was soft leather, and almost big enough for an orgy. She lost the kitten heels and her toes curled in the plush carpet as he slid a second finger into her.

'Not appropriate footwear for a nature reserve.' He nodded to her shoes. Then he pulled her down and shifted her until she lay full length on the seat. 'You could have broken an ankle.' He lifted her foot to his lips, bathing her heel in his hot breath. 'What were you thinking?' His words slurred as he ran his tongue up over her instep and suckled each toe in turn, causing her to buck against the seat and her pussy to grip his fingers like a hungry mouth.

'Ticklish, are we?' He continued the trail of kisses and nips and love bites over her ankle and up the inside of her thigh while she squirmed and giggled.

Shoving aside the crotch of her knickers until they were stretched uselessly over one arse cheek, he lapped at her clit and suckled her labia until she was heavy and distended, still gripping his probing fingers. There was the sound of a zipper, the swish of clothing, and he pushed into her with a grunt. 'You shouldn't have come here.' He held very still, making her wait with his fullness inside her. Making her want. 'It's a complication neither of us needs.'

'Please,' she whimpered, and tried to thrust against him.

Still he didn't move, but he let her squirm beneath him feeling like her cunt was on fire. 'You didn't come for me, did you? You came for Tino.' He rocked against her just enough for his body to rake her clit, and the shock of it felt like electricity jolting through her pussy. She clenched down hard on his cock.

'Please!'

He lowered his mouth to her nipples as though they had all the time in the world, nibbling them to the tetchy place between pain and pleasure just as the limo turned towards Portland. Then he raised his dark-brown eyes, suddenly so unlike Tino's, and met her gaze. 'You want Vincent?'

'Please! I want Vincent.'

He chuckled softly, then gathered her to him, cupping her buttocks in his hands to push deeper into her. She raised her arse, wrapped her legs around him and hung on for the ride.

He was pitiless. He battered her with exquisite force until she was almost there, then he stopped, holding her so tightly that she couldn't satisfy herself, she could do nothing but yield as he kissed her until her lips felt bruised, and nibbled her throat and neck until she trembled like light on the surface of water. Then he battered her again.

And just when she began to wonder if she would even survive the trip to Portland, he shifted his embrace and pulled her on top of him, nearly toppling them both off onto the floorboard in the process. 'I'll make you come now, Anne.' His voice was raspy at the back of his throat. 'Vincent will make you come.'

Perhaps it was some magic formula, she didn't know, but with the gentle rocking of his hips like waves on a calm sea, and the stroking of his thumb against her clit, she came in whimpers and sobs. A few more thrusts and she felt him clench beneath her and his cock spasmed inside her.

'Where are you taking me?' she asked. The street lights indicated that they were in the suburbs of Portland, and time was running out.

Still naked, he knelt on the floorboard, wiping the wet folds of her vulva with his white handkerchief. 'The airport.'

She pushed his hand away. 'I don't have a ticket, and look at me, I'm a mess.' To her irritation, she was suddenly fighting back tears.

He rose on his haunches and kissed her, cupping her cheek and pushing the hair away from he face. 'I think you look exquisite. Now hold still. I'm not finished with your pussy yet, and I'm enjoying the view.'

She felt as though she would burst as the first signs for the airport came into view. She had gone to Lincoln City for answers, but she had got only more questions. 'There's so much I want to ask you, Vincent.'

'Don't. Because I won't answer, and I don't want to ruin what we've just shared.'

'Will I see you again?'

He forced a smile. 'You weren't supposed to see me at all.'

Panic suddenly rose in her chest. 'Will I see Tino?'

'That's up to the Kennel Club.'

The limo pulled to a stop, and the driver opened the door and helped her out. To her surprise, they weren't at the departures drop-off point, with its manic coming and going of cars, disgorging people with too much luggage. Instead they were on a darkened runway. For a second, panic rose in Anne's chest. Perhaps Vincent was schizo after all, perhaps his intentions were more sinister than a flight back to London.

But before the thought was fully formed, he handed over her bag and nodded above the roof of the limo. 'The plane's there.'

'Bloody hell!' Beyond the car was a sleek private jet, smartly dressed staff standing at the ready near the foot of the stairs leading to the open door.

'Come on.' He slid an arm around her. 'Your bags are already on board. You'll have time to freshen up. Pilot expects a smooth flight into London.'

Then everything happened so fast. He gave her a brain-melting kiss at the bottom of the stairs, turned her over to the smiling attendant and, by the time she was at the top of the stairs, the limo was already pulling away.

Stella sat curled on the end of Anne's couch watching her pace. 'I can't believe you cancelled your flight and went chasing after some tree-hugging tycoon.' She handed her a tissue mid-stride and Anne wiped her swollen eyes and blew her nose.

'Well, I did, and look what it got me.' She nodded towards her laptop open on the coffee table. 'My weekend with Tino has been cancelled, and my Kennel Club privileges have been revoked. I can't get on the website at all, and I haven't heard from Vincent either.'

'You said it yourself, Vincent's a recluse.' Stella poured herself a glass of wine and sipped while Anne paced. 'And you really can't expect him to be Tino for you now after what you know. It would never be the same. That's the reason for the strict Kennel Club rules.'

'Don't lecture me, Stel, all right? I just don't understand why a man like Vincent would become a pet.'

'Who knows?' Stella said. 'Maybe he needs something different, like we all do sometimes. Maybe he needs not to always be in charge. Maybe he needs someone to take care of him for a little while.'

Anne plopped down on the couch. 'I have to see him again, Stella. I have to.' Her eyes misted, and the empty space inside her felt vast.

'For fuck's sake, Annie, be sensible. You don't even know him – whoever he is. Tino's a glorified hooker, and Vincent's a bored rich bloke who got a good shag out of you. God, if I'd known it would cause you this much grief, I'd have never introduced you. It was all supposed to be in good fun. Pull yourself together.'

Anne ignored her friend's reprimand. In fact she barely heard it. 'I need you to do me a big favour, Stel. I need to use your Kennel Club password.'

'Are you crazy? Annie, this just isn't healthy. You need to let it go.'

'Please, Stel. I have to see him one more time. I just have to.'

For a long moment, Stella held her in a gaze that would have penetrated iron, then she shook her head and heaved a sigh. 'Tino or Vincent or whatever his name is, he's not the nutter, Annie. You are. But you're also my best friend.' She grabbed a biro and a piece of paper from her bag, scribbled the password and handed it to her. 'Try not to get me banned from the site, OK?'

As soon as Stella left, Anne pulled the computer onto her lap, entered the Kennel Club address and waited impatiently until a password was requested. She typed what Stella had given her, holding her breath. Suddenly she was in, scrolling down through the bios and photos of pets until she came to Tino, and her heart somersaulted as she recalled the shy man, unable to meet her gaze without encouragement. How could he be Vincent? How could Vincent be him? The body was the same, there was no mistaking it, but they were so different. Even the way they made love was different.

She clicked on Tino's diary. He had already been rescheduled for this weekend. She felt an empty ache beneath her breastbone. He should have been here with her, in her arms, in her bed. His diary was now full for the next six months, so she couldn't even schedule him under Stella's name. Six months was an eternity.

She Googled Vincent Evanston for the hundredth time.

He was thirty-five years old. He'd made his wealth in his father's shipping business, then turned everything over to his employees and disappeared, donating massive amounts of money for environmental and wildlife causes. He was nicknamed 'the Invisible Man'. He was seldom seen, but his money was always hard at work.

Nothing she didn't already know. She poured herself another glass of wine and paced the floor some more. Then she pulled up the Kennel Club website again. She was about to scroll to Tino's bio when she noticed the logo at the lower left-hand corner of the Kennel Club home page. It was small and highly stylised, but as she squinted down at it, she could tell that it was an owl. Underneath it in minuscule letters were the words 'Night Owl Services'.

She released breath she didn't know she'd been holding. Suddenly she was as certain as she was of her own name. Vincent Evanston owned the Kennel Club! She stared at the logo until her eyes could no longer focus. The Kennel Club was simply high-class hookers with a twist, and Vincent was one of his own pets. Why? Was it really because he needed someone to take care of him?

She had to admit it took courage for Vincent to be Tino. She thought about the other Annes living inside her; Annes whose existence she had denied. Was it possible for her to learn to share power? On the other hand, perhaps Vincent was just an entrepreneur providing a much-needed service for pathetic people like her? Unfortunately she would never know. She finished her wine and went to bed.

The next morning she discovered a letter from the States lying on the mat in front of her mail slot. Inside was a newspaper clipping from the *Denver Post*. She read the first paragraph.

> *Vincent Evanston, reclusive West Coast philanthropist, will make a surprise appearance at the annual charity banquet for the Natural History Museum, Saturday night.*

It was the night Tino would have been with her. As she unfolded the article, a ticket to the banquet dropped onto the table.

Feeling suddenly weak, she lowered herself into a chair. For a long moment she sat staring at the ticket, then she called her secretary. 'Claire, I need a flight to Denver.' As she hung up, she wondered just who, of all the people living inside her, would join Vincent Evanston for the banquet.

Short fiction by K D Grace appears in the Black Lace anthology *Liaisons*.

Fancy Feet
Heather Towne

Matt watched as his wife pulled up her knee-length black skirt, unhooked the red-ribboned black garter straps from the lacy tops of her sheer, black stockings. Watched on his knees, on the bedroom carpet, his blue eyes wide and unblinking behind the lenses of his glasses, his thin-lipped mouth hanging open. Watched as an obedient dog anxiously watches its master, fervently hoping for the promise of play in her movements.

Lela tossed her long blonde hair over her shoulder and coolly regarded her kneeling husband for a moment. Her silver-glossed lips parted slightly in a frosty smile, and she sat down on the edge of the bed, slowly unfolded a long, lithe, stockinged limb and extended it towards Matt.

He gulped, and rushed forwards on his knees.

She rested her slender ankle on his shoulder. He carefully slid his trembling fingers into the darker stocking top and delicately eased it down his wife's sculpted leg. The silky material whispered to him as it descended her leg, revealing more and more of her gleaming ivory skin.

And when, at last, he had the gossamer material wispily bunched at her shapely ankle, she lifted her leg off his shoulder and arched her stockinged foot at him, long, slim toes pointing. He swept the stocking off her foot with a sigh, placed the puddled leg garment on the white towel to his left (to be lovingly unrolled and stretched and stored later on), and stared at his wife's bare limb.

He performed the same procedure on Lela's other sheathed leg. Unfortunately, there was no time now for him to exultantly scoop up the piled hose and bury his nose in it, nor to thoroughly soak the woman's feet in warm water as he normally did; for Lela had come home late from the office again, and was tired and anxious to sleep. So he was just as anxious to perform the joyous, late-evening ritual of preparing his wife's lower limbs for bed.

His tools were laid out on the white towel to his right: lotion, which he caressed into Lela's smooth, porcelain skin – from long, lean thighs over slim, hard-shelled knees and down onto lightly muscled calves; pumice stone, which he rubbed against Lela's delicately rounded heels and balls, washing away any dry skin; emery board, which he brushed over the tips of Lela's shiny toenails, sanding them smooth and convex; and finally, foot cream, which he massaged into the tight, silken skin of her feet – up and over the sky-high arches, in between the limber, nail-crowned toes, and down under the curvaceous soles.

Sadly, there was no jewellery or toenail polish to remove tonight. She'd eschewed those adornments in her rush to work that morning, when he'd carefully dressed her legs, and shod her feet.

Now, with her limbs and peds properly primped and pampered for bed by her footman, Lela let a tight smile flicker across her pursed lips. 'Stand up,' she told Matt.

He sprang to his feet. Naked, he faced his wife perched on the edge of the bed, his cock straining obscenely hard and long at her. He hung his head, hoping against hope.

And his feverish prayers were answered, for Lela leaned back and slowly unfolded her stunning legs, reached out with her shining feet, clasped his jumping cock between her agile toes and stroked – once.

'Jesus!' Matt blurted, jerking.

Hot, pent-up semen burst out of his slit and sprayed Lela's knees, her calves, her ankles. Like a fiercely devout worshipper inculcated with hours and hours of fiery gospel and then rushed down to the river, he jumped in blindly and unabashedly, unable and unwilling to control himself. Her beautiful legs were the beatific vessels of his lust, and he anointed their glory over and over, rapturous at being blessed with a foot job.

Until, finally, Lela withdrew her semen-striped legs and Matt stumbled, shamefaced, into the bathroom. He staggered back with an armload of wet and dry towels which he used to cleanse his wife's heavenly limbs.

Come morning, as Matt was dressing Lela's legs – painting her toenails a bright crimson and softly blowing them dry, slipping a pair of snow-white stockings onto her limbs and securing them up with pink garters, sliding her peds into a pair of scarlet leather pumps – he received another surprise gift from his wife, which he surely didn't deserve.

Looking down at the hunched-over man still fussing with her shoes, straightening the seams in her stockings, she stated, 'There's a woman from work I want you to meet tonight.'

He tore his eyes off his wife's legs and glanced up at her face, startled.

'Have dinner ready at eight,' she added, before pirouetting and strolling out of the room.

He stared intently at her long, lean lower limbs, every step of the way.

Matt was glad that his wife had finally made a friend. It was his hometown, and she'd only been living in it for a year, coming from a much larger city after they'd gotten married. They'd both agreed that his job at his mother's footwear factory was just too good to give up.

And Matt was even happier, downright ecstatic, when he met his wife's friend – Sophie L'Esperanza, a fellow paralegal at the law firm they both worked at. She was a tall dark-haired woman with flashing brown eyes and a dazzling white smile, skin the colour and smoothness of poured caramel, her slim high-breasted body supported by long luscious legs.

Matt openly stared at the woman's bare, gleaming limbs spilling out of her brown leather skirt, pouring down into a pair of gold, high-heeled, open-toed sandals, which perfectly displayed her spectacularly curved arches and slender, gold-tipped toes. His blue eyes were wide and unblinking behind the lenses of his glasses, his thin-lipped mouth hung open.

They sat down to dinner. Matt had prepared a small feast of leg of lamb and russet potatoes and string beans, thin slices of chocolate cheesecake for dessert, a light red wine throughout. He served the two lithesome ladies eagerly, anxiously, almost totally silently, unquestioningly. Just happy to the point of giddiness that his wife had brought into their home such a leggy companion.

They adjourned to the living room, the two women sliding onto the white leather couch and crossing their legs, Matt hanging onto the edge of a hard-backed chair right in front of them. He had turned on all the lights, so that he had a clear, close view of the women's supplely folded limbs.

And then he spat up some of the chicory coffee he'd made and served in fine-bone china cups, when Lela casually remarked, 'I've told Sophie all about your . . . fetish, Matt. And she's expressed an interest in experiencing it.'

He stared at his wife in utter astonishment. 'I . . . I . . .' spluttered. He couldn't finish. He was just too choked up.

'I want you to do to her legs what you do to mine, when I first come home.'

His knees hit the polished hardwood before she'd even finished her instructions. Brushing aside the glass coffee table, he dived his head down at Sophie's left foot on the floor and licked her exposed big toe.

'Oh, my!' she gasped, coffee cup rattling in her hand, as Matt lashed his tongue back and forth across her gold-clasped, gold-tipped toes.

He vigorously tongued them, joyously tasting the smooth-nailed, leather-spiced piggies with his sensitive buds, the woman's airborne right foot jumping up and down in sympathy to the oral onslaught its sister was receiving. He dragged his flattened tongue up and over the bare, bronze arch, painting it glistening with his saliva, stopping his sensuous ascent only when he reached the strapped-in ankle. Then he descended her wicked arch with his wet, swirling tongue again.

Sophie placed her sandalled right foot on the floor, and Matt licked those toes, that arch. Then he tongue-levered her big toe off the tilted leathern platform of her sexy shoe and took it into his mouth, and sucked on it. Eyes closed and lips working, chin scraping the floor, he sucked and sucked on Sophie's bulbous big toe, like a hungry baby nursing at its mother's breast. Then he popped that toe out of his mouth and popped the other one in, tugging on the trembling woman's left big toe.

Still sucking, he opened his eyes and looked up at Lela. She nodded, and he disgorged Sophie's slathered toe and stripped away her footwear. Expertly and rapidly, he unstrapped and slid the high-heeled sandals off the hard-breathing woman's peds, leaving her gorgeously, innocently barefoot. He sniffed at the damp, tangy-scented soles of her shoes, inhaling deep and dizzy, before placing the golden ped-holders to one side and scooping up Sophie's buff, brown feet, then cradling them like twin trophies in his knowing hands.

He stared at the long, outstretched toes and shiny, soaring arches, the soft, delicate balls and heels and contoured soles. Then he placed the light-as-a-feather peds together side by side and opened his mouth up and consumed the tapered tips of the woman's feet.

'Oh my God!' Sophie shrieked, her legs quivering, feet jumping in the kneeling man's mouth.

Lela clutched the woman's hand, feeling her vibrations. Riding the hem of her black minidress up and sliding her other hand into her black satin panties, and rubbing, she watched her husband reverentially suck on fully half of her friend's delectable feet.

Matt didn't notice the effect he was having on the two women. His watery blue eyes were on the tops of Sophie's feet so close – the gleaming, rising portions of the arches that refused to be swallowed – his throat and tongue working desperately. He sucked on the woman's spicy peds, swabbing his tongue back and forth across the balls and bottoms of her feet. Saliva spilled out of the corners of his outrageously stretched mouth and splashed down onto the floor. He ran his hands up and down Sophie's clenched calves and dug his fingers into the quivering taut muscles.

Both ladies moaned with pleasure, as Matt finally, slowly, pulled Sophie's feet out of his mouth, disgorging the curvy peds inch by dripping inch. Then he held and gazed at them, the slickened brown skin all but blinding him, preventing him from noticing his wife lean in closer to Sophie. The two women softly kissed each other.

Matt parted the sparkling feet a couple of inches and then popped a big toe into his mouth and sucked on it again. Then did the same to the other big toe, his thumbs rubbing the baby-smooth soles of Sophie's feet. She moaned into Lela's mouth, the two women kissing more urgently now.

Matt began sucking up and down the rows of foot-digits, savouring their ripe, silken texture, their blossomed tops and tapered stems, the way they delightfully wriggled in his mouth. He sucked and pulled on each and every toe in turn. Then squirmed his tongue in between them, bathing and scouring them, up and down the line, before popping the cute little pinky toe into his mouth and gently biting into it. Sophie slid a hand into Lela's dress and found the woman's breasts, and squeezed.

The two women's tongues excitedly entwined over and over, Lela grabbing onto Sophie's shimmering curtain of hair and pulling her even closer, Sophie fondling Lela's firm, pointed breasts. Matt was joyfully oblivious to their passion, his own passion building and boiling, as he greedily fed on Sophie's feet and toes, unknowingly stoking the women higher and hotter with his unadulterated leg lust.

And he had just traced the stunning peaks and valley of Sophie's deliciously crinkled sole with his lapping tongue, when his reddened ears rang with the harsh pronouncement, 'Let go of Sophie's feet! They're mine!'

He looked up, dazed, from the woman's peds. His wife was nude on the couch, glaring at him, an arm covetously clutching Sophie's shoulders. He instantly replaced Sophie's soaking feet back on the floor, where they sprung up prettily on splayed toes.

Then he watched in anguished amazement as Sophie jumped to her feet, wriggled out of her gold lamé dress and, naked, rejoined Lela on the couch. The women shifted over sideways, so that their legs were up and extended towards one another in open, erotic invitation.

Lela grasped Sophie's right foot in her hands and briefly stroked it, caressed it. Then blatantly stuck it in her mouth and sucked on it. Sophie did the same with Lela's presented right foot. The two women ardently sucked on each other's foot-tips, their long legs tangling together, right before Matt's very widened eyes.

He could hardly capture it all, or comprehend it all. His wife had always allowed him his leg fetish – more so with each passing month – but she'd never seemed to appreciate it very much. Tolerated it, yes; enjoyed it, no.

But here she was sucking on another woman's toes, all at once and individually, squeezing her tongue in between them, lapping at Sophie's foot-bottom. Moaning with desire, shaven pussy glistening with moisture, as her dark-haired co-worker sucked on her toes, licked at her soles.

Matt watched in wonderment. He was shocked back to consciousness only when Lela yelled at him, 'Pull your cock out! Jerk yourself off as you watch Sophie and I foot-fuck!'

His zipper was down and his iron-hard cock out in the flick of a toe. He fisted furiously, unbelieving, watching his wife pull her moistened ped-tip out of Sophie's hands, and mouth, and trail it down the woman's heaving tits and stomach and onto the damp, black fur of her pussy. She jabbed her toe inside, and pumped. And Sophie cried, 'Oh, God!' rattling Matt.

He torqued up the pressure on his cock even more – his hand a poor substitute for Lela's feet – as Sophie dipped her own big toe into Lela's pussy and pushed back and forth. The two women clung to each other's bent legs, their other legs working, quivering, more toes penetrating slickened pussy lips and plunging in and out. Their moans and gasps came faster, harder, in rhythm to their pointed, pistoning feet.

Until Lela's sleek, pale body suddenly arched, and shuddered, electric orgasm arcing all through her. Sophie's tawny body spasmodically shivered with her own savage orgasm. The two women convulsed violently in the throes of toe-fuck ecstasy.

Matt jacked ropes and ropes of white-hot jism out of his pulsating cock, staring at those yards of shimmering leg flesh, that plethora of shining peds and toes.

He found the note propped up in the leopard-pattern sole of his personal favourite pair of his wife's black stilettos the next morning. It read:

Matt,
I've run off with Sophie. Your fetish has become my fetish.
Thank you and goodbye.
Lela

They were the kindest words he'd ever received from his wife. He clutched the sexy shoe to his chest, thanking Lela for the parting gifts she'd bestowed on him the previous two evenings; proud of her choice in women.

Then he rushed back into the bedroom and flung open the dresser drawers, the closet door. All of Lela's stockings and pantyhose and shoes, toe and ankle accessories, were gone; the collection he'd so earnestly helped her build over the past year – taken away.

He sighed and sat down on the bed. Then took a deep breath and picked up the phone on the nightstand, punched in a number.

'S-Sophie?' he said, his voice cracking. 'I-I can still see *you*, can't I?'

He held his breath, shaking all over.

'Yes, Matt,' his hometown sweetheart – the first pair of legs and feet he'd ever worshipped – finally replied, her voice firm but warm. 'Nothing has changed between us.'

The short fiction of Heather Towne has been featured in numerous Black Lace short story anthologies.

Wet and Wild

Shada Royce

I stripped in the shadows. The cool evening breeze provided a welcome relief to the sweltering heat of the mid-August night. In the shade of the trees near the edge of the fence I knew I'd be well hidden from view, but once I stepped from the darkness and until I made it to the water, I'd be exposed. Naked. Vulnerable. The thought thrilled me, my nipples budding as blood coursed through my body, heightening the awareness of my nudity.

Stepping from the protection of the trees, I forced myself to walk slowly to the edge of the pool, basking in the possibility of being caught. The pale glow from the lamp post gave my skin a milky, bluish tint. I looked flawless in the forgiving light, beautiful – sexy even. Something I only felt here, in this place.

Easing down to the edge, I slipped into the water, careful to create no more than a gentle disturbance to the even, quiet surface. The water licked along the length of my legs, pulling me into an enchanted rippling of sensual waves and swirls. I sighed as I sank lower and the water lapped against my pussy, moaning as I dipped further and the coolness caressed my breasts, like the delicate tease of a tongue. Drawing in a breath, I dived beneath the surface and swam to the opposite edge, to my favourite spot.

The Property Owners' Association had to be wasting a ton of money by running the pool pump all night. Although it cycled on and off, the electricity alone had to be costing the swanky, private swimming pool a small fortune. I didn't pay any membership fees so I couldn't care less, and good thing I could climb a fence.

I swam to the far corner, nearly vibrating with need as I neared the jet that swished and gurgled along the surface. Already my blood hummed through my arms and legs, coursing through my chest. My breaths came shallow and fast as the boiling motion of the water brought a wave of remembrance to my body of the pleasure to come. The water cooled as I swam further into the darkened corner, nestled on the other side of the diving board. The jet sprayed a heavy, strong beam of water that beat against my stomach as I swam closer. Warm, thick cream slid from between my legs, wetting my body in anticipation. Heart pounding fiercely in my chest, I only glanced briefly around the pool area before I lay back in the water and set my legs out of the water along the tiled edge. Floating to the surface, my breasts bobbed out of the water, the warm night air sending cool caresses along my wet, heated skin. I scooted forwards until my knees were settled securely over the rounded lip of the pool. The angle brought my pussy in direct line with the water pushing from the small orifice on the pool wall.

Pounding swirls of bubbles coalesced into a pulsing stream of energy, focused right on my clit. I closed my eyes as my nipples beaded from the sheer ecstasy lapping between my legs. The parts of my body floating beneath the surface of the water felt hot while the exposed parts tingled under the summer breeze. A slow, drumming swirl of heat gathered in the pit of my stomach, gathering at my chest and pussy. Everything along the length of my body tightened as I tried to hold the orgasm at bay, wanting to enjoy the pleasure of the jets longer. I scooted closer to the wall, the pressure increased, the swirls coming in faster, quicker tugs.

The hard contractions of the release washed over me, like the surf beating against the beach. Fierce. Sudden. Wave after wave of what felt like a velvet tongue trailed down my entrance, as my lips sucked in and out. I fought to stay afloat as I stayed centred over the jet and a second orgasm pushed over me. Not as strong as the first, but just as potent as my body twitched with the tremors. As my body stilled, I forced my breathing to settle, then I pushed away from the wall and floated towards the centre of the pool. The whispering night air teased my skin, releasing the tension and heat. I closed my eyes and relaxed.

As I neared the centre, the lights flicked on in the pool. I could hear the faint click beneath the water.

Shit, I'd been caught. Someone would see me, find me and these late night escapades would cease. A saddening sense of loss and disappointment washed over me before a flutter of fear, mixed with excitement, coursed through the baser emotions. I floated upright and turned until I saw him standing there, the top half of his body shadowed beneath the pool building overhang.

'Enjoying the swim?' he asked, his voice a deep murmur in the darkness, the baritone quality of his voice flowing over every jazzed nerve.

Squinting towards him, I tried to make out his features. He was wearing slacks and dress shoes but everything above the waist was shrouded in the shadows. He could be the security guard who only occasionally passed by, a pool member, a neighbour. I didn't care. He'd found me and I needed a way out.

'How long have you been standing there?' I asked, forgoing any inclination for an explanation or a question of who he was.

He rocked back on his heels and stuffed his hands in his pockets in a nonchalant sort of way that told me the answer long before he spoke.

'Long enough.'

Treading water in the centre of the pool had caused my limbs to feel like lead so I swam towards the edge, careful to keep the water lapping at my chin. But I knew he could see every curve of my body below the crystal-clear lighted water. I knew how I looked. Although I would never pass for any size three supermodel, I knew I had plump curves in all the right places. Think hourglass rather than ruler.

Contemplating his silhouette, I pulled up on the edge of the pool and crossed my arms under my chin. 'Enjoy the show?' I managed through the excited mortification clogging the back of my throat. How long had he really been standing there? From the minute my feet landed on the concrete after I climbed the fence? Or only recently? Just recent enough to watch me coming twice up against the water jets.

'Yes,' he stated without a hint of remorse. His body had tensed and he shifted again. He hesitated for only a moment before stepping forwards.

The overhead lights cast his face in stark, angular planes. His dark hair looked like inky waves in the ocean at midnight. Eyes glittering mischievously from beneath his lowered lids, his full, devilishly curved lips kicked up on the ends. I wanted to press my mouth to his and slap his cheeky face all at the same time.

'Good. Now if you'll turn around so I can get out, I'll be leaving.' I started to push out of the pool but he stood his ground, holding my gaze captive.

Then he began a seductive, slow prowl towards me. A fluid movement that screamed he knew he had me trapped and would enjoy watching me squirm.

I fought the urge to push away, back towards the deep water. My breath rushed from my lungs. Would he call the police? Would he ask me to leave? Would he yank me from the pool and have his wicked way with me before letting me go?

I stilled, tensing as he squatted down near me, realising in a sudden flash of clarity how bad I wanted this man to fuck me.

He was even more handsome up close, all broad shouldered, blue eyed and dark haired. His thigh muscles bulged against his slacks, his black dress shoes glittered in the light. I pulled my gaze away, caught the rippling muscles in his forearms, sprinkled with a light dash of hair. I'd always been a sucker for forearms and the thought of those arms straining to hold me up against a wall flashed through my mind.

Meeting his hooded stare, I wet my lips as I contemplated the wicked curve of his mouth. His lips kicked up on one side as he glanced down at the cleavage of my breasts pushing together at the edge of the pool. He tore his gaze back to mine.

'I came to swim, not see you naked,' he replied, standing again.

My stomach plummeted as a sense of disappointment and relief washed over me. Did I really want him to drag me from the pool? A man I didn't know.

The answer – yes.

My attention was diverted as he reached for the top button of his slacks, undid them and then pulled down the zipper.

'What are you doing?' I asked like an idiot, then forced my mouth closed.

'Swimming,' he stated matter-of-factly, then his mouth quirked again.

I unabashedly gaped as he pulled his shirt over his head. Who knew a stiff-necked polo shirt could hide such muscles. His great barrel of a chest gleamed in the moonlight, each ripple and cut highlighted by the starkness of the street light. He stood there, glistening in all his glory, like one of those half-naked models on the beach in an Abercrombie and Fitch magazine. I practically drooled. To save myself the embarrassment, I turned and swam away.

'Off to your corner again?' he called after me, the question echoing across the water.

I whirled, heat burning my cheeks, as he dived into the pool. I just caught a glimpse of the dark thatch of hair between his legs. He was as naked as I was.

Just the thought of all that sexy muscle in the same water as me had my body tingling. The place between my legs grew heavy.

He broke the surface within a foot of where I trod water. Shaking the water from his head, he wiped his face and settled those electric-blue eyes on me. A hot, heavy cream slipped from my pussy.

Water droplets glittered like diamonds in his hair and on his dark skin. The pale-blue water made his eyes appear like crystals and his jawline seemed harsher, more cut. I swallowed the gasp of pleasure as he swam a little nearer and the heat from him seeped into my bones.

'No reason to swim alone,' he murmured, his voice a throaty masculine rasp.

My nipples beaded as the water lapped at my neck, sending delicious waves of awareness down my torso and straight to my molten core.

I felt as if I stood on the edge of a cliff, where I could choose to leave and go back to my safe life with no surprises and all the delicious dirty little secrets of my midnight swims. Or I could jump, dive into the unknown and the possibility of darker pleasures.

I jumped.

Taking hold of my wavering bravado, I swam closer. 'Everything's better in pairs,' I purred as I reached out and traced a finger down his shoulder.

His lips twisted as the planes of his face hardened with blatant passion.

My lungs froze as the desire, so obvious on his face, turned his blue eyes to bright blue flames, threatening to engulf me.

He reached out and pulled my hand as he swam towards the steps leading out of the pool. I went willingly, unable to resist the unspoken promise of pleasure.

We reached the shallow water and he stood, bringing me with him. His broad shoulders expanded beyond my vision, appearing as wide as the horizon. His skin looked to be a vast expanse of tanned silk. I reached out and placed a hand to his chest, feeling the muscles jump beneath my feathered touch. Bringing my gaze back to his, I suddenly felt very small. Fragile and delicate like a thin piece of ice under the sweltering summer sun.

The side of his mouth turned up on one corner, the half-smile not quite reaching his burning, pointed gaze. He stretched out his hand and ran a finger from my collarbone, down my chest, along the side of my breast before circling my distended nipple. Dropping his hand back in the water he repeated the caress on the other side. My insides clenched, turning to a rolling ball of molten need. The heat radiated from my chest, pricking to my quivering pussy.

I caught his appreciative gaze before I closed my eyes and dropped my head back. The water rippled as he stepped closer. I could feel waves of warmth from his body reaching out to me, promising to relieve the chill from my skin. His hands gripped my hips and pulled me towards him. I leaned into his muscular frame, sighing, as my soft curves pressed into his hardened body.

The hold on my waist tightened and I felt the rigid length of his cock pressing into my stomach. Raising my head, I looked into his eyes. His face had grown harsher in the few seconds I'd closed my eyes.

I traced my hands up along his biceps, then circled one hand around his neck and the other around his head, pulling his mouth towards mine as I rose up on my toes.

'Kiss me,' I breathed across his lips, craving the taste of him, the feel of his tongue massaging mine.

He released a low growl before pulling me fully against him and planting his lips to mine.

I gasped in surprise, his barbaric action drawing out the woman who fantasised about being possessed, begged to be devoured. He kissed me as if he wanted that too, as if he couldn't get enough of me. My entire body hummed as I clung to him. Never wanting the feeling of being so intensely wanted to ever dim.

His tongue slipped into my mouth, then danced in and out in a swirling rhythm. With one hand he held my head still so he could suck and lave everything from my mouth. His other hand lightly trailed a path down my arm before slipping around to my back and down to my butt. He kneaded my ass, his fingers digging into my flesh, threatening to hoist me around his hips and impel me on his rigid cock.

I stood high on my toes, wanting more of his mouth, more of his body. He suddenly became like a drug, an aphrodisiac – addictive and delicious. And I didn't even know his name.

But the thought only increased my hunger to have him screw me. That was when I realised I'd slowly inched my way from bad to naughty – and I couldn't wait to dive deeper.

His fingers drove between my ass cheeks, scooting along my crack until he touched my swollen, aching pussy, budding and creamy between my thighs. I bit his lip as he circled one large finger over my entrance, smearing my slickness over my lips. Releasing my mouth to kiss his way down my chin, over my jaw and down my throat, he made his way to my ear. Then his hot breath was breaking over the shell and his tongue lashed out to dive deep.

I bucked against him as my pussy clenched and my nipples tightened against his chest.

I wrapped a leg around his waist and my lips brushed against his rock-hard cock. He groaned in my ear as the tip of his dick kissed my entrance, the welcome heat of my body teasing him.

He backed towards the stairs of the pool, then turned and set me on the first step.

'Turn around,' he said, his voice gravelly.

I looked into his blue gaze and licked my lips, missing the taste of him. I reached out and wrapped my hand around his cock. He sucked in a breath.

I smiled and then sank down in the water.

Working my hand along his length, he pumped against my fist. I glanced up as I lashed out my tongue to lick the tip of him. His body stiffened, waiting to see what I'd do. I could see the hope in his eyes, the silent prayer that I'd sink my mouth down over him and suck him.

Giving him a saucy smile, I turned my attention back to his manhood then opened my mouth and buried his thickness in it. He groaned again and his hands went to my head. His fingers flexed along my scalp as I began a slow slide up and down his cock. I sucked and licked his length before I began working my hand. He flexed his hips as I sank down and I felt him slide down the back of my throat. His fingers grew tighter and he flexed harder and harder. A deep sense of satisfaction settled through me that I could bring this sex god of a man to climax with my mouth and hands. I drew off of him, intending to dip my head and suck on his balls, but he grabbed my elbow and pulled me to my feet.

'Enough,' he ground out, his face lined and hard, but oh so sexy. 'Now turn around,' he said.

I did as he asked, bending over on my knees on the steps so my ass was level with his thick, pulsing cock. I had hardly noticed the lapping, cool water while I played with him, but suddenly, without him touching me, I felt the erotic swirl of the liquid as it slipped over my skin, like satin sheets teasing every body part it touched.

I closed my eyes when he placed his hands on my hips, waiting for him to slip inside. Yearning to have him buried to the hilt.

But instead he circled my pussy with a finger and then his tongue darted out and lapped at my entrance. I jumped, the delicate lick sending delicious waves of heat over my body. With one hand on my hip, he slipped two fingers inside of me, working them in and out. He licked around my lips before pulling my clit between his fingers and pinching. Then his tongue swirled on my pussy and he flicked my clit. Every nerve in my body was on fire as I came in a rush, bucking against his probing, pinching fingers. Before the last tremor left my body he bent and kissed the back of my neck, running his tongue down my spine. When he reached my ass, he shifted and drove inside me.

A heavy breath rushed from my mouth as the sudden fullness of him inside me plunged me closer to another orgasm. I gasped, his cock stretching me to the limit. His fingers dug into my hips and he slid slowly in and out of my body. Each stroke was an even, measured thrust – made to drive me wild. I bucked against him, needing more than the easy, deep penetration. I needed him pounding into me, his balls slapping against my clit.

'Harder,' I begged.

He tightened his grip on my hips and stayed his even course, drawing out my pleasure like a thin web. Stringing me along the path of passion. I slammed back into him, but he held me tighter in place.

'Harder, please,' I whimpered, so close to begging.

Faltering, he paused, then shifted and slammed into me. He increased his tempo, igniting a dangerous longing inside of me. Each stroke wound me tighter and tighter. A hot sweat broke out over my skin, and then chilled. The water lapped at my clit and coated my nipples each time he pushed in and pulled out.

My arms shook. My tunnel tightened around his cock in a silent plea to take me to the edge and toss me over. One of his hands slid up my back and tangled in my hair, pulling lightly. Then he pounded into me, hard and quick in long strokes.

The night sounds came into sharp focus for a moment – the slap of his body against mine, the gentle swish of the water on my breasts and between my legs, the whisper of the wind rustling the leaves, and the quiet singing of crickets. But just as quick, every sound disappeared as he tugged my hair harder. My pussy tightened and I felt the hot honey drip down my inner thighs. Slapping into me, his balls pounded on my clit and his cock angled to touch that one spot inside me. The heat started at my belly button, spiralling out like a hurricane until the ferocity of the storm engulfed me, pulling me under and stealing my breath. I screamed as I came, bucking and pulsing against him as he drove home once, then twice, before my pussy milked him to his own release. He slipped from inside me, spilling himself in the water.

My vision blurred and I felt dizzy. I sank further down in the water with him. He held me against his chest and we floated out towards the centre of the pool. The water cooled my skin and I was sure, if I looked, I'd see steam rising from the surface.

After I caught my breath, I turned to look at him.

He cocked a brow, as if to ask, 'What?'

'Still believe in the pleasure of pairs?' he asked, still swimming close to me.

I took in his glistening model-like appearance – the moulded lips, the breathtaking blue eyes, that square jaw. I knew I was pretty, in an exotic way with my dark hair and green eyes, but never would I have put myself in his league.

'Why me?' I blurted. A blush burned my cheeks.

He grinned, then shrugged and looked contemplative. 'You're different.'

Not what I expected. 'Different?'

He nodded. 'Yeah, you experiment and you have a whole bag of sexy secrets.'

I scoffed, but then turned on him. 'What do you mean, "a whole bag"?'

His face turned still but something glistered behind his eyes – mischief perhaps?

'I know you come here every Tuesday night, at midnight, and ... uh ... swim,' he said, the last part with a quirk of one dark eyebrow.

'What? How do you know that? Have you been watching me?' I suddenly felt ashamed, guilty, and just a little pleasure at the thought.

'I live across the street,' he murmured, indicating the dark mansion with a tilt of his head.

I turned, taking in the large brick home with the big picture windows. The house was still, no light showing in any windows. I'd always envisioned some elderly couple living there that retired early in the evening.

'OK, so why didn't you just call security instead –'

'Instead of screwing your brains out?' he cut in.

I shook my head. 'No, instead of coming out here yourself.'

He laughed. 'I did.'

'You did what?' I asked with a sinking feeling.

'Called security.'

I waited for him to continue, but he levelled me with a dark stare. 'And?' I asked, a little afraid of the answer.

'They set up surveillance.'

'What?' I looked around, trying to find the cameras.

'Over there,' he said, indicating the snack stand. Sure enough, a small red light flashed. One small enough that anyone would have hardly noticed without knowing the location. A hot flush of embarrassment ran through my body.

'So am I under arrest? What now?' I hated to ask.

'Let me just say that at first I had come out here to only watch, but something in your face when you came on the jet of water had me wishing for a taste of you.'

My heart fluttered. He swam nearer and I couldn't move away from the hungry look in his eyes.

'I had no idea you'd put a trance over me,' he murmured, reaching out.

I hesitated, but the possessive gleam in his eyes had me simmering with a second wave of need. So I swam to him, coming into his embrace.

'And no, you aren't under arrest. And as for what now, I plan to have you again.'

My body melted, silken cream dripping from between my thighs. Every pore of my body yearned to absorb this man, to sink into every part of him. I wanted him to have me again, video be damned.

'Who has the videos?' I asked, wrapping my body around him.

'I do,' a voice from the darkness stated.

I whirled, surprised, and my heart constricted. Clinging to my swimming partner, I peered into the darkness.

From the inky-black night stepped a god of a man, tall with dark-chocolate skin. He was bald, though it looked as if he shaved his hair away. His face appeared to be carved in granite – long, lean and sharp. His full mouth slid into a small smile. I looked back towards my man; the two nodded at each other.

'Do you two know each other?' I asked, looking between the two of them.

My partner chuckled, a deep rumbling in his chest. 'You could say that,' he murmured, looking at the man.

'What are you going to do with the videos?' I asked, turning my attention back towards the handsome black man.

The man shrugged, his hands buried in his khaki slacks. 'Watch it, sell it, post it on the internet.'

I groaned. My partner chuckled.

'I'll buy them from you, all of them,' I blurted in a rush of air.

The man shook his head. 'Don't want money,' he replied, his deep rich voice so quiet I was unsure if he'd spoken at all.

'What do you want?' I asked.

My partner looked at me, then back towards the man. He arched a brow. 'Yes, James, what do you want?' he asked, his voice as smooth as honey.

The man chuckled and shook his head. He looked down at the pavement then back up, his gaze locking to mine. 'I want to watch you make her come; this time I want her to know I'm watching.'

I stilled in the water, not sure what to think. I really should have felt indignation, maybe a little embarrassment, but tonight I'd become someone else. More adventurous – free and unbound.

The truth of the matter was I'd only started breaking into the pool a few months ago, the first time on a dare from friends for a one-time naked swim. And I'd initially been naughty enough that I'd broken into the pool to skinny-dip, but that first sink into the water I felt myself begin to change. On the second swim I'd found my corner and the jet, then the thrill had taken hold and I'd returned again and again, like a moth to an irresistible flame. And don't get me wrong, I'd had my fair share of one-night stands and wild sexual escapades, but never had another man watched as I was screwed by someone else. The image of James, all smooth like black velvet, relaxing in a lounge chair while my mystery man fucked me brought a flutter of anticipation tingling over my body to melt between my legs. My pulse quickened and my heart thundered in my ears as I replied before my partner could. 'OK, but I get tonight's tape when it's done.'

James nodded, my partner unmoving in the water. I swam towards the stairs, then led my partner out of the pool and over to a lounge chair. James sat in a chair facing us and leaned back, his long, dark fingers interlaced across his stomach. He looked as if he was ready to watch a football game.

I pushed Mystery Man down on the chair. 'What's your name?' I asked him, suddenly wanting to know.

'Does it matter?' he asked as he leaned back on the chaise. I surveyed his muscular, deeply tanned form so elegantly relaxed over the lounger. He reminded me of a sleeping lion, always on the verge of attack but manageable as long as the tide was in his favour.

'I want to know what name to scream while I'm riding your cock,' I said, straddling his waist, his hard, thickened shaft poised at my entrance.

His eyes widened, and then he smiled. 'Blake,' he murmured as he traced his hands up my outer thighs, along my waist to cup my breasts. 'And yours?'

I sighed as he tweaked my nipples, tugging at them with his thumb and forefinger. 'Misti,' I managed, choosing to give my middle name rather than my first.

He leaned forwards and lashed out at the budded peaks, flicking his tongue over and over the distended tips. I arched into his mouth, forgetting about James and the video. All I wanted was this.

With his other hand he traced back to my pussy, trailing one finger in the crease, smearing my dew over my swollen, aching lips. I moaned, the sound even guttural to my ears, like a mating call. A plea really.

I felt Blake smile against my breast and then he parted me and lanced two fingers inside my entrance. My body clamped around him. He nibbled at my breast, alternating with a tugging suction. The smooth, fevered pace of his hand and the gentle suckle of his mouth drove me higher.

I rose up so his fingers fell away, because I needed more. I needed something stretching me, filling me, touching every silken nerve along my tunnel.

Positioning myself over Blake, I tore my gaze from his and turned to meet James's hot, steady stare.

His face was a mask, etched and hard. Holding his gaze, I sank slowly down on Blake's shaft, burying him inside me. As my lids dropped on a sigh, James moved and his chair scratched along the concrete.

The sound brought back the sensual reality of the situation. My riding one man while another watched. Rippling pleasure, like the sun warming my skin, coursed over my body.

Rising slowly, I started the same even tempo Blake had used on me in the pool. He gripped at my hips and pushed when I sank, trying to increase the rhythm and the pressure. He moaned beneath me as I slid along his body, swaying my hips and tightening my pussy to milk his length. With each rock of my hips I rubbed my sensitive nipples against his chest, abrading my skin on the coarse hair matting his. My clit ground into the hair circling his cock, sending rivulets of silken sensations up and down my body to pool at my core.

'God, Misti, you're going to kill me,' Blake ground out as he once again tried to quicken the pace by bucking beneath me. I smiled down at him, his face half-shadowed in the dappled midnight shade of the large trees surrounding the pool.

Leaning forwards, I flicked out my tongue to lick his flat nipple. 'Good way to die,' I purred as I rose back up.

His face hardened and James scooted in his chair again. I wasn't sure if he made the movement to bring back my awareness of him or not. Shifting my gaze, I turned back to James and rose up on Blake. Preparing for the fall and the path to release.

Then I rode him, undulating on his cock, drawing out his pleasure by working the muscles of my body. Rubbing and caressing with each touch of my skin to his. Blake circled a finger over my clit as I rode him. And I kept my eyes on James, imagining them both fucking me, as heat pooled at my centre. James's black stare bore into mine, heightening my awareness of Blake's body beneath me, each flinch of my own skin, each twitch of my pussy.

James stood and removed his clothes; the fabric of his pants swished as they pooled around his feet, and he stepped from the pile. His cock stood erect against his abdomen. The dark length jumping as he stood and let me look over him. I rose slowly up on Blake, then sank down, never taking my gaze from James.

'Are you going to just watch or do you want to play?' I asked, moving slowly again.

James walked towards us, his bronzed body rippling in the pale light. The lounge chair dipped as he bent down on his knees behind me, between Blake's legs. My hair moved away, bringing a chill to my body and then his hot mouth pressed gently against the crease between my shoulder and my neck. Chills swept over my body as he suckled, his hand moving around to scrape against my sharp nipple.

Sucking in a breath, I leaned my head back and Blake gripped my hips, pressing me down on his dick. Every muscle in my body quivered. I rose up and began a slow ride on Blake. Opening my eyes, I looked down at James's dark hands gripping my creamy breasts, the shades stark against one another. Again my body rippled, wetted, as I continued to move up and down. James's hands left my breasts, one wrapping gently around my neck, the other pushing me forwards, exposing my ass.

Blake buried a hand in my hair and pulled me roughly against his mouth to suckle on my tongue and nip at my lips. My mind was on overload and I focused on riding the engorged cock buried deep inside me. James ran a thumb over my asshole, just tweaking the rim with a gentle probe of his finger. Then his hand left my ass and they were pushing me up. I stood and Blake guided me so I turned around towards James. I sank back down on Blake's cock, his hands wrapped around my hips. James leaned in and trailed his tongue over my lips. I quivered as he cupped my face between his hands.

Licking my lips, I glanced down at his dick, huge and pulsing against his stomach.

Leaning forwards, but keeping eye contact, I folded over slightly as James stood and put his cock in my mouth. Sinking deep over the head, I swirled my tongue then reached up to grip the base. As I pulled back, I sank down on Blake's cock. I worked the two men, one with my mouth, the other with my pussy. Blake gripped my hips, guiding me on his dick. He swirled his thumb over my asshole, just a tease of penetration, causing my pussy to tighten on his length. James buried his hand in my hair, gently keeping the strands from my face so he could watch as his dick disappear inside my mouth. I sucked and swirled, working my hand up and down his wet length.

The tempo escalated, my ass slapping against Blake, and I pounded down hard on his cock. James tightened his hand in my hair, keeping the pace even. I couldn't break away, not when I felt the orgasm twisting inside me. Blake moaned, his cock jerking inside me; the sound almost triggered James's orgasm as hot come spurted against the back of my throat. Blake's cock stiffened and pulsed. My own body broke and shattered. I jerked with the force of the release, my body tightening and relaxing in quick waves. My skin tingled, like yards of satin winding around each limb to slide down and pool at my hips. James slid from my mouth. I heard him putting on his clothes, the chair scraping again. I took great gulps of breath, my eyes closed as I tried to focus. I stood, my legs wobbling beneath me. Every bone in my body felt made of rubber, threatening to bend and I'd melt in a heap on the concrete.

'Think I'll get that video now?' I asked turning to James.

Except no man stood in the darkness. Nothing but the night. I had to wonder if James had been a dream, an orgasmic induced apparition.

'He's gone,' Blake replied, standing and looking around the pool.

I nodded. I turned towards the pool and dived in, swimming across to the edge where I'd begun tonight's swimming journey. The lights in the pool flickered out. I broke the surface, wiped water from my eyes and turned to find Blake. But he'd gone too. The pile of his dark clothes was no longer there beside the pool. Just mine, where I'd left them, neatly folded on a nearby chair.

I pushed from the water and, shivering in the night air, pulled on my clothes. I looked around one last time, then headed for the fence.

Making my way in the dappled light towards my car, I wrapped my arms around myself and shivered in the night. The pool parking lot was empty, eerie in the moonlight. I pulled my keys from my pocket and I clicked open my door, the interior light coming to life. A dark shape on my windshield drew my attention. I picked up the video box and pulled out the tape. A note and a key dropped to the ground. I picked up the note and the key.

So you don't have to jump the fence – J

I looked around at the surrounding darkness, my body heating with the remembrance of the passing night. Of two men, their hands roaming my body, licking every crevice, buried deep, and I knew, without a doubt, that I'd be back. And they would too, and together we'd get wet and wild.

Short fiction by Shada Royce is featured in the Black Lace anthology *Seduction*.

Have Sex Will Travel
Delilah Devlin

The Russian's fingers did it for her.

As annoyed as she'd been with his arrogant set down on the train platform before they'd boarded, one look at his hands as he clutched his newspaper in front of his face and she was mesmerised, unable to drag away her gaze.

He had large hands, shaped like shovels, dark, sparse hairs sprouting below the second set of knuckles. His fingers were long – the tips blunt and thick. His nails were clean, trimmed, but not filed or buffed. He had a man's large and capable, but unfussy hands.

Evie surreptitiously clenched her thighs. Two of those thick, blunt fingers would equal the girth of the last cock she'd had thrusting up inside her. Three would stretch her to the point of delicious pain. His palms would be slightly calloused, but she could already imagine the feel of them rasping over her breasts. Her boyfriend's hands had been as soft as hers.

The newspaper snapped, and her gaze shot up to meet his over the top of the pages. The same narrowed glance he'd given her on the platform now seemed to hold a hint of challenge.

Evie's cheeks grew warm. He'd caught her staring. At his hands. At the long fingers curling tighter around the paper he held in front of him. He probably knew exactly what she'd been thinking.

She glanced away, reached for the backpack at her feet and pulled out her itinerary to review it for the hundredth time, staring at the pages, but not really reading.

Something deliciously unexpected arced in the air between them. An electric charge of sensual curiosity that didn't dissipate the longer they sat, side by side, on their red-upholstered bench, pretending not to notice their deepening breaths or the number of times they restlessly shifted in their seat. It wasn't the vibrations beneath them from the train ripping down the track, even though the steady even hum added a subtext to their restless movements.

Evie crossed her legs, wishing she'd worn something less comfortable than her favourite pair of faded blue jeans and a Three Doors Down concert T-shirt. She dressed like a grad-school student in a state of arrested development, which she was. Or a teacher who'd saved her meagre salary to splurge on museum tickets rather than a holiday wardrobe. Also true.

The Russian wore a dark-brown business suit. A summer wool that fitted him well without an overly tailored cut that would hug his frame. He'd left off the tie. His dress shirt was opened at the neck to reveal the base of his throat and give a hint of the dusting of dark hair that clothed his broad chest. Comfort seemed to be his priority over style.

The paper lowered to his lap, and Evie suppressed a groan, caught again. His gaze rested on her – telling her silently he knew she'd been watching him.

She lifted her chin. 'It's not as if I have anything else to do,' she muttered, knowing he didn't understand a word she said.

A soft snort was his response. Then he folded the paper and stuffed it into the handle of his brief bag. He crossed his arms over his chest, then began a slow perusal of her body that left her slightly outraged – and incredibly aroused – beginning with her breasts and sliding slowly down her body.

Was he truly attracted? Or did he think he could intimidate her into giving up her berth? That he hadn't wanted to share the small compartment with her had been apparent in the low, heated argument he'd had with the attendant who checked their tickets and collected their passports.

Having been shocked that she'd been given such a nice accommodation in the first place, no doubt a mistake but one she wasn't going to admit, they'd have to prise her cold dead fingers from the sides of the cabin door to remove her now.

She'd withstood her cabin-mate's irritation, ignoring both men as they spoke and gestured towards her until the Russian had uttered a low curse, unmistakable by his tone, raked a hand through his straight brown hair before finally, grudgingly, taking his seat. He'd made a great deal of noise opening and slamming his case, drawing out his newspaper and raising it so high she knew he wanted to tell her she didn't matter. He would simply ignore her.

Only it seemed he found it impossible to dismiss her. Was his predatory stare simply his new tactic to drive her out?

Oddly, Evie found herself growing amused. *Let him stew.* Let the tension grow so thick that neither of them could pretend something wasn't happening here. 'I'll be out of your hair by morning anyway,' she drawled.

While his dark gaze lingered on her breasts, she eased back in the seat, straightening her shoulders so that her breasts lifted subtly. If he kept looking, he wouldn't miss the sight of her nipples beading beneath the thin material of her bra and T-shirt. She unfolded her legs and crossed them again, drawing his gaze down to her long legs. She might not have fully fleshed-out curves, but her slim body did manage to pull male glances everywhere she'd travelled so far.

One asset in particular seemed to hold their attention longest.

Knowing she was being a little devious, Evie bent over to rifle through her pack, pretending to reach deep for something while her cropped T-shirt slid up her back to reveal the upper edge of her turquoise thong.

When she straightened, she caught his glance sliding away from her bottom. Feeling smug, she couldn't help the slight smile that tugged at the edges of her lips and turned her head to lock her gaze with his, returning his challenge without blinking.

Only maintaining that stare proved hard. The longer she looked into his face the more she took note of his strong, square jaw, the dark, slashing eyebrows that overhung deep-set brown eyes, the thin sensual lips that firmed while she continued to look.

Suddenly, he stood, his height towering over her. He shrugged out of his jacket and folded it, laying it atop his brief bag. When he sat and pulled off his shoes and socks, Evie's triumph wilted, wondering what he was up to now. Without glancing her way, he stood and opened the cabinet above her head to fold down the upper bunk.

Evie quickly ducked to keep from getting bumped. 'You could have given me a warning,' she said grumpily.

Another soft snort had her tilting up her face to meet his steady stare. His hands pulled open his belt, unbuttoned the top of his pants, and he efficiently pulled his shirt tails free.

Now, the air inside the compartment grew stifling. Her heart thudded dully in her chest as he stripped away his shirt and folded it neatly over his discarded jacket.

His naked chest drew her gaze. Helpless to resist, she conceded his body was attractive even if his behaviour made him seem a total jerk. Broad, rather than lean, thickly muscled, his waist narrowing proportionate to his size – she knew he'd blanket her completely, press her deep into the thin travel mattress if he lowered his body over hers.

Unwilling to let him mock her a single moment longer and needing to move now that excitement hummed through her body, Evie gave him a disgruntled frown and slid her bag along the floor with her foot. She stood in the small space between him and the bed, and then sidled towards the sink near the entrance of the cabin.

She watched him in the mirror, saw his gaze rake her back, lingering on her buttocks and thighs, and reached a decision she was sure she'd regret later.

Right now, however, her body was beginning a slow burn that quickened her breaths, tightened her nipples and softened her sex. She'd started this journey needing to fill her life with experiences she'd never have back in her own prosaic little world.

Experiences. New challenges. Obstacles for her to overcome on her journey to discover herself as a single woman in charge of her own destiny.

Her boyfriend's defection, which had forced her to make this trip on her own, had stung. Her self-esteem had dents large enough to park a Hummer inside – but the Russian had been checking her out. She thought that just maybe she was ready to put to rest any doubts she had about her ability to attract and seduce another man.

She quietly twisted the lock on the door to ensure their privacy. Then without looking back, she slowly drew her shirt over her head and dropped it beside her feet. Unfastening her bra, she let it slide off her arms, not caring where it landed either. She slipped out of her leather slides and unbuttoned her jeans, pushing them down to her thighs. When she bent to push them the rest of the way down, she heard a throaty murmur behind her, and her body reacted immediately, urgently, dampening the crotch of the panties, which were the only item of clothing she still wore.

She straightened and tucked her fingers beneath the bands at her hips, and drew a deep breath for courage, then started to push them slowly down.

Hands closed over hers, halting her. Had she misread his interest? Evie's breath rasped as her courage fled. Heat filled her cheeks, and she closed her eyes.

His large hands squeezed hers, pressing them to her sides, telling her to keep them there. Then he slowly glided up her ribs. When his long fingers nudged beneath her breasts, she couldn't help the shallow, breathless moan that escaped her lips.

Heat encompassed her back and buttocks as his body pressed against her. They stood for a long moment, tension keeping both their bodies stiff and their breaths deepening. Evie waited to see whether he would follow through on the promise of his touch. Did he wait to see whether she would change her mind?

Wanting to make sure he understood her compliance, Evie clutched his hands and lifted them to cup her breasts.

His murmur – thick, guttural, incomprehensible – turned her on every bit as much as the way his fingers tightened on her breasts. He didn't give her a tentative, exploratory massage. He held her breasts and squeezed while his knees nudged the backs of her thighs and his cock rutted at her bottom through the trousers he still wore.

Always a 'talker', Evie let her head fall back against his broad chest. 'Again. Do it again,' she moaned, welcoming the rock of his hips with an undulating caress that rolled across his thick cock.

One hand dropped from her chest to slide down her belly. His fingers slipped beneath the elastic banding of her panties and glided straight through her curls to cup her sex.

His fingers rolled across her pussy, tugging and tightening against her outer labia, coaxing more moisture to seep from her and coat his fingers with her honey.

Evie reached up, sliding her hand behind his neck, surrendering to his manipulations, widening her legs to give him access to stroke deeper.

One finger slid between her lips and thrust inside her, swirling, circling, driving her crazy because she wanted that second thick finger, needed that fullness sliding inside her to get off. 'More,' she moaned, rolling her head on his chest, rubbing a hand on top of the one clutching her breast, following the length of his arm with the other to encourage him to give her what she needed.

A harshly muttered epithet, one she understood, was all the warning she got, before he withdrew from inside her and turned her quickly in his arms.

Staring up into his face, Evie's head fell back and her chest pushed against his, her nipples tangling in the hair furring his chest. Chest hair hadn't been something she'd ever given much thought, but now she knew she preferred a chest clothed exactly like his. The crisp curls abraded her spiked nipples and scoured her areola. A delicious shiver shook her body. She gasped as he hauled her up, his hands gripping her waist.

And because there was no way in hell she was letting him change his mind now, she wound her legs tightly around his waist and swooped down to take his lips in a searing kiss.

His lips held firm, not opening.

Undeterred, Evie softened her own, gliding them wetly over his mouth, sliding along his cheek and jaw as she wound her fingers in his hair and tugged. She tightened her legs, pressing her open sex against the front of his pants, confirming his hardness.

Whatever his problem, it wasn't because he didn't want her.

She rubbed against him again, and lifted her mouth to stare into his narrowed gaze. 'Don't you want this?'

His stare was so intense, so dark, she hesitated for a moment. It was the same expression he'd worn on the platform, but now she knew it wasn't annoyance. His hands left her waist and she wrapped her arms around his shoulders. He pushed his trousers down. She groaned as his cock sprang free beneath her, nudging her pussy.

He stepped forwards. Her back met the door. He rutted against her, his cock sliding between her folds in long glides, but not entering.

'Don't tease,' she gasped, letting her head fall back. 'I thought all men were wham-bam studs.'

He rutted again, grinding against her sex as moisture slid down her channel and coated them both.

'It's OK. Come inside,' she whispered. 'Fuck me. You know that word? Fuck?'

But he continued to move against her, driving her crazy. All that thick, hard cock right there between her legs but not plunging deep where she needed it.

'Please,' she whimpered.

The Russian stepped back and pushed her legs down until she stood in front of him. He bent and reached for his pants, slipped a hand inside his pocket and withdrew a leather wallet.

Her lips began to curve. Not so different from American boys. He wasn't ending it. He was just being smart.

Evie took the small plastic-wrapped square he withdrew, ripped it open with her teeth, and extracted the latex circle. Then she went down, ringed her lips and pressed the circle just inside, showing him what she would do.

His thick, blunt fingers dug into the top of her scalp, holding her as she grasped his shaft and pointed the blunt, full head towards her mouth. Then she glided down, using her lips and tongue to slide the condom over his cock, following with fingers to stretch it until he was covered.

When she glanced back up, he indicated the bed with a jerk of his square chin. She slid around him, stowed the upper bunk, deployed the lower bed behind the bench seat, and climbed on all fours onto the mattress. Then she glanced behind her as he stepped out of his pants.

He turned off the light glaring onto the mattress, but left the softer one glowing above the travel sink. That single soft bulb gilded one side of his body, leaving the other defined in shadows.

With his longish, dark hair falling forwards, his eyes darkened by his heavy brows, the Russian looked like a conquering warrior, minus the animal furs and horned helmet. So different from the scholarly men she'd dated and taken to her bed. Broad, muscled chest, slabbed thighs – a cock as deliciously proportioned as the rest of him . . .

She licked her lips and raised her glance to meet his. Again, a small smirking smile curved the corners of his firm lips. He knew what she was thinking. That she couldn't wait to feel the difference between what she'd always settled for and what he offered – raw, animalistic sex.

Sex with a man she'd never see again.

His hands reached out and cupped her ass, fingers digging into her soft globes, his gaze falling to her sex. His cheeks drew tight over sharpening, bladed bones and he brought one knee then the other onto the mattress, mounting it behind her, his cock and thighs gliding up behind her, pressing towards her.

She pushed back, arching her back and giving him the best target possible because modesty was the last thing she was worried about now. Her body ached; her heart beat fast. Her pussy clasped air, inviting the sexy stab of his dick. 'Jesus, please, just fuck me now.'

He swatted her with his open palm. One cheek then the other. He slid his hand between her legs and fingered her sex, stroking into her with those blunt fingers she'd fantasised about, then withdrawing. When the head of his cock fitted to her opening, she bit her lips to keep from crying out. She didn't think she'd last long.

The girth of the cock he thrust into her stretched, pinched, heated. A harsh jumble of consonants punctuated the air, and she smiled because she felt the same way. Something powerful was happening.

His large shovel-like hands clamped around the tops of her hips, and he shoved her forwards and back, controlling her movements, shafting her slowly. She knew he watched his cock slide into her, because he barely moved behind her, using her to masturbate himself like a tight fist stroking his cock.

Evie was OK with that. She felt boneless, wet, helpless within his strong grip. She'd never considered herself the submissive type, but he'd dominated her from the start, compelled her to act, to strip, to offer herself with a sexy, challenging slant of his lips and brows.

She was quickly coming apart. Her inner walls rippled around him, caressing him in strengthening vibrations. Liquid heat spilled from her pussy, adding a moist, nasty softness to the sounds of his blunt, harsh strokes.

He pushed her forwards, off his cock completely, and then turned her with his hands until she lay flat on her back.

She lifted her knees, splayed them, and reached down to caress herself while he came over her, his broad frame blocking out the light. His cock touched her inner thigh, and she grasped it, fitting the tip to her opening, funnelling the shaft as he pumped into her, withdrawing when she wanted all of it cramming deep.

Her gaze rose to meet the deep shadowed sockets where his eyes glittered.

His jaw remained tight, his lips closed and firmed into a narrow line. Was he pleased?

Did she really care if he was? She'd wanted an adventure, a new experience. This scary, intense man thrusting into her was more than she'd ever dreamed.

Evie dropped her feet and planted her heels into the hard mattress. She lifted her hips, grateful for the freedom to oppose his strokes and work up some sexy friction where her body craved it most. Deep inside her. All along her inner walls.

His breaths deepened, his body tightened, and she grew alarmed that he'd leave her behind, leave her wanting if he came now. She snaked her hand between their bodies and ringed the base of his cock, squeezing tight.

A sharp, guttural complaint blasted from his lips, but she tilted up her chin and dared him to make her stop.

At last, a smile curled one corner of his mouth, and he paused his steady, heavy stroking to screw into her, his hips circling, delivering a delicious pull and drag against her sensitive tissue.

Her head dug into the mattress, her mouth opening around a long moan. Her hand slid away from his cock.

He paused, gathered her knees beneath his arms and pushed them higher. Now she had no leverage, couldn't help herself to find her orgasm. He powered into her, his movements so harsh he scooted her up the thin mattress. She reached above her head, braced her hand against the back wall and held on.

He slammed deep, tapping her womb. Then holding there, he ground against her, rubbing the crisp hairs at his groin against her clit. She exploded, stiffening under him, her mouth opening around a breathy, endless groan.

They both came, bodies gliding in sweaty, sex-drenched motions until she collapsed under him. He continued to rock inside her, and she enjoyed the comfort of those intimate caresses, praising him with soothing glides of her hands over his shoulders and chest, until he slowed and stopped.

With his chest heaving above hers and her shattered breaths rasping, they stared at each other.

Evie worked up a smile and offered it. Feeling a little shy now the excitement had palled. She'd fucked a stranger she'd never met before. A man whose name she didn't want to know. Someone she knew she'd probably never have liked as a friend, much less a lover, because he was arrogant and overbearing.

But he'd been just what she'd needed when she'd boarded the train. She'd been alone. Felt disconnected.

The most primitive of connections still bound their bodies together. When he slid out, she closed her eyes. Abandoned at last.

He spoke, a deep rumble of garbled words. His hands gripped her shoulders and shook her.

She opened her eyes and gave him a glare, but he was only asking her to scoot over.

When she moved, he stretched on his side, facing her on the narrow mattress. His heavy arm fell across her waist. He was breathing softly beside her in seconds.

'Un-fucking-believable,' she muttered.

A hand swept from her belly to a breast, and he squeezed it.

Evie turned her face to see his sleepy eyelids rise. His face seemed large beside her. But then again, everything about him was over-sized. Even the hand groping her gently.

She eased to her side and scooted backwards, giving him more room. He filled the space she vacated and rolled onto his back, bending his knees to place his feet at the end of the bed, because he was too tall to fit otherwise.

An arm slipped beneath her, bringing her flush against him. She accepted his offer, cuddling close to the comfort of his warm body as the train continued to rattle and hum beneath them.

Light spilled through the windows the next time Evie opened her eyes.

It was morning. She wondered how long they'd slept, and how much longer it would be before they reached their destination.

Feeling a little less bold in the glaring light, she lifted her head to find the Russian staring at her.

A single dark brow lifted.

'Were you waiting for me to wake up?' she asked, even knowing he didn't understand, but conversation filled the awkward silence.

In the morning light, his features seemed a little less austere. Younger. But no less arrogant.

His gaze raked her naked body then dropped between them to where his cock prodded her belly.

'Yeah, first thing I noticed,' she murmured. 'Hard to miss.' She gave him a cheeky grin. 'But I'm not sure we have the time.'

His scowl deepened and he growled then cupped her face with his wide palms and dragged her towards him.

His kiss was hard, fast, and left her breathless.

When his lips backed away, she blinked owlishly. 'Guess we have time if we're really quick.'

Only he hadn't been waiting for her to agree, he was already pulling on her arm, urging her to straddle his hips. She braced her hands on his shoulders and rose on her knees, waiting as he quickly guided his cock between her folds.

He cursed and shoved her back, then reached to the floor for his wallet again, this time doing the honours and cloaking himself. Then his cock was back, pushing into her.

By now, her pussy was accustomed to his size. She slid down, fitting around him snugly.

Her sigh of pleasure was met with a thin-lipped smile, then his hands encouraged her to move, pushing her up and down. 'I get it,' she said, giving him an exaggerated huff. 'You want me to move.'

A short, sharp rap sounded on the cabin door, and she froze.

The Russian's eyes narrowed, and he shouted something to the porter. Telling him to move along? That they were awake?

She didn't know, but the thought that the porter might have an inkling why they hadn't yet unlocked the door fuelled her excitement.

Again she was caught in the delicious excitement of doing something forbidden. She began to move once more, not checking the sounds she made, letting her moans lift around them, and loving the low, seductive murmurs he returned.

'Sure need to learn some Russian,' she gritted out as his hips began to lift, driving up his cock in counterpoint to her downwards thrusts.

The train's smooth motions slowed; the humming seemed to grow louder. 'Must be getting close,' she whispered. She sure was. Close enough that her body was beginning to quiver and melt, fresh arousal drenching his cock and easing the friction growing between their genitalia.

When he removed a hand from her hip, she shortened her strokes, her knees weakening, shivering. The raspy pad of his thumb slipped over her clit and rubbed, pressing harder when she cried out and held still.

Her orgasm bloomed, spreading outwards from her cunt. Her

head fell back and she ground down in shallow rocking motions until the internal reverberations waned.

She peeked at him, noted the sweat breaking on his chest, the redness and tightness of his features. He'd pleased her so much. Now she wanted to return the favour. Lifting off him, she climbed off the mattress and knelt in the narrow space between the bulkhead and the edge of the bed.

He didn't need sign language to understand what she offered. He jackknifed up and spread his legs on either side of her, then leaned back on his hands. His cock was right in front of her, riding his abdomen and pulsing. He rolled off the glistening condom and tossed it towards the sink.

She gave him a smile, glanced at the cabin door, met his glance again then shrugged. 'That attendant's gonna come back with a key any moment now. I don't care if you don't.'

Her position wasn't optimal for what she wanted to do. She bent to one side, grasped his shaft and licked up one side, leaned the other way, and went down, wetting him with lush brushes of her tongue.

Then she wrapped both hands around him, one on top of the other and stroked up and down his reddened, satiny shaft. The full head had a nice flanged ridge, and she paused to lave the underside, glancing up to read his expression.

The man didn't give a lot away. His heavy, rugged features were set, grim even, but the colour staining his high cheekbones, two bright spots, encouraged her.

Stretching as far as she could, she came over him, sinking on the cap, gliding her mouth downwards, past the glans, deeper until his cockhead butted the back of her throat. She placed one hand beneath the lowest point she could take him, and began to slowly twist on his shaft while she drew a deep breath and bobbed, suctioning hard as she came up.

The Russian muttered and pushed her hand away, clasping himself. His thick fingers tightened harder than she would have thought comfortable. Then he waited until she resumed sucking, his hand coming up to meet her downwards strokes, moving over his cock in harsh glides.

Watching those fingers again, she grew more excited, moaning around him and lip-stroking faster.

He eased forwards on the bed and clamped his free hand on the top of her head, pushing and pulling her harder and faster.

The raw, wet sounds of her mouth and soft choked gasps at the back of her throat escalated until at last he pulled her off his cock. He held her face poised above his cock and came, ejaculating short, ropey geysers of come that she stuck out her tongue to taste.

The train slowed, then rumbled to a stop. Her gaze lifted to his, and a smile crooked one corner of his mouth. He bent towards her, his tongue licking her lips and chin, then his mouth brushing over hers before he drew a deep breath and pointed towards the door, telling her to move.

As impersonally as if he hadn't just licked his come from her face, he stood and stowed away the mattress. She bent for her clothing, drawing it on with shaking hands, not caring about the sticky moisture gathering between her legs.

When she'd finished, she glanced back up. He was tucking in his shirt, his gaze going to the window, and his brows drawing into a frown as though worried about making his next connection.

Evie reached for her pack and slung it over one shoulder, then unlocked the door and drew it inwards. The corridor was busy, but she kept her gaze on the traffic, waiting for her break. Then she was out, striding away without looking back, trying not to think about the fact he'd let her go without even giving her a goodbye in his Russian gibberish.

The tryst was what it was. Not a deeply moving experience. Just sex. Not the sort of adventure she'd planned, but something to add to her list of life experiences.

Sex with a sexy stranger aboard a moving train. *Check*.

Never mind her stomach felt queasy, and her breaths were rattling they came so fast. She'd felt hurt by his dismissal. But what had she expected?

She'd wanted a kiss, a gesture of regret. Something to tell her she wasn't just a willing pussy. Despite the fact that's exactly what she'd offered.

She stepped off the train and headed straight for the bench facing the train and set her backpack down. She unzipped it, pulled out her itinerary, and glanced up to check the station's clock.

Glancing back at her itinerary, she froze. A big blue asterisk sat beside Saturday's destination. Not a mark she'd made – or that had been there before yesterday.

A smile tugged at her lips, and she cast a quick glance up and down the platform. The Russian stood at the top of the steps leading into the station. His steady gaze on her.

Evie lifted the itinerary and waved.

His gaze went back down the steps, and then he turned back, striding quickly towards her.

Her smile told him everything he needed to know.

His kiss promised her a fresh adventure.

Holding on to his lapels she grinned against his mouth. 'Saturday.'

His large, roughened palm cupped her cheek. 'Saturday, Travel Girl,' he said, in thickly accented English. 'Don't keep me waiting.'

She turned her head and bit one of those thick, meaty fingers that had got her into trouble in the first place. 'Not nice.'

'So I played a game.' He shrugged, not the least repentant.

'You know what they say about payback,' she murmured, then soothed the indentations with her tongue.

Those wicked, dark brows of his lifted. 'I'm not that fluent. You will have to show me.' He kissed her again, then turned and walked briskly away.

She strolled to the opposite side of the platform and took a seat to wait for the next train.

Nothing on her plan – not a church or museum or grand plaza – would ever compare with the beauty of the feeling that swept through her.

It wasn't love. Not by a stretch.

But it sure felt sweet and lifted her heart.

Evie sat back, stretched her arms across the back of her seat and laughed, already looking forward to her next naughty rendezvous with the Russian.

Sexy Little Numbers features the first appearance of short fiction by Delilah Devlin in Black Lace.

The Perfect Distraction

Rachel Kramer Bussel

It's hard to get distracted from watching an orgasm relay race, but Charles and Amanda manage to distract me quite easily. We're all standing watching five women get fucked by powerful, giant machines that are intent on bringing them to orgasm. The room is filled with the collective energy of held breaths, wet pussies and hard cocks, as we partake in the highlight of the BDSM conference. Except for, well, me. I've come here on my own, and the two of them are the hottest thing I've seen all weekend, outstripping even the motor-powered climaxes just waiting to happen. Real live flesh will win out over machinery anytime, though in this case it's pretty close.

Still, it's undeniable that they are creating their own quite powerful energy right in front of me, the kind that you feel more than see, the kind that makes your pussy tingle and your brain go to mush. He's got a sexy short brown beard and pinchable cheeks, and she's got red hair, glasses and a cleavage-baring red dress, but it's not just their looks; it's the energy they give off that makes me want to escape from the crowd and get them alone. They're whispering and giggling and she's running her hand under his shirt; I imagine she's running a fingertip over his nipple. I can't make out their words, but I don't need to; I can tell they're plenty dirty.

We keep turning towards each other, the attraction palpable, as if we've already dispensed with the getting-to-know-you small talk and moved on to getting-to-fuck-you. He's rubbing the back of her neck, and I picture him grabbing her there and shoving her onto her knees. I step closer to them and get in on their whispering.

'Charles wants you to spank him,' Amanda says to me, then looks away. She's made me blush, and I tell her so. I may put on a good front, but I'm never quite sure what to do when people so boldly proposition me. Clearly they've heard about the impromptu spanking demo I gave the day before, one that was fun, but nothing to write home about. It was a momentary bit of pleasure, but it didn't make me ache as watching the two of them does.

Amanda grips my hand as we watch one girl after another get pounded to orgasm, their screams echoing through the room. The spanking demo hardly slaked the lust I'd been wanting to reveal, to the right person, or people, as the case may be.

I lean over and tug on her ear lobe with my teeth. 'Which one of those devices do you want in your pussy?' I ask her, then look up at him to make sure he knows I'm not excluding him. To me, the whole point of a threesome is to get everyone involved, so we all feed off each other.

'The fucksaw, I'd say,' he answers for her.

I smirk at them, the kind of smirk that says I just might have a fucksaw of my own. 'Really?' I whisper in her ear as I massage the back of her neck.

She squeals again, an utterly girlish sound that makes me long to get her to do it again, if I'm not stuffing something in her mouth to muffle it. Both are equally enticing possibilities. She looks up at me with wide eyes, her extra-long lashes seeming to emphasise her mock fear. I know she's not truly afraid, even though she's biting her lip and trembling just a little. That's not fear, it's desire, and I love seeing it on her face. I reach between her legs and brush lightly against her pussy. We're in a room full of people, sure, but they're all fellow perverts – I know they understand.

'Yeah,' she moans as I play with her through her panties. I take his hand and place it on her breast, which is conveniently accessible, right there, taunting us with its presence. Soon she's writhing between us, her breathy moans attracting attention.

Thankfully, I decided at the last minute to stay an extra night. Thus far, I haven't seen more action than my hand and my trusty vibrator getting me off – not that there's anything wrong with that, but I'd felt a little lonely in my queen-size bed. I pull my hand out from under her dress. 'If you want more of that, take me to your room,' I toss out at them, knowing they will.

We walk out to the sound of the buzzing machines and, by the time we get to the elevator, are practically glued to one another. I hardly know where to start first. We could do anything – and everything.

'Show me how she likes her breasts played with,' I dare Charles, spying elevator guard or potential passengers be damned. 'Go on,' I add, helpfully pulling down the V-neck of her dress enough to display them in all their glory. 'Good girl. I like that you're not wearing a bra,' I tell her, waiting to see what he will do.

Then he grabs one in each hand, getting a solid grip with thumbs and forefingers, and twists. Then pulls. What he's doing has to hurt, but I can tell from the noises she's making that she wants more. Her nipples go from placid little pink pearls to screaming red nubs getting flattened by his fingers. She lets out shuddering breaths as he turns her nipples into his personal playthings. Then he stops, and they seem to pout just as she'd been earlier. I'm torn between watching them and getting in the middle of things.

The elevator chimes, and Amanda tucks her breasts back in. I'm sorry to see them go, even though I know I'm about to torment them to my heart's delight. Her red hair is perfectly tussled, as if she's just been fucked, except that hasn't happened – yet. I am giddy with excitement, as if I've never done anything like this before. I have, of course, but Charles and Amanda bring me back to my first threesome, when everything was new, every touch a thrilling discovery. I'd always thought sexual knowledge built and built, like acquiring a PhD, but maybe my stretch of celibacy – a few months that had felt like much longer – had somehow wiped my slate clean, purified me in a way that now makes me tremble as Amanda deliberately brushes her ass against me as she gets off the elevator.

I blush as an older couple walks around us to get inside. Can they sense what we've been doing? Is it obvious? Will they return later only to hear us fucking? Part of me wants them to, the rest of me hopes we'll have some semblance of privacy.

But when we get to their room, I find that I don't care about anyone else; they are more than enough for me, with their flirty glances, her luscious breasts, his barely contained desire. I want to fuck them and have them fuck me and watch them fuck; any and every permutation we can think of. I grab Amanda by the back of her hair and pull her towards me, smashing our lips together for a kiss, the kind meant to sting. She moans and I pull her hair, then reach for those nipples.

'Get over here,' I say to Charles and, when he does, I reach for his cock, fondling it as Amanda takes her breasts back out of her dress. Suddenly, as I massage his hardness and slap at her breasts, I know what I want.

'I want you,' I say to Charles as I unzip his pants, 'to take this beautiful cock of yours, and fuck Amanda's breasts. Slide it between them, back and forth, while I watch. But don't come just yet.' I can't help but move into organiser mode. I want to touch, and taste, and fuck, but I also want to watch. These two beat any porn I've watched or ever will watch. He places his hand over mine on his cock and suddenly I get a different idea. 'No, I take that back,' I say.

'You want to suck his cock, don't you, Amanda?' I ask, grabbing her by the back of her neck. Her breasts arch upwards temptingly.

'Yes, I do,' she says.

I do too, but I want to watch her first. I have him sit in the chair in the corner of the room and push her to her knees. She goes to grasp the base and I pull her hands behind her back, then ease her panties down and twist them around her wrists. They're wet, and I like that she can feel her own arousal against her wrists while her bare pussy is open to me.

'That's better. Now get to work,' I tell her. He groans and looks up at me, his eyes filmy with desire as she opens for him, opens herself, not just her mouth. Her lips move slowly, pressed so closely to his skin it's like they have truly merged. 'I like that,' I tell them, more softly, and he looks from her face to mine.

I lean down and kiss him, his bristly beard pricking my skin, while the sound of her slurping fills the room. It's not just that she's doing it so lustily, it's that I've ordered her to do it. I love this, but part of me wishes I could watch them at home, hidden away, to see what they do when they don't think anyone's watching. I look down at Amanda and caress her cheek, and she looks up at me even as she takes all of him down her throat. In that instant, I wish I had a cock so I could feel the divine pleasure Charles is feeling. Oh, yes, I have plenty of dildos and love getting them sucked by guys or girls, but it's not quite the same thing.

Before he can come, I ease her off of him. 'Stand against the wall with your arms above your head,' I order her. Immediately, she does what I tell her, her face flushed, hair messy, her body ready for whatever we want to do to her. There I am, getting distracted again, daydreaming about all sorts of luscious possibilities rather than going after this ridiculously sexy vixen who's just asking for ... well, everything. I walk over to Charles, facing him and blocking him from Amanda's view. I grab his cock and whisper in his ear, 'What should we do with her?' It's a conspiratorial whisper; I want him to know that even though they are the couple, he and I could pair up in the name of sadism.

I put more pressure around the base of his cock, and his face contorts with desire. I know I'm making it hard for him to think. 'I'll make her suck your cock until you come ... after,' I whisper again, sucking on his ear lobe for good measure. I'm pretty sure he's used to having her do his bidding, to pulling her hair, ordering her around, spanking her pretty ass. I want to do all those things, too, but I don't want to usurp his role.

'Well ... she does like to have her pussy spanked,' he says, his voice pitching lower as I shift so I can play with the wetness at the tip of his dick.

'Then why don't you go over there and show her a good time? But wait, I have something for you.' I fish around in my bag – glad I still have all my supplies – for a small shiny slapper, perfect for some punishing blows to a pretty boy's or girl's ass – or, in this case, pussy. 'Use this,' I say, pressing it into his hand. Then I dig out a special treat for myself and tuck it into my palm. I walk over to her first, and slam three fingers inside.

'She's very wet,' I call out to Charles. 'She feels like she could use a really hard fuck,' I continue as I add another finger and feel her clench around my hand. 'Or a spanking.' I pull out and wipe her cheek with my wet fingers. I motion Charles over and smile at Amanda. She smiles back, a little hesitantly, clearly uncertain about just what she's getting into.

This is becoming more intense than I'd thought it would be at first. It's longer than just a romp, but an intense session where anything can happen. They keep darting glances at each other, as if to ask if what we're about to do is still acceptable.

'You have beautiful breasts, Amanda,' I say, giving them each a light slap to emphasise my point, 'but I think they'd look even more beautiful with these, don't you?' I ask as I reveal the clamps. They are shiny and bright, and their jingling makes her eyes go wide. 'Don't look at me like that, Amanda. You know you like the pain. You like it when your big hard nipples get flattened into nothing. You like it when it feels like they might get pinched right off of you. It makes you want more and more, doesn't it?' I trail the cool metal along her belly, letting it dip briefly against her hot pussy.

'Charles, dear, don't delay,' I tell him. 'Keep your hands above your head and spread your legs, Amanda.' She does what I say, even though the position isn't the most comfortable. I want her to know this isn't about her comfort. She's the kind of girl who likes to be challenged, who likes to be told what to do and then rushes to obey so she can get high off her ability to follow orders. She doesn't even need me to tell her she's doing a good job, but I do. It's simply being worthy of being ordered around that does it for her.

I fasten one tweezer clamp around her right nipple, then slide the tong up, up, up. Charles moves towards her, the paddle in one hand, but he preps her pussy with a few smacks of his hand. His dick is so hard that I know it must be almost painful not to be touching it, and the promise of two women sucking him off simultaneously is gone, at least for the moment. I pull on the chain attached to Amanda's nipple while her boyfriend spanks her pussy, the noise ringing out in the air. She's gasping, not for breath but for survival, to find a way to make the pain even hotter for her.

I'm engrossed in what I'm doing, but I'm still making sure Charles is doing what I want him to. Soon he replaces his hand with the slapper. She winces, then whimpers, and starts to slide downwards. I prop her up, my hands under her arms, giving me the chance to engage in a little tickling. She laughs, and I realise I've forgotten to put the other clamp on. I make quick work of it, fastening it more tightly. She's not laughing any more, but that was such a sweet sound, I return to her smooth, shaved, slightly sweaty underarms while Charles spanks her cunt harder and harder.

'Having fun?' I ask her, then kiss her roughly. My pussy is soaked, but that can wait. When I'm busy with a gorgeous sub like this, the foreplay of taunting her, topping her, is enough to suffice.

'Yes, mistress, I am. Oh God . . .' she groans as he keeps on smacking her. I let her go and pull on the chain, raising my free hand to her neck. It's so soft and delicate, it makes me want to press harder against it.

'Make her come, Charles. You do that, then you'll get that pretty cock of yours milked but good.' This is language I'd only use right here, right now, lost in the tempo of our play. He says, 'Yeah,' under his breath and then bites his lower lip to focus as he keeps smacking her while I pin her to the wall by her neck and torture her nipples. She's going mad now, grinding and twisting, but we don't let up until her cries echo through the room. She comes so fiercely I'm almost thrown off her, and Charles works his fingers into her pussy to spur her on. They emerge coated with her essence.

I ease my grip on her neck, but keep my hand there as we kiss. 'Now I'm going to fuck your boyfriend, Amanda,' I tell her. She opens her mouth, as if she might protest, and I give her a light slap across the cheek. She trembles, and I almost give her another, but she can't be too greedy, can she? Instead, I tie her wrists behind her back and stuff my panties in her mouth and make her watch. I'm separating this crazy-hot couple, but only temporarily, and their apartness seems to make them seek each other out in new ways. I'm on top of him and his eyes alternate from my face to my tits to his bound and gagged girlfriend. When she moans against the gag, he pumps into me harder. I like that feedback loop, and pull her closer to us, add another little tickle. Her muffled giggles are what do it for me, and I come on Charles's cock, which makes him do the same.

We separate and he helps me untie her. Then we're all free, tentatively reaching out hands, Amanda blushing, Charles with one arm around me, one around her. I realise now the disadvantage to being the domme; there's no room in that role for cuddling, and all I want to do is turn towards him. That's what Amanda gets to do, and he wraps his arms around her to cradle her. I watch them for a few moments before slipping out and into the tub, the hot water soothing all the stinging parts of me but my heart. If I'm forced to admit it, I'm a bit jealous of them, even though I know they're ravenous for me. Isn't that always the way? The grass is always greener and all that. When they drift off to sleep, I slip out of their room with my bags, as quietly as possible, and hope I'm leaving with at least some of their couple's magic on my very single skin.

Sexy Little Numbers features the short fiction of Rachel Kramer Bussel for the first time in Black Lace.

LOOK OUT FOR THE ALL-NEW BLACK LACE BOOKS – AVAILABLE NOW!

All books priced £7.99 in the UK. Please note publication dates apply to the UK only. For other territories please contact your retailer.

Also To be published in August 2009

UP TO NO GOOD
Karen S Smith
ISBN 978 0 352 34528 8

Emma is resigned to attending her cousin's wedding, expecting the usual excruciating round of polite conversation and bad dancing. Instead it's the scene of a horny encounter which encourages her to behave even more scandalously than usual. When she meets motorbike fanatic Kit, it's lust at first sight, and they waste no time in getting each other off behind the marquee. They don't get the chance to say goodbye, however and Emma resigns herself to the fact that she'll never see her spontaneous lover again. Then fate intervenes as Emma and Kit are reunited at another wedding – and so begins a year of outrageous sex, wild behaviour, and lots of getting up to no good.

THE CAPTIVE FLESH
Cleo Cordell
ISBN 978 0352 34529 5

A tale of decadent orgies amidst the sumptuous splendour of a North African mansion. Nineteenth-century French convent girls Marietta and Claudine learn their invitation to stay in the exotic palace of their handsome host requires something in return – the ecstasy of pleasure in pain.

To be published in September 2009

MISBEHAVIOUR
Various
ISBN 978 0352 34518 9

Fun, irreverent and deliciously decadent, this arousing anthology of erotica is a showcase of the diversity of modern women's erotic fantasies. Lively and entertaining, seductive and daring, *Misbehaviour* combines humour and attitude with wildly imaginative writing on the theme of women behaving badly.

NO RESERVATIONS
Megan Hart and Lauren Dane
ISBN 978 0352 34519 6

Kate and Leah are heading for Vegas with no reservations. Both on the run from their new boyfriends and the baggage these guys have brought with them from other women. And the biggest playground in the west has many sensual thrills to offer two women with an appetite for fun. Meanwhile, the boyfriends, Dix and Brandon, realise you don't know what you've got 'til it's gone, and pursue the girls to the city of sin to launch the most arduous methods of seduction to win the girls back. Non-stop action with a twist of romance from two of the most exciting writers in American erotica today.

TAKING LIBERTIES
Susie Raymond
ISBN 978 0352 34530 1

When attractive, thirty-something Beth Bradley takes a job as PA to Simon Henderson, a highly successful financier, she is well aware of his philandering reputation and determined to turn the tables on his fortune. Her initial attempt backfires, and she begins to look for a more subtle and erotic form of retribution. However, Beth keeps getting sidetracked by her libido, and finds herself caught up in the dilemma of craving sex with the dominant men she wants to teach a lesson.

To be published in October 2009

THE THINGS THAT MAKE ME GIVE IN
Charlotte Stein
ISBN 978 0352 34542 4

Girls who go after what they want no matter what the cost, boys who like to flash their dark sides, voyeurism for beginners and cheating lovers . . . Charlotte Stein takes you on a journey through all the facets of female desire in this contemporary collection of explicit and ever intriguing short stories. Be seduced by obsessions that go one step too far and dark desires that remove all inhibitions. Each story takes you on a journey into all the things that make a girl give in.

THE GALLERY
Fredrica Alleyn
ISBN 978 0352 34533 2

Police office Cressida Farleigh is called in to investigate a mysterious art fraud at a gallery specializing in modern erotic works. The gallery's owner is under suspicion, but is also a charming and powerfully attractive man who throws the young woman's powers of detection into confusion. Her long-time detective boyfriend is soon getting jealous, but Cressida is also in the process of seducing a young artist of erotic images. As she finds herself drawn into a mesh of power games and personal discovery, the crimes continue and the case becomes ever more complex.

ALL THE TRIMMINGS
Tesni Morgan
ISBN 978 0352 34532 5

Cheryl and Laura decide to pool their substantial divorce settlements and buy a hotel. When the women find out that each secretly harbours a desire to run an upmarket bordello, they seize the opportunity to turn St Jude's into a bawdy funhouse for both sexes, where fantasies – from the mild to the increasingly perverse – are indulged. But when attractive, sinister John Dempsey comes on the scene, Cheryl is smitten, but Laura less so, convinced he's out to con them or report them to the authorities or both. Which of the women is right? And will their friendship – and their business – survive?

ALSO LOOK OUT FOR

THE BLACK LACE BOOK OF WOMEN'S SEXUAL FANTASIES
Edited by Kerri Sharp
ISBN 978 0 352 33793 1

The Black Lace Book of Women's Sexual Fantasies reveals the most private thoughts of hundreds of women. Here are sexual fantasies which on first sight appear shocking or bizarre – such as the bank clerk who wants to be a vampire and the nanny with a passion for Darth Vader. Kerri Sharp investigates the recurrent themes in female fantasies and the cultural influences that have determined them: from fairy stories to cult TV; from fetish fashion to historical novels. Sharp argues that sexual arche-types – such as the 'dark man of the psyche' – play an important role in arousal, allowing us to find gratification safely through personal narratives of adventure and sexual abandon.

THE NEW BLACK LACE BOOK OF WOMEN'S SEXUAL FANTASIES
Edited and compiled by Mitzi Szereto
ISBN 978 0 352 34172 3

The second anthology of detailed sexual fantasies contributed by women from all over the world. The book is a result of a year's research by an expert on erotic writing and gives a fascinating insight into the rich diversity of the female sexual imagina-tion.

Black Lace Booklist

Information is correct at time of printing. To avoid disappointment, check
availability before ordering. Go to www.blacklace.co.uk
All books are priced £7.99 unless another price is given.

BLACK LACE BOOKS WITH A CONTEMPORARY SETTING

☐ AMANDA'S YOUNG MEN Madeline Moore   ISBN 978 0 352 34191 4

☐ THE ANGELS' SHARE Maya Hess   ISBN 978 0 352 34043 6

☐ THE APPRENTICE Carrie Williams   ISBN 978 0 352 34514 1

☐ ASKING FOR TROUBLE Kristina Lloyd   ISBN 978 0 352 33362 9

☐ BLACK ORCHID Roxanne Carr   ISBN 978 0 352 34188 4

☐ THE BLUE GUIDE Carrie Williams   ISBN 978 0 352 34132 7

☐ THE BOSS Monica Belle   ISBN 978 0 352 34088 7

☐ BOUND IN BLUE Monica Belle   ISBN 978 0 352 34012 2

☐ CASSANDRA'S CONFLICT Fredrica Alleyn   ISBN 978 0 352 34186 0

☐ CASSANDRA'S CHATEAU Fredrica Alleyn   ISBN 978 0 352 34523 3

☐ CAT SCRATCH FEVER Sophie Mouette   ISBN 978 0 352 34021 4

☐ CHILLI HEAT Carrie Williams   ISBN 978 0 352 34178 5

☐ THE CHOICE Monica Belle   ISBN 978 0 352 34512 7

☐ CIRCUS EXCITE Nikki Magennis   ISBN 978 0 352 34033 7

☐ CLUB CRÈME Primula Bond   ISBN 978 0 352 33907 2   £6.99

☐ CONTINUUM Portia Da Costa   ISBN 978 0 352 33120 5

☐ COOKING UP A STORM Emma Holly   ISBN 978 0 352 34114 3

☐ DANGEROUS CONSEQUENCES Pamela Rochford   ISBN 978 0 352 33185 4

☐ DARK DESIGNS Madelynne Ellis   ISBN 978 0 352 34075 7

☐ DARK OBSESSIONS Fredrica Alleyn   ISBN 978 0 352 34524 0

☐ THE DEVIL AND THE DEEP BLUE SEA Cheryl Mildenhall   ISBN 978 0 352 34200 3

☐ EDEN'S FLESH Robyn Russell   ISBN 978 0 352 32923 3

☐ EQUAL OPPORTUNITIES Mathilde Madden   ISBN 978 0 352 34070 2

☐ FIRE AND ICE Laura Hamilton   ISBN 978 0 352 33486 2

☐ FORBIDDEN FRUIT Susie Raymond   ISBN 978 0 352 34189 1

☐ THE GALLERY Fredrica Alleyn   ISBN 978 0 352 34533 2

☐ GEMINI HEAT Portia Da Costa   ISBN 978 0 352 34187 7

☐ THE GIFT OF SHAME Sarah Hope-Walker   ISBN 978 0 352 34202 7

☐ GOING TOO FAR Laura Hamilton   ISBN 978 0 352 34526 4

☐ GONE WILD Maria Eppie   ISBN 978 0 352 33670 5

❑ WILD CARD Madeline Moore   ISBN 978 0 352 34038 2
❑ WING OF MADNESS Mae Nixon   ISBN 978 0 352 34099 3

BLACK LACE BOOKS WITH AN HISTORICAL SETTING

❑ NICOLE'S REVENGE Lisette Allen   ISBN 978 0 352 32984 4
❑ THE SENSES BEJEWELLED Cleo Cordell   ISBN 978 0 352 32904 2   £6.99
❑ THE SOCIETY OF SIN Sian Lacey Taylder   ISBN 978 0 352 34080 1
❑ TEMPLAR PRIZE Deanna Ashford   ISBN 978 0 352 34137 2
❑ UNDRESSING THE DEVIL Angel Strand   ISBN 978 0 352 33938 6
❑ A GENTLEMAN'S WAGER Madelynne Ellis   ISBN 978 0 352 34173 0
❑ THE BARBARIAN GEISHA Charlotte Royal   ISBN 978 0 352 33267 7
❑ BARBARIAN PRIZE Deanna Ashford   ISBN 978 0 352 34017 7
❑ THE CAPTIVATION Natasha Rostova   ISBN 978 0 352 33234 9
❑ DARKER THAN LOVE Kristina Lloyd   ISBN 978 0 352 33279 0
❑ DIVINE TORMENT Janine Ashbless   ISBN 978 0 352 33719 1
❑ FRENCH MANNERS Olivia Christie   ISBN 978 0 352 33214 1

BLACK LACE BOOKS WITH A PARANORMAL THEME

❑ BRIGHT FIRE Maya Hess   ISBN 978 0 352 34104 4
❑ BURNING BRIGHT Janine Ashbless   ISBN 978 0 352 34085 6
❑ CRUEL ENCHANTMENT Janine Ashbless   ISBN 978 0 352 33483 1
❑ DARK ENCHANTMENT Janine Ashbless   ISBN 978 0 352 34513 4
❑ ENCHANTED Various   ISBN 978 0 352 34195 2
❑ FLOOD Anna Clare   ISBN 978 0 352 34094 8
❑ GOTHIC BLUE Portia Da Costa   ISBN 978 0 352 33075 8
❑ GOTHIC HEAT Portia Da Costa   ISBN 978 0 352 34170 9
❑ THE PASSION OF ISIS Madelynne Ellis   ISBN 978 0 352 33993 4
❑ PHANTASMAGORIA Madelynne Ellis   ISBN 978 0 352 34168 6
❑ THE PRIDE Edie Bingham   ISBN 978 0 352 33997 3
❑ THE SILVER CAGE Mathilde Madden   ISBN 978 0 352 34164 8
❑ THE SILVER COLLAR Mathilde Madden   ISBN 978 0 352 34141 9
❑ THE SILVER CROWN Mathilde Madden   ISBN 978 0 352 34157 0
❑ SOUTHERN SPIRITS Edie Bingham   ISBN 978 0 352 34180 8
❑ THE TEN VISIONS Olivia Knight   ISBN 978 0 352 34119 8
❑ WILD KINGDOM Deanna Ashford   ISBN 978 0 352 34152 5
❑ WILDWOOD Janine Ashbless   ISBN 978 0 352 34194 5

BLACK LACE ANTHOLOGIES

| ❑ POSSESSION Various | ISBN 978 0 352 34164 8 |
| ❑ ENCHANTED Various | ISBN 978 0 352 34195 2 |

BLACK LACE NON-FICTION

❑ THE BLACK LACE BOOK OF WOMEN'S SEXUAL FANTASIES ISBN 978 0 352 33793 1 £6.99

    Edited by Kerri Sharp

❑ THE NEW BLACK LACE BOOK OF WOMEN'S SEXUAL

    FANTASIES   ISBN 978 0 352 34172 3

    Edited by Mitzi Szereto

To find out the latest information about Black Lace titles, check out the website: www.blacklace.co.uk or send for a booklist with complete synopses by writing to:

Black Lace Booklist, Virgin Books Ltd
Random House
20 Vauxhall Bridge Road
London SW1V 2SA

Please include an SAE of decent size. Please note only British stamps are valid.

Our privacy policy
We will not disclose information you supply us to any other parties. We will not disclose any information which identifies you personally to any person without your express consent.

From time to time we may send out information about Black Lace books and special offers. Please tick here if you do <u>not</u> wish to receive Black Lace information. ❏

Please send me the books I have ticked above.

Name ....

Address ....

....

....

....

Post Code ....

Send to: Virgin Books Cash Sales, Black Lace,
Random House, 20 Vauxhall Bridge Road, London SW1V 2SA.

US customers: for prices and details of how to order
books for delivery by mail, call 888-330-8477.

Please enclose a cheque or postal order, made payable
to Virgin Books Ltd, to the value of the books you have
ordered plus postage and packing costs as follows:

UK and BFPO – £1.00 for the first book, 50p for each
subsequent book.

Overseas (including Republic of Ireland) – £2.00 for
the first book, £1.00 for each subsequent book.

If you would prefer to pay by VISA, ACCESS/MASTERCARD,
DINERS CLUB, AMEX or MAESTRO, please write your card
number and expiry date here: ....

....

Signature ....

Please allow up to 28 days for delivery.
....